Praise for Nuruddin Farah and *Secrets*

"Nuruddin Farah, the most important African novelist to emerge in the last twenty-five years, is also one of the most sophisticated voices in modern fiction."
—Neal Ascherson, *The New York Review of Books*

"The plot is rich and the language is superb, exotic and consciousness-expanding. It's enough to make you home-sick for a country that is not your own."
—*Los Angeles Times Book Review*

"In spellbinding, luminous prose, Farah unpeels layer after layer of family history."
—*The Baltimore Sun*

"Daring, lush, urbane. . . . Beneath the playful sensuality of *Secrets*, Farah is raising a cry against the old bonds of kin-ship that, transformed into ideology, have done so much recent damage to Africa. Love, he is saying, matters more than blood."
—*The New York Times Book Review*

"Decadently rich in myths, metaphors and sensuality."
—*The Wall Street Journal*

"Hypnotic . . . *Secrets* is a shape shifter—murder mystery, family saga, magical realist thriller."
—*Newsday*

"[*Secrets*] seethes with the threatening potential energy of nearly lost histories and nearly revealed secrets."
—*The Star Ledger*

"Farah is a captivating imagist, whose language teems with the earthy physicality of Africa. He creates a startling, con-vincing portrait of Somalia as a place of primitive ritual and taboo, shape-shifting and witchcraft, jumbled with computers, automobiles and European clothing."
—*The Seattle Times*

"What [*Secrets*] achieves . . . is a demonstration of what art needs to achieve: It offers an er
vincing portrayal of human ex
—*Emerge*

ABOUT THE AUTHOR

The 1998 laureate of the Neustadt International Prize for Literature, Nuruddin Farah has been described by some of the world's foremost writers not just as "one of the finest contemporary African novelists" (Salman Rushdie) but "with *Secrets* . . . as one of the world's great writers" (Ishmael Reed). Farah chooses to write in English.

Farah was born in 1945 what is now Somalia (what was then the Italian Somaliland), in Baidoa, and grew up in Kallafo, under Ethiopian rule in Ogaden. The ethnically and linguistically mixed area of his childhood contributed to his early fascination with literature. He spoke Somali at home but at school learned Amharic, Italian, Arabic, and English. Farah worked in the Ministry of Education in Somalia before leaving for India to study philosophy and literature.

His first novel, *From A Crooked Rib*, was published in 1970; it has since achieved worldwide cult status, admired for it's empathetic portrait of a Somali woman struggling with the restraints of traditional Somali society. It was followed by *A Naked Needle* (1976).

Farah's next three novels. *Sweet and Sour Milk* (1979), *Sardines* (1981), and *Close Sesame* (1983) comprise the trilogy known collectively as Variations on the Theme of an African Dictatorship. Upon the publication of *Sweet and Sour Milk*, which won the English Speaking Union Literary Award, Farah became a persona non grata in his native Somalia. In exile, Farah began what has become a lifelong literary project: "to keep my country alive by writing about it."

The Variations trilogy was followed by the Blood in the Sun trilogy, which consists of *Maps* (1986), *Gifts* (1992), and *Secrets* (1998). In the summer of 1996 Farah was able to visit Somalia for the first time in more than twenty tears. *Secrets* is his first novel since that visit.

Farah lives in Kaduna, Nigeria with his wife and two children.

SECRETS

NURUDDIN FARAH

PENGUIN BOOKS

PENGUIN BOOKS

Published by the Penguin Group

Penguin Putnam Inc., 375 Hudson Street, New York, New York 10014, U.S.A.

Penguin Books Ltd, 27 Wrights Lane, London W8 5TZ, England

Penguin Books Australia Ltd, Ringwood, Victoria, Australia

Penguin Books Canada Ltd, 10 Alcorn Avenue, Toronto, Ontario, Canada M4V 3B2

Penguin Books (N.Z.) Ltd, 182–190 Wairau Road, Auckland 10, New Zealand

Penguin Books Ltd, Registered Offices: Harmondsworth, Middlesex, England

First published in the United States of America by Arcade Publishing, Inc., 1998
Published in Penguin Books 1999

10 9 8 7 6

The author wishes to acknowledge the following:

My thanks to the many persons who have helped me: to Tsigie and Seyoum, Haile
Kiros, Shamsuddin Ahmed, Tsegu Belay and Worku Shatew; to Leena, Arne Ruth, and
Ingemar Karlsson; to Pili and Bob Coover, Rashiidah Ismaili, Bill and Anna Colaiace;
to Joachim Sartorious and Barbara Richter; to my parents-in-law, Eli and Margaret
Mam; and finally to my partner in life, my wife, to whom lots of love.

   Thanks also to Nigel Varty's *The Mammal Community of the Riverine Forest in
Southern Somalia* (1988) and Yuri Dimitriyev's *Animals on a Pedestal* (1989), translated
from the Russian by Raissa Bobrova.

PUBLISHER'S NOTE
This is a work of fiction. Names, characters, places, and incidents either are the products of
the author's imagination or are used fictitiously, and any resemblance to actual persons,
living or dead, events, or locales is entirely coincidental.

THE LIBRARY OF CONGRESS HAS CATALOGED THE HARDCOVER EDITION AS FOLLOWS:
Farah, Nuruddin, 1945–
Secrets/Nuruddin Farah.
p.   cm.
ISBN 1-55970-427-6 (hc.)
ISBN 0 14 02.8045 6 (pbk.)
I. Title
PR9396.9.F3s4   1998
823—dc21   98–11464

Printed in the United States of America
Set in Walbaum MT
Designed by Sean McDonald

For Mina
with all my love

PROLOGUE

One corpse, three secrets!

My name Kalaman conjures up memories of a childhood infatuation with a girl four and a half years older than I, memories on the heels of which arrive other recollections. Like an easy answer to a seemingly difficult riddle, my name evokes surprising responses in many people, especially when they hear it for the first time. Some, at the risk of sounding ignorant, have been known to wonder aloud, "But what sort of a name is it?" Give them a clue, as I am prone to do, nudge them in the right direction and you will observe that slowly, like a mysterious door opening, their faces widen with grins as self-conscious as a sparrow dipping its head in the river's mist. Then my interlocutors say, "Now why on earth did we not think of that?"

There was a brief period when I thought of altering my name altogether. I had been infatuated at the time with Sholoongo, whose animal powers were mightier than mine. I resented my squeamish behavior not only because of our gender difference, but also because my mother held the girl's guts in ominous awe. Nonno, my father's father, appeared at times to go out of his way to encourage my cultivating her friendship, arguing that it was salutary for me to meet a woman who was my equal. Then he would change the subject and engage my interest in the stars and, between irrelevant asides, point the Milky Way out to me and explain the myth behind it, indicate the twenty-odd stations along the path of the moon and how each of these affected the weather and a person's destiny.

Sholoongo was so domineering I could never say my own name in her presence without stammering. My mouth would open a little and my tongue would push itself up against my palate, only I would either fail miserably in making the K-sound, or be incapable of getting to the L before finally seizing up altogether. Unable to unjam my tongue, I would become aware of a feeling of despair and inner rage.

Months went by before I asked Nonno why I could not stand up to Sholoongo's mysterious power, or couldn't just shrug off her spells, like water off a crow's back.

He said, "I gather that Sholoongo was delivered of her mother when the stars were bivouacking at a most inauspicious station. She was born a *duugan*, that is to say, a baby to be buried. And that was what her mother tried to do: she carried the infant out into the bush and abandoned her there. But Sholoongo survived, and lived to haunt the villagers' conscience, especially her mother's."

As he paused, perhaps to catch his breath, my mind jumped further ahead and was able to recall other versions fed by other memories.

He said, "I cannot vouch for its truth, but in the version I heard, a lioness adopted and raised her together with her cubs, then abandoned her at a crossroads, where some travelers found her. These took her to the nearest settlement, which happened to be her mother's hamlet. You might think this far-fetched, but this is the stuff of which some people's misfortune is made, myth galore!"

"Then what happened?"

"Rather than own up to any of this, Sholoongo's mother committed suicide in the version I have. Now this is considered a most heinous crime among peoples of the Muslim faith, and the mother was most ruthlessly punished. Her corpse was left to rot out in the open heat of the sun. It was remarked by those present in the hamlet that even vultures did not dare to go anywhere near the dead body."

Shocked, I remained silent.

"The girl's father turned up," Nonno went on, "a seaman on leave. Bizarre though it may seem, the villagers did not tell him the whole truth. Only that he had to slaughter several goats as part of a sacrificial ceremony for his own safe return, nothing about suicide. Nor did anyone bother to inform him that his daughter was born *duugan*. Remember, he was away, at sea, when she came into this world."

"What happened after he slaughtered the goats?"

"He left the hamlet soon after that, taking his daughter away with him to a town, where he married again," my grandfather explained. "The new wife supplied him with a son, Timir. But then, all of a sudden, for reasons unknown, his young wife went insane. The relatives of the woman, who had heard rumors about the *duugan* girl, pointed a superstitious finger at Sholoongo. The father consulted a savant, who prescribed ostrich eggs as a cure."

"How do you know all this?" I asked.

He had a mischievous glitter in his eyes as he said, "I've managed to glean all this from the ears of a legion of untold secrets."

I took a sip of chilled water with a dash of tamarind in it, the same concoction being the wondrous secret drink with which Nonno wet my lips at birth. My larynx loosened up, so did my pharynx, my voice organs bounced into action, with the Adam's apple jerking to life, functioning with the ease of a recently greased engine. And I sang the songs Sholoongo had taught me.

"Do you have any idea why she makes you stammer?"

I explained in the hesitant language of a child of eight-plus that I believed that I had occasional seizures. Then I compared my stammer to hiccups with which it shared at least one feature: that I responded positively to chilled water with a dash of tamarind juice.

As though impressed, Nonno said, "Well done!"

One day, following hard on the heels of an exchange between myself and Sholoongo about my name, she and I had a no-holds-barred quarrel. As was usual, Nonno's name came into our conversation, and Sholoongo, who could be very mean, inflicted an obloquy on my ancestry. She described my grandfather in the vilest language, referring to him as a "closet literate." Even though I did not know what the phrase meant, I felt affronted. Leaving her in a huff, I traveled to Afgoi where Nonno had his estate, with the express intention of asking him what the phrase "closet literate" meant. In the event, I got carried away and egged him on to tell me why he had named me Kalaman.

We sat in the shade of a mango tree, Nonno and I, eating our fruit salad out of the same wooden bowl with our fingers. He had prepared the macédoine himself from the produce of his own orchard. We shared our talk in measured quantities, and paid regal attention to each other. He was a very large man, with an oversized personality, a most agreeable character whose charisma charmed many a woman in the very spot where some are thought to be hard. Although young, I observed that a lot of women were not averse to being teased all the way to his bedroom, laughing, with half the knots of their *guntiino* robes undone. I loved him all the more for his occasional self-abandon, which was as guileless as a child's, and adored him for the wicked grin which often blemished his features.

Part of me suspected that I was committing a flagrant disloyalty by insisting that Nonno tell me why he had named me Kalaman; the other part was weighed down with a curious dismay at my inability to ask him why Sholoongo had called him a "closet literate." How I loved his company, how I adored the wisdom of his silences: for he sat majestically, his mouth thronged with unmade sounds, a harvest of nearly three score years of memories of which he had been a faithful repository. At last he said, "I named you Kalaman because it is a cul-de-sac of a name."

I did not understand his meaning, and said so.

We fell under the spell of a silence that had something of a hissing quality to it, a sound not too dissimilar to that of a snake moving over wet grass. I stared for goodness knows how long at a small bird with a nervous twitch, a shrill whistle, a creamy white abdomen and a grayish chest, a bird which held me spellbound until it flew away, vanishing in the hollow of the hillock beyond. I was trying to decide if I had seen the bird before, or what its glorious name might be, when his voice interfered with my thoughts.

"Commonplace names need propping up," he said, and paused. Maybe because he too was having difficulty identifying the bird, I thought to myself. He went on, "Commonplace names need to spoken in conjunction with a father's name, or a grandfather's. Or better still,

they need to have a custom-made nickname added at their tail ends.
Otherwise they do not feel right somehow, as if there is something in-
complete about them. Name a child Mohammed, and everybody is
bound to ask 'Mohammed Who?'" He fell quiet, and stirred in his
chair restlessly. After a while he added, "I had the foresight to call you
Kalaman because I knew it would stand on its own, independent of
your father's name or mine."

Borrowing a few of his complicated words, which I had half understood, and propping these up with a few of my own, I wondered
aloud what had prompted him to give me such a name. Was there
something he was hiding and of which he was ashamed? I didn't mean
to be disrespectful, but maybe I was. Some of these things are too difficult to judge, especially if you are only nine and the girl with whom
you are infatuated prods you with pointed questions. Mark you, a
number of people, including my own mother and also Sholoongo,
were of the opinion that Nonno was withholding a secret. A friend of
my mother's had the crude habit of alluding to the smallness or large-
ness of manhoods, Nonno's and my father's, both of whom, according
to her "hung down a ton!" Why was it that I didn't? Was I or was I not
of that line, the son of my father, Nonno's grandson?

"Unless . . . !" I said, and trailed off.

Maintaining a stately silence, Nonno refused to rise to my challenge. Earlier, I had rehearsed the scene in the bus on the way to him
and in my script he had asked "Unless what?" and I had prepared a
tentative response. However, my grandfather, faithful to his agenda of
priorities, knew how best to lead our conversation to safety. You could
tell from the way he spoke that he was conscious of where he was
headed. He said, "Curse the day!" This was one of his favorite phrases,
and he employed it when he was upset. The Lord knows he had a
plethora of these phrases, shibboleths pointing to his nervous or joyous state. He repeated, "Curse the day!"

"You see, Nonno," I said, "I am eight-plus, a big enough boy to
know that there are adult secrets which are unwise to share with a
child of my age. I understand."

I could tell from the restlessness which swept over his features that
he would change the subject. He dragged long on his unlit cigarette
and, realizing what he had done, shook his head in amusement. He

then said, "Speaking of trust," and he talked in haste as though I might interrupt him, "Your mother's worries are contagious, and I for one cannot help being contaminated with them. But tell me, has Sholoongo taken you into her feminine trust?"

I made a disparaging remark about my mother.

"That's not a nice thing to say about your own loving mother," he advised. "She is worried, and may have her own reasons for her distrust of Sholoongo."

I returned to the conversation as I had scripted it in my head on the bus to Afgoi. Surprising even myself, I told him that I doubted very much if Sholoongo had anything but respect for my mother. Why, she had suggested that I drop my father's name and take my mother's, as is done in some other countries.

He lit his cigarette and pulled on it long and voraciously, inhaling a chestful of smoke and exhaling only pencil-thin jets through his nostrils. He wheezed and coughed a series of convulsions, like a cat choking on a fish bone. "The girl is making a fool out of you, can't you see?" he said.

I argued that Sholoongo meant no ill.

In the silence which followed, Nonno and I listened to a small flock of starlings communicating with one another in liquid squawks, their whistles fruity. To exonerate my calf-love of blame I explained that since Nonno's and my father's and my name were all dead ends, would it harm anyone if I added my mother's name to this odd mix? Because not only was this fair to the woman who carried me for nine months, but in more than one sense it was also a daring thing to do in a country where nobody contemplated such a step. I put this across as though it were my own idea, not Sholoongo's.

He was firm. "You're ill advised to do so," he said.

"Why?"

"Because you would be attracting the kind of dastardly comment you would do well to avoid. I'm sure I needn't remind you that children of unknown male parentage are, in our part of the world, referred to as the 'misfortunates.' Quite often they are burdened with nicknames bearing associations with their mother. You know of the one exception to this: the Somali prefix *bah* indicates a mother's name with which a woman ancestor is identified, in the context of house-name siblings in a polygamous situation. This does not apply to you. After all, you are an only child of a monogamous union. And surely you do not want anyone to think you are an illegitimate child?"

The adult in me took over with unprecedented punctiliousness as I retorted that our society was unfair to women, this being a view I had often heard Nonno advance, and with such eloquence. I went on, "Fancy the unfairness of it all! Imagine the outrageousness of it, not to be allowed to take one's own mother's name!"

He nodded his head but said nothing. Nonno was given to drawing pleasure from my changes of mood and to appreciating my habit of abandoning my child's nature and assuming that of an adult, not only in the register of my language, choice of vocabulary, but in my bodily gestures too. For I was a good mimic and was adept at becoming other persons if I chose to.

"That'll make your mother most unhappy," he said.

This wasn't the first impetuous confrontation I had had on the nature of fatherhood. I was barely seven when I insisted that I had made a woman pregnant, and no one succeeded in persuading me that I had not. At four years of age, I remember seeing a drawing of the sun which my father had done in very bright colors, and ascribing to my old man immense powers beyond a mortal's. I believed, in those days, that girls were molded into feminine shape in their mothers, who were able to procreate their daughters without help from a man, and that boys emerged as boys out of their fathers' penises.

Nonno was saying, "If you do not wish to displease your mother, then you must abandon the idea of drawing anomalous attention to your beginnings."

My mind was elsewhere, concentrating on the erratic movements of a flycatcher perched on the dead branch of a nearby tree, a flycatcher hesitating whether to pursue its insect prey, which was restless and frightened, a victim in flight.

With neither speaking, Nonno and I sat eating our fruit salad in the afternoon's lacework of bright sunshine and crisscross shadows. And I watched birds flying solo or in pairs or in flocks, my grandfather's stare fixed almost all this time on a singular bird which moved its head in the repeated figure of seven.

"What's so special about Sholoongo?" he asked.

I started to say something, but stopped just in time.

I dared not betray Sholoongo, my secret-sharer whose daredevilry never ceased to amaze me, who would sneak into my bed in the dark after her half brother had started to snore in his bed in the same room. I dared not speak of how thrilled I was when I thought of the diabolical nature of what we were up to, so excited that I was able to meet her challenges with equal bravado. Where other boys' braggadocio underlined for me their overly explicit male self-awareness, with her our secretiveness redeemed us, or so I believed. I doubt that I enjoyed the sexual aspect of our relationship, considering my sex had not *broken*. But then nor had my voice.

I had my first taste of her one night when I dared the lark in her, after slipping into her bed for what seemed to be an innocuous cuddle. Innocent or not, her abundance sought me out, she touched my groin, and I was all erection. I must have know what I was doing, for I held my sex between my thumb and forefinger and asked if she could find some cavity for it to dip its head in. She chuckled in derision and spoke loud enough I feared Timir might wake up; but he didn't. She said, "My, my," as she pinched my sex where it hurt, "yours is no bigger than a navel button. Are you sure you are your father's son? Because he hangs down like a leather strop."

(Looking back, it embarrasses me to think how my male ego was hurt whenever women whom I desired happened to be so indiscreet as to emphasize my smallness. Insulted and naturally annoyed, I even called one of them a whore. But that was years later.)

Nonno was now saying, "What's so special about Sholoongo?"

"I like her for her outlandishness," I said. "Full of fun!"

Maybe to hide his discomfort, Nonno prevaricated, and then equivocated, and finally spoke like an elder addressing a few words of advice to a youngster. He said, "Apart from the obviousness of there being a blessing or a curse, you as an offspring are there, I suppose, to reform your progenitor's arrogant ways. And you've done wonderfully!"

Maybe he felt that I understood his meaning, because he spoke at length as though he were at an elders' council meeting, rhetorical, quoting proverbs, paraphrasing poems, supporting his arguments with a rehashed myth here, a legend there. He was a great orator, quite impressive. If I paid little heed to what he was saying, it was because I was of the dubitable view that he was talking to himself, not to me. And I let him. But I began to talk to myself too, and I said, as to myself, "She is fun, Sholoongo is. She is great fun."

The expression on his face darkened at first. A moment later his features widened with a ghost of a grin, one which was meant to perform a specific task, the kind of grin that might transform itself into a frown.

"You take care!" he said.

In his way he was telling me to leave. And I rose.

Then we heard a huge blast coming from the direction of the river, a little to the right of his woods. We had barely given ourselves time to think what it might be when Nonno's housekeeper arrived to announce that a crocodile had swum away with one of his laborers. More men arrived, one of them guessing that the gunshot we had heard came from Fidow's matchlock, Fidow being Nonno's general factotum. Nonno went into the bungalow and came out armed with a gun, and made to leave with several of his farmhands brandishing spears and all manner of clubs and axes. I sensed that he was determined either to recover the man from the crocodile's jaws or to kill it. It was common knowledge that this particular crocodile was a nuisance, a greedy beast which, having tasted human blood and made off in the recent past with two little girls and their mother, was bound to return. In my grandfather's village in those days, the crocodile was suspected of having swum away with lots of other humans, in broad daylight at that.

He remained outside the excitement generated by the threat posed by the voracious crocodile. His voice calm, he spoke in the tone of a man who may not come back soon. He said to me, "I suggest you take home with you the pot of honey, and that you take care."

Alone, I felt light in the head and in my heart too, and was rather too eager to be reunited with Sholoongo, my calf-love, whom I would feed on the honey collected by Fidow and given to me by Nonno. The question was, would she take *me* in?

A glint of yet another piece of daredevilry now glittered in Sholoongo's left eye as she pulled me away from where a woman neighbor was engaging her half brother Timir in meaningless banter. A gossip, Barni was giving the latest about the son of a neighbor, whose parents had married him off before his fourteenth year to his first cousin and playmate. I knew the woman to be childless and thrice divorced, I knew her to be older than my own mother, and it was common knowledge that she had her own place in a rooming house a couple of gates away. Barni had no profession as such and, like many women in urban Somalia, had no obvious means of support.

Sholoongo told me that Barni was rather keen on establishing closer ties with her and Timir, her half brother, in view of her interest in their father, Madoobe. I cannot remember who explained to me that their father had charmed the underpants off Barni. Once a sailor, Madoobe made his living taming wild horses, which he exported to the Middle East and out of which, it was rumored, he made a mint. What's more, he was reputed to have been the first Somali ever to employ an ostrich as a guard to mind his horses and zebras, a feat which turned him into something of a celebrity.

"Listen to her," Sholoongo said, glancing in Barni's direction in derision. "Bla, bla, bla, my God, she never stops, and doesn't take my father's no for an answer."

I quoted my mother's wisdom that love is subservient. No one could explain what Barni saw in Madoobe, whose moods were determined by the rise and fall of his fortunes, whose disappearances tended to be shrouded in mystery, away one month, back the next, never condescending to be questioned about what he had done in the intervening period. I knew that Madoobe was asleep at this hour and that Barni would hang around all day if need be, patient like a groupie waiting for an instant's sight of her idol.

But now that we were out of Barni's and Timir's hearing I could tell that Sholoongo was up to some mischief. For she held right under my nose a piece of paper on which someone had sketched in pencil

what I took to be a pair of prominent lips, with a thumb protruding
out of a corner. Not knowing what to make of it, I looked at her grin.
To me, she wore the expression of a pirate who had made a sortie into
a treasure trove.

"Tell me what you see!" she ordered.

I grunted out a few words, because I didn't wish to admit defeat, or
that I might get it wrong. On my second attempt at working out the
meaning of the sketch, I saw a figure seated in yogic communication,
a sadhu with a missing leg. Scarcely had my thoughts formulated than
I realized that I was actually holding the drawing upside down. To
cover my embarrassment, I said, "What did Timir think? Have you
shown it to him?"

"My half brother sees the hand of a vet busily pulling out a calf's
forelegs in an attempt to deliver it of its mother," she responded.

Silent, I concentrated all I had by way of a gaze on her chin, which
sported a singularly long hair, so lovely to fondle. Then at her insistence I demonstrated what I saw, now that I had the drawing the right
way up. To do so, I extended a middle finger, with nearly all the other
fingers remaining folded away, then pouted my lips as if I were suck-
ing a half-bent forefinger. Finally I rubbed my index finger against
my lower lip.

She said, "Fingers, mouths and lips, corks!"

I felt hot blood running into my cheeks and toward my eyes. For a
moment I could not see anything, neither could I hear anything, not
even my own heartbeat. Meanwhile Sholoongo, who had numerous
inelegant ways of reaching for my crotch, was suddenly fondling me
until I rose. She whispered that I was a cork and she a bottle, as her finger caressed my fly. In her idiom she used to say that she was the hole
in a flute and I the finger. It was much, much later, with my ears
drained of the tepid blood of lust, that I could hear Barni's voice. I
cannot be certain of what she said, but it sounded like "When you
have no luck to ride!" In my memory then I was able to taste my for-
tune in my own saliva, a river of blood, thimblefuls of the finest quality, Sholoongo's, finger-licking savory!

When next I picked up the thread of Barni's conversation with
Timir, the woman was speculating that Madoobe's heart was "as hard
as the calluses on a camel's tongue." Timir nodded his head, not

because he agreed with her, but because he wished to get away from her.

For my part, I was prepared to pursue Sholoongo to the ends of the earth, hoping that she might be in the generous mood of taking me into her. "A thumb in a mouth, teeth closing in on the nail!" As she did, I heard a shout "Ouch, you're hurting me! Go easy, please!"

I sensed from the first instant my mother set eyes on Sholoongo that she would disapprove of her. In fact she said as soon as the girl was out of earshot, "Beware, she is as dangerous as live wire." And her advice? "If I were you, I would treat her with caution, and wouldn't touch her with my bare hands, as if she were static."

In those days I was interested in the origins of things, how rivers came into being and why they ran and where. I put a legion of questions to Nonno about where babies began and how, where the dead ended up, and whether, once interred, the buried awoke in the dark of their tombs and were immediately reborn, and if so in what form, child or another grown-up, or did they stay curled up, like baby snakes knocked senseless on the head? I was a self-questioner, my head teeming with the drone of unpacified anxieties buzzing inside it, like angry bees. Was maybe this why I wanted to change my name, because its origins made no sense to me? If every given name had its tensions, I used to muse, and every newly acquired one its birth pangs, why, so did every new friendship. Then surely my and Sholoongo's friendship was no exception?

It upset my mother to hear me speak fondly of anybody except my immediate family. ("There is nothing like blood," she would say, her loyalty to her family imbued with such conviction I would wait until I was out of her view before a smirk spread across my features. After all, I knew of a different kind of blood, Sholoongo's, of which I partook, a secret ritual to which my mother was not privy.)

As far as I knew, I was not an unhappy child, but my mother had reasons to suspect that I should be. Perhaps she could not help it, being a worry pot, bubbly and bursting with aqueous energy. At the sight of me and Sholoongo, especially on the days when she was under the weather, my mother would be transformed into a flood of words, an avalanche of emotions, the corners of her eyes mere assembly points for her tearful expostulations. After dark, when asleep, my mother's cheeks would prove to be stained. Could it be that she wept as she dreamt? At daybreak there would be vapor circling just close enough to her eyes, moist like early morning mist.

My mother suspected others of wanting to undermine her influence over me, her only son. She took pride in her intuitive powers, which she claimed alerted her in good time to the inwrought patterns of Sholoongo's long-term designs on my destiny. On occasion, Nonno would intercede. Not that his interventions, his attempts at allaying her unfounded fears, ever worked. I recall hearing him once when I eavesdropped, "Come, come," he said, in the tone of a parent silencing a plaintive child, "the boy is not yet ten, for goodness' sake, and Sholoongo is only fourteen!"

My mother didn't find Timir vulgar or threatening. To her, he was the saintly figure in a household of fiends. Her instincts never warned her of his unhealthy influence over me. "In my dreams," my mother once said, "Sholoongo is long-nailed, and is endowed with a stout head, protruding teeth, with legs that are abnormally short, with rounded ears which resemble a ratel's. She is busy forever digging, without a moment's break."

Even though all attempts to persuade her that Sholoongo had no long-term designs on me proved unfruitful, the fact is my grandfather and father never tired of trying. Pale with fright, my mother, when cornered or asked to see reason, would repeat one of her frequent nightmares: of a honey badger chewing its way into her viscera. My father would speak a gentle rebuke, suggesting that she relax. Nonno would counsel self-restraint, reminding her that she might be accused of untoward prejudices. "It isn't the poor girl's fault that she was abandoned to a suckling lioness," he would argue. "Besides, what evidence have we that she has the power to alter her human nature to that of an animal?"

My saliva thickening as though it were dough fermenting, I would explain to my mother that it had been at her own insistence that I was introduced to Sholoongo, her brother and father too. I would remind her that it was my father who had described them, when he first got to meet them, as "a threesome of originals, as unique as they are fascinating to know, clowns of a tragic reenactment of a sexual farce."

Her head slightly inclined in the attitude of someone who is hard of hearing, my mother would listen very intently to every bend in my every phrase, register my pauses and watch the curves in my words: she might have been listening for some evidence that I had been bewitched. Then she would cry out most passionately, "I lie in the haunted darkness of my sleep, separated as I am from your father by my nightly visions of horror. Hardly have I fallen asleep than I have a night filled with ominous dreams in which ratels chew their way into my viscera, elephants go amok, their huge ears raised in fury, nightly visions in which a hippopotamus crashes through the flimsy fences of my slumber. Where there are graves, these are desecrated, the bodies dug up, exhumed and then buried anew, not in the ground but up in the trees, in nests meant for birds the size of owls. In the blink of an eyelid, the mounds of the newly dug-up earth assume the appearance of anthills, with many openings woven with spiderwebs. My fear is most intimate, and I wish I could rid myself of it, but I can't."

I sought Nonno's opinion. Why was it that the girl's presence fed my mother's unconscious with a fodder of frightful dreams? In his reply Nonno drew my attention to "the idea" of ratels, which, he said, were "partial to the pupae of wild honey, nocturnal animals with the habit of making deep burrows in the earth." There was a subterranean link, he went on, between a ratel's feeding on carrion and my mother's belief in Sholoongo's animal powers, the power of transforming her human nature into the animal of her choosing.

As for Timir, her half brother!

He arrived, his skin as flaky as the arid desert from which he had come, some provincial capital in the interior of the country whose residents were as immune to thirst as camels. I had been infatuated with his sister, and didn't have many friends in those days. Because my father liked Timir, my mother acquiesced to the suggestion that I strike up a friendship with him. My father was present on the day we first met, and he gave me a valedictory encouragement, suggesting that I teach the city ways to Timir, from whom I would learn the culture of the pastoralists who form the majority of our country.

How could I ever forget the detailed attention paid to all the arrangements to ensure that my meeting with him would be crowned with immediate success! It might have been a marriage, my father assuming responsibility for its being consummated. There was a period of supervised courtship lasting almost a month, with my father present in his role as an overseer, a counselor. In the meantime, our two families were in each other's houses like the hands of thieves in one another's pockets. Nonno was persuaded by my mother to lend Madoobe, their father, half of the required funds for him to finance his horse-taming business.

The truth about the boy was sadly more complex, for not only did he help me precious little, nor teach me anything about the culture of the nomads, but he was more interested in what he referred to as his "sex eruptions" than in the burgeoning fabric of my ideas about the origins of things. At least Sholoongo and I shared a keenness of spirit, a genuine interest in the beginnings of things. She unraveled mysteries, taught me the basics about what I took to be something akin to the Sufi tradition, offered the clearest feminist interpretation of the Carraweelo myth yet. Carraweelo is the queen to whose reign may be traced the period when the male order of society in the Somalia of old replaced the country's matriarchal tradition, with women accused of betraying the vision of society and of failing to rule in a just manner.

The benefits I gained from being associated with Timir were of doubtful value. Even so, his kind interventions helped prevent Sholoongo from interfering with my mother's unconscious. But then at the very time when my parents were at their most relaxed, Nonno advised caution, "because volcanoes, although they may not be active, are never extinct. For they explode, and turn into deadly lakes of lava."

Timir would have his eruptions. I never saw anyone looking as pleased with himself as he did on the very instant of his final coming. He took his eruptions as seriously as his father did the smoking of his water pipe, rituals ensuring their unflagging vitality. Timir beat his five when dejected, gave himself a dry quickie when under stress. He admitted to having done it with other boys before, and to having made love to older women, some of them prostitutes. But he argued that there was nothing as enjoyable as coming in your hand with a little help from the leaves of a *gob* tree. Only once did I join him in chewing a palmful of leaves, and although we exploded together, my eruption wasn't as satiating as when I had an escapade with Sholoongo. Even though I never dared ask either of them, I did wonder if he and Sholoongo had had it off too.

To find out I spent a night at their place.

Tense, I stayed awake for much of the night, feeling drowsy just before dawn. I am a light sleeper and remember stirring in my half sleep and sitting bolt upright when someone walked past my bed. Dawn hadn't quite broken, nor had I heard the muezzin waking up the faithful Muslims to their duty. Madoobe, their old man, went out of the room, his movements quiet as the night. I presumed he rounded the hut to make water.

Unable to contain the upsurge of my curiosity, because no sound issued from him for a long, long time, I got out of bed and out of the room, and searched anxiously for any change in the general makeup of my surroundings. Stiff with attentiveness and noticeably uncomfortable, I relaxed only when I saw Madoobe standing ebony dark in the near distance. He was stark naked. He had in his hand an object resembling a wand with which he was rubbing his back, up and down, up and down.

To see better, I moved closer, half crawling on my haunches. But I frightened one of the cows, which, assuming my posture to be threatening, dug its hoofs into the ground with menacing repetitiveness, its horns at the ready, ears rigid from fear, like an angry elephant's. I ceased moving, and remained in a half-bent position for some time before getting up to show my two-legged nature. The cow then lost interest and turned its back on me.

And where was Madoobe? What was he up to?

He dipped the wand in a metal pail which I presumed to be full of water, and as before rubbed the stick between his shoulder blades. He repeated the same process several times and then finally walked away from the pail. Now his nakedness was prominent with an erection. In a moment he was standing behind a heifer, saying something, his voice even. The nearer I got to him and the young cow, the clearer his voice was, only I couldn't decipher his words, maybe because he was speaking to the cow in a coded tongue, comparable to children's private babble. Was he appeasing the cow's beastly instincts by talking to her in a secret language?

A little later and after a lengthy invocation, he inserted his erection in the heifer, still talking but also breathing hard. I might have been listening to a man and a woman making love, for the cow was *muttering* something too. When at last he came, Madoobe returned to where he had left the metal pail, to wash. He kept uttering a louder salvo in a secret tongue.

A few days later I broached the subject with inordinate caution. I didn't expect a windfall confession, and was surprised to be told that I had misunderstood the symbolic nature of a ritual involving Madoobe and what I took to be a heifer. After all the cow wasn't a cow.

"No?"

"It was a cow," Sholoongo said, "whom my father has decided to domesticate, that's to say, take as his wife."

A couple of days later, Madoobe brought home a young bride.

When I pressed for a more acceptable explanation of how a cow metamorphosed into a woman and the woman became a cow, Sholoongo took refuge in prevarications. But I wouldn't let go, insisting that she tell me more. To dissuade me from pursuing the matter any further, she told me a folktale her father had learnt from a Nigerian fellow seaman.

In the tale a hunter stumbles on a skull while chasing game, and exclaims aloud, more to himself than to anyone else, "I wonder how this skull got here." To his surprise, the skull talks. "Beware of divulging secrets, because that is what got me where I am, dead."

Confused, the hunter returns to his village to share his worries with his wife and friends. Eventually the king hears of the hunter's story and asks to be taken to the talking skull. But the skull won't respond either to the king's queries or to the hunter's appeals. Put out by what has occurred, the king orders that the hunter's head be cut off right there and then, and that it be left there, unburied. When the king and his men are departed, the skull asks the hunter, who is dead now, what got him there. His unburied head replies, "Divulging secrets got me here, dead."

PART ONE

CHAPTER ONE

I felt there was something afoot as soon as I opened the door to my apartment, something to do with an alien aroma. I had scarcely crossed the threshold when a pageant of odors invaded my senses, odors reminding me of Taj, the Ethiopian honey-beer. Also I was struck by the odd presence in the flat of a fly, whose helicopterlike drone taxed my frail nerves.

An instant later I encountered the startled expression on the face of my elderly housekeeper, who, meeting me in the shadowed half-light of the corridor, placed her forefinger close to her lips in an effort to hush me. But what was she doing this for? I was a bachelor, I lived alone, I had no children and, so far as I knew, no guests. Don't ask me why, but the thought uppermost in my mind as I stared at Lambar was to run a comb through my unkempt hair, suspecting that, in any case, the clue to this urge lay elsewhere, something to do with the pectinal nature of a number of matters coming to a head. My housekeeper Lambar whispered as she approached, "Why didn't you warn me of your visitor?" I felt there was a touch of blame in the tone of her voice.

It was quite some time before I knew what to say. In the meantime I heard the drawn-out cooing of the telephone ringing with the quality of a homing pigeon calling to one of its own. Temporarily nonplused, I went past my housekeeper in inelegant haste to answer the phone, and as I did so bumped against two chairs placed upside down. In all the years that she had worked for me this was first time I had returned home to find her job undone to my full satisfaction. From what I could see, it seemed she had not finished mopping the floors. With my mind opening a parenthesis, which housed both a thesis and a counterthesis, I reached the telephone in its last breath, just before it died. I panted "*Pronto?*" and waited, convinced that I had arrived too late.

In the inventory of voices stored in my memory I couldn't for the life of me place my mother's, which was rather an odd thing to happen. But there was something agate-hard about her voice, and that wasn't how I remembered it. "Are you all right, Kalaman?" she said.

Before I was conscious of it, I had gained entry into another universe and there was no turning back: my mother's confederacy of demands, her legion of requests, of pleas, her do-be-carefuls, on account of the possible violence on a large scale, as she predicted the federations of clan families taking on one another. She could date the day when she became certain that there would be civil strife in Somalia. It was two o'clock in the afternoon, right in the heart of Mogadiscio. She was driving her pickup and, it being a hot day, had all the windows down. She stopped at a traffic light, waiting for the green to come after the yellow. Before she knew it, she had two gunmen in civilian clothes in the cab of the pickup, one of them brandishing a revolver and asking her to stop the vehicle, get out, and hand over the keys. She did no such thing. She drove on and on and on, faster and faster, confident that one or the other of them would get dizzy and plead for her to let them go. In fact that was how she saved her vehicle and her life. When asked how she thought of doing what she did, she simply responded, "The man's accent told me he was not familiar with cars and how they worked, and would be frightened of speed."

Already there had been intimations of a civil war erupting and of civic society collapsing into total anarchy. But whereas many of us thought these were early days yet, my mother held the view that we were approaching a collapse, what with the rumors reaching us that armed vigilantes were in the outskirts of Mogadiscio. It was as if someone had sold an idea of doom to her and she bought it as offered, wholesale. And she started to acquire all manner of weapons, preparing herself and her family for the worst. My mother did not wish our family to be caught by surprise, following the inhumane destruction caused to the people and property in the northern regions. The second largest city of the land was bombed by Siyad's regime, its residents massacred, almost all its buildings razed to the ground. From the day we received the news of the massacre, my mother remained on edge, a suitcase packed, and herself ready to depart at short notice. She would call me every now and then on the phone and inquire as to my preparedness for the approaching collapse. So what did she want today?

"Why do you never return my calls?" my mother said.

"I was going to come and see you," I lied.

Did she sense the proverbial limp in my walk: proverbial as the Somali adage in which it is said that a lie has a lame leg, truth a healthy one. I would have been the first to concede that my voice was wanting in firmness, its quality unsteady, that it was comparable to a limp in one's gait.

"Why do you lie to your mother?" she asked.

"Where are you?" I said.

"You should be ashamed of yourself, lying!" she said.

I derived comfort from remembering the proverbial black pot with the additional spout which, being tongued, called the other kettle all kinds of mean names. I said, "Mother, you have no reason to accuse me of wrongdoing. Because when you rang me at the office three or four times earlier today, I was busy with clients with whom I was tying the loose ends of a contract worth a lot of money to the firm."

"Are you still planning to take a week's holiday?"

If my mother approved of my planned trip to Nairobi, it was because she hoped that once I was out of the country, I might decide not to return to Mogadiscio. She urged me often enough to leave, suspecting that the civil strife might start any day. I kept postponing my date of departure, giving my workload at my computer business as the reason.

"I am planning to go, but I haven't a date yet," I said.

"Is anyone going with you?" she asked.

The question wrong-footed me. "I'm not decided. Why?"

I could hear a touch of hurt feeling in her voice as she said, "There you are, my thirty-three-year-old son Kalaman. In spite of your grown years, you have never stopped lying through the gaps of your teeth, cozy as a whirl of wind entering a keyhole."

We say, in Somali, that you don't ask someone whom you know to tell you about themselves. I knew where my mother was coming from. Maybe by calling me a liar she hoped to club me into a tight corner, so I would tell her everything she wanted me to, no secret withheld. I knew what she would do if her strategy did not produce a satisfactory result: appeal to my sense of filial loyalty.

She said, "I know you're not going away alone."

"I wish you wouldn't provoke me," I said.

Having completely forgotten about the alien aroma which greeted my senses upon my reentering my apartment, and having for the time shelved away my housekeeper's worries somewhere, I made myself as comfortable as I could under the circumstances. But then Lambar entered my peripheral vision and I began to see myself as a victim of my women's proclivities, of their wish to look after me better than I did myself.

"Who are you going with?" my mother said.

"Do you never tire, Mother?"

"How could I tire thinking of you?"

My housekeeper was hanging about me too, wanting to tell me something. I wondered if what she had to say might have any bearing on my conversation with my mother.

"I'd hate to hear about your news from a third party!"

My mother had a way of denigrating my women, whom she turned into a subject worthy of being celebrated in a limerick. Not that she was religious, but she didn't approve of seeing me with a woman I had no intention of taking as my lawful wife, proof enough that I intended not to offer her a grandchild. When she liked one of them, the poetics of her enthusiasm would entice her into a rapturous intensity. The words *Give me a child* were starting to haunt me. And in my memory I am a child and am requesting that my parents *Give me a sibling!* The words may have changed, possibly the speakers too; it wasn't I repeating the give-me plea, it was now my mother, who had never given me a sibling. Presently things were so quiet I thought my mother had hung up on me.

"Mother, are you there?"

"I am here, at your maternal beck and call," she chanted.

I had asked Nonno if he knew what caused my mother's exuberances. He said, "People with secrets have such an overabundance of energy for which they must find an outlet. My suspicion is that your mother talks unceasingly to hide her worries, whereas your father's silence is a tunnel in which he finds solace."

And then all of a sudden my nose felt clogged with the sweet scent of as pure a potful of honey as you were likely to find anywhere. Meanwhile my mother spoke on and on. And Lambar's shadow spread itself right before me, hovering in the attitude of a vulture in the vicinity of an abattoir.

"You're not getting married, Kalaman, are you, my darling?"

"Not that I know of. What makes you ask?"

"For several nights now I've been having dreams in which you get married. I just thought I should ask."

"You hear of all-out war between the autocrat's army and the militias wanting to overthrow his regime," I said, "and you have night visions which have to do with the impending disaster. I am thinking that these nightmares are brought about by an individual's private, un-thought-through reaction to a major crisis which is likely to disrupt the life of the whole society."

"In one of the dreams," she continued, "you are a mere child in every aspect save the fact that you invite us to your wedding, but your wife-to-be stands you up. In last night's dream, you slash open a vein of your middle finger and make a pledge of trust with your partner, a woman whose face bears a striking resemblance to Xusna, once your favorite pet, the vervet monkey." She paused. "You remember Xusna the monkey, don't you?"

"How could I forget!"

"But the weirdest thing is that Sholoongo's name is repeated by everyone I talk to in all these dreams. Have you any idea where in the world she is or what she is up to?"

"No," I said and, discerning the quiet movements of a short afternoon's shadow, which I assigned to Lambar, I resorted to the strategy of appeasement. I said, "I'll come and see you soon, because I must go now."

I held the dead receiver in my hands, not certain who hung up first. Anyhow, my eyes were misted over with a dejection of spirit. I was contemplating the idea of ringing her back, if only to apologize to her, when my entire world became all smells: putrid invasions of undomesticated odors, alien scents everywhere in the apartment, as if a cat had brought in a mouse and abandoned it, the rodent rotting under the sofa or the kitchen sink.

I hoped Lambar would explain the origin of the odor.

I found Lambar sitting in a huddle at the dining table in the kitchen, wrapped up in lengths of sorrow. She got up when I entered, her shadow as tight as a mean person's fist. I said, "I'm sorry, but did you mention something about a guest I hadn't warned you about?"

I occupied a first-floor two-bedroom apartment in one of Mogadiscio's most sought-after residential zones, and seldom entertained anyone claiming to be from either side of my parents' extended families, clansmen and clanswomen whose demands would range from being put up and fed for months to having their medical and their children's school bills footed. I had no time for them and didn't hesitate to show them the door. I would remind them that I was no member of a clan, that I was a professional. I had never had any of them come and stay as my guests, fearing what their nimble fingers might remove between the time you went into the shower and the moment you got out. To me they were pickpockets who arrived empty-handed but whose departures were as lucrative as corruption money. And social blackmail was their ploy!

"I have no idea how to explain," Lambar now said.

She was in her early fifties, and had been with my parents for years before coming to work for me. She had known me since my early teens, and I had always been impressed with her orderliness, her diligence, and her self-pride. She was from the River People, two villages farther down the Shabelle from Nonno's estate, and had a bedridden husband whose condition had remained unaltered until his death several years ago. And although she received full pay, she worked for me three half days, mopping the floors once a week, dealing with my laundry likewise, and preparing the traditional specialties cooked in the lean-to kitchen in my backyard. We got on very well, Lambar and I, and I loved her cooking, even if it was a bit too oily, with the vegetables overdone to the point of death.

When she didn't speak, I asked, "What gender is my guest?"

Her lips moved. If they managed to formulate the faintest of sounds, I didn't hear what she said. Lip reading is as difficult as deciphering hand signs drawn in the air. I am good at neither. I requested that she repeat what she had said. It took some time before I worked out that I had a female guest, who was not Talaado, my current woman-friend, whom, in any case, Lambar knew only too well. What's more, my guest had apparently let herself in, with her own key.

We were becoming more tense by the second, especially because Lambar was having difficulty getting her words out. I wished I knew, and learnt soon, what was causing so much discomfiture. Now we were nearly touching, and as I listened to her halty breathing, almost that of an asthmatic, it occurred to me that I was inhaling an odd mixture of odors with histamine caution, my nostrils gradually flaring, my lungs turning into a pair of bellows in expansive flames. I stood rock still, my head inclined backwards, as I held back a sneeze. Whereupon Lambar sneezed. This inspired me with an uncanny feeling. I blessed her. A moment passed, then another. Then the alien smell insinuated itself again and started to interfere with my thoughts.

"Where is she, then?" I asked. "My guest!"

Not a word out of her. She was the darkness of a tropical night filling one's eyes with dusky obliteration, her eyes wide open but unseeing. For an instant I took hold of the lower portion of her bony elbow in the attitude of a drowning person grabbing a watery foam, only to let go of her arm abruptly, all the more because I couldn't work out the *meaning* of the scent, or if my guest had something to do with it. We were now in the part of the flat which received more sunlight (how we got there I had no idea), the afternoon's brightness shining in and the contagious allergy of worry abating temporarily.

"Did you see her come in?" I asked.

"I didn't let her in, and didn't see her enter either, I swear." And the brown of her eyes became a shade paler, as if she had sighted an ethereal being.

"You must have been out of the flat when she got in?"

"I was in," she said, "from when I came in, working."

In my impatience, I walked away from her toward the corner room where I presumed my visitor to be, some poor clanswoman from some famine-stricken region of the land, out to make proprietorial demands of some kind. If I stopped in my tracks, it was because I thought of other possibilities, such as that the woman might be not a relative but a former lover, come to rekindle a romance that was dead.

Lambar lowered the volume of her voice to a near whisper as she came closer. "I thought you supplied her with a key. Not that I heard her enter, I repeat. But anyway," she said, and then lifted her shoulders in a meaningless way. I knew from previous experience that she was no good at lying or hiding her fear.

"You insist you were here all the time?"

"I was engrossed in mopping and other chores and then she was *here*." As if I failed to follow her meaning, she corrected herself by looking in the general direction of the corner room, and she rephrased it thus: "Or rather she was *there* between one instant and the next." She invested a variety of significances in the word "there," a concatenation of linked associations with space, time, and place too. With her arms wide apart you might have thought that she had at that very instant brought the cosmos into being, and along with it a sense of mystery and an attendant enigma.

Lambar's pupils were like the eyes of needles, as if the sun shaft joined them with the dark threads of my imagination, in and out, fast as a sunbird swooping across a pond. I stood right in the center of an open parenthesis, in a time without past or present or future. Then I felt something scratchily pulling at the hairs inside my nostrils, and sneezed so loud the world shook on its stilts. My nose was runny with mucus, my lips were wet with saliva and the palms of my hands moist with a motley of discharges; I thought, what histamine inelegance!

"It could be that I hallucinated," she said.

As I dried my hands, mouth, and nose with a handkerchief, her lips stirred. This put me in mind of a bird frightened in its sleep. An instant later Lambar's eyes fluttered with the pained slowness of a fledgling lacking one of its wings but attempting to fly. Lowering her whole body into a crouched position, she now inserted her head in the embrace of a bracket which she formed out of her own hands. Was she fearful that I might hit her? I took a step away from her.

"Wait, Kalaman, wait," Lambar said.

When I turned around, Lambar's eyes flickered like those of an animal vaguely conscious of approaching peril. "Be very careful," she advised.

A dangerous woman? An armed woman from one of the *other* clan, the enemy clan — how stupid can you get? — ready to make me do her bidding, prepared to put a gun to my forehead, in my own apartment and in broad daylight, to order me to empty my bank savings, make me sign on the dotted blood line, arguing my clan had been robbing hers blind for centuries? (My mother would say, "Serve you right," and in an I-told-you-so wisecrack after the fact, she would point to the animalness of these people!) Surely she couldn't belong to one of the militia groups using women to infiltrate the dictator's corrupt citadel? If so, why me?

Not only could I discern a change overcoming me, but a sudden feeling of fear was beginning to play all manner of tricks on my perception. I was seeing a cow in the semblance of a woman; I was seeing a woman in the ethereal flimsiness of a ghost which entered my apartment, in broad daylight, without being heard, seen, or suspected by Lambar. Suddenly I knew who my visitor was.

When I put it to Lambar, she appeared to support my thesis. She said, "Your visitor has the quiet, confident look of someone who has chosen *to be*, if you follow my meaning. It was as though she chose to be a woman today, but that she could as well have been a man in another life, or a ghost or a goat."

And no sooner had her gaze steadied itself as burning wicks do after the breeze has ceased blowing than she added, "When I last went in, she was sitting quietly, head bent over a piece of paper, drawing ugly *things*."

There was no need to engage in a whispered conference anymore: my guest's composite face called on my consciousness in bursts bright as shafts of lightning, in fits and spasms intimidating as doors opening in the squeaky dark of a Hitchcock horror film.

"Please ask her to join me for lunch," I said to Lambar, who moved to do just that, but hesitantly, as if struck with fresh fear. "After that," I went on, "you may leave us alone. We can set the table and serve ourselves."

My housekeeper stared at me in disbelief.

"I won't be needing your services for several weeks," I said, "so I suggest you see my assistant at the office, for your pay. She has instructions to pay you a full month's salary and bonus."

For the first time since entering my employ, Lambar was on the verge of disobeying my command. I saw this behavior as a most inauspicious omen, and I got very close to unsaying all I had said.

She pleaded with me, "Let me be here, please!"

"Do as I say," I ordered.

"Let me feed her with my own trusted hands," she said.

Firm, I said, "Please. Leave!"

Sholoongo had the smell of grass freshly cut, the odor of spring. She had the look of a cow smeared with its runny waste, green as the season is wet. This sent a shiver of hirsute allergy up my nostrils, and my hay fever was back. I was utterly miserable, I was short of breath and incapable of relaxing enough to let go of my sneeze. And the more I searched for something to say, the more the pollen count of my anxiety increased and along with it my sense of agony, my general discomfort. I stared helplessly at her, thinking that, unlike the nails on the fingers of the dead, Sholoongo hadn't grown an inch taller in the twenty-odd years since I last set my eyes on her. But she was heavier in the chest, like a woman meant to bear many children; her hips had widened too, as if she were intended to carry a roomful of them. Yet I deduced, the Lord knows how, that she hadn't borne a single child. Broad-featured, not bad-looking, but full of stir, Sholoongo had an inexplicable vitality. But she had too short a neck for a human, more like a bird's and just as agitated, forever moving back and forth, up and down, perhaps tracing mystical sevens, or else tying the knots of eights, or drawing the top loop of a nine.

She had a spot of brown stain on the tip of her nose. Also she had a startled stare as she returned my fixed gaze. She might have been a ratel, disturbed in the act of digging up recently interred carrion. I wrinkled my forehead with concern, part of me objecting to an unfair judgment of a woman I hadn't set eyes on for almost twenty years. Just because my mother distrusted her didn't mean that she was all evil. I decided to take the initiative myself, so as not to allow her to draw circles around me, or to dominate the conversation.

I said, "Would you like a glass of tamarind juice, chilled?" My tongue rubbed itself against my fricative palate without stumbling on any of the consonants. But my sense of triumph didn't last long, for I sneezed several times and in quick succession soon after speaking. She showered no blessings on me. In fact she looked away as if she might have been partly to blame. Even so, I led her into the kitchen and poured out a generous glass of tamarind juice and passed it to her. She received the drink with both hands and sat down at the table. I was thinking about how I might disown the common past of our youth, when I sneezed with allergic inevitability.

She took a sip of her tamarind juice, the look in her eyes as distant as someone savoring an ancient memory in the flavor of a drink. I had the suspicion that for an unguarded moment she wore an impish grin, but her tone was matter-of-fact as she said, "It's been a long time, hasn't it?"

Her voice had become harder, I thought, more like my mother's. It had a metallic edge to it, as if somewhere inside it half a razor blade had been buried. I dreaded to imagine what sparks my mother's and Sholoongo's head-on collision would produce when the sharp corners of Sholoongo's blade encountered my mother's, which was hard as a pebble. I sneezed yet again.

"I hope you're not allergic to lice," she said.

I had heard it said that the most efficient way to stop people hiccuping is to shock them. Which explained why the absurd question — was I allergic to lice? — had a salutary effect on me. My nose was suddenly cleared of its itchy irritability. "Why ask if I am allergic to lice?"

"Because I am carrying a couple on my person," she said, sitting rather solidly in the squat posture of a pigeon cooing. There was no twitch in her anywhere, she was all seriousness.

With curiosity outweighing my discretion, I said, "But pray, where on your person are you carrying the lice, and why?" I might have been a U.S. customs officer inquiring if she had brought along with her some maggot-infested fruit from across the oceans.

"Don't be a bore," she said, leaning away, all *shakara* mystery. She didn't seem likely to divulge where on her person she had hidden the lice, nor give the reason why.

My mother endowed me with an overwrought sensibility. In other words, I tend to infer that evasion is tantamount to telling lies, or hiding a secret. "I don't believe you," I said. But all she did was smile.

Annoyed, my head was abuzz with memories born of a moment being relived, these fraternizing with other remembrances from a remote past. I rummaged through the recesses of these recollections. Too embarrassed to recall them, I hoped nobody would ever get to know what Sholoongo and I had been through together, childhood mischiefs which were bound to put me to utter shame. Blood oaths there were, the veins of fingers cut, flints used, vows taken, till-death-pull-us-asunder promises made. Put it down to a sense of guilt weighing on my conscience, but the truth was I felt trapped in a universe of knots, which the more I tried to undo, the more the clove hitches loosened up and the more the reef knots and the bowlines got more and more entangled.

"Is Fidow still alive?" she said.

I nodded my head lamely.

She drank her tamarind juice in small draughts, as I saw visions of the world tumbling around my ears, and of me falling, collapsing, and taking along with me Nonno, my parents, perhaps Fidow too. Imagine: a woman whose name hadn't crossed my mind or lips for years turns up in my mother's dreams, then shows up in my apartment into which she lets herself. My mother rings, asking if I have any idea where she might be. Now she is here, in my kitchen, a real blood-and-bones irritation. I dreaded to think what a novelist might say if a mere creature, and a weakling character at that, were to challenge his powers of invention!

"Is this all the welcome I'm going to get," she said, "a glass of oversugared tamarind juice, just that, no hug, no kisses, nothing but questions and dead-end stares?"

I didn't answer her for fear that my voice might sound hoarse, and didn't move, wondering if my manner would strike her as intimidated. I countered by regarding her with malice. She stared back at me with the self-confidence of a woman in whose eyes the majesty of an afternoon sun has found a residence.

"How did you come in?" I asked.

Her lips burst into a daredevil bud of a smile. "Did you expect me to use a back entrance, as if I were the day's hired help or something? How did I come in? The cheek of it!"

"My housekeeper says she didn't let you in."

A fresh fit of panic took a tighter grip of me, the moment the words left my lips. And for some reason I was remembering a murder committed, Nonno fleeing southwards, away from his birthplace in the city of Berbera, then in the British Somaliland Protectorate. He ended up in Afgoi of all places, to don a new identity and emerge into an altered perspective. Why on earth was this woman making me revisit in memory some of the things I had clean forgotten? There was no way of knowing what her visit might bring forth, what mysteries it might unravel, what manner of disastrous debates it might generate between myself and my mother on the one hand, and between Talaado, the woman I was seeing, and myself on the other. In other words, there was no telling how much havoc Sholoongo would cause.

"You have no idea," she said, "how much the blood in my forefinger's veins thrilled at the thought of touching yours after so many years. You shock me. Because all you seem to be interested in are mere mundanities: how I managed to enter your apartment, or why I was carrying lice on my person, or where. Have you forgotten how to think big? Are you fearful stiff of what the impending disasters might do to your lifestyle, your clan pitted against mine? Is this uppermost in your mind?"

Reduced to a flutter, I stared tongue-tied and in dumbfounded frustration. Doors cracked open in my head and then just as suddenly were slammed shut with a loud thud, as I abandoned the attempt to speak in self-defense.

Now she flung a question at me. "How's Nonno?"

"He is like a well-tuned drum, his skin still tight on his body," I said. "He looks a great deal younger than eighty-three, and going stronger, with a great deal of spring in his gait."

"And your father?"

"Attending to a world in messy disrepair."

"I won't ask about your mother," she said.

"Why not?"

"Perhaps you can offer me a stronger drink?" she replied.

I have no idea why, but as well as thinking of Chinese rice-names, I mouthed the French expression *nom de lait*, remembering that just before naming me Kalaman, Nonno had wet my lips with a drip of

tamarind drink. Only afterwards did my mother breast-feed me.
"What stronger drink would you like to have?"

"Two fingers of any available liquor," she said.

As I moved toward the drink cabinet, I wondered if Sholoongo had
been my invention, reminding myself that a quarter of a century is a
long time to account for. A pot of honey lasts not forever; a glass of
tamarind juice, chilled, sours within a couple of days into a stimulant,
a bar of chocolate melts into a smudge soon in the tropical heat of the
day. Two fingers of liquor, indeed! I brought out an assortment of bottles,
which I placed before her, suggesting that she help herself. Obliging,
she poured into her glass more than several fingers' worth of whiskey.

"Why didn't you alert me of your coming?" I said.

"How you are bourgeois and boring!" was her cutting reply.

I felt oddly secure in my silence.

"What have I meant to you all these years?" she asked.

I dared not tell her that I had celebrated her absence by allotting
it a central place in the scheme of my life; or that her ubiquity extended to every opening of every door I entered; or that I thought
about her whenever I looked at a hole in a wind instrument, or played
it, stopping it with a finger!

She said, "Remember the maxim: Finders keep!"

"Finding and keeping what? Or whom?"

"We played that as children!"

"And so?"

"I was eleven and you were ten," she said.

"You were fifteen, I was nine," I corrected her.

"Not in my passport," she said.

"I didn't think you had one in those days," I retorted.

"In my U.S. passport I am only two years older than you."

The thought occurred to me that perhaps she was flaunting her
U.S. passport, assuming that I would be interested in her as a holder of
it. After all, it would provide one with a way out of the crisis in Somalia, should the country collapse into total anarchy. I let that pass without comment.

She was reminiscing. "We had so much fun, didn't we, when
young, you and I? We lived a free-for-all life, didn't we? And things
being what they are today, we can maybe look forward to a lifestyle

unhindered by today's narcissistic banalities, where I am *faciis* and you are a member of the other clan confederacy!"

"America, the land where differences are made to melt?"

She was suddenly irritable. "You can do better than that, clichés stood on their heads! Where is the Kalaman with the restless intelligence, the cork to prevent the genie from flying out of the bottle, into the smoke of dissipation?"

No witticism came pat to me. Helpless as a cockroach on its back, a cockroach with all its tiny feet searching up in the air for something solid to latch onto, I sat staring at her.

"You don't recall much, do you?" she challenged.

I said, "The landscape of my memory is strewn with discarded bits of a life as useless as driftwood. A host of these hang askew, picture frames too heavy for the nail holding them up."

"Do you know why I am here?" she said.

If there were byzantine traps lying in wait for me, let them, I thought. I replied, "You'll tell it all to me, won't you, sooner or later." Hoping I sounded convincingly indifferent to why she was here, I got out the plates. I set one down on the kitchen table, then the other, and dished out the meal, giving her a larger portion. I took a spoonful, food as prophylactics!

She said, "It is curious how food played an important role in our relationship. You gave me food and I gave you my *self*. Pots of honey, a bar of chocolate, a morsel of this or that. And what did I do? I served you a young woman's soul, mine, in exchange for these edibles. Very tragic! Or is that how things are between men and women, men providing for women's easy-to-meet necessities, and in exchange receiving the women's souls?"

"Damn you," I cursed, my voice sounding as if it originated underwater. I got up, and came closer to touching her than at any other time since seeing her. Could I bring myself to hit her or throw her out of my apartment? I cursed because I didn't know how else to defend myself against these preposterous generalizations about men and women. Eventually I got back to my side of the table and seated myself before my plate, but hadn't the will to eat.

"I won't eat alone," she said.

We ate, she faster and faster, and as she did so she spoke, chanting

every single word with the slowness of a sorceress uttering potent in-
cantations. "We've come, Timir and I, to bury our father," she said.

I extended my condolences.

"But there's another reason why I am here."

As she took her penultimate mouthful she choked on her breath,
and coughed. I wondered if I should give her a slap on the back. There
was a rush of sudden anxiety in her throat, her hands reaching for her
Eve's apple, which she massaged gently. I sat tight, waiting.

"What did your housekeeper put in the food?" she asked.

I made a search-me gesture, and as I did so I noticed a smudge the
size of a shilling on her left cheek. Apparently I mistook the smudge
for a shadow her nose cast. Now she was scratching the very spot. I
remembered then how my mother had once described Sholoongo as
having the look of a predator, the blood-and-raw-gut appetite of a
wolf, the sweet sting of a honeybee, the cunning of a fox, and the de-
viousness of a hyena.

"I'm here for a few days," she said. "Can you put me up?"

I greeted the news with the full compliment of a genuine smile. I
thought of my mother; I thought of what my father might say; I
thought of what Talaado might think; I thought of Nonno.

She went on, "I am here to bear a baby."

She had the clearheadedness to reveal in few words what it was
she wanted very badly, and I envied her. I envied her how everything
was there, the poetry, the pathos, the rhetoric of breeding. After all,
whereas I had difficulty working out how I was going to say no to her
request to stay with me, she had moved on. She was here to have a
child? How? Unable to determine my role in her desire to bear a baby,
I asked, "In what way may I be of assistance?"

"I want you to be the father of my child," she said.

"Why me?" I asked, and flinched at the thought of what she
might say. In my imagination I heard a voice charged with a mix of
bitterness and sarcasm. The answer came out pat: *For the genius in
your gender, my handsome genie!*

"The reasons are too manifold to go into now," she said. Then a
mean look spread across her face.

I couldn't think of anything to say, so I asked, "Where is Timir?"

"He has been wearing his out-of-the-closet colors lately."

Her meaning evaded me. "What are they, the colors?"

"He is an active member of the American gay movement."

"Is he here to set up a branch?" I asked.

Crocodiles have tears to shed, Sholoongo had none. "He's come to buy a woman, preferably one with an infant and who, out of gratitude for his wealth and his American passport, is prepared to slave for him and his artsy boyfriend in San Francisco in a threesome setup."

The telephone rang. My wristwatch confirmed my own suspicions: I was decidedly late for work. As it was, I was delighted to get away. I spoke to my secretary at my firm and dictated a couple of brief messages.

I said to Sholoongo, "I am off and will see you later."

And I fled.

My hand has an atavistic memory of a script with mysterious loops and curves. I trace these, my thumb rubbing against my index finger as I write this imaginary script. I do so whenever I cannot concentrate on my self-allotted workload in my office. Drawing helps me to minimize the tension within me. Now and then I do the cross of Lorraine, and at some point join the top strokes to the bottom ones. This way faces emerge, of owls with eyes forever shut, or fishes with their mouths open and feeding. My father is the artist in the family, capable of depicting what others are unable to imagine. I am not much of an artist, I am a computer freak, and that is my business and primary concern. I run my own business, and have some fifteen people working for me. My office is in the annex, and I have an efficient deputy-director, a former lover, named Qalin. We all rely on her.

I start on a Lorraine, with memories of Sholoongo's odor overwhelming me time and again, fastidiously flatulent, like the odious belch of palm oil. I am wondering whether to go for a walk, if only to clear my lungs of the terrible belch, as I ring my secretary for messages. Among the callers is Timir. He has been and gone, promising to return, maybe tomorrow. Would I like her to call his hotel? No. Even so, I won't deny that a part of me is eager to call Timir and talk to him, if only to find out the truth about Sholoongo's motives. Why me?

With the air conditioner in my office humming in the background, my hand traces out more strokes in a Lorraine and obtains a set of interlaced pinnate patterns: of leaves of a tamarind tree, its foliage immaculately green, soft to touch in the way feathers are, and having a similar influence on the beholder. The afternoon sun loses its harsher edge and more of its rage. Somewhere in the grooves of the design I am able to work out the shape of a lamp, forever lit, burning!

In my memory I am a child. Sholoongo's father, I know, is with a woman, on a bed whose sheets haven't been changed for days, in a room whose windows haven't been opened for almost a week, the two giving each other a whale of a week's honeymoon, the weft and warp of their bodies so interwoven you couldn't tell which leg or arm belonged to whom, except you might be able to see the difference if you concentrated on the hirsuteness of the male's, and even then you would be mistaken, for Madoobe hadn't a single hair on his chest and legs and had the habit of shaving his beard and pubic hair. He is with a Yemeni woman who is darker than he, and he is dark all right. Because I cannot tell who is on top, who is the one covered all over with stiffish hair, I go closer. I am eight years of age, a frequent voyeur. I got into trouble more than thrice with my own parents, who caught me spying on them. But not Madoobe, Sholoongo's father.

Timir and Sholoongo are in their room, having it off without ever letting on. My only evidence is Timir's say-so, after I overheard him say that he would not "give it to her anymore." Give what? I surprised them one late afternoon, and instead of choosing to remain unseen and staying quiet in the safety of a voyeur's secret place, I decided to show myself.

"Would you like it too?" she asked.

That was not how *it* all began!

On another day I rummaged in her satchel and in her pockets in search of evidence of witchery. Finding none, I invited her and Timir for a swim at Nonno's. I made certain we took our dip in the spot of the river where we were likely to irritate a crocodile into enraged action. My idea was that if, as was rumored, she were capable of exchanging her human form for that of an animal, what better way to prove it than to risk her life? Alas, we did not meet any danger. I tried to catch her out again and again, but to no avail.

All three of us, on another occasion, went out for a walk in Nonno's woods. I took them up the route where packs of hyena were said to prowl. We waited, again to no avail. There is not much fun sitting it out in the dark, stiff with fright, your heart beating faster than Fausto Coppi's when breaking a world record.

Now, years later, a couple of hours after having lunch with Sholoongo in my apartment, I give a start when the telephone rings. I don't answer, because I don't wish to talk to my mother, to Timir if he is the one phoning, to Talaado if she is the one, or to Sholoongo. When the telephone bell ceases sounding its long, rather drawn out scare-monger's alarms, I take a worried look at the drawing in front of me: a parrot, and in its beak a young moon.

I didn't get back to my place until late. But I called my mother's retail business before she closed for the day and made peace with her. I didn't divulge Sholoongo's whereabouts. Nor did I tell Talaado about her even after I picked her up on our way to see a film with a confusing story line, something I put down to my own state of mind. And when my friend and I were at a drive-in sandwich joint and she inquired why I was in such a quiet mood, my answer was evasive.

My apartment was quiet when I reentered it, the lights out. As far as I could tell, my guest was asleep in the spare bedroom, whose door, I sensed, was pushed shut. I moved about in the dark and then lay in my room, unable to sleep, torn by the conflicting demands on a man in my situation. I fell asleep to the hooting of an owl, wishing me and all the other insomniacs in my neighborhood a good night.

CHAPTER
TWO

A memory of singular significance supersedes all others. This memory is centered around a man in his early seventies, thick-set, with a shock of gray hair. He is wearing a robe dipped in dull red acacia-bark dye and is riding a stallion of sterling handsomeness. At his approach there is pandemonium. The women separate themselves from the men. They ululate. The men rise to their feet in apparent awe of him. He dismounts. A young man leads away his horse.

The old man with the shock of gray hair is given a stool, which he takes. To show the high respect in which he is held, the village barber shaves his hair off. A procession of women arrives, bringing along a high chair. One of the young women offers him the high chair with great deference, as if she were offering herself to him. He mounts the high chair.

There is an undercurrent of tension between the old men and the young men in the community. One of the old men speaks about the queasy times, a young man makes reference to a drought which has killed three-quarters of the community's livestock. All this while the old man, still on his high chair, his shaven head shiny with a coating of oil, remains silent, as if uninvolved. But his lips are touched with the static charge of his devotions, most likely a rosary in praise of Allah.

As a mark of respect, he is now asked to distribute milk among the members of the gathering, first the young, then, if there is more milk to be had, among the old. He gives half a gourdful of milk each to a group of children. Curiously, the more milk he gives out, the fuller the receptacle becomes, until it spills over. To ensure that not a drop is wasted, the young ones assign several of their number to lick the outside of the milk vessel. Those farthest from it make smacking theatrical sounds with their lips, while those close by go on their knees and work their tongues into the most awkward positions, catching the overflow in any way they can. Otherwise the entire place is in a silence as reverential as that of a sadhu performing a Hindu ritual. "Like a hole," whispers the young boy who led away the horse, to the girl who offered the high chair to the old man, "that grows larger the more earth you take out of it."

The sun is setting. There are crocodiles everywhere, crocodiles with wings. There are also snakes engaging wide-hipped dragonflies in a never-ending dialogue of drones. When another lot of youngsters have had sufficient milk, they line up to receive their share of bones with no meat on. On the smooth meatless bones are engraved centuries-old designs. The youths chew the softer end of the bones with no patterns on them. They do this with as much enthusiasm as a thirsty person drinks up, in imagination, all the water in a distant mirage.

The atmosphere is serene. The rituals appear to have been stripped of all pretensions. Then the gathering hears a whimper, which at first it can't locate. The old man, from his vantage high chair, spots the whimperer, a boy, whom he requests to approach. All silence. The old man asks the youth what's amiss. The boy shakes his head in sadness, unable to speak. His companion, the girl who earlier offered the high chair, approaches and explains, "He has been very greedy."

"But why the whimper? Are you in pain?" asks the old man.

Raising her voice to drown her companion's sobs, the girl says, "He has swallowed his Adam's apple, mistaking it for a bone with a smooth body with centuries-old cowries engraved."

Someone asks, "And what is to become of him?"

"From now on," responds the young girl, "he and I will perforce belong to an outcast clan with whom most Somalis will not intermarry. Because he momentarily swallowed his Adam's apple, mistaking it for a bone, his failure to restrain himself has cost us most dearly. Our family is assigned an inferior position in the scheme of clan politics."

The old man ponders in silence for a long while. Being new at the job, he is not sure if it is in his power to replace the boy's Adam's apple. But will that set things right, alter the way society treats those whom it considers to be "deviants"? A moment's lapse, and we are in the land of tragedy, where it no longer makes sense to think of the boy as just a boy, to whom you may suggest that he moderate his intake of food. Why do the rites with which food is associated cause possible damage to society? Why is food important in the way we think of ourselves, some inferior, others superior? We live in tragic times, thought the old man helplessly, when a chance birth can make so much difference to how one is viewed, where a secret ensconced in the recesses of untapped memories assigns one to an inferior or a superior position.

As the newly chosen wise old man, I . . .

It was seven in the morning.

Sholoongo joined me in the kitchen for breakfast. She came in with the quietness of a conspirator the very moment I had throttled the kettle's singing. I paid her no mind, in fact did not bother to greet her until after I had emptied the coffee from the grinder into a pot for it to brew. She told me, with little ado, that she preferred tea if tea was "in the realm of the possible." I asked how she liked her tea, and she said, "As dark as you can make it, no milk. No sugar, unless you have Fidow's honey to hand."

Then she greeted me, wishing me a *"Subax wacan!"*

I was fully dressed, hair not as yet combed. She was in a silk kimono with eagle-patterns. The eagles made taking-off motions whenever she lifted her arms, and made descending gestures when she crossed her legs, only for the unwinged birds to feel frustrated when, shortly thereafter, she recrossed her weighty thighs or entwined her fat fingers in an intricate way. As for honey for her tea, I doubted that I had any collected by Fidow, Nonno's general factotum. I knew I had bought imported honey recently from a supermarket, but not where the jar might be. I opened one cupboard after another, reading the labels on the jars, now Zairois *pilipili*, now Ethiopian *berberre*, now Indian curries, ground cinnamon, or nutmeg.

"You can't find it?"

"Nothing remains hidden forever!"

"Not even secrets?"

"Nothing remains hidden forever without losing its original identity, and no secret is forever a secret: it has to be known by someone who places a value on it, no matter whether it is divulged or not." I paused, if only to ask myself what I was looking for. Then I wondered to myself why I was engaging in a semiphilosophical argument early in the morning with a woman I barely knew. What was happening to me?

Honey found, but not Fidow's, we lamented the changing pattern of our neocolonial economies, when we import honey, bottled in jars, from Europe, when we have plenty of the commodity locally available and at a cheaper price, and many Fidows to collect it. I placed the two pots — coffee for me and tea for her — side by side, and poured out hers. I watched her put three spoonfuls of honey in it. Two sips later, she smacked her lips in approval. "I am sorry it is not Fidow's, but . . . !"

"Did you sleep well?" I asked.

"I heard you come in," she said.

"But you slept well, and you were comfortable?"

"I woke up several times," she said, "because I could hear the exchanges of gunfire, some coming from as close as a kilometer away. How long has this been going on?"

"You get used to hearing the sound of automatic weapons," I said, "and you sleep through it. For several months now, the armed militias have been closing in on Mogadiscio, but Siyad and his men are unimpressed. There are so many irregular armies operating within the city, some of them under former army officers, out to loot. You cannot tell who is shooting at whom."

"Some kind of gang warfare," she said.

I wasn't sure whether to challenge that or to let it ride. At this stage of the strife, almost every act appeared to be informed by the politics of the parties waging a struggle. I let it go as I often have let go foreigners' throwaway remarks spoken in ignorance, foreigners who held the view that "Somali politics is clan politics." It would take me years to convince them otherwise. So we sat in silence, like lovers who had a quarrel the previous night, who slept in separate beds, but whom the morning's sunshine found in no conciliatory mood.

"Were you at all tempted to come into my bed when you got back late last night?" she asked. She sat in her silence, as time sits in the sunlight, marking the passage of time in dust.

To myself I quoted the Somali proverb that, having met once, a penis and a vagina seldom turn down the chance to be reacquainted. I was confident, however, that mine would rather remain dormant than be entertained by hers. Remembering that I had difficulty getting it up the previous evening even with Talaado, I said, "I was not tempted to come to you at all."

And as though squeamish, I looked away from the extended bulginess of her hips, her folds of navel extensions, and her partly exposed breasts. She had a mole where the breasts parted, at whose singularly long hair she pulled the way some men caress their beards, presumably thinking. I wondered if that lone hair was artificially grown, in an America where sex is an industry supplying on demand what a client needs.

"What did you do yesterday after I left?" I asked.

"I changed some money, for starters," she said, "got myself a bagful of local shillings in large denominations, took a taxi to a car rental agency, where I paid for a week's rent in cash and in advance. Then I went places."

"Where?"

"I researched into your private life."

"What did you come up with?" I asked, not curious.

"I dug up a beauty of a discovery, name of Talaado."

I tried in vain to speak normally. I rubbed my wrist as though it hurt, which of course it didn't. Anxiety caught at my throat. I thought of roping her neck with a hangman's noose, right now, in my kitchen. Would her corpse lose the warmth that was its blood before our cups of coffee or tea got cold?

"What point are you making nosing into my affairs?" I said.

"It's just for the thrill of it, I suppose," she said. "The things you discover, the secrets you uncover, just for the intimate thrill of it. It is like having a bat for a pet, and wearing it wherever you go, the bat dangling from your necklace. I saw a woman on TV with a bat for a pet. Anyway I bet you thought I would not know about your hush-hush affair!"

We went to lots of bother, Talaado and I, to have our rendezvous where no one knew either of us. Whereas my mother had not found out about us, even though we had been going out for several months now, it took Sholoongo only half a day to do so.

"Just the thrill of it," I repeated.

"A bat for a pet," she said. "Imagine the excitement."

I had my omelette in silence, she her scrambled eggs. She talked and I listened with all my body as if searching for clues. I suspected she felt the anxiety in my eyes and in the way I held my hand still, as if worried I might become violent.

"If you want me to leave," she said, "I shall do so. I'll go on your say-so, no sweat. I would hate to impose myself on you. Tell me when to leave."

I made some more tea and coffee, and availed myself of the opportunity to alter the course of the conversation. I said, "What ever have you done with the lice?"

She might have been speaking about her children who were sleeping next door. She replied, "They are in a tiny jar, the size of a matchbox, which is in my handbag. They have enough jelly-stuff to live on. It's the jelly which smells awfully."

I felt delicate as I listened to the detailed care she was giving to the lice. Possibly this inhibited me from further pursuing the matter, and I dropped it altogether. Perhaps she sensed my unease, for she said, "Relax, Kalaman. We've done more hilarious things together, you and I, weirder, more out-of-the-way, bloodcurdling stuff. What are lice in a jar, with jelly in it? This is kid stuff compared with what you and I have been through together."

The hard reality of my childhood secrets dissolved in my coffee. I could savor it, in the way I smelt an amalgam of odors with a savage bitterness to them, smells-as-spells, the scent of jujube's dried wood. It was to the smoke of jujube wood that Sholoongo used to expose her private parts, in the traditional belief that such fumigation would help protract her sexual performance. These animant revisits to our childhood were so overpowering that I suffered the anxious dilation of a sinus cavity. I sneezed and sneezed and sneezed and sneezed, and got myself a wounded membrane. I hurt badly. When my eyes cleared of the fog bedeviling me, I asked, as though nothing untoward had occurred, "What do you do for a living, where you are?"

She was silent for a long while, as if she were shuffling her words in her head, deciding which trump card to show. "I am a shape-shifter," she replied.

"A shaman, in a manner of saying?"

At her nod, doors opened in my imagination, houses shifted. The earth moved, the sky came nearer, birds flew in and out of human skulls, discarded by the roadside of my memories. One of the birds flew higher and higher into the seventh heaven of my expectations, and I waited for it to return with a secret, about Sholoongo, clutched in its beak.

"I mean to do no one harm," she said.

"Have I accused you of planning to hurt anyone?"

"Your mother will."

"Have you seen my mother since coming back to Mogadiscio?"

"I understand she's had problems adjusting to your refusal to give her a grandchild," she said, "and I am told she has been seeing nightmares. Not that I don't have nightmares myself, we all do, now and then."

My inner anxiety pressing in on me, I found it difficult to breathe. It felt as if, hurting badly, my lungs were expanding into the very space of my heart. "Who's your source?" I said. "Because you appear to know a lot about my private life."

"I reiterate that I shall leave the very instant you tell me to," she said. "I would not countenance the thought of being accused of all manner of evil when I mean no harm, only good. The proof of my goodwill rests in the fact that I've come to bear your baby."

"But that is out of the question," I said.

Like a broken vase her smile leaked droplets of sadness.

I was grateful for the arrival in the room of a fly, large enough to be mistaken for a dung beetle. It circled above the honey jar and wouldn't be shooed away. Meanwhile I busied my mind with more homegrown thoughts: about a moral blur, of Sholoongo being accused of stealing a document from my mother; of Sholoongo as a mistress of lascivious wantonness. And there was of course the matter of her mysterious entry into my apartment. How did she do that? Shifting shapes, altering her own nature? Or changing the shape of things? Or was she a burglar with a master key? Could Lambar have left the door ajar, and forgotten, or lied about her oversight?

"I've been to your mother's shop too," she said.

The fly flew out of its own accord with no help from us.

"When did you do that?"

"The day before yesterday."

"She didn't see you, did she?"

"She didn't recognize me."

No wonder my mother had seen her in a dream. My mother saw her, but didn't recognize her there and then. Only later did she acknowledge her presence in her unconscious, by dreaming about her. After all, she was not expecting to see her, was she?

Now there was a snarl in Sholoongo's eye's tangle. She appeared slightly confounded, like a traveler coming to the fork in a footpath, not knowing which one to take. Examined closely, she had the dusty look of a cow that had just given itself a sandbath after drinking from a trough. Her features, which had earlier been smile-paneled, were presently austere-looking and of a darker hue that suggested dead wood soaked in water. In my mother's unconscious, perhaps she was the bride who stood me up? Because I wouldn't give her a baby?

She fixed me with her fury of a stare. But I didn't feel at all intimidated. Then she became fidgety. Restless, she moved her flowing gown about until I could see an eagle's silver-lined wings spreading fully, a bird of majesty, the kind which seldom descended before nightfall, whose sense of privacy was exemplary. I got up with as little caution as an absentminded cook putting more salt in an already salted stew. I opened a kitchen drawer and pulled out a bunch of keys on a chain. I said, "Here are the keys to the flat. You may stay for as long as you please."

Soon enough I felt wretched, asking myself why I was giving her a set of my keys, why I was getting myself into the murkier end of already muddied waters. My mother would argue that Sholoongo had bewitching powers over me.

She said, "By the way, my husband knows that I'm seeing you, but I would appreciate it if you were discreet when it came to the others."

"I'll be damned," was all I said.

A fresher unease made me jittery. My head itched and I scratched it savagely. When I looked at my nails, they had dandruff under them, traces of eczema, a trail of it, the untreated patches of dry disease. "I'll tell who I like."

My unexpected hostility shocked her. But she was silent.

"I will see you later," I said, and quit the apartment.

Noon the same day. And I am at work.

I started my company, Birders, with an initial capital supplied by Nonno. I began it as a small two-table affair, meant to provide a letter-writing service to Mogadiscio's residents, the majority of whom are illiterate, or at best semiliterate. Once successful, I soldiered on with the help of my then secretary, Qalin, and provided more and more services, including document preparing, typing, photocopying. After receiving a bank loan, Nonno putting up his estate as collateral, much of which I've since repaid, I expanded into computer programming. More recently I've set up a data-processing network, a venture which now boasts a clientele among foreign-run nongovernmental organizations and foreign embassies, both lucrative, the bills paid in hard currency, preferably into an account bearing Nonno's name in Italy. Thanks to the dedication of my fellow workers, this is a flourishing business. In fact, we're stretching in uneven curves with the liveliness of a bird breaking out of its natal shell. If we are moving into dollar-making ventures, it is because this country is becoming a land of ruin. And we are working against the odds of survival, in possible exile, out of Mogadiscio, when it all collapses.

Apart from Qalin, a most capable executive, we have three assistant deputy managers, two of whom are women. We also have seven full-time scribes, three doubling as typists. As support staff, we employ three simultaneous translators (a first-rate Arabic specialist, a second specializing in English, and a half-Italian woman). The scribes take dictation notes in Somali. The job then is passed on to the relevant person, depending on the language the letter is be rendered into. The scribes themselves do an excellent job for those wanting missives in Somali because they are illiterate.

We occupy three floors in a high-rise. (We are the first to go when Mogadiscio collapses, predicts Qalin.) Now many people ask why we named our company Birders, in much the same way as they say "Kalaman?" To her credit, Sholoongo did not put either question to me now or at any time.

Why Birders? In response, I tell the story of a Yoruba-speaking man from present-day Benin, in West Africa, whom the French had detained together with his coconspirators, some of whom were released earlier than he. Before they parted, one of them offered to take a message to his wife. The prisoner requested they take to her a stone, a bit of coal, a sniff of red pepper, and a rag. When the would-be bearer of the message asked what each item meant, he was informed that the wife would supply him with the clue to the riddle.

I suggest you make up your own clue to, Why Birders?

I couldn't concentrate on my work and, restless, paced back and forth in the corridor separating my office from the foyer. I had the ominous sense of descending a declivity, only I remembered the age-old Somali wisdom in good time: that little lies had bigger ones on their false heels. If truth was the first casualty resulting from my reticence, then discretion was the second. Moreover there were bound to be disasters as a consequence of these lies, future heavy losses, of face, of dignity, of self-pride, of family loyalty, and eventually even of life. Why did I not call up my mother? Why not tell her, Sholoongo *is* my guest? What I was afraid of? I was wise enough not to set much store by the questionable idea that I was buying time. After all I was not. I was merely affording myself the luxury of a pause, as I waited in anticipation of a storm brewing, which I hoped would blow over without harm to any of us. From the sound of her, Sholoongo was a traveler in possession of an air ticket with no expiration date. A guest, my guest. Forever.

If I wanted to stop this lie-telling, then why not take the first step: since journeys start with the first pace, why not speak up? I pressed Qalin's numbers on the intercom. She came into my office, a little nervous. She was nearly as tall as I, six years my junior, with intelligent eyes and handsome bearing. She stared at me now with bewilderment, and now with affection. I thought of her as the one friend who wove a kind of webbed continuity around me. We were once lovers, but we parted with our friendship intact, something quite rare. Discreet, she aborted my baby and never bothered to tell me, for fear I might bear her ill feeling. Such a generous soul! I knew a lot more about her life than she about mine, knew that she was seeing a man but, in my heart, suspected that she would have dropped him if I suggested she and I marry.

Now I was fretted with inarticulateness, for I did not know how to tell her about the complications in my private life. I was tentative in my approach, and spoke, with long pauses and a couple of stammers, about the fact that my problems might not go away soon. And that I might not go away on a ten-day vacation to Nairobi, as I had hoped, because of these complications. I noticed disappointment lift itself up out of the calm of her eyes. I was touched.

"Is there anything I can do?" she said.

"I'm not sure," I said.

There were shadows under her eyes, shadows abounding in interstices. Were these dark eye-bags the result of staying up, an insomniac having night visions?

"Are your worries about your mother?" I sensed a hint of ambivalence in her voice.

"What makes you ask?"

"Because she came to see me last night," she said, "at my parents', and wondered if I knew that you were planning to elope with a woman. Was I the woman? If not, did I have any idea who it might be? I told her that you were not planning to marry." A pause. "Are you?"

I shook my head, no.

Without saying anything, Qalin now placed a bunch of keys on my desk, then stood at a distance, back straight, formal. I was taken aback by this, wrongly assuming that she was tendering her resignation. I stared at the ring holding the keys together and thought of other rings, including the one Qalin had on her middle finger, a gift from me when we believed we were to marry to each other. Until this day, I couldn't tell why we decided not to. Or who called the engagement off. For the sake of our friendship.

She halved her attention between me and the keys, now focusing on my eyes, now on the ring. "Is there any point my keeping the master keys if you aren't going on vacation? In particular, the coded ones for the safes and the generator," she explained.

"Please hold on to the keys," I said.

"Sure," she said, as she picked them up with the care one uses to pick up a grenade. Then, with a worrying suddenness, she raised a wall of privacy around her. She consulted her watch and was gone, fast as a woman responding to her baby's cry in an adjacent room.

Alone, I felt Sholoongo weigh on my thoughts. It wasn't in my nature to be unkind to women, and for whatever this was worth, Sholoongo had already disabused me of some of my earlier misconceptions, proving, as the folktale has it, that I was as powerless as a dik-dik picking a fight with an elephant. I turned these burning questions over in my mouth with the same touch-and-drop wariness of a child handling hot potatoes. Then I overheard the voice of a man rejoicing in the name of Timir. He was insisting that the receptionist announce him.

It was a few minutes before she buzzed me. As I waited, my door ajar, my hands and my eyes fidgety like an anxious rabbit's, a scatter of ideas gathered around me. These were as insubstantial as the shadows of a man in whom disparate thoughts formed and unformed the way seasonal clouds in the sky do, now knotting themselves into fists of dark ominous rain, now dispersing before a finger of water has pointed earthwards.

I remembered how Timir described Sholoongo, saying, "My half sister is a consummate trickster. She insists on you paying up what she thinks you owe her, but fails to honor her vow." Yesterday she posed as a victim of my male machination, seeing herself as a woman giving her *self* in exchange for a morsel of food.

And Timir?

He was the first to speak. "My God, Mogadiscio is a dangerous place, what with all these heavy weapons randomly being fired! I hear Muuse Boqor and two of his companions have been blown up in their vehicle. Do you know if Siyad is responsible for these deaths? Or are the armed militias the culprits?"

We shook hands after an uneasy pause. He said, "How good to see you," his voice making a reluctant admission of our strained reunion.

I made pleasant noises about seeing him too.

Fretful, my fingers entwined in the fashion of a child's crisscross game played with threads. I sensed I itched all over as if I had come into contact with a poisonous ivy. Maybe the thought of having his sister as my guest had brought about an allergic tendency in me. I sneezed. I hoped Timir's presence wouldn't cause my body to break out in rashes.

He looked rough, stubbled with a day's growth of hairs, his eyes feverishly active. He was taking in everything all at once: Nonno's framed photograph, which occupied its place of pride on my office wall, a portrait of my parents, my personal computer, printer, and all the paraphernalia that came with my responsibility as a programmer, not to mention the highly customized interior design of the room where we were. Uptight, I stood upright. My forefinger was on duty, as it were, tapping away nervously. I felt dwarfed by the large thick-bodied escritoire which lay between us, a referee stopping a fight. I sat down.

I pointed him to a chair, but he wouldn't take it. Was he planning to speak his part and leave forthwith? You could say this in Timir's favor: he had as much gumption as Sholoongo had stir. Nonno had once commented, "The boy and his sister between them have shared out a large portion of the world's stir and gumption, lizards forever alive to the changes of the shades in the surroundings."

After a great to-do with his hands, and a homely expression with as brief a life as a recently struck match, Timir, as if he couldn't help it, fell into the chair. I scratched my head, and thought of a well in a semiarid land, dandruff dry. My neck, with which the palm of my hand came into contact, felt rough as a giraffe's coat of stretchy skin.

"We received a telegram to come and bury our father," he said, "and we obliged, Sholoongo and I. Only to discover that the poor sod had been dead a month and a week."

"Did it take that long for the cable to reach you?"

"I suspect we were made to come for a different purpose."

"And what's that?

He said, "Our clanspeople want us to contribute toward the arming of the militia which is to fight in the interest of our people. They have the weapons, not the ammunition. Since we come from America, we are being asked to make our contribution in dollars."

I spoke my condolences, and only then inquired as to what had caused his death.

Timir said, "He wasted away, like an AIDS victim. He died a skeleton."

Now that we were within arm's reach of each other, I saw his hair was a tangle of bushes on his skull, with not a spot of thinness showing nor a single gray hair. Even though younger than he, I was going bald, and my eyes crawled with crow's feet, shallow furrows on a skin otherwise smooth, like the scent of aloe. Timir had the sour smell of beer drunk hot at midday.

I thought how America had changed him.

He said, "How does death strike you?"

"How do you mean?" I said.

"I ask because Nonno must be getting on in years."

His question sounded to me a little too contrived, at best a cue-providing ploy. It struck me that by putting such a question to me, he was in his mind paying homage to a yoga-practicing latter-day hippie with arty pretensions, the kind of thing you might say at a party in California. I imagined Timir having chilled Californian wine under an awning in Malibu; I imagined him in tight-fitting jeans, his chest bare, a key chain hanging on his trouser belt: I imagined him speaking this very line to a famous actor, or actress.

"Death does not induce as much sadness as dreamlessness," I said, pretending I too was in the California. "Death is the tragic, sorrowful acceptance of an irredeemable reality, a notice served that one will no longer figure in the dream of one's beloved."

I could see that he was impressed: his state of inaction told me so, in a silence as compact as thumbtacks. I wondered what life would be like if I ceased to see Nonno in my dreams. This, I thought, was perhaps the most apt definition of death, not seeing one's departed in one's dream.

I asked, "And Sholoongo?"

He said, "I thought you would know."

His voice was even as the waters of a placid river, with no ripples anywhere. Or was I being hoodwinked into believing that no secrets were concealed in the serpent's coils, the serpent ascending from the mist of a *mother-descended* river, each of its moltings having the likeness of a tree-stump floating down a dusk-engulfed body of water?

"What?" I said. "What did you think I would know?"

I breathed the sourness of beer drunk when stale. He was fat in the face, his eyes getting more and more bloodshot by the second, his expressions emptying themselves of every iota of the worldly awareness they had contained when he first walked in. His lips had something unformed about them. It was as if, unlike the rest of him, the lips had ceased growing during his infancy. His jaws, ending in a strong pointed chin, had the shape of an ancient hoe in rusty disrepair. But when I looked into his beady red eyes, they held me spellbound in spite of myself, in the same way they did in our youth. And because I couldn't bear the silence, I asked, "Have you any idea what your sister is up to?"

"Sholoongo's waywardness is as mysterious to me as it is to you," he said. "I learnt only this afternoon that she had checked out of Lafaweyn Hotel and vanished. For all I know, she may be putting up with you."

"Tell me, what does she do for a living?"

"She is the chairperson of the New York branch of the All-America Shape-shifters' Union, a body as powerful as the Artists' Guild of the USA. She likes to describe herself as a Somali-born shaman married to a Moroccan-born fire-eater."

"Did someone tell me that you are an active member of the gay movement in San Francisco —" I said and worked my face cunningly into a friendly smile. And waited.

"I am her half brother, come to buy a wife, she will tell you, were you to run into her, all the better if the said woman to be bought has a three-month-old baby and a recently deceased spouse," he said.

Timir had his sense of humor, I thought. He could raise a laugh in someone's eye, could even make a wisecrack at his own expense. "Death is . . . !" I said, and trailed off.

"Is that where she's ended up, at your place?" he asked.

"Obviously I am not too difficult to reach."

There was a silence with a disturbed meaning.

"Why is she having someone else's baby if she is married?"

He had as blank a look as the space a meteor has vacated. "Apparently you don't know my sister," he said.

"Please help me to get to know her a little better."

"My half sister appeared to me as a maggot in a recent dream I saw," he said. "With maggots, you can never tell where they've entered or where they've exited. Likewise, you discover that my sister has visited a place only when she's already left the area, reasons undisclosed, motive unexplored."

I decided to swap Sholoongo-induced nightmares with Timir.

"In one of my dreams," I said, "she was a species of rat, the type of rodent with almost mythical qualities which is said to bite your toe and then blow on the spot, as if helping to reduce the pain. Only it claws you again and again. Pain and comfort, fingers entwined, the thorn on the pulpy fruit!"

But then I thought, Damn! Here we were, two men, one half a brother to her, the other once infatuated with her, mean men bad-mouthing a woman whom they called a bitch, witch, a whore.

He continued in the swapping vein, and I did not stop him, despite myself. "When last I talked to Sholoongo, she told me of a dream she had in which your mother wore a crocheted wrapper dyed in blood, and arrived looking visibly under stress. Did she say she looked insane? Anyway, your mother argued that she had been invited to her son's wedding. But there was no bride. Then the most bizarre thing happened."

"What?

"Your mother put on the wedding garment. When someone got up to call a qadi to officiate at the ceremony, your mother tried to make light of the matter. It was tragic, Sholoongo commented, to see a son marrying his mother in such a bizarre fashion."

I changed the subject. "Have you seen Fidow?" I asked.

The name made him look dispirited. I hadn't suspected a veil of sadness could descend so fast on him. "Fidow? No, I haven't seen him. Why do you ask?"

Just then the tea lady arrived, bringing in coffee and biscuits. As he rose to help the young woman, two ideas called on me, like unexpected visitors. These were: magic and taboo.

"Magic and taboo," I said. "Fidow and Timir!"

He cursed under his breath.

"So what do you do?"

"I am an all-around theater person," he said. "I teach the theory of theater, I act semiprofessionally in plays whenever I have the time or the opportunity. I review now and then under a pen name for one of the local weeklies."

"A shape-shifting sister in cahoots with an actor brother!"

His lower lip shrunk back to a dwarfish size, like a sheet of plastic too close to the tongue of a red flame. I was debating whether to apologize for my below-the-belt comment when he began to speak, his words having to them the numbed affectedness of someone out of a dentist's chair.

"Magic and taboo are linked," he said, "as centers of tension, their theatrical qualities infinitely enriching. But then the two notions are not subject to rational justification. Let me give a pedestrian example. X has magical powers. It follows that you do not approach X with the same ease as you might approach others without. On the other hand, taboos are connected principally with a woman having her period, or someone dying; taboos point in the main to uncleanness, sacredness, or fear. A person returning from the precipice of death performs certain rituals, a woman giving birth undergoes a standard set of purification rites. The idea is to remove the impurity which is attached to their 'status.' Now savoring a woman's monthly, or for that matter messing with the magical nature of a passage from the Scriptures or violating the sexual norm of a Somali: each of these contains aspects of magic as well as taboo. As a man in the theater, I seem to appreciate the qualities that are inherent in magic and taboo."

"There is truth to magic, but is there truth in taboo?" I said. "Like acquiring a strand of someone's hair with a view to bewitching its owner? Or getting through to a mother newly delivered of an infant via a tendril stretch of her afterbirth? Or simple blood-drinking voodooism? You're not speaking of these truths, are you?"

"No, I'm not."

"What are you saying, then?"

"That there are push-start magical formulae such as *as above, so below*, key phrases spoken as shibboleths, which are said to lead one to a witch's domain."

"My mother used to make me wear on my upper arm an amulet folded in leather on which was inscribed the numerical power of my names," I said. "Apart from its prophylactic value, as when she would plait into the charm a braid of her hair, fastening it with a drop of her menstrual blood. Equally, the tamarind concoction administered by Nonno following my birth contained a protective charm, a secret drink more potent than any magic."

"It occurs to my jet-lagged brain that you are making a fool of me," he said. "Are you leading me up some kind of a path? Talking of magic and taboo, similar to the kind you watch on TV or which is performed by circus hands. I've come here not to speak of these, but about you, me, and so on."

"Does Sholoongo have the power to commit the demons to doing her bidding?" I asked. "Is your sister truly a shape-shifter, a shaman capable of altering her own and other people's nature?" Then I told him all that had come to pass, from the instant I walked into my apartment and found her there. However, I chose to underplay Sholoongo's role in my mother's nightmares.

A surge of energy made him rise. He was up on his feet, clearly eager to say something important and then leave. Timir, it seemed, had other pedestrian preoccupations on his mind.

"I haven't come to talk about Sholoongo," he said.

"What has brought you here, to my office?"

He said, "If I asked you to be the witness as well as the best man for my wedding, would you agree? That was why I came, because I cannot think of anyone else to ask."

That took the wind out of my lungs.

"What sort of a wedding?" I asked, as if this mattered.

He assured me it would be a very simple affair.

"It is my honor to accept."

"And my pleasure to ask."

He dashed out of my office: a child with a toy to show off.

As soon as I was by myself I telephoned Talaado to tell her I wouldn't be seeing her that day after all, the first of many appointments I would cancel. It would be hard to remember a day when she and I didn't touch base at least once. She wondered if she might be of help, being still under the impression that we were leaving for Nairobi in less than a week. The vaguer I was when answering her question, the more eager she was for us to meet and talk. But I did not wish to talk. Nor did I want to raise the antennae of her suspicions. I lied so as not to cut her short, suggesting that my troubles were work-related. We agreed to meet on the morrow.

She said to call her. I knew I wouldn't.

Another memory intrudes, from the remote past.

Timir and I hanging around too close to where a mother crocodile was guarding her nest against predators, the eggs ready to hatch. You could hear the crocodiles' squeaking appeal to clear away the soil with which they had been covered during their incubation. Neither Timir nor I was keen on testing a crocodile's patience. Dusk was gathering. And yet we wouldn't leave, in expectation of Fidow showing up. We knew that, as a hunter of crocodiles for their skins, he would come, armed with a huge spear, his chest and the whole of his elbow neatly sheathed with layers of metal, this strengthened with a Goodyear tire stitched end to end. All because he wished to protect himself from imminent crocodile harm. Fidow used to kill crocodiles, hippopotami, and rhinoceroses on commission, and doubled as a collector of wild honey. I also knew that he would sell all the items found in the killed animals' second chambers, silver bracelets, gold earrings, watches, belt buckles and suchlike, which the crocodile's digestive systems could not handle, to my father.

Nervous, Timir and I knew the tropical night's wont to fall with the suddenness of an eagle descending on its prey. Lest we enrage a hippopotamus emerging out of the waters or an entrapped crocodile returning to its watery habitat from a sunbath among the shrubs fringing the river, we hid in the bushes, waiting. All the same I managed to suppress my fearful instincts by showing off how much more than Timir I knew about crocodiles.

I was the lucky witness to marvelous sights: of a marabou stork digging with its beak deep into the open mouth of a crocodile taking his sunbath; I saw a wading bird which, without fear of being harmed, pulled a fish out of a crocodile's mouth. I was fascinated to learn, from Fidow, that crocodiles had friends among the birds. Like the water bird, a spur-winged plover, who was not afraid to pick leftover food from between the crocodile's teeth. Usually silent, the plover will make a shrill yak-yak-yak flying-away cry when disturbed in its own nesting area, alerting the crocodile of impending peril. I being younger and of a disposition to boast, Timir did not believe what I was telling him about the relationship between the birds and the crocodiles. "Are you taking me for a fool?" he said.

"You and your sister pull such incredibly tall tales out of the stilts of a beanstalk," I said — alluding to but not saying that I didn't trust Sholoongo's story about their father, the cow becoming a woman, and the woman metamorphosing into a cow — "and you want me to believe you all the time? My friend, at times, you insult my intelligence. Now if you don't trust what I am telling you, ask those who know. Ask Fidow."

"I will," he vowed.

"Ask him too," I went on, "if just before embarking on his search for wild honey, he blows through an appropriately perforated snail shell, which produces a high whistling tone. Ask him if he means to alert the honeyguides to lead him to where the hives are hidden."

"What's all this?"

"If you were not such a fool," I said, "you would know that the honeyguide helps Fidow by leading him to where the hives with uncollected wild honey are. You would know too that the spur-winged plover, being generally on friendlier terms with the crocodile, is protective of his friend."

"I'll ask Fidow," he promised.

Timir and I spotted Fidow's figure. He was bringing with him a bedraggled smell, an odor charming enough. I thought about the tale of a robber who has in turn been burgled. At Fidow's approach, there were ugly stirs in the vegetation fringing the river. All the crocodiles, especially the young ones, moved fast, returning noiselessly into the river, except for the nest-guarding mother. Readying herself to attack, she wouldn't budge, but waited while Fidow, unafraid, went forward toward her.

"What is the putrid odor?" Timir whispered.

"Fidow has the habit of smearing his body with the very strong odor crocodiles emit just before mating," I said. "It is his intention to confound them."

In an instant, Fidow would be issuing a bellow similar to that of a bull preparing to mate. And as if on cue, the female crocodile would open her mouth and make a throaty sound which, as Fidow had explained to me, was that of a female responding to a bull's lusty advances. Stark naked now, except for an immense amulet dangling from the upper part of his arm, Fidow came closer to where we were, as though to validate the truth of all my claims. He moved toward the aroused crocodile. And while we waited for Fidow to go on the attack and for the mother crocodile to defend her territory, I shared a gossip with Timir: that according to what my father had told me, Fidow went both ways in matters of sex.

A silent spell, hollow like a vase with many perforations, and into which more sound is purposelessly poured. This put me in mind of Sholoongo, and therefore of fingers playing a flute with unstoppable holes.

It was all happening right before us: Fidow holding a short dagger, sheath unremoved, in his left hand. In his right hand he had a long spear. Years ago Fidow had earned the mellifluous nickname King of the River of Leopards. Now he moved royally toward the confused crocodile, with its diffuse stare on the hunter's laurels for bravery, immense scars now healed, which he displayed as one did medals acquired in battle.

We watched his studied movements with awe. The King of the River of Leopards turned his back on the crocodile. He stopped at the edge of the water, his right foot in, his left out, and his lips atremble with Koranic prayers overlaid with additional salvos in gibberish Shi-idliana. He waded farther and farther in, until the water was navel high, whereupon he washed his body with ritual attentiveness. This was to provoke the crocodile into hasty action. Now that the beast was moving toward him, he walked backwards, taking each step with the caution of a man ready to defend himself, all the while spraying the river with a magical fluid which he had brought along in a container. In his wake Fidow left a pathway clear as the Milky Way. At last he was in the shallower part of the river, where the water was knee-high. First one, then two, and finally a dozen or so crocodiles emerged out of the river, and they all swam toward him in Indian file. Appearing mesmerized, they looked as harmless as a baby's fist. They came to him one at a time to receive pats on their heads, and for Fidow to call them by name. All this time the mother, watching over her nest, refused to trust his motives but still seemed confused. Then, all of a sudden, he was aware of her menacing growl as she moved from behind the bushes to attack him. The King of the River of Leopards wrong-footed her. She raised her tail to throw him in the water before grabbing him with her open jaws. But he stuck a dagger and a spear in her belly before she could do so.

"Quick as a crocodile coming," I said.

"*Arriva, arriva!*" chanted Timir, a reference to a brief eruption, no doubt as joy-giving to him as one that required a longer time.

The following morning, we joined Fidow to help in the skinning of the crocodile, in whose second stomach we found a manikin of unknown origin, no bigger than my thumb, made of some sort of ceramic, perhaps Russian, Nonno guessed, when I showed it to him that evening. The manikin became mine. *Finders keep!*

A few days later I saw Fidow and Timir together, having it off.

They were in the river and were at it, assuming that no one would see them. It was very early in the morning. Their bodies clinched together like dogs, Fidow behind, Timir in front and half-bent, Fidow in in-and-out motion, Timir submissive. The King of the River of Leopards came at last. Timir then took his turn mounting Fidow from behind.

The afternoon is longer than the shadow it has cast, a shadow which, in turn, has something disfigured about it. There is a heavy, uneven drone of an air conditioner, and I listen to the vapory water dripping into the bucket outside my office window. And in the imagination of my recall I hear the sound of an oar going in and stirring the river into action, a raft up and down steep waves. All is a splash. All is wetness. I feel an ugly chill in my bones. I get up and switch off the air conditioner. The room is stuffy with humidity when I go out.

I get into my car and drive, with no idea at all where I am headed. I can see smoke in the distance as I drive north, smoke spiraling upwards. What I cannot tell is whether, as a result of a militia attack or a reprisal by Siyad's regime, a bombshell has struck home and in a deadly way, setting people's houses alight, or whether it is wood smoke rising. Like a cow knowing where it is going after a day's grazing in the green grass on the outskirts of a village, my car leads me somewhere but I know not where.

CHAPTER THREE

My exasperation with myself heightened to the point where I began to hate what I was doing to myself. I came close to being hit by a sniper as I drove around at night, trying to delay returning to my own apartment. Nor did I feel like seeing Talaado, or being in the company of other friends. Once or twice I parked my car at the marina, switched the engine off, and listened to my favorite jazz records, with the ocean breeze caressing my cheeks. I sat, not knowing why I was exposing myself to so much peril; I sat, wondering what was making me suicidal. After all, there were marauders stalking the night with their guns at the ready, their fingers on the trigger, prepared to kill and blame the death on the armed militias or on the evil men the regime fielded to counter their attacks.

I arrived home after midnight and let myself in, quiet as a secret. I could not decide whether Sholoongo had deliberately left her door ajar, on the off chance that I might join her in bed, or whether she slept in innocence and the draft pushed it open. I could see into her bed if I craned my neck slightly. She lay in a fetus curl of clumsy sleep.

As I made breakfast the following morning, I watched eagerly for a silk sleeve with as wide a circumference as the fully opened wings of an eagle. In fact I positioned myself so as to spot her the instant she swung into view. Five minutes of waiting, six, but before the hand of the seventh made it to the dot of the eighth, I sensed an alien shadow scattering the rays of the morning sun's light into fragmented beams. And there she was, a clearer stretch of light coming toward the kitchen. Dry of scents, she was scratching her eyes awake. Was she itching?

Which reminded me, where were the lice? The human nostril and the human mind, I thought, can domesticate any odor, familiarity breeding a dullness of the senses, the damping of enthusiasm, perhaps a lack of interest in hairsplitting distinctions. The human mind annuls these differences, leaving one with two principal categories, bad smell and good smell. Sholoongo was bad, so was her smell, lice or no lice.

But on seeing her, I welcomed her as a well-brought-up host welcomes a guest. I got up, and remained on my feet until she took her seat. Whereupon (I couldn't determine if she meant to do it or not) her left hand let go of her unbelted kimono. This afforded me a glimpse of the terraces of her flesh, to me a sign of ill health. No way, I thought, would I entrust my future to a body so besieged by fat!

In silence I chased a most elusive question about lovemaking: why some people preferred it in the morning, why some were nocturnal romantics, why some liked having the lights on as they manufactured it, why others the dark. I knew a woman who liked it best in the afternoons, the curtains drawn, the radio playing loud rock music; I knew another whose body enjoyed rising to the morning's flirtation. Perhaps there was more logic to sex than many of us realized. If my body had its own timetable, then surely Sholoongo's was no potential partner of mine.

"I went to see Arbaco," she said, sipping her honeyed tea. Arbaco was one of my mother's closest friends.

"How's she?" I asked.

"She wonders why you never bother to visit her."

Arbaco's name now took me back to the days just before I met Sholoongo. But for the moment I had to put my memory on hold as I listened, with feigned interest, to the latest news about Arbaco. Not that I learnt much from Sholoongo's babble. In fact I edged our conversation to Timir's visit yesterday afternoon as soon I felt it was politic to do so.

"What did he talk about?" Sholoongo asked.

"He wants me to be his best man," I said.

"Have you accepted to be his best man?"

I felt wicked saying, "I told him it'd be my honor to be associated with him in the hour of his wedlock to the woman of his choice." I meant to provoke Sholoongo's venom. I got what I wanted: she was all hackles, her bloodshot eyes darting every which way like an enraged porcupine's quills.

"But that's scandalous!" she said.

"What's scandalous?"

"Because you are abetting him in a fraudulent crime against women," she said. "The man has the self-serving idea of buying the gratitude of a woman no better than a slave, a woman who won't interfere with his false life, considering that he bought her."

I said, rather actorly, "Aren't you yourself pursuing self-serving motives, coming to me as you've done, when you are married to a Moroccan fire-eater? Why have you come to *me?* As a self-serving woman, you have no right to be occupying a high moral ground."

"There are essential differences," she said.

"How?"

"You and I enter into this as equals," she said.

"I haven't entered into anything," I said.

She said, "That's my point. You are under no obligation to do my bidding. No money changes hands. And then, in any case, if you choose not to oblige me, I know I am free to go to someone else, and you have no way of stopping me. The woman, once she is wedded to him, has no free will."

I moved to a less contentious subject. "Why is it that you and Timir come to Somalia, the one to get married to a woman with a baby, the other to be impregnated with one?"

"We both feel unfulfilled," she said. Her teeth gleamed, reflecting the sun in their shine. For a second I mistook that for a smile, and almost responded to it. "What else did Timir talk about?"

"We talked about magic and taboo."

"Did he talk about his African-American boyfriend?"

"What's interesting about his lover?"

"Because they get up to bizarre deeds," she said. "They swap roles and call each by the other's name, and now and then stand in for one another. Wayne loves to pass himself off as an African, Timir as an African-American. Timir introduces himself to people as an actor,

Wayne presents himself as a substitute teacher at an elementary school. They keep exchanging roles, they wear each other's clothes, and because they resemble one another to some extent, this can be quite confusing."

"Isn't Timir in the theater, an actor?"

"He's not. He's done walk-on parts, that's all."

I don't know by what circuitous route we got to our next topic: sex, which we were now approaching with the courtesy of a courting couple. Was she aggressive in bed? Was I quick in coming, like a crocodile? Or did I take my time as frogs do? We came round eventually to her fire-eating Moroccan husband. Was he bisexual? I garnered from what she said about her man that, in various ways, their partnership had left inordinately positive impressions on her. I remarked that sex had its logic, and she agreed with the sentiment. I added that, at its pinnacle, sex had a tense center, lavalike: a hot body cooling, the phases of the moon entering a decisive turn. *Give me a child!* I asked myself, would our sexual encounter, if I were a willing partner, end in a bonanza harvest, a healthy Somali-looking baby with round cheeks and dark brown eyes?

The phone rang. I felt mean, and chose not to answer it, knowing it was my mother who, courtesy of Arbaco, now knew not only that Sholoongo was in town but that I was hosting her. When the alarm bells of the telephone ceased sounding, I got up and said, "Just a matter of detail. Supposing I consent to father your dream-child, and supposing you have a baby, what position will I occupy in the scheme of things?"

"The way I see it, fathers are an outdated irrelevance."

"So what is in it for me?"

She said, "Maybe I should quote the hyperbole you yourself coined as a child: that *fathers matter not, mothers matter a lot!* You were then passing through a phase when you debated whether to add your mother's name to the tail end of yours."

"Have a good day, madam!" I said, and took leave of her.

As I drove, I felt I was traveling through layers of time, in lengths of colorful clothing, each length representing a given phase of my youthful years: now menstrual-blood scarlet, now dark as the fertile earth near the Shabelle River, now green as the walks in the woods of my daredevilries, now quick as the termite crawling out of the coziness of its nest of powder, and now watchful as my Xusna, my pet, my vervet.

There was a certain method to my reveries, though. For I could at last see where I was headed, toward my childhood, in concrete terms my parents' house. I was behaving, oddly enough, as though I too were a recent returnee to Mogadiscio, calling in memory on the scene of my earliest years. The impulse to react to the presence in my life of Sholoongo and Timir had little to do with my behavior, I thought. No, I was at the wheels of my own destiny, guiding it left, then right, straight, then down a bend, all in the hope of going to my own watering point.

An imagined sound reminded me of a honey collector. A child resisting its mother's instruction took me back to my own infancy when my father washed me, or when Arbaco teased me. A smile pinched my lower lip as I recalled a vignette of a dream in which, with baby fingers, I had closed shut my father's eyes, my father who had the habit of sleeping with his eyes wide open, their whites dominating, their darks hardly visible. I recalled now that I had woken up, that dawn, from a nightmare in which two immense, crowned eagle hawks swooped from a great height. The eagle hawks took turns, now one, now the other, with the aim of frightening and eventually flying off with Xusna, my handsome vervet. My cries for help had been as jarring as the hawks' calls. And in my dream I had hoped that by closing my father's wide-awake eyes I would startle him; that once awoken he would come to my aid and Xusna's. Reminiscing, I drove in circles. Then I saw my father's features in the windshield, figures etched in the wipers' stumbly scrawls in smears of dusty artistry.

Finally the dirt alleyway in which I grew up. This lured me with its labyrinthine bends, seduced me with its sweet memories. In my recall I am six, and climbing a *baar* tree with a hollowed center located directly above a spot where the honey collector has built a fire. As his errand boy, I have cut maize stalks or green plants with which he means to choke the flames. Bless Fidow who lets me munch crunchy mouthfuls of the honeycombs, the occasional egg or piece of coagulated wax finding its way into my system. Standing at the threshold of dawn, eager like a groom joining his bride, I look into a hole in which aromatic herbs have been burnt to give the honey a touch of piquancy. With the odd odor at the beck and call of the my memory, I am the scent, the whiff of incense curling its way into the evening's idol worship.

I drove as I created an Identikit of a face out of the hesitant windshield wipers' to-and-fro motion. I drove as I quoted a Somali proverb with the gist that a woman's vulva never forgets the penis it has known.

My father was on the porch, engrossed in mending a silver bracelet of elaborate design. Standing, he was stooped in concentration. From where I was, I assumed that he was dealing with a broken chain, a scroll of patterns, geometric curves pursuing the ideals of a system of syntax. Or perhaps I was meant to see a termite submerged in its sand dune? Or a stone figure with a raised fist, chanting salvos of triumph? Or a spiral within a circle where, in the ascending bend, winding around the principal point, rather fringing it, my gaze was meant to follow a bird half lifting its body but not quite making it, a bird in half motion, its posture suggesting a breath withheld? Wait, feathered one, wait!

Intuiting, I stayed silent, a shadow falling on his worktable and its scatter of tools. With his serpentine tongue out of the corner of his mouth, a lizard's on a fly-hunting errand, searching before returning to base, you might have mistaken my father for a child tracing the alpha and omega of his literacy initiation. My father now held a wedge-shaped instrument, which he used to give delicate restoring touches to a spot on the work before him, a spot looking grayer than the rest. When he first looked up, he either didn't see me or didn't recognize me, his eyes widening in the manner of a man choking on a gizzard. Being as orderly as I was disorderly, he put away the bracelet in a polythene bag marked "Fidow" in red. Only then did his face open with a smile of wondrous acknowledgment, and we embraced. He was in his fifties, slim. He was handsome.

"Are you taking care?" he asked.

I responded I was.

"There are many stray bullets lately," he said, "which are in search of where to lodge. There is talk, too, of the armed clan militias choosing to victimize the members of other clans. I suppose you know what that means? You must take care and stay out of the bullets' way as best you can."

I lied, saying I was staying out of the bullets' way.

"How's your visitor?" he asked.

My thoughts were a shambles. My scabrous head itched. I scratched it. I reminded myself that it was the second time in as many days that I had been disabused of my naïveté. My father then teased me, comparing me to an ostrich which, burying its head in the sand, imagines it can't be seen. He volunteered that he had come by the news of my guest's arrival courtesy of my housekeeper. "Lambar has been here," he said.

When I gave my father a summary of what had transpired so far between me and my visitor, his eyes, like the surface of water, rippled with the sun's reflection which rose and fell in them.

"I am glad you could come and visit," he said. His voice had in it a touch of discomfort. Had Sholoongo's coming unseated his composure? It was unlike him to talk a great deal. "And how does she plan to make you give her a child? Does she envisage making you do so at gunpoint?"

"We haven't come to that yet."

"What on earth have you come to, then, in two days?"

I explained that she and I were having a civil discussion about the matter, that we had breakfast in the mornings and that I got home late every night. I waited anxiously to see if he would ask where I spent my hours at night, since I was avoiding returning to my apartment.

He looked away from me, focusing on one of the pigeons pecking at an assortment of grains. Now he plunged clumsily into what caused him irritation.

He said, "I wouldn't know what to do if I were you." His eyes partially closed, their rainbow white more prominent than the dark hemming it, he continued, "Mark you, she is as cheap as a popular rag dishing out pornography in the sophisticated idiom of a highbrow program."

It was good to see him in such a devil-may-care attitude.

When I didn't say anything, he shouted, "Why doesn't she ask Timir to give her a child? You know that Arbaco always believed that they were doing it, right under their father's eyes."

Still I said nothing.

"From whichever angle you look at it, you are staring at an incongruity," he said, "a pack of half beasts engaged in an incestuous orgy, just like their half siblings the animals. My feeling is . . ." and he trailed off, like a man who has given away more secrets than he ought to.

I dipped my hand in an old tobacco tin and fed the half dozen or so pigeons in my father's courtyard. Nonno had trained several of this species as message carriers, our feathered friends traveling between Nonno's and my father's compounds, a million times more trustworthy than the nation's mail services, which were nonexistent, and much cheaper and more discreet than humans bearing verbal messages between father and son. For this purpose my father had constructed a palatial dovecote in each yard. The homing birds were made to convey messages tied with rubber bands to their legs between Mogadiscio, where my father lived, and Afgoi, where my grandfather's estate was. Unconfirmed gossip had it that, envious and eager to gain access to their secrets, one of the neighbors waylaid and fed on them. And he was taken ill.

"Timir has gone to see your mother," my father said.

"When I think of the trouble you took to help Timir and me to become bosom pals," I said, "what would your reactions have been if I now showed the same sexual preference as he?" A young pigeon landed on my shoulder. My attempt to feed it off my palm failed, maybe because it sensed that I was no Franciscan.

"Your mother would've been most unhappy."

"What about you?"

"I've known about Fidow, and that has never bothered me."

"But you knew about me and Sholoongo?"

"I knew that you would outgrow her."

"It appears as if she won't let me outgrow her."

A pigeon balanced itself on my right shoulder and tried to peck into my ear, perhaps seeking my untapped wax. Irritated, I shooed it away.

"There's something worrying me about all this," he said. "Your mother is pricing a firearm, and is intending to take a crash course in how to use it."

"That's an exaggerated order, surely?"

His eyes popped open and there was a mad severity to his stare. Years back my father had described himself as "a silent situation." Myself, I interpreted his silences as the fudges of a man knowing a lot while refusing to speak. He was said to have *arrived* five months to the day after he was conceived, sporting, in addition to his unusually short forefinger, a wick of silver hair, which crowned his skull. He was endowed with a pair of watchful eyes, forever suspicious. Nowadays a couple of dark strands in the silver bestowed on him a look of distinction.

As we sat in silence, I remembered that for years I used to fall asleep to the coos and cackles coming from my parents' dovecotes and chicken coops. I would wake up to the cock's predawn cries. How I loathed the fowl's filthy odor, their fleas! I hatched a quiet plot to get rid of them by sneaking in a stray dog. I hoped the dog would worry the poultry to fright, and the pigeons to flight. But Nonno talked me out of my mischief.

To Nonno, my father was a boarded-up house. With eyes brown as the floodwaters of a muddy river, my father sat, his lower lip drooped downwards, heavy like an unpicked jackfruit. My grandfather told me how once, in a rage, he had nearly kicked his son's teeth in.

Nonno, a respected member of the Afgoi community, had earned the nickname Ma-tukade because he wouldn't pray. My father, to cut a different figure in the eyes of the villagers, spent a great deal of his time in the House of God, never missing the weekly Friday get-together and never failing to take part in the activities marking the days of the saints. Then some riffraff accused my father of stealing a pair of shoes from the mosque. As was his wont, my father refused to confirm or challenge the charge. Nor would he respond to my grandfather's speculation that he was being framed, and why. He would not speak a single word in self-defense. More baffled than irritated, Nonno did everything, even threatening to disown him. Nothing. Nothing doing.

As a last resort, my grandfather sought my mother's help, it being believed that my father was garrulous in her company, when the two of them were sharing secrets. Nonno might as well have spoken to the cackling hens in my parents' backyard. For regarding honor, a husband's trust in his wife, my mother did not deem it "honorable" for a woman to divulge to other persons secrets her man had entrusted to her in marital confidence.

"But I am not *other persons*," Nonno had cried.

"If I speak of this to you," she said, "I feel as though my pact with my husband would melt."

"Just fill in the background for me, will you?" Nonno had pleaded. "Is Yaqut a kleptomaniac? Does he specialize in shoe-pinching? Or is he being framed by men from a different clan who have it in for him?"

My mother responded that it wasn't her place, as daughter-in-law, to interest herself in a quarrel between a father and his son. Nonno left, accusing her of having no sense of family honor.

But the origin of my father's falling out with Nonno had lain elsewhere, in Yaqut's being a poor dreamer, with ideals and aspirations hard to attain. Nonno put it thus to me years later: quoting another favorite maxim of his that living is ambitious dreaming and that if you don't dream beyond your reach, why, you may as well give up living, Nonno explained that, insofar as he was concerned, his son was a failure because he had no ambition. He fell to wondering why his son made his living in such bizarre ways. Why did he invest time and money in commissioning crocodile hunters to fetch him skins and any unclaimed jewelry found in the beasts' second chambers? Why would he set up a grave-digging business? Why place a tender with the local government to bury the city's dead whenever relatives hadn't enough funds to meet the funeral fees? Yaqut would present the bills after burial to the authorities for refund. "What manner of a curse are you, my son?" Nonno would harangue him. "You're no less vile than a hyena which, smeared with its own excrement, feeds on carrion. What manner of a curse are you!"

My father quit school early to become an apprentice to an Italian marble engraver. The Italian specialized in the carving of gravestones, and in lettering these with the appropriate Catholic words of benediction: *Mori il debole servo, sperante nella misericordia di Dio!* Nonno didn't approve of his son's meddling, at the age of seventeen, in the affairs of the dead, because he had done so himself and had suffered its sad consequences. "But you are continued in me!" Yaqut would retort. "I am doing what you did, at my age, meddling in the business of the dead, and making money out of it."

When Somalia gained its independence and the Catholic burying business was at a lower ebb, Nonno helped my father to buy the Italian's workshop, intact. Yaqut then received orders for the lettering of marble from the Somali government, jobs often requiring engraving on stone the pompous titles of the autocrat. To supplement his income he mended broken items of silver and gold. In his leisure time he worked with leather, carved wood, or did a little carpentry. If he put his mind to it, he could paint well too, in watercolors or oils.

Presently my father put away his tools on a shelf where he preserved many items which others who knew no better had discarded, and for which he would find eventual use. Among these items were the odd earring, a rusty ancient piece of metal, tins in which he stood his brushes and crayons. My own interest in the origin of things, I felt, linked me to my father and my grandfather.

He asked if I would like my tamarind drink chilled. But he did not wait for my reply. He ambled away, cautious as lizards are, looking this way and that, eyes darting a rush of vitality, before venturing on and into the house.

The faint sound of bells ringing.

My parents' maid arrived. She had a face wider than a boulevard, a face with a smile stretching across it. I remarked that her muddied *kurta*-frock was sodden with stains at the oddest of spots. Hard of hearing, she spoke loudly. Such was our rapport that I too pitched my voice a couple of notches higher. In a moment my pulmonary efforts were totally committed not only to getting the words out but to rivaling her volume. She had brought out a tray with two tall glasses, one obviously mine and containing tamarind juice, the other my father's. I had no idea what was in his.

Now that he was back, my father looked from me to the maid, his lips curled and bemused. He sat down, his forefingers hovering near his ears. I took this as a sign that I should lower my voice. I brought the conversation to an abrupt halt, my ears ringing with the hollowness of wind blowing through them. And soon enough I heard the knock-kneed collision of two metal manikins inside, a sound that wasn't too dissimilar to the kee-kee of a kingfisher when searching for prey.

A pigeon came closer. Slow-witted, it continuously pecked at its feed, which after every failed attempt moved farther from it. Anxious to have its feed whatever the cost, the bird kept giving it another shot and missing it, then looking up before plotting its next move. My hand went up to scratch the dandruff of a Sholoongo-related memory. The bird, misunderstanding my intentions, flew off in a flutter, only to perch on the ping-pong table a couple of meters away.

My father was saying, "Your mother woke me up earlier today to rehash her version of Lot's story in the Koran. Then she spoke of a punishment being meted out to half-human-half-animal deviants. Afterwards she informed me that she had acquired a firearm on an impulse buy. Now, it's not unusual for people to own guns in a land run by gunrunners, or even to resort to carrying them in self-defense. I asked your mother why she had bought the firearm, and waited for her to deliver the spiel one hears so very often these days about Mogadiscio being in the grip of a collapse. Looking me in the eyes, she responded, 'I know whom I intend to kill, a woman messing with my dreams.' I didn't need her to name her victim."

Talking was causing him visible discomfort. I knew too that sleeping did something akin to that. My father was at his most relaxed when working on a repair job. No wonder he had his eyes owl-open when the rest of him was asleep. His head dropped on his chest with the quick naturalness of a turtle's neck vanishing.

"There's a lot of ground to cover," he said, "scores of secrets to part with. To begin with, why didn't I explain myself to my father? There are a couple of questions which had better be answered. Why did some riffraff claim that I had stolen his sandals from a mosque? You deserve to receive answers to these questions even if you've never asked them. In a manner of speaking, the questions are comparable to bones with no flesh on them. Questions aged, they lose their relevance, but do bones? Do skeletons hidden in closets age, on account of the dust with which they are covered? The marrow in these bones may have dried, but they are not lifeless. And when bones have remained buried for years, it may be unwise to dig them up, for they may have changed shape, so will the questions about them."

"What if I don't want to have the bones dug up?" I asked.

He appeared agitated. He rose, irritating several pigeons into flight, their wings beating the wind, noisy as a washing line with clothes on it. He had a gangling posture for a man who wasn't all that tall, nor that young anymore. I heard the bells of memory tolling inside the house, tongueless ones knelling the sad departure of my own innocence.

"A stone standing stationary for some time will have all manner of life under it," he said, "insects nesting or mating, scorpions with inactive tails. Move that stone, shift a rock, and you expose a mysterious world. Now why is Sholoongo making us behave like scorpions whose hiding place has been disturbed? Why is your mother purchasing a firearm? What manner of secrets are we guarding?"

I caught myself picking my nose with an outrageous indifference, as I was led away by the hand of memory taking hold of mine. I was a child in this very house, sneaking into no-go areas and touching the items my father had bought secondhand on a no-questions-asked basis. My father used to buy stuff from men of dubious backgrounds. He was, as a result, taken by the police for questioning twice, and was let go because my mother pleaded with a cousin in the police force, who interceded.

Inside the house, the breeze rang the bells of one knock-kneed manikin against another, souvenirs of metal clashing against amulets covered in similar material, ancient tongueless talismans, silverware someone had "found" somewhere and which my father acquired dung cheap. Some of these included amber beads reputed to have come from the bed of the Baltic Sea, copal resin, a beaded belt from Mauritania bought from a sailor from those regions, seashells, ostrich eggs. As a child, I heard the sea in the shells dangling down from above my father's workroom. As a child, I listened to the sounds of the desert by placing my ear against the hole in the ostrich egg. Busy, my father didn't mind if I rubbed bits of copal together to produce electricity, or a scent reminiscent of honey and lemon. His work fetched plenty of money. Moreover, no burglar was ever tempted to break into our house, because people credited the items with juju powers.

In my father's fudge of silence, the world went up in jingles. He said, "Under a stone not lifted for almost thirty years, one finds a scorpion in one's memory. Secrets cling to the earth beneath the curled-up scorpion. Now I will tell you something no one else knows, save your mother."

"What if I don't wish to know?" I said.

"Your mother made me promise that I'd tell you."

"Father, I doubt that there is any sting left in the tail of a scorpion hiding for thirty years. So why bother?" I said.

He wouldn't be dissuaded. His voice as devoid of its natural energy as a tape recorder functioning on low batteries, he said, "When I met your mother, she had problems originating in a misunderstanding with a man who had courted her. And soon after we married, I was accused of stealing a pair of shoes from a mosque. For years neither of us has wanted to see what has lain under the stones, fearing that, once disturbed, the scorpion might sting."

My father's eyes were moist, and there was a softness to them like late afternoon light. He rose without ceremony and walked inexplicably off, as clumsy in his bodily movements as a child taking his first walk. One of the pigeons almost flew right into him, not realizing he was coming. The bird lost a few feathers, my father mislaid his groggy gait, and I the grim expression on my face.

He was gone for a little over two minutes and was back with a posse of his tools. He had in his hand an awl, a chisel, and a three-branched candelabra.

I thought about my cul-de-sac of a name. Years earlier, I had come around to the idea that there were atavistic stresses in the string of names a Somali child recites as his or her own, emphases of a linear listing of ancestors in the male line. You might say that in every *abtir-siino* there is the implicit genesis of divine omnipotence. Somewhere in the background, there is Satan's exodus, evidence of humankind's loyalty to a God-given point of law, a supreme being not begotten and who Himself does not beget. But what makes one kill another because this mythical ancestor is different from one's own: this has little to do with blood, more with a history of the perversion of justice. What makes one refuse to intermarry with a given community has to do with the politics of inclusion and exclusion. Forming a political allegiance with people just because their *begats* are identical to one's own — judging from the way in which clan-based militia groupings were arming themselves — is as foolish as trusting one's blood brother. Only the unwise trust those close to them, a brother, a sister, or an in-law. Ask anyone in power, ask a king, and he will advise you to mistrust your kin.

I said, "Father, I meant to ask . . ."

But when his brown eyes looked at me with muddied apprehension, I fell quiet. He might have been regretting that he had employed inapt mixed metaphors to elucidate his points. After all, whereas scorpions cause exemplary pain, a stone feels none.

"What's with my mother and Sholoongo?" I asked.

"How much do you know of what took place between them?" he said. I felt he was suppressing a secret that was wanting to be let go.

"I know of a series of score-settling sprees," I said.

Attending to the candelabra as one might to the needs of a crying child, he looked up. Then he spoke with the deliberate slowness of a man who didn't wish to divulge secrets which ought to have stayed buried. "You probably had no idea that your mother arranged for Sholoongo to be fingerprinted, on suspicion that the prints on the flower-canister on our mantelpiece were hers," he said.

"And were they?"

"The stolen document was never recovered."

"Why has nobody ever told me of this?"

"I didn't learn of it myself until a few years ago," my father said. "When I did learn of it, it was thanks, as a matter of fact, to my having done a favor for the very officer who had taken Sholoongo's prints. You see, he referred to the incident in passing, imagining I had been privy to it all along."

"What a dreadful mess!" I said. "But who was the officer?"

"Someone to whose sense of clan loyalty your mother has of late appealed. It's he who has got her the firearm." His voice had an indistinct but sad pitch to it.

The smart hurt made me get up.

My feet were wobbly, my head giddy, my ability to reason nil. I was going away from my father, because I wanted to find somewhere to hide my shame. The toilet extended its generosity to me in the shape of a bowl, ready to receive my worry, my vomit or my other wastes. I shared one feature with Nonno: we both had delicate stomachs. These ran when our mental balance was upset.

In the WC: reminiscing . . .

As an infant I was physically inseparable from my father. I would fall asleep with his finger in the tight clasp of my fist. My mother wasn't around a lot. He was — often indoors, often practicing a profession with a greater flexibility than my mother's. She went out daily, busy running the family business, including my father's souvenir stall, a shelf of assorted items, the product of his magic wonders. She made more money than he. It was just as well, he would comment, because she was always running around, a scorpion without a tail. But he was more content doing what he did, prolonging the lives of objects. When he was praised, my father's eyes lit up, like formidable flames.

He would strap me to his back as he lettered the headstones he had been commissioned to etch, as he engraved names on slabs of marble. He fed me, washed me. On occasion, my mother's friend Arbaco looked after me when he was, for some reason, unavailable. When I couldn't breathe because my nasal passages were clogged, my father took my nose in his mouth and, at a single drag, sucked the unease out of me, phlegm and mucus and all.

In those days, my father spoke seldom. It was explained to me that he used to stammer until his early teens. I feel as if he has never fully recovered the confidence to talk normally. With his Adam's apple atremble, like the chain of an elevator in a high-rise, an elevator about to plunge down in one unstoppable slide, he would abandon a sentence in the process of speaking it, or a thought before completing it. The radio was on almost all the time. It entertained me with an adult's register of language, and with music, to whose rhythm I danced. On returning home in the evenings, my mother imposed a curfew of silence upon us. She would switch it off. Stone silent, he would stare at her. Vexed, she would try to outstare him, and would fail. No maid ever stayed in my parents' employ for more than a week, because my mother's tempers chased them away.

With the radio off and my mother's high-pitched voice on the run, I would cry until my weeping dislodged all they had in the way of nerves. Cursing us both, she would storm out of the house, vowing never to return. He would pick me up. We would play at his being my mother, and I would pretend as if he were breast-feeding me. We dwelt in a world of make-believe, my father and I, pleased with each other until my mother returned. When my mother was in an agreeable mood, then all three of us showered together, jets of shivery water, with me standing between them, playful, full of rejoicing.

I loved falling asleep to my father's lullaby singing, a lullaby he himself would compose. I didn't like it when he chanted the traditional one, in which the mother of the baby goes away to a place no one knows about. Nor does anyone know if she has been raped by camel herdsmen or if she has fallen asleep in the shade of a tree. In my father's version, Mother rides away on an elephant traveling northwards, to a country devastated by internecine wars and famines. At three I could write my name in the defunct Somali script, in Arabic, and in Roman orthography. I could read faster than I could speak an entire sentence in any tongue.

With his eyes open and mouth closed, my father slept in my mother's arms, her eyes closed and mouth open, snoring. Their late-night whispers were *cuud* music to my half-alert ears. So were the grunts of their lovemaking on which I eavesdropped. Now and then I received an unintentional kick from one or the other of them, as they rolled on their backs. If they became conscious of my awoken state, they would cease their lovemaking and act prudently.

I didn't dare ask, but somehow I sensed deep in the flow of my blood that my parents had no intention of having me. Things my mother said suggested this. Because my father spoke less vociferously, and invested all his energy in his vocation and in looking after me, I never knew from him one way or the other. My mother had venom. I feared the hate in her eyes. My father took care not to involve me in his doings, if he could.

My mother had loads of ambition. Because of this, she was often bad-mouthed by other women, who described her either as pushy or as lacking in the grace of femininity. My mother equally displeased men, many of whom couldn't stand her guts. A man I knew compared her to a bee-eater, with its ungregarious nature, its fretfulness. Bee-eaters are birds known for hunting on the wing and for snapping up the weaker airborne insects. I could understand why men were fearful of her, but not why other women were hostile to her. This was anathema to me. "To think that she won't look after her son herself! It's a real shame."

My father wasn't alone when I reemerged. He had a visitor with him, a woman.

By then my head had cleared. My father was on his feet, with his back to me, repairing a belt bedecked with Venetian sequins. The belt mounted on an easel, he placed himself at an artist's distance, his shorter than usual forefinger moving like a lizard's head, up and down, his bifocals on, his whole body stooped as though paying homage to a pagan deity. I watched him in appreciative quietness, comparing him in my mind to a man engaged in writing a very long disaster signal in codes. He was as still as a man tying such a disaster signal with a string to a pigeon's leg, the bird blessed with *nuuro* power. When my shadow fell across his vision and he turned around to look at me, I remarked that a scowl was wreathing the frontiers of his face. Silent, he moved toward a chair padded with cushions, into which he dropped. "It won't take long," he said to me apologetically.

"I am sorry for barging in like this," the woman said to me. "I didn't know he had another customer."

"I am not a customer," I said. "I am his son."

Nervous and because she had nothing better to do with her hands, the woman bundled her hair into a huge topknot. This contrasted with her gold earlobe disks and her silver anklets.

My father, holding a cloth in the loose grip of his left hand and making a hurried effort at cleaning away some dirt, looked rather bemused when the woman asked, "Is this Damac's son?"

In my mother's inexactitudes Yaqut was "the father of my child." I don't recall ever hearing my mother refer to him as her husband. Now, this is not unusual in a country where women resorted to all sorts of coded nomenclatures when it came to their husbands. Women were more adept than men in defining the hidden in the obvious, and of ensconcing the apparent in the inapparent. Unless my mother was underlining the importance of something altogether different.

My father concentrated wholeheartedly on what he had been hired to do. His hand in his toolbox, and not moving, he reminded me of an artist recalling a fault in a work long completed. I felt he was regretfully bothered by something, his inability to correct an error. He held a trowel in midair, and he brooded. There was a kind of piteous sadness about him as he pulled out a screwdriver. He held both in the same hand and thought what to do next.

The woman and I chatted randomly about this and that. From her accent, I could tell that she came from the Central Region, which is where my mother hailed from. And Timir and Sholoongo too.

After a while she said, "Your mother was ranting and raging all day apparently about an evil woman who holds your soul in her witch's clasp."

I didn't contest it, because this sounded like something my mother would say. My father's eyes avoiding mine, he did something not in keeping with his character: he provoked a client. He said, "This lady is our neighbor, and an acquaintance of your mother's. Now I cannot vouch for the truth of what some of our other neighbors say: that she manufactures stories, which she then attributes to other persons and spreads these as truths."

"People are just mean," she said.

"You are in search of a confirmation for a gossip you've picked up somewhere, aren't you?" my father said. "And it is your intention to learn more. Is that not why you've hired me to repair this?"

Shocked, the woman got up, snatching her beaded belt out of my father's grasp, and left.

Neither of us spoke anything for a long time.

"Would you throw out Sholoongo if you were me?" I asked.

My father talked about the possible consequences, mainly negative ones. In a roundabout way he got to the Somali mystical notion of *nabsi*, whose boomerang effect is said to produce very unenviable results in the person choosing not to return another's loving advances favorably. If a man or a woman shows interest in you, Somalis suggest, treat them with civility lest love's *nabsi* should cause you irreparable harm. *Nabsi* is both a weapon and a means by which the weak turn the fight to their benefit. "Give Sholoongo a couple more days," he said. "And if I were you, I would seek Nonno's counsel. He might know what to do."

A fat, squat pigeon sat on my lap, unafraid.

My father said, "You see what happens when you visit and stay a long while? Even our feathered friends aren't scared of you anymore. Imagine!"

I got up to leave.

"I would love you to stay for supper," he said, "only your mother may be in a fire-breathing mood. I wouldn't be here when she gets back if I were you."

We hugged. I left.

I went home, intending among other things to speak with Sholoongo. Alas, she was not there, but there was evidence of her presence in the apartment. This comprised several sheets of amusing reading matter in her longhand. I browsed through it, undisturbed. In one sense, it could serve as a key to her state of mind. Here I give the relevant passages from the piece. It is entitled "The Kettle Calling the Crow Black."

> *I believe K was ten when, in his eagerness to seduce me, he disrobed in record quickness, faster than it took me to enjoy the flavor of the chocolate he had brought along that day. He associated food with sex, and would invariably ask if I had eaten, or if I would like to. He was perverse, taking relish in the sound of munching food, claiming that this turned him on. Food before sex!*
>
> *He would then drag me to a secret corner, to whisper an earful of obscenities. He would boast about his voyeuristic exploits: a man mounting a woman from behind, an African-American woman taking the manhood of her landlord in her mouth. He was obsessed with sex all right, but he was decent enough to withhold the names of the persons involved.*

K has a sadistic side to him, one day wanting to bind my feet in a bandage, another day insisting that we make love in a particular position, for we would enjoy it more. One night he applied one of Fidow's herbal concoctions to my private parts, just for the heck of it, and later he said he would want to try it again, with some improvement. Because my left foot was smaller than my right, he said that a slight defect in a partner's feet might interfere with the access, that is to say with the penetration.

His obsessions were food, feet, and sex!

But I remember the day I dissuaded him from coming into me because I had my monthly. You cannot imagine how keen he was to question me about my period. Half in earnest, I told him that a woman's monthly was in so concentrated a form that if one froze it, one could mold a human out of it. He wondered if his father, who was adept at giving shapes to things, might make a baby out of it, a sibling for him, to whom he would do what he believed Timir and I did to each other.

At some point he wondered what the blood of the menses would taste like. Mischievous, I encouraged him to try it. "Not bad!" he said, having tasted it. Then I told him (I learnt this from my father, who was well-traveled because a seaman) that there were some countries whose people called a woman's blood red milk. They drank it in the belief that they would attain longevity. Before I knew it, K had emptied the blood that was in the thimble in a gulp. He asked for more.

"Now you will become pregnant," I said.

He was most pleased!

I stayed up until the small hours, waiting for Sholoongo. I was vexed. Eventually I went to bed, thinking that tables were being turned: a mirror seeing its reflection in the quicksand of another mirror's mercury. And I couldn't help observing that Sholoongo was, on the one hand, presenting herself in a good light and, on the other, employing corrupt tactics to influence my decision. Blackmail. In other words, she was truthful to her memory, and I to mine. Truth, after all, has its dynamism, and memory its momentary lapses.

On his way to a festivity Kalaman (in a dream) comes across a heap of
elephant bones, partially but hastily covered with a scatter of broken
trees and other debris. Not far from this devastation there is a
tamarind tree. The tree has died recently, it appears, from being ring-
barked by a woodpecker. On the distant horizon a pillar of sand shoots
heavenwards, its summit culminating in a shape resembling a mush-
room's head. Farther east, a mirage forms and unforms, salt efflores-
cences, vapory, an obstinate fog refusing to be lifted.

In all, there are about a hundred persons, most of them women,
with children of either sex. A feast is being held, as if in homage to an
ancient deity. The day is clear, the weather pleasant, the sky dressed
here and there with the whitest of clouds. These cast dark shadows on
the ground, dark flutters of a candle in nervous agitation. A select
number of the women and the men are busy attending to a huge fire.
Others attend to the cauldrons already bubbling over with water, to
which they add salt. Now and then, the people look expectantly up at
the heavens, apparently anxious to feed their famished inner demons
on a manna of hope. They all, every single one of them, act as if they
are waiting for the late arrival of a divine promise.

There's a lot of rejoicing. The younger ones sing nursery rhymes,
those a bit older challenge one another in games requiring a strong
spirit of competitiveness, and those in their twenties dance, the expression on their faces becoming more eager the longer they court, the
brightness in their eyes reflecting the true joy in their hearts. Some of
the women burn sweet-smelling incense in stone urns, which they

pass around. Some of the other women apply cinnamon-scented oil to their skins. An older woman, with a flying fish on a line, is shaving the hair of a girl with a honey badger on a lead. After she's cut the young woman's hair, the older one digs a hole in the ground. She performs the act as solemnly as a devout Parsee prepares a corpse for the carrion eaters. In the meantime the young girl draws a crude representation of an ostrich, a totem whose significance is known to the attentive barber.

All of a sudden, a mass of locusts, migrating in myriads, covers first the forehead, then the flanks, and finally the full extent of the heavens' body. Obviously excited, the men and women strip down to their underclothes, hoping to gather robefuls of the windfall. They behave as if they look forward rather anxiously to the moment when they might satiate their inner hunger. There has been a famine in the region, a drought lasting for a long time, cattle decimated, humans reduced to skeletons, emaciated hands outstretched, begging for food.

Presently everyone's ears are filled with the sound of the locusts flying across the brow of the sky, and everyone's eyes with the sight of locusts in motion. No sooner have the people begun to fear that the locusts will just fly over them, and that they, the victims, will not have the opportunity to take their vengeance on them, than the insects lose their balance and fall in cataracts, wings first, straight into the boiling cauldrons. To everyone's utter delight, it turns out that the catch they collect in their spread-out garments becomes ever more bounteous.

Taken out of the bubbly pots, the cooked insects are laid on the grass to dry. After this they are peppered, salted, and then passed around. The eaters have as many helpings as they please. They remove the heads, pull apart the stomachs, and tail the locusts with the expertise of an adept shrimper plucking off the inedible segment of a shellfish. A great many of them gorge themselves with abandoned relish. Those with seasonings are generous in sharing them with those without. Those who have brought along other additives or pickled condiments do likewise. A couple of the unreconstructed men dictate outdated instructions to their womenfolk to prepare their portions in the best clarified butter. Others insist on supplementing their share with browned onions, garlic, and boiled basmati rice.

But there is an old man, with a crow for a totem, who does not partake of the feast. This lowers a damper on the spirit of those in his circle, especially that of a young man standing near him. While eating voraciously, the young man is making a proud display of a mantis in religious meditation. It is he who asks the old one why he is not partaking of the meal, why he is not rejoicing.

In reply the old man says glumly, "We are witnessing a tragedy, a community frenziedly placating an unease in its mind by filling its belly. We are bearing testimony to the foolish doings of a community doggedly refusing to take notice of its spiritual drought, which it mistakes for another type of want. If I refuse to eat, it is because I am asking, is it worth our humbling our human status by feeding on the locusts? Are we not engaging in a lowly form of self-abuse, eating the locusts because they have wrought havoc on our lives, because they have deprived us of our harvests?"

The boy with the mantis says, "Why does that worry you?"

"It worries me, and I hope I am not alone in thinking this," argues the old man, "that we are preparing ourselves for the day when we will feed on our neighbors, in boiled versions, on account of suspecting our age-old neighbors of dispossessing us of our share of food, or of denying us our rightful place. I hope, too, that we do not consider anyone refusing to eat with us to be a deviant, worthy of being ostracized."

A man with a chameleon on a leash reacts hostilely to the non-eater's remarks, which he describes as utterly simplistic. The man says, "Does it occur to my honorable peer and age-mate that the members of our downtrodden society cannot help being vengeful, that he who has suffered untold injustices may not know how to express so much pent-up frustration? What are these forsaken people to do but eat the insects that have ravaged their crops, given there is no other way of avenging so much injustice? How are they to keep body and soul together if they do not eat the locusts? In any case, who is he to preach from a high moral ground? And how dare he blame our people for being incapable of telling a physical hunger from a spiritual one? Pray, what are they expected to make of the ubiquitous famines, which have not only rendered the marrow in their bones dry but have also deprived them of their self-pride, the power of reasoning, their humanity?"

"Like dictatorships," retorts the old man with a crow for a totem, "famines produce a boomerang effect among other things, a beastly backlash. Where dictatorships reign, famines reign too. However, I doubt if we should be debating about finding an outlet for people's anger, or about placating their hunger, but about squaring the circle, in expectation of dealing with the root causes of famines, of ignoramus dictatorships, injustices."

A woman who has not spoken till then says, "We're doomed if we do, and damned if we don't." This speaker has in her embrace a lizard with an agitated head, with eyes darting outbursts of nervous tension.

The man with the chameleon on a leash utters his lines as though they are excerpted from a longer dirge. He chants, "We are the drought, the breeders of these monstrous dictators; we are the sons of the sycophants, the offspring of the accursed. We visit the havoc of famine on our heads. No rivers rise in us, no good blood runs in us."

Hardly has he finished talking than a cataclysmic shock is felt, heard, and then seen, in that order, an earthquake with an epicenter which might be plotted on the ocean floor several kilometers to the east of the festival site. All of a sudden, the sky caves in, and there is a huge flood, the earth turning into a cavern. On the precipice of the opened cavern hang a lot of screaming men, women, and children who anticipate, with fear and horror, the prospect of falling into the tumultuous waters below.

Between two mouthfuls of water a woman and a man, both drowning, exchange their last hyperboles, the woman saying, "This is death giving notice!" and her companion lamenting, "A famine followed by floods, the eye of a hurricane in an ascending whirlwind culminating in a storm."

Then, just as suddenly, the sky clears. On the far horizon a mirage is retreating. It is replaced by a rainbow, on whose heel drifts of sand rise in apparent fascination toward the sun, a tsunami of seismic tremors, mere waves undulating the sequined waters of the ocean's surface. A tidal blend of crows' cries come and go faint. None of this makes sense to the sleeper, the dreamer, Kalaman, who, in a startle, shouts the bisyllabic "*Waaq!*" He sits up, rubs his eyes red, irritates them awake.

As I showered I remembered reading about a hungry hermit who coveted his neighbor's lamb chop. His teacher advises him to brand the chop with a cross before consuming it. The hermit does as his teacher instructs him. Later the following morning, the hermit remarks, to his amazement, that he has in fact tattooed a cross on his own body.

A little later, in the kitchen.

I prepared breakfast, asking myself if I should throw down a gauntlet in Sholoongo's direction. I was thinking about some of the passages she conveniently left for me to see and read. The passages had hurt my ego, even though I might not admit it. It hurt that she could distort the picture of our rapport, presenting herself as an innocent and a victim, on top of being a woman giving herself in exchange for snippets of throwaway food.

I had fallen asleep the previous night nurturing a fantasy: that I might end the whole affair in a couple of days without prejudice to my or anybody's dignity. As I ran through the events so far, I was overwhelmed with my father's generous comportment, for answering some of the questions I hadn't put to him about "scorpions" and their poisonous place in our lives, and for enlightening me on matters I had no knowledge of. Now I let the kettle sing longer, hoping that its whistle would bring Sholoongo into the kitchen, fast.

I had hardly decided not to call out her name when I heard the key turn in the outside door. This was followed by the footsteps of somebody approaching. Assuming Sholoongo to be the person coming from outside after an early morning walk, I said, "I was beginning to wonder what had taken you so long, Sholoongo, or why you hadn't joined me for breakfast."

Morning surprises aren't my favorite pastime. Not only had I prepared my mind for a different complexion but I had not expected to encounter Talaado's fury. She was shouting at the top of her voice, "Where is the bitch?"

Struck dumb, and thinking ahead to an ended relationship, I moved toward Talaado. I intended to assure her of my total affection for her, in spite of what she thought, or might do to me or to Sholoongo.

Riding the high stallion of a rage, she would not give me the comfort of a soft gaze. She said, "Where are you hiding her?"

If I could, I would have given Talaado a loving embrace. This would have ended my worries and hers too, and I would have thanked her for saving me from the evil clutches of Sholoongo's designs. But Talaado stood apart from me, slim, trim, a quarter of a head taller than I in her high heels, her light brown skin glowing in the morning sun, eyes on the larger side, small-breasted, on the whole radiating not her usual charm but a body of disjointed messages. She was twenty-nine going on thirty. She was ugly when she was so furious.

"Where is she?" she asked again and again and again.

Angry people repeat themselves, but then so do people wanting to exonerate themselves of blame. Talaado reiterated her censorious remarks. I repeated my innocence. (You wouldn't think there were as many ways as I found, to express the idea of blameless innocence.) In the end, I got tired and chose silence. Which made her more furious. She shook further with the irritation of betrayal as she said, "Tell me where you are hiding her!" Sad, I stared at the threadbare reality of a ruined friendship, Talaado's and mine. Then I watched her, my love, do a half pirouette and walk away from me, in the direction of my bedroom, where she suspected Sholoongo to be ensconced. I sat down to have my coffee.

When she got back, she sounded angrier, maybe because she didn't want to admit defeat, having not found the object and subject of her rage. I wondered where Sholoongo might be, if she had not come home the previous night, or if she had done another vanishing act, more miraculous than the previous one.

Talaado said, "This marks the end of everything." Even though sounding angrier, she also sounded unconvinced as to her emotions. I doubt that I understood the meaning of the word "end" when Talaado used it, in the way one comprehends the same word conveniently placed on the screen after a man and a woman in love have ridden off into the sunset. I stretched out my hand to touch Talaado. But to no avail. She avoided all contact with me.

I suggested that she take some tea. I suggested that she sweeten it with plenty of honey; and that she listen to me. I spaced my words to make sure that I kept the consonants and the vowels from slurring into one another, as on a tongue sodden with alcohol.

She hollered, "How can I bear the thought of having tea with you?"

"Because I still love you," I said.

"And you want me to believe you?"

I asked, "Who told you that Sholoongo is staying here?"

"Your mother," she said.

I kept silent.

Speaking more furiously, she added, "And the shame of it is that not only are you admitting your guilt, but you do not sound in the least apologetic."

This brought a smile to my lips. I remarked to myself that she still loved me. Otherwise, why were her eyes runny with mascara, why did her face resemble the slate of a Koranic pupil having difficulty with his alphabet, with the letters growing extra legs and arms which caused them to merge with one another?

She had a keen wit, Talaado. She worked for a new idea come to town: she sold "space," placing ads in newspapers or mural ads on people's walls. With socialism out of fashion and with capitalism still in an embryonic state, billboards became the possibilities of custom. We had met more than two years ago. We took to each other instantly, and she gave me her visiting card, with her name and telephone number on one side and, on the flip side, the valediction: *We sell space!* My deputy was responsible for buying the space on behalf of our firm. Qalin and Talaado and I went out for a meal to talk things over. After the meal, she and I made a detour while I was giving her a lift, because I was calling on my father, I cannot recall why. And she and my father got on like a thatch hut caught up in a summer fire. To date I had never actually introduced her to my mother, suspecting that either the two wouldn't get along or, if they did, I would be asked to marry her right away.

Talaado now stormed out of my apartment without saying any more. Strangely, though, I wasn't at all disturbed by the spontaneity of the melodrama. Maybe because she didn't leave her set of keys behind. Nor did she return my ring, or ask that I return her photographs.

Stranger still, there was no sign of Sholoongo even after the door had slammed shut behind Talaado. I behaved very blasé, confident that Talaado's storm would lose its fury once we met again, in the calm, and had a chat. Eventually she was bound to come to her senses. Then I would apologize.

As I cleared my breakfast table, I felt that my life had suddenly taken a decisive turn. I rang my office, spoke to my deputy, and told her that I was going off to Afgoi to visit Nonno. Being very fond of him herself, Qalin asked if all was well with the old man. I assured her that it was. So far as I knew.

I was on the move when I first heard *it* on my car radio.

As I pieced the story together, and listened to variations of the same tale, I decided that it was cast in the vein of a dream sequence with a centerpiece. The tale was ankle deep in ominous consequences; it had a mythical quality to it. When placed under scrutiny, the woven fabric of the fable had huge gaps. You might even discern some elements of speculation introduced into the tale the moment the journalists reporting on it for the world press got hold of it.

Again I ran through it in my head as I drove.

A gray moving mountain appears before a couple of villagers who take note of this extraordinary happening: an elephant, behaving like a human resident, walking by as if he knew where he was headed. One of the men telling the story to the radio journalist adds that the elephant seemed to be in haste, like somebody with a job to be done before sunrise.

By the time the television lights are switched on, more villagers have come out of their compounds. They all speak to the reporters, to confirm what they have seen. They tell how one of their number has emerged out of his compound, half clad, and run into this larger-than-life elephant, in and of itself a frightening sight. A neighbor, reminiscing, remembers thinking this can't be an elephant, maybe several people holding up a cloth and walking under it in a synchronized manner, the way they do in animated cartoons. Meanwhile another who happened to be passing by narrates how, returning from his usual early morning swim in the river, he runs into *him*, an immensity of worrying proportions. Yet another recalls having had the suspicion that the beast had escaped from a zoo somewhere. For her part, a breast-feeding mother asserts that it is her child who sees *him* first, her child who screams frightfully loud. Old and young alike, the villagers marvel at what has come to pass, one of them boasting that, because of the elephant, they are famous now all over the world, the BBC, Radio Cairo, the Deutsche Welle, and the VOA falling over each other to give their tale a lead-story status. Imagine!

Many more villagers, who have seen an elephant for the first time in their lives, give absurd exaggerations regarding his size, weight, and height. One of them describes him as "a fundament!" Another, elaborating, alludes to the term "firmament," because of the elephant's hugeness. He felt as though the sky was obliterated from his vision. The last to be interviewed by the local TV station swears that he sensed the world lean forward as the elephant came closer and tilt backwards as the beast walked away.

This large mammal ambles on purposefully. He pays no heed to the crowded silence following him in stealthy consciousness. One of the villagers, a woman often suspected of dabbling in witchcraft, talks of her inspired theory: that this was no elephant, more like a human on the holy mission of avenging justice. Two other witnesses, neither having had any contact with the woman, speak in substantiation of the woman's claims, giving as evidence the observation that the elephant turned around when someone said something in Somali. Several villagers will not comment, afraid of a fitting retribution should they do so.

Finally, those following him in stealthy curiosity report how the elephant comes to a decisive halt, right in front of a compound belonging to a villager named Fidow. He stands his ground for a long while, the elephant does, momentously huge and yet so aware of his surroundings that at one point he steps aside to let the women and children run past him and out of Fidow's compound. These join the curious onlookers outside, waiting and watching. The elephant issues a rank roar, then silence. He repeats the roar several more times, and waits, maybe for the master of the house to come out. His height almost doubling, his trunk and tusks going up, his weight seemingly heavier, the elephant now engages provocatively in a display of nerves, a display which makes the crowd run away for cover. As if to convince those refusing to be scared, he smashes through the high concrete wall of the compound, tearing off the metal gate and tossing it in their direction. Clearly worried for their lives, many of them flee. An instant later, many return, to watch.

It is at this point that Fidow comes out of his compound. He retreats, fast, only to reemerge, armed with a stout gun. The elephant goes berserk, and as quick as death, thrusts his tusks into Fidow, whom he throws to the side before trampling the corpse into a pulp. He steps over Fidow's dead body, the crowd, aghast, still watching him, and enters the room out of which Fidow emerged earlier. By the time the villagers see him again, the elephant is carrying with him dozens of tusks.

The world's wirelesses are broadcasting the news in as many languages as there are. To a radio, they are repeating the amazing feat, the wherefores and mystery of an elephant avenging his kin. They are speaking of an elephant stalking a man who had shot dead half the members of his immediate family, taken their tusks, and hidden them in his house. Not only, they say, has the elephant killed the hunter, but he has reclaimed their tusks. Some of the journalists speculate that the elephant means to give his massacred kin a decent burial. Many of the radio commentators sound triumphant. One of the local radio reporters boastfully predicts that from this day on we will have a green movement in Somalia, the first genuine one of its kind in the world.

I was stopped at the checkpoint on the outskirts of the city. My car was searched for weapons, I was frisked and let go.

I sat in a long queue of cars on either side of the motorway, no fewer than fifty vehicles, and as many as a hundred Red Beret soldiers, the dictator's special regiment, trained to frustrate the ambition of the armed militia movements to take the city and the tyrant along with it. A number of the drivers with identifiable regional accents were made to park to one side, to step out and wait for further checks, in the sun.

As I gave a hurried glance at the clutch of men listlessly standing by their vehicles and humiliatedly waiting to be asked questions and frisked and taken in, I thought they were suspects because of their intonation of Somali. This was why they were being singled out and, no matter what they said, were thought to be sympathizers of the local armed militia grouping, with vigilantes who infiltrated into the city nightly. It is not uncommon for a stone thrown at the guilty to strike the innocent. And many of us innocents would fall victim to this head-on confrontation between the dictator, at the head of his Red Berets and his army of thugs, and the leaders of the vigilantes, who claimed to be fighting for the overthrow of the regime, though they were bearing arms with a view to advancing not the interests of the nation but their own.

On the road, moving, I thought of the elephant story . . .

Was it worth my imaginative while to look for Sholoongo or Timir in the labyrinths of the tale about the elephant? Such was the mixture of sorrows I felt, with Fidow dead, Talaado alienated, my mother so very unhappy, that an abyss opened below me, and a smart hurt imposed itself on my mind. Something was eluding me, but what? I had a problem locating Sholoongo in all this. Was I to see her as a catalyst, setting off chains of catastrophes? Or was all this coincidental, she happening to be in town when these occurred? What was I to make of the unsubtle glimpse I had, in my dream, of a heap of elephant bones?

I drove toward Afgoi on a road which for thirty-odd years had seen me come and go, a road the sight of which made me burst with the fidgetiness of a sparrow harrying its playmate. Today there was a bee in my bonnet, a bonnet with invisible strings like a puppeteer's. I had no idea what good pulling at the strings would do. In fact, I wished I could alter my human nature, exchange it for that of a bee so I could fly freely, or become a bonnet so I might lend my services, as a hat, to Sholoongo. Then I might have known more, might have got to the bottom of all these secret communications.

For me, Afgoi meant Nonno, who was more of a place than a person, an octogenarian with whom I associated the locus of my joys, their primary source. Nonno: the vase in which, as a child, I hid my toys. Physically vast, Nonno was endowed with a spacious laughter, with numerous chambers. In more ways than one I had his ears, and in more senses than one my father was heir to his feet and the size of his sex. One of my aunts was born with hands identical to Nonno's; an uncle inherited his bulkiness. However, if Nonno had a heart, he appeared to have buried it with his late wife.

What a pleasure it was for me, as a child, to know the geography of his person. What a delight it was for me to touch base with the symmetry of his vision, through contacts I made with his mind. I kept him company, and sat on his lap as he gazed at the stars, repeating to me myths of old. He would make up new ones to edify me, his favorite grandchild. Nonno was a need evocative of other necessities. He was an ambition making other wishes deserving of deference. He was an epoch reminding you of other eras, times that had come and gone. He had many names, which he kept changing, ultimately placing his preference on Nonno, a descriptive designation of his status, that of being a grandfather, mine. He lived for an eternity of years, each year a joy to those close to him.

There was a great deal left of Nonno even after everyone appropriated the parts they claimed for themselves. He had larger-than-myth proportions, so that when excited, half of his face would expand into a grin of vaudeville richness, the other half remaining rigid like a lagoon, quiet in its depravity. I would remember with narcissistic incredulity, recall with reverential humility, how as an infant I wished I had been the dew in the bent leaf of his hand, a leaf touched with dawn's distilled wateriness, my grandfather's smile as clear as amniotic fluid.

He was a birder. Such was our relationship that he knew my mind better than I did myself, presenting me with a parrot for my fourth birthday. Nonno helped my imagination grow wings and fly to the seventh heaven so I might return to the planet Earth with a bounty of secrets. He used to point out to me the Hal Todobaad constellation, whose sighting presaged rain. He would talk of how the clouds darkened and why, how come the sky rolled mats of thunder across its brow preparatory to pouring the season's monsoon of torrents. Often things happened just as he had predicted. It was he who spoke of the *Isninta qorrax madow*, an eclipse portending a massacre. Or of the Year of Saturday, which alluded to the arrival of the Italian colonialist Captain Bottego in our country. According to him, I was born under the auspicious Gudban, in the Scorpio constellation. He explained I was meant to be an orator when I became a man.

I interrupted my thoughts, for I had arrived. I parked in the shade of a tamarind tree and, as I did so, quoted to myself a line from a poem by Ted Hughes, in which a hawk makes the bold claim of holding creation in its claws!

I strode with the agility of a bird to whose pointed claws the secret of the cosmos clung. I reiterated to myself how, ever since Sholoongo's arrival, I had the feeling of being outpaced by the events unfolding. Time, I told myself, dwelt in the soft squawk of a sparrow, as I saw a sparrow. Time resided in the whisper of an African-American woman, Nonno's secret lover; anxious time was transferred from one hand to another with the swiftness of a hot potato dropped by a too eager child. Time was in the child's mouth, the child sneaking his way through the mist in the woods toward the river, where he would set traps on behalf of Fidow, his mentor; the same child, curious as his young years, would blow a large snail to attract honeybirds. Time conjured up a girl, busy drawing monkeys touching their fingers to their lips or blocking their ears or pretending not to see. But where were the boy's fingers, the ones not helping the three monkeys? In the boy's memory, the fingers were either crawling up the girl's skirt, or feeding her.

Now I favored the scene ahead of me with a contemplative stare. To the right of the mosquito-wired sunporch there was a little zoo: pet rabbits and stray cats, the odd peacock displaying its colors to an appreciative crowd including a couple of crows, three ducks waddling back and forth, in and out of the shallow pond, a stork with hurt wings, several pigeons. There was also a monkey, the only pet with a name, Hanu, short for Hanuman, a grandchild to Xusna, for a time my most beloved vervet. Named, he was pampered too, the monkey, as though human. Hanu stayed in the main house most of the time, wearing the old man's shoes or shirts. It had never occurred to me that Nonno raised animals and kept them for my own diversion. Years later I learnt that my grandfather had an irrational phobia of snakes, and the presence of these animals guarded him against their intrusion.

Hanu was the first to spot me. He dashed in my direction with the eagerness of a child reuniting with one of its absentee parents. We embraced rather clumsily and he gave me a smacky kiss and offered me a bite of his half-chewed corn. The other members of the circus joined us. They gathered at my feet too, ducks and crows as well. The pigeons, however, elevated their status by getting up on my shoulders, one on my left, a second on my right, with a third, cooing in cozy comfort, perched on the crown of my skull. Together we moved toward the bungalow, a circus unlike any other, my shirt and trousers stained with Hanu's irresistible charm, his fingerprints of adoration, my skull drippy with pigeon droppings.

"You're treating them as though they were born out of the flow of your own marrow and water," Nonno's housekeeper was saying, in a tone meant to convey friendly censure. "Look at you!"

She turned and shouted at the animals as if they were children misbehaving in the presence of a guest. Obedient, the ducks waddled away in their hip-swaying fashion. Even if slow, the pigeons flew off, leaving a few feathers in their wake. The peacock strode off, offended. Only Hanu remained, his head buried in my chest. I said to him, "That's all right." Zariba did not approve of my lavish pampering of Hanu.

She was a squat, heavily built woman in her late forties, with a heart large as the African continent. She had been in Nonno's employ for more than twenty-eight years, a fact of which she was proud. My mother took this as a hint that Zariba was claiming to be more than the ancient man's house-minder. When I got closer she repeated, "Look at you, you must be ashamed of yourself." I wasn't sure whom she was addressing, Hanu or myself. Not until I heard her bark the command "Get down, you!" was I certain she was talking to Hanu.

"Don't worry," I said. "I have a change of clothes here, do I not? Besides, it's wonderful to be so welcomed, when only a couple of hours ago an elephant's rampage minced Fidow to a pulp."

"God bless the dead," she said and was sadly silent, as if mourning. Hanu looked sad too. It struck me — and not for the first time — that Hanu understood every single word we spoke. (I remembered the earlier supposition by one of those interviewed on the radio, that the elephant comprehended human speech.) Hanu lowered his beady eyes now, and this put me in mind of a flag at half-mast. Was he too mourning? He knew Fidow, and loved him, didn't he?

I said, "The tragedy of it all!"

"Those were Nonno's very words," Zariba said. Here for the sake of stress she shook her head, maybe in memory of how Nonno had reacted to the news when he had been brought it.

I surveyed the scene around us and saw nothing but the signs of successive droughts. I concluded that the elephant's anger had a lot to do with man's indifference to nature, humankind's exploitative greed.

Hanu was his usual self, mischievous, with a scarf tightly drawn over his nose and eyes. "Whose scarf is this?" I asked Zariba, as I lifted him up to give his hairy cheek a kiss.

Self-conscious as a bride in the presence of her in-law, Zariba demurred gently at Hanu's inability to explain his actions in words. She dipped her head in a slight bow, her lips touched with an undecided grin. She said, "The scarf belongs to Sholoongo, who spent last night in your room."

It was then that I took leave of Zariba.

It was often said that when in Nonno's bungalow, the seasons, like a tamed tigress, fed off the palm of your hand. Built at the beginning of the century by a most adept Italian architect-turned-farmer who was keen on ornithology, it had four porches in addition to a more recent extension. This new extension, where guests were put up, had its own private entrance. Until a decade ago, a wooded patch of land encircled the bungalow on all sides. Nonno would quote a poem by Cali Dhuux, a Somali poet, about the interdependence of the human and animal worlds; how human beings, by studying a gazelle's mating-time, may decide as to the auspicious nature of the seasons.

As a child I used to get to the river faster than anyone else, because I had all the secret approaches to the area at my fingertips. I knew how to find the logs in which Fidow would site his hives. Moreover, it was here at Nonno's estate that I acquired what knowledge I had about astronomy and astrology, here in these erstwhile woods that Fidow had taken Timir, here that night after night I sneaked in on men and women engaged in illicit lovemaking. Fidow, a Casanova, had many mistresses.

Now I sat in Nonno's ancient rocking chair in the west wing, remembering the thrills and chills of my childhood discoveries. In my memory, a curtain is billowing. I am a child of seven, hiding in a cupboard in Kathy's room, Kathy being Nonno's African-American tenant. I watch her as she takes off her clothes, as she weighs her breasts, as she reaches down in an attempt to kiss her nipples. Then she lies on her bed, naked, fingering herself. A little later, Nonno tiptoes into the room. They shower together, scrubbing each other's backs. I try to leave, but can't for fear of being seen. I stay behind the curtain, waiting for an opportunity to sneak out.

Kathy was a Peace Corps volunteer. She taught English in the Afgoi school system. A big-boned woman, she had a crack of a loud laugh which had more body to it than even Nonno's. When they were together, showering or scrubbing each other's backs, Nonno's residues of youth kept resurfacing. They were good for each other. Nonno had been a widower several years when she came on the scene.

On the day I hide in the cupboard, Kathy takes him whole, in her mouth. As she does, she chants, "Heaven is heavy, quick-coming is hell." After their shower, he takes her several more times. I am still in the cupboard, hiding.

No doubt Kathy helped Nonno to perk up his fragmented spirits. One idea leads to another. One moment I am recalling Nonno's frequent visits to Kathy's annex. Another moment, I am congratulating myself for having sneaked into Kathy's room earlier, and for having made cuts in the curtain, holes large enough for me to see through without being seen. Suddenly, before I wise up to what I am doing, a most delightful thought dawns on me, and I am thrilled to infantile distraction. No longer hiding in the cupboard, I am talking to Nonno, asking him to see what I am admiring: the contours of an eagle in flight, whose movements I discern in the cuts in the curtain. Kathy and Nonno stop their lovemaking. Sitting up, he says to me, "What are you doing here?"

I sat on the porch, waiting for the rising dust on the horizon to settle down, or for the whirl of dust to materialize eventually into Nonno's jalopy. For a good while I couldn't see much, as though clouds had lodged themselves in my sight. To clear my eyes of the gauzy fog residing in them, I rubbed my scratchy eyelids, recalling that Sholoongo had spent a night in my room. Where was she when the "elephant" paid his visit to the village, not far from here? Did she have an alibi? Did she, in fact, have a hand in Fidow's death?

Nonno's rackety vehicle came into view. He parked it next to my car and, alighting, banged the door shut. However, he stopped in his frisky tracks when he heard a cacophony of birds gathered in the high perch of an exceptionally good-looking royal palm, birds flying up in fright.

I got up to welcome him.

Nonno's voice rode the wind. He said, "He lives an owl's cry away from death who messes with elephants!"

"Or deals in ivory —" I said, moving toward him.

"Or receives a lucrative payment in wads of Hong Kong dollars," Nonno went on, "lucrative payments in exchange for a heady gauntlet-running which makes you massacre half a herd of elephants."

His ventriloquy gave way to a tall smile horizontally erected on his face, a lodestar of welcome, shining as it did in the eye in which the setting sun was reflected. He was as vast a man as a seagoing vessel might be large. We met halfway and hugged, and I kissed him on the right cheek. He smelt of tobacco. I said, "I should've liked to drive straight to the burial grounds where Fidow was being interred, but I didn't know which cemetery."

Nonno said: "Fidow's death, however deserved, dumbfounds those of us who have survived him. How do you explain an elephant behaving as we ourselves might have behaved? Rumors are being circulated that the murderer was not an elephant who ran amok, but a human being disguised as one. People cannot comprehend how an elephant could journey so far from his base, cross an international boundary, kill a man in a beastly vengeance, and then leave with the remains of his massacred kith and kin!"

I remembered my dream of the previous night, and dismissed the idea that Sholoongo had altered her nature to carry out an act so absurd. A chill ran through my body.

Momentarily Zariba joined us. She brought along two chairs which she balanced on her shoulders. She said to Nonno, "How are things where you've just come from?"

"I would say Fidow jumped the queue," he said, lighting a cigarette and puffing on it. "He was younger than I, and should've waited his turn."

"What nonsense!" Zariba demurred warmly.

Of late, news of death, whether of somebody he knew or did not, affected him more and more, as if he were too tired to indulge in stargazing, too exhausted to survey the sad state of his estate. I always imagined that when the Angel of Death finally called, Nonno would receive him as an old friend whose tardy arrival he would compare to a familiar figure coming, clad in the Messiah's unfamiliar garb of a leopard skin.

Nonno said, "Fidow couldn't say I didn't tell him!"

I tasted salt in the wind. Nonno too had a bitter expression on his features, an expression which put me in mind of a dragoman being fed on pork.

I thought he might have been speaking to himself as he said, "He came to see me a week before he went to the border area between Somalia and Kenya. He told me that he had struck a lucrative triangular deal with some Kenyan, Somali, and Hong Kong businessmen. He spoke of a one-off jackpot, on which he hoped to retire. I advised him to pay heed to the position of the stars. I warned him not to proceed. I said to call it off."

I was sad, all right. But I was angry too. Angry and also confused, still not knowing what Sholoongo's role in this might be. My sorrow and confusion were brought into sharp relief the moment Nonno made a reference to divination. Did she, in her capacity as a shapeshifter, have a hand in his death?

Nonno shouted to Zariba, "Are you not offering us something to drink?" He sat in a sad reverie. Neither of us spoke until we heard the clinking of glasses approaching. He stubbed out his cigarette and received his drink. After a sip, he said, "Thirty-three years ago, to be precise on the day you were born, a crow made a cameo appearance in our lives. A stunned crowd of villagers later that day watched the almost comic scenario in which a vast middle-aged Nonno maintained pace with a crow. Many other creatures had preceded the crow's arrival, many more came after his departure. I can think of an ostrich or two, a monkey named Xusna, mail pigeons, a peacock, ducks, a skyful of birds, *and* Hanu. The question has often been asked, how is it that carrier pigeons orient themselves both in the sky and on the ground?"

I said, "Maybe they memorize the road while going?"

"How do they return?"

"It is all easy when they remember the layout of the road?"

He puffed on a new cigarette. He went on, "You can put them in a basket blindfolded in the back of my jalopy. You can drive around and around at whatever speed, but they will find their way back to this place. So how do they achieve this?"

I said I had no idea.

"We believe that a pigeon's homing sense is infallible, because all animals are blessed with *nuuro*, which aids them in their effort to know. God has given them this instinct, no mean attribute, comparable to human intelligence."

Being adept at uttering bird noises, Nonno now made them. In a little while, there were movements in the bushes, in the low shrubs, movements high up in the trees. All manner of birds were now assembling, as though they had been invited to a conference. Ants came too. So did the odd dog. A giraffe turned up, maybe just to have a look. A stallion neighed as if wishing his high-pitched call to be remarked upon. Hanu appeared to be the busiest, herding them forward.

Then Nonno sounded a deep coo-cocoo appeal, in pigeon parlance. There was a hush. He repeated the same sound. We waited awhile. Most of the other birds flew away, very few staying. These watched from their high perch. Among them you had crows, vultures, hawks, and a canary of sterling beauty. Was Nonno a Solomon calling a pigeon's meeting? At his bidding the feathered creatures came closer. At his prompting they formed a semicircle. He put his hand in the pocket of his jellaba and began to feed them. He might have been Adam on the first day of creation, naming all the animals.

I remained quiet in this atmosphere of mounting tension, hoping that in good time Nonno would work his way to a relevant conclusion: about an elephant traveling a great distance to reclaim what had been his clan's; an elephant killing the man who had massacred his whole lineage.

Now he was saying, "If we acknowledge that plants have their secrets, and if humans, as we know, have their own universe of them, then we must assume that birds have theirs too, secrets which help them to avoid danger, to distinguish those who are wicked to them from those who wish to do them no harm, an instinct which enables them to feel not only the sense of peril but also where to migrate and when. In Somali, we have a word to describe this notion too. We call it *nuuro*, and animals are blessed with it; so are babies, imbeciles, the insane, and any human whom misfortune, in some decisive way, has affected. One category specially blessed is those who return from the verge of death and live to tell their tale. I don't have it, you haven't got it, why? Because our working faculties require no supplementation. Now, since every coin must have a reverse side, *nuuro's* flip side bears the name *nabsi*, a means by which human activities are governed, a way of maintaining equilibrium: if you please, the overall communal peace and stability."

"*Nabsi!*" I repeated the word as if I had heard it for the first time. At my own prompting, I was remembering yesterday afternoon's conversation with my father.

"*Nuuro!*" said Nonno, pronouncing the word clearly.

This time I didn't repeat it.

He continued, "When I think about *nabsi*, I think of you and of Sholoongo too. I think of how you should behave, and how you should treat her with due civility or not. Never forget that you were once infatuated with her, which makes her entitled to a fair hearing and a good deal of respect, especially now that she has come around to paying her belated affection in return."

"But that's not what she's come for," I said.

"She's thrown in her lot with you, baby or no baby?"

I couldn't think of an answer. Silence.

"You can't walk away from this *nabsi*," he said. "It's like walking away from a civic responsibility. *Nabsi* raises its head, puts a stop to unfair treatment of persons weaker than oneself. *Nabsi* brings the torturer to his senses, *nabsi* makes sure that massacres of animals, wasteful murders are brought to a retributive end. I would hypothesize that if *nuuro* led the elephant to Fidow's door, it was *nabsi* which killed him."

It seemed as though Nonno was on Sholoongo's side, granting her both *nuuro* and *nabsi* powers, the one because of the misfortunes which had befallen her at birth, the other because she was the weaker, the needier one, from whom I was not supposed to walk away.

I asked, "What's her secret?"

Looking upset, he remained silent. The pigeons flew off without him shooing them away. Then he excused himself and went into the house "to change," he explained, and returned after a few minutes.

He said, "A man locks himself in a dark room and raises his index finger, pointing at the ceiling. Reemerging, he challenges the community members to tell him what he did in the dark room. Another man describes accurately what he did in the dark room when alone."

"*Morale della storia?*"

Nonno said, "Let me tell you something else. The Prophet Mohammed was once asked to define Allah. Responding to the question, the Prophet said that God is different from any Identikit that a human being is capable of constructing!"

What was I to say? Or what was I to make of the folktale, in which a man shuts himself away in a dark room, raises a finger, and is informed by another about what he did? What had defining God to do with all this? It had been a day of shocks. First thing in the morning, Talaado's surprise arrival rendered me speechless; then the elephant story and Fidow's death; then I learnt from Nonno's housekeeper that Sholoongo spent a night in my room.

Nonno and I were joined by Hanu. All three of us, in our different ways, appreciated the self-consciousness of a bee engrossed in its drone, a bee engrossed in its somersault search for a safe spot to perch. I thought, here was an instance of *nuuro* in action, two of the weaker species encountering in the folds of a human understanding or misunderstanding of what they were up to. Hanu and the bee!

Nonno said, "I won't pontificate on the Prophet's rhetoric as to the definition of Allah, but will confine myself to the *morale* if there is any in the *storia* whose wisdom lies in the simple idea that nothing is unknowable so long as another human has knowledge of it. It is my guess that, on a pedestrian level, the folktale's purport is that when a secret is known to two humans, such a secret will be known before the death of both parties."

I felt a storm gathering in Nonno's head. I sensed the violent turbulence from the tremble in his voice, his eyes going far beyond what was visible to me, his nose twitchy as though he were smelling high winds from afar. Would he explode or implode? Would his death cause the earth to reverberate with a seismic instance of total shock? My memory of last night's dream called on me again. I couldn't help remembering the gentle breeze with which it all began, followed by the dreamer's sighting of a heap of elephant bones. I remembered how a lone locust revealed itself, very tiny, sad in its aloneness, until it was joined by more and more insects, a skyful of locusts, a view which overwhelmed the central consciousness of both the tale and its teller. The dream ended before I had heard the rank roar of a beast in vengeful fury, a *nabsi* catching up with the perpetrator of a massacre, a *nuuro* coming in aid of a weaker mammal.

But now a less ferocious storm was brewing in Nonno's pupils. These appeared dimmed in one corner and very bright in another, with a lightning coming on and then going off at regular intervals. He blinked his eyes, and I felt a chill deep in my viscera. I had the impression that the signs were not good. The cold in my belly was getting to my head, my thoughts frozen in a winter of incomprehension. The marrow circulating in my bones went icy suddenly. The air had a moistness to it, like a breeze bringing in rain from beyond a mountain.

He said, "Most societies have myths in which a nonhuman gives birth to their ancestors. There is a plethora of further possibilities, of an egg containing the cosmos in embryo, of humanity beginning at a specifically named date, of bulls' horns keeping the world in perfect balance, you know the lot. But in most myths, one has a part-human ancestry. It follows naturally that those who are capable of regaining their animal self and merging it with their human self are deemed more powerful. They are worthy of our envy, not our disdain."

I wished to defend myself. I wished to remind him that I had often envied Sholoongo the power of altering her nature, if that was what she did, exchanging her humanness for an animal one. What's more, I had not been wicked to Sholoongo. I had been civil. The fact is, though, that a pain which avoided definition was gaining a foothold in my body. I had no inkling where the pain originated or what it might be. I kept quiet.

Comforted by the parenthesis of quiet, I excused myself.

CHAPTER
FIVE

Kalaman my grandson *was* in finger-deep trouble!

I returned home with a hint of daylight still aglow and found Kalaman on the porch. He was hugging a shortwave radio to himself, listening to the news. His face loosened itself into a charmful grin when our eyes met, his features spreading into a buttery smile. There were traces of dried sweat marking the boundaries of his chin. My grandson had a forehead smooth like the inside of a seashell. I made a waving gesture as he rose to welcome me, and suggested that he wait. Because my irrational fear of snakes overwhelms me when I think they might be about, I lifted my feet off the ground with extra caution, lest I step on one. This aversion is so bizarre it used to be compared to that of an African who admits to being frightened of insects. But there you are!

A silk shawl was draped over my left shoulder. Since the occasion of Fidow's funeral demanded it, I was in formal attire, including a crocheted conical hat which Zariba, my housekeeper, had presented me with to mark my seventh threshold. I also had on my favorite Egyptian jellaba, of the finest silk, this a gift from Kalaman. My feet boasted the loveliest pair of thonged sandals, a most handsome affair, designed by Yaqut, who made them himself with his own filial hands to celebrate my eightieth birthday. They had a special place in my wardrobe and heart, considering they were the only pair he had ever made from start to finish. That Yaqut is not born the son of a shoemaker is a fact I needn't stress. But I hope this point is taken in the manner I am presenting it, Somali clan rivalry and lineage obsessions of *begats* being what they are. It would upset me terribly if a clannish snob were to behave loutishly toward him and treat him with haughty contempt.

I stand over six and a half feet. I am large-boned for a Somali and heavily built. One of my tenants, an African-American, used to point out that there was too much of me to take at a gulp. One chokes, she explained. I knew what she meant.

Although I may not be of noble blood, whatever that means, I am of a noble age, a man who has lived for a mountain of years. I am using "mountain" to pay homage to Kathy, my African-American tenant and, for a time, my lover and a Catholic at that. She would pray that I might live, as she put it, for an Everest of years. In a roundabout sort of way, I am asking if somebody of my age nobility, my description and disposition, has an identity outside the perimeters of the one which other persons have invented, each constructed identity having a value, the mintage of a made-up currency. To Kalaman, for instance, I am a place, a vase capable of receiving the affections with which he fills it. To Yaqut, I am the threshold of an imagined hurdle of self-appraisal, an offspring's tread traversing the face of a huge mountain, a most risky undertaking, especially when there is no foothold. To Kalaman's mother, I am a serpent of the aquatic variety, dark as the mysteries it guards. To Kathy, I am membered, my sinusoidal body a precious stone, color ochre. To Fidow, I might have been a crow, uttering an unheeded prophetic cry. In short, I am many in one, and I am *other* too.

Ever since learning of Sholoongo's presence in the land, and more especially after Fidow's death, I've thought of Kalaman as my legatee, for reasons that are to do with my imminently awaited death. Anyway, he and I hugged.

"He who messes with elephants by massacring half the members of their immediate clan is bound to dwell within the radius of an owl's cry from death," I said. "How I wish Fidow had paid heed to my counsel not to accept the commission to poach elephants. How I wish he was not tempted by the fat fee in Hong Kong dollars. Now he is no more, and no ivory either. The Kenyan middlemen who hired him are at a loss, so are the Chinese dealers in tusks. And we are mourning a friend."

Kalaman struck me as being anxious about something, I could not tell what. It was unlike him to speak in terrible haste and loudly for my comfort (a man of my noble age is touchy when others assume he is hard of hearing, or losing total power over his bodily functions). Why speak fast, as if he had paid for a three-minute transatlantic telephone call with a cash deposit in advance? Or had he meant to say his say with speed, fitting all he could into the already paid-for time, and then quit, *vamoose?* I recall how conscious I was of the embrace which came after the oration, as we hugged.

We often teased each other, he and I, about our respective sizes. I loom large. He is small. A pygmy to my Dinka stature. We sat down, and got to talking about his parents. Even though there was no call for it, he made several oblique references to death. Somehow he worked Sholoongo into our talk. He alluded to scorpions hiding under rocks, to dreams weighed down with elephant corpses. I spoke with sadness about my fraught mental state: how the door to the vestibule might open shortly, and then *finito*, before my ninth threshold, bringing to an abrupt termination my Kilimanjaro ascent of annuaries! It was no secret that I read the obituary pages first in newspapers and the front page last. Curiously, I'd begun to observe that the pages giving death notices, in dying autocratic states like Somalia, expressed a more popular form of newspaper reporting, far better than the first pages, which invariably concentrated on the despot's or his deputies' misleading doings.

Ever present in our thoughts and preoccupations, the odor of death overwhelmed us. I wish I had a way of linking the pungent smell to the country's slow march towards collapse. Item: the bombings of cities, like Hargeisa, which was razed to the ground, its residents massacred, their corpses lying unburied where they fell, the survivors reduced to refugees. Item: Mogadiscio's current daily civilian casualties, their bodies hacked to death with machetes. Item: the environment. Item: Fidow and his trampled-on body. Deaths everywhere I looked. Corpses bearing the name of a clan. No one innocent. No one of us. If I avoided mentioning Sholoongo's name, it was because I feared it might upset Kalaman, who, while welcoming me to my own home, had the appearance of a man who had put his major personal problems on a back burner. Not that I was certain how we might broach the matter of Sholoongo when we finally did.

The late afternoon held sufficient brightness for my eagle eyes to notice that Kalaman had been to a dentist. As I prepared myself to light a cigarette, I remarked how, with the residual tobacco stains removed, Kalaman's teeth looked TV-commercial clean. My hand, in a purposeful detour, tapped gently on my shirt pocket to ascertain that I had enough smokes to last me until the morning, a near-full packet. This prompted my grandson to provide me with an ashtray, and I indulged my smoker's appetite in quiet as I dragged on my fag, a present from the Nairobi Airport Duty Free Shop bought by no other than Kalaman. "If you must smoke, you must," he would say, and present me with lighters and the nicotine in its pleasantest form, in addition to packets of the rough-hewn tobacco of a Gauloise and the Italian Nazionale, and throw in something of a Turkish blend, unadulterated wonders of smoke, so I would burn in my own heaven!

Restless, Kalaman pushed around the chairs and turned off the radio, which he put next to a ceramic plate full of fried cassava and a vinegar-and-salt dip. I ate a charred slice of cassava and took a mouthful of water to gulp it down. I asked him if he would be spending the night here, or did I question Zariba? I can't be certain.

Again I can't be certain if it was then that Kalaman repeated his conversation with Timir the day before. One or the other of them speculated that "death stipulated dreamlessness, the tragic acceptance of a great loss. Those whom you love, when dead, will no longer figure in your dreams." Perhaps I am not quoting correctly. Even so, I sensed that he appeared bothered as he revisited his and Timir's respective positions. When next he fell silent, he wouldn't speak for a long time, as if his tongue had been turned into a tangle of thorns. Possibly the idea of Sholoongo living and figuring in his mother's dreams was at last getting to him; or maybe Fidow's death had begun to sink in just then. He looked his years, a youth caught in the trappings of his age.

Before his teens, Kalaman had the habit of carrying a conch shell with him wherever he went, a conch shell to which he spoke in an invented language of sorts. Holding the conch shell close to him, he would ask a question, then put it near his ears, as if listening to an answer. He insisted that, this way, he received secret whispers from a distant surf, and that he was in touch with the beyond. Infatuated with Sholoongo, who had built her house of stone inside him, he pleaded that I feel his stomach to confirm that he was irredeemably pregnant with "the baby of his affection." I thought, frankly, that he had given us the best description yet of a child's infatuation.

When not awaiting private communications from the conch shell, or whispering received secrets to his manikin, Kalaman spent the greater part of the day with Xusna in my woods, now and then attaching himself to one of the farmhands, and now and then joyfully serving as apprentice to Fidow, then a crocodile hunter and my general factotum. A child of obsessions, Kalaman fell asleep with the conch shell in one hand, a palm-filling talisman in the other, and Xusna either beside him or embracing him.

Our conversation that late afternoon straddled several subjects. For one thing I meant us to have a good reunion. For another, I felt that there was no benefit to be had from speculating either about scorpions or Sholoongo's intentions or whether it was wise to censure her for Fidow's death. The man had been an obstinate fool, and fools die wasted deaths. But because many things were coming to a head, what with the ruin being visited on the nation as we spoke, I put my effort into finding a safe haven in abstractions. Hence I touched on the notions of *nuuro* and *nabsi*. I cannot for the life of me remember by what circuitous route we got to the abstractions.

Kalaman gave me in a parenthesis a rundown of his news so far, because I wanted him to. When he finished, I detected a sense of regret. I felt that the grieving had to do not only with a capitulation — appeasing Sholoongo by granting her what she had come for — but also with a loss, Talaado. Once infatuated with Sholoongo, he had long outgrown, her and was currently in love with Talaado. It was most unfortunate that Talaado showed up at his apartment unexpectedly, and in tears. The beast of the mystery was: how did Sholoongo gain entry into his apartment? And how did she manage to insinuate herself, demon that she was, into Kalaman's mother's nightmares a couple of days before turning up at her shop? I put down much of these happenings to a simple coincidence.

Ridden with uncertainties (his mother pushing him one way,

Talaado and Sholoongo pulling him in different directions to their respective bosoms, the one small and neat, the other complicatedly cluttered with multiple contradictions), Kalaman decided not to postpone his ten-day trip to Nairobi with Talaado. After so many years, the prophetic significance of throwaway phrases as in *fathers matter not, mothers matter a lot* was getting to him. He was confronted with no easy matters, and was having to reexamine his beginnings. You cannot help entertaining your past as you entertain an unwelcome guest, when you cannot think of a pleasant association with which to celebrate the present. You cannot help wanting to construct the solidity of a future with the female companion of your choice, when the world, in the form of a haunting past, is collapsing around your ears. Before rounding it all off, Kalaman alluded to yet another circle of boomerang cycles: all in the construct, mystical concept of *nabsi*. I might have been wrong, but I was under the impression that he was holding back from me a secret, he was not telling all. But what was he withholding from me, and why?

The scene changed. So did our moods.

Kalaman's eyes lit with the candles of memory.

He asked, "Who was the riffraff who accused my father of stealing his shoes from a mosque?"

I attempted to dampen his enthusiasm for this sort of talk with a dismissive face-drying gesture, in the attitude of a devotee whispering secret salvos to Allah. But he wouldn't be discouraged. Shaking my head in sorrowful remembrance, I said, "You do not have to worry yourself, or to recall the incident, because I am certain that it has no bearing whatsoever on the present crisis." He was not impressed. Then I chose to be economical with what little I knew, which I shared with him, seemingly out of the generosity of my spirit. He listened most attentively. He might have been a computer saving an item in its memory, to which it gave its own directory heading.

"Things look more complex than they seem when you study patterns," I said, taking refuge in abstractions, "of a bird's cycle of migration and return, of the moon's phases and how they affect human relationships. If Sholoongo and you had never made a pledge of mutual trust by cutting open each other's forefingers and touching the blood of each to the other's, if —" Here I paused, to ask, "Just out of curiosity, what curses did the two of you invoke, when making your pledges to each other?"

He was ill at ease. He shifted in his chair. "Touching the tips of our bleeding fingers together," he said, "Sholoongo and I spoke the words of the oath, she leading, I repeating: 'May death rock the fundament of our earth, if either of us breaks this vow.'"

"The *fundament* of the earth?"

He nodded his head.

I discerned a distillation of an abstraction from the text of the oath, my apprehension taking me to a different plane. I couldn't help remembering how both the elephant and I were referred to, in our particular ways, as "fundaments." I thought about the prophetic qualities of the vow, how the two young people had set a history in motion, in canny prediction not only of what might happen to them but of what might happen to the nation in its hour of imminent dissolution. It also meant that I could no longer dismiss this heavy-handed reference to my own death, I who had been described as a fundament by no less than Kalaman, fundament in the sense of being "grounded."

"After Fidow, who?" I said.

He rejoined, "Not who, but *what*?"

The fact that in his calculations Sholoongo had a hand in Fidow's death was not lost on me. I had to reinterpret his "Not who, but what?" in an altogether different light. It was as if he was pointing to "the collapse of history," which was, in and of itself, more important than the catalysts deemed to have set it off.

I frame a scene in front of me, then listen to the gentle slapping of the river a few hundred meters away.

The scene is one in which Kalaman is bathing in the sweet memory of a dream, naked, in Sholoongo's company. Out of the alluvial land, a muddied figure emerges. The figure has found a treasure in the deposited wash on the riverbank. Then, at the "Sesame" command, a door is pushed open to reveal another treasure trove of remembrances. I see a seventeen-year-old once-upon-a-time ambitious scholar from the environs of the northern city of Berbera. The youth is fleeing the scene of death. Dressed in near rags, he is heading south in flight. The youth will overhaul his identity, he will adopt a made-up name in the new environment, in order to break with his past totally. He will find a low-paid menial job, denying that he has ever trained as a scholar. He will marry a woman from the southern River People. This will help him bury his past in the tomb of oblivion.

"Could you get *it* up?" I asked him.

My words were lost on him.

I rephrased my question. I said, "Could you, Kalaman, get up sufficient enthusiasm to absolve yourself of your and Sholoongo's pledge? Might you not produce a sliver of sperm, bang, bang, zoom, and then *basta?*"

Kalaman's features relaxed as he got my meaning. I watched his incomprehension transforming itself into a frown, then into a startle, and finally into a bemused grin, all in a manner of seconds. A little later, I could see whom he was staring at: Hanu. My favorite vervet — I almost said child — was performing a series of athletic feats as if he were entertaining a guest in a sad mood.

Kalaman said, "Not that I didn't give that a thought."

I remarked that the ways of the human body are mysterious, and that you never know what it might or might not get up to. I continued, "Yet I assumed all along that you and she had shared something more substantial than a verbal pledge made as children. I thought she had hidden hands able to afford her blackmailing powers over you, some evidence against your mother."

"I always believed that, her judgment being untrustworthy, my mother was misled by a rank paranoia," he said. "How I wish this were untrue."

"Still," I said, "Sholoongo is probably in possession of, in her inflated opinion, a secret of earth-shattering quality, whose divulgence would make the planet shake in the eggshell of its foundation. A world collapsing at the seams, leaking weighty blood, clans at the throats of contending myths!"

We were silent for a few moments.

"I doubt that local scandals have earth-shattering properties to them," I resumed. "Besides, she's intelligent enough to know as much, having lived in New York, where a progeny of scandals are reared in every adult's imaginings." I chain-smoked, lighting a cigarette from the stub of another before I dropped it into an ashtray filled with water to its brim.

"What do you mean by 'local scandal'?" he wondered.

"Local in the sense of it being limited in reach," I explained. "Let's imagine your mother is having an affair, or your father is committing adultery, or some other unpardonable perfidy, maybe something involving Sholoongo. Remember the fuss surrounding your own name, Kalaman? In other words, she is only too aware of the fact that people guarding a secret with their lives become frightfully paranoid. Is your mother guarding a secret with her life, and is this the reason for her paranoiac behavior? You see, sooner or later, secrets sabotage the very purpose for which they are being withheld, they give away the very thing one wishes to protect."

"What's your opinion?"

"The more I think of this," I ventured, "the more I suspect that it is a pledge-breaking boomerang that is causing so much unprecedented havoc."

He spoke cautiously, saying, "Do you think that Sholoongo and my father were ever involved with each other?"

He sat waiting uncomfortably, as if he didn't wish to know the answer. We were both conscious of treading sensitive ground here. I remained silent for a while, maybe to let my thoughts mingle with his dejection. I said, "Why do you ask?"

"I ask," he replied, "because I know that sometime before her sixteenth birthday, Sholoongo was pregnant with an older man's child."

I smarted, because we were painfully plunging into the deepest reverie, family secrets being dragged out, blemishes, warts and all. This saddened me no end. My mind traveled out of my body and walked in the land of my youth. I was listening to heartrending cries, of goats being slaughtered to feast us, my youthful self barely seventeen among the Wandering Koranic Scholars. Scarcely had I pulled myself out of the reverie than I remarked that Hanu too had sensed the gravity of our silence. He was stone still, ceasing all movements.

"What makes you think Yaqut impregnated her?" I said.

"I remember the charged looks which my father and Sholoongo often exchanged," he said, "looks with something furtive about them. I suspected they might have shared a secret lust for each other." He paused. "I mean no disrespect if I compare their charged exchanges to the looks you and Kathy shared with each other, in public. What's more, my mother kept accusing Sholoongo of all manner of evil doings. This made me wonder if my mother's accusations were decoys meant to mislead others."

"Then you think we have a family-centered scandal, local?"

He was in apparent discomfort. "You have a hell of an earth-shattering scandal if you put together all the things my mother did to her, including her being fingerprinted, and, to pepper it, throw in the charged looks. And let's not forget my personal involvement with her."

I told him then, with deliberate slowness, about my conversation with Sholoongo the day before, when she explained to me that she was not interested in ruining her memory of the fun times she had had with him. "On the contrary," she had gone on, "I've come here to *con-nect* with him, not to *dis*connect. Nor do I wish to alienate him or his mother."

"Nothing makes sense anymore," Kalaman admitted.

I smiled to myself, confident that Hanu's antecedents, given the chance, could have given us another image-shattering secret, of a girl not yet sixteen who failed in her attempt to seduce a sexagenarian. The seductress had joined the old man in his early morning bath in the Shabelle River. Even at that tender age, Sholoongo was an expert in the department of persuasive seduction. She went for his manhood — a hill rising to a mountain! He kicked her hard and unkindly. Hurt, her lower lip began bleeding from the kick. The sixty-one-year-old man swam away, caring not a bean. As her young blood, fresh from her wound, flowed into the waters, small fishes congregated around her, some following her, rubbing themselves against her thighs as though they were cats whose stretched felinity teased the flanks of someone feeding them. To the old man's knowledge, Sholoongo never spoke of the incident to a living soul.

From that day on, I viewed her with suspicion, partly in awe of what she might do and partly in deference to the strength of her spirit. Someone once said about Sholoongo that you sensed you were in the presence of Carraweelo, the mythical queen who, in her day, was nicknamed the castrator of men, the murderer of boys. There was a difference between her and the mythical queen: Sholoongo was keen on men not gelded of their sex but only of their prudence, the queen on advancing the cause of women, albeit controversially.

"What if the elephant wasn't an elephant?" Kalaman said.

"Hold it there," I said, my prostate urging me to leave.

Ultimately Kalaman's sense of unease got to me and, like paranoia, ran away with me.

As I took a sip of my drink, it felt as if my cup were filled up not with tamarind juice, even though that was what I had poured into it, but a bitter disillusionment. I feared that before long I might end up with a wraparound of xenophobia.

"I might have thought Hanu was human," I said to Kalaman, apropos nothing I could put my finger on, "if he had not such hardness to his gaze, a stiffness almost sequinlike, which puts me in mind of a firefly in celebration of night life."

I stubbed out my cigarette and, for the first time in a long time, thought about abandoning the habit of smoking altogether. But what obsession would replace my obsession with chain-smoking? An inner voice, my late wife's, suggested, "Why not start saying your prayers, that'll keep you fit and busy!"

Now, Kalaman was a peculiar mix of the ebullient and the fey. "It is one of life's ironies, isn't it," I said, "that someone is pleading with you to give her a child, and when you run, you come face-to-face with a death, Fidow's?"

Kalaman reminded me that, when he was a child, he used to plead with his parents to supply him with a sibling. He never forgave them for that. Presently he rose to his feet and remained for a long time leaning against the metal fence, his back to the pandemonium the go-away-birds were making. I topped up his tamarind drink and passed it to him. He took the cup in both hands, murmuring his thanks. I hoped that a few sips would have a calming effort on his nerves.

He said, "Does the mother of our story begin thirty-three years ago with my first sip of tamarind juice, from a tree whose seed germinated in elephant dung brought to you in a shovel by Fidow, whose very death we are now mourning?"

"You could begin the story there."

He continued, "Is it far-fetched to draw attention to the resemblance, in shape, between tamarind seeds and human heads?"

I can't recall if I concurred by nodding my head.

"You will have noted, too," he said, "that Sholoongo has helped to make death stand out in bold relief, death and all one associates with it, burials, massacres, civil strifes, death becoming more and more ubiquitous: in my dreams, in my mother's nightmares, in my father's choices of vocation, in Madoobe's and Fidow's deaths, and their inhumation."

Pale like the underside of a fish, I stayed silent. I smoked chains of cigarettes, each stub looking like the stump of an amputated toenail, the spilled tobacco growing darker as it came into contact with the water in the ashtray. I shouted Zariba's name. She came. I instructed her that we would have our supper after our showers, and that under no circumstances should we be disturbed. As an afterthought I added, "Kindly take Hanu away with you too."

"Is Kalaman spending the night here?"

"Please prepare the spare bed in my room," I said.

I had no sense of why I wanted Kalaman in the spare bed in my room. Because I dared not take chances, as if something might happen to him, if he weren't nearby? Because a number of unusual things had started to happen? Perhaps I believed that death might even be emboldened by my dreamless state?

Zariba bent down to pick up Hanu, who at first resisted, the way children being taken away from their parents kick up a fuss. A mere nod of my head and he succumbed, allowing himself to be carried away. Zariba whispered something in his ear, perhaps a promise of his favorite food, I had no idea. Myself, I was struck by fear, I was frightened by the residual light-in-the-dusk out of me, I admit.

I said, "Shower. And after shower, supper."

"A wonderful idea," Kalaman agreed.

We ate our supper. Then, in reverent silence, we listened to the cacophony of an assembly of white-bellied go-away-birds in their favorite high perch up in the tree near the east wing. When their cries died down, I said, "Sholoongo came here straight from the airport, smelling of airline refreshing towelettes. For some reason her behavior in the few minutes we spent together convinced me of her matured comportment."

Kalaman's voice emerged out of the recesses of silence as he asked, "Was it you who told her where I lived?"

"She assured me she would check into a hotel."

"What day would that have been?" he asked.

We counted the days, and agreed that she came to call at my place three days before her arrival at his, presumably after she had sorted out a few things to do with her father's funeral.

Kalaman, meanwhile, reiterated that she had been preceded by a powerful set of signals, including rank nightmares in which his mother, Damac, was invited to a wedding reception at which the bride was not present, to the irritated consternation of the groom and to the embarrassment of the guests. Damac then volunteered to don the wedding-gown meant for the bride. "What do you make of that? Weird?"

"If this isn't loaded with the occult, I don't know what is! I concede the whole thing is bizarre. I doubt there is a way of explaining these incidents in isolation from the tension all around, the persistent rumors of a civil savagery about to be embarked on, and numerous other bizarre happenings in the land. They are all connected."

"I couldn't agree more," he said.

In the ensuing silence, I thought that if there were dual strains tugging at Kalaman's heart, these emanated from the civil strife syndrome: if Somalia were to collapse right into it, we all would, the lot of us. If there were to be dual comforts, these could be supplied by Yaqut and me.

Then with an alarming suddenness, like a child overtaken by exhaustion, a child abandoning a game in the middle, Kalaman spoke the one word "Madness!" But I did catch a glimpse of self-doubt as it made its way into his physical posture. He winced. I saw him shift restlessly in his chair, and felt a chill starting to spread all over him. But what I could do to help?

"How did she gain entry to your place?" I asked.

"She wouldn't give a satisfactory answer."

I didn't like what he was getting at, and feared the consequences of a feeling of dislocation. If Sholoongo could will her way into his mother's dreams; if she could insert herself into my consciousness; if, to murder Fidow, she could alter her human nature into an elephant's — well? If one were to accept all these as given, then one might as well believe that Hanu was her accomplice, a spy performing an inside job and accomplishing it superbly.

In which case, we were sitting ducks to her elephant running amok. And there was nothing anyone could do, or say. She might as well do to us what she pleased!

Kalaman didn't eat his food.

His not-eating had its effect on me, like a man striding speedily but who has to slow down because he knows his son's short legs won't catch up unless he waits. I took mouthfuls, hoping that would make him less self-conscious.

I said, "Sholoongo is unpredictable."

He said, "She has come home, Gehenna is let loose, Satan unchained, elephants cross boundaries to avenge their kin. A shape-shifter married to a fire-eating Moroccan, with a half brother who heads the Bay Gay. Madness!"

In a moment of truce, I said, "There's AIDS too."

At first he didn't follow my meaning, just like earlier, when I had inquired if he could get it up at all. But when he did comprehend, he said, "I'm not likely to jump into bed with her. No, thank you. I wouldn't, even if there were no AIDS. Now, if child-conceiving weren't part of the contract, I might have worn a condom. Disregarding any emotional or health hazards, I might have done it as quick as a crocodile. Come and go, fast!"

He looked worried.

"But you have to admire the woman's guts," I said. "I am floored by her outrageous defiance of the ethos of the very society which castigated her at birth, as part of her mother's rite of self-absolution. Is it part of her revenge-taking ploy to punish us, because society made her bear the consequences of her inauspicious stars?"

"As for my infatuation?" Kalaman asked.

I offered him a kind of a makeshift grin. "You were passing through a growing-up phase. I remember that at the time you felt a more pronounced spiritual kinship with animals, less with humans. If my memory serves me right, you had lost Xusna, your pet and love, and, grieving, were prepared to return to the human fold. It was then you were introduced to Sholoongo. You did what I expected you to: transfer your pent-up loyalty from a dead monkey to Sholoongo, a human with the potential, if we believe it, of animal power."

He said, "My mother advised against her!"

"All the same, there was no denying that she had a calming influence on you. It was very clear to us. We thought she was the thing, that she was very good for you."

"Maybe she was."

"Would you listen if we disapproved of her? I doubt it."

There was a symmetry to our conversation. We kept skirting, we kept going around topics, we kept going back to them, we kept teasing them in the belief that we would light on the key to the secret which had so far evaded us. We tapped on as many doors as possible, a touch of disappointment altering the complexion of our faces whenever access was denied to us.

Blood was central to my mental wanderings. Had someone other than themselves known all along about his distasteful habit of savoring her monthlies?

As if to assure him of my understanding sympathy, I placated him by saying, "Every living being has as many secrets as there are hiding-places, to which occasionally others obtain a key. We eavesdrop, we gossip, we spread rumors, we place ourselves behind keyholes when the doors are closed."

I hoped by speaking in this way I wasn't causing a graver shock than he had already suffered; or admitting that I too had stood behind keyholes, spying, or behind windows, eavesdropping. Sholoongo made one do stupid things.

"Have you any idea where she might be now?" he asked.

"My guess is as good as anyone's," I said.

He appeared to be losing his hold on reality. If he used the spare bed in my room, within an arm's reach of me, I might have a positive influence on him. Certainly I would worry less about him, if he were physically so close to me.

His lips were now amurmur with faint sounds. Was he talking to himself? To his unseeing eyes, I might have been a squat shadow cast by a jinn smoking chains of cigarettes. I didn't like what I was imagining.

"Listen to me," I said. Somebody was going mad and, for the life of me, I couldn't tell who. He sat in his laid-back way now, a man waiting for his turn in a friendly exchange with a grandfather.

He interrupted what I meant to say, for he said, "I wonder what they are up to." Not a question, a categorical statement.

I touched him. "Listen to me," I pleaded with him.

Not listening, he was talking. "I wonder, what if I had not seen a heap of elephant bones in my dream? Or if she had not insinuated locust-eating scenes into my sleep?"

He fell silent as if he might never speak again, ever. Which was why I didn't ask him to listen to me anymore. There was no point in that. I encouraged him to make a ceremony of his silence. I moved away from the table where our uneaten food was, and then went around so that my hand rested on his right shoulder. His breathing was slim like a napping baby's.

Silence was now his refuge.

I hadn't the heart to remind him of the year and a half he'd spent in a detention center, more or less incommunicado. Kalaman had risen courageously in defense of my liberty, against Somalia's then autocrat. He got thrown into a dungeon of detention, solitary. A year and a half in an African jail marks you for life.

We watched Hanu come into the room, dragging behind him Kalaman's duffel bag. Agitated beyond instant recovery, Kalaman said, "How does Hanu know that I won't be staying in my usual room, and that I'll be sharing yours?"

Not waiting for my reaction, he snatched away the duffel bag from Hanu, rummaging in it. It was as though he knew what he was searching for. Hanu's deep guttural croak, a noise emanating from the pit of his throat, gave Kalaman further reason to search the bag more thoroughly. I was trying to remember where I might have heard a croak as harsh as a crow's. As if intending to rub salt into a festering wound, the monkey was hopping around, putting us in mind of crows trotting about among human dwellings, ready to take off at the slightest hint of being stoned.

"See you shortly," Kalaman said, going out of the room.

"Where are you going?" I said.

"I'll have another shower," he said.

I afforded myself a fumiferous solace. I deserved a comfort-offering fag end, hoping that every drag would increase my willpower. Calm as a column of smoke, I convinced myself that Kalaman was all right.

A long hot shower restored charm to his face.

Hot baths did him wonders, as an infant. I recall how he loved to be submerged totally in the vapory mist of a hotter-than-usual *baaf*! Myself I prefer cold to hot showers. I prefer an early-morning or late-in-the-evening dip in the river to both. And prefer taking an afternoon siesta to showering. My siesta to his showers! After a shower, he would look a changed man, with no wildness in his stare. Nor, I hoped, would he be speaking in a disjointed discourse. Because he had me worried earlier, he had me thinking ahead to a future in which he had gone insane, the very Kalaman who had survived a year and a half in solitary confinement in a Somali prison. I couldn't imagine what my life would be like if something were to happen to him, my Kalaman. I would contemplate murder, no doubt about it, none at all.

I might as well confess here and right away that I had felt I was failing in my duty as a grandfather not to have envisaged all this when I provided Sholoongo with his current address. Was it possible that she had helped herself to a set of his keys to his apartment? There was no way of knowing how many sets there were in his room, and therefore no point in checking if any was missing. And now the shame of me, the dishonor of me: I had committed an indiscretion.

I pried. I spied on him. I stood on a stool and peeped into the bathroom while Kalaman was showering. Scenting my presence, Hanu joined me in my naughtiness. He hopped onto the chair, cuddled himself between my feet, and had the gall to pull at my robe, wanting to see what I was seeing. I took him down rather roughly, for I wanted to punish him. I locked him in a room, with a key. Then I returned to my voyeurism.

Patience paid its dividends. The shower curtain removed, Kalaman coaxed an erection out of himself, and then whispered an incantatory self-hypnosis as he beat his flesh. I dismounted when I saw Zariba in the vicinity of the corridor where I was. The shame of it all. I had to make up a story about a stomach upset, but didn't name the sufferer, Kalaman or me.

The west porch of the bungalow was where we met. This porch was capable of containing our divergent moods. Not only did we feel protected from mosquitoes, but no casual visitors ever dared come that way. It was here where I liked to sit, to meditate; here where I would spy on the movement of the stars, and eavesdrop on the watery sounds emanating from the river five hundred meters away.

We sat in silence facing an open-air clearing. We were fenced with neem trees, with a wide entrance, that is to say a clearing adjacent to the woods. This was the clearing in which we organized dances and other kinds of village activities. What had been once a fertile land had now turned to fine dust, an earth as lifeless as a cut wire. Trees and forests devastated, wildlife decimated, we had a generation of farmers dead from starvation. Many former farmers were, as of now, dependent on meager handouts from their immediate families or reliant on Oxfam and the like.

Through an opening in the night's darkness, I could see the shape of a huge drum the villagers aptly nicknamed Rhinoceros on account of its likeness to the two-horned animal, long ago a frequent visitor to these parts. A story trafficking among the residents had it that a hippo had suddenly come upon this rhino and gone into action, insane with the mad energy of a duelist not being challenged. It was Yaqut who had cast the rhino's horns and flanks and back in iron. My son, when sculpting, had given the figure the proper height and its steadfast physical sturdiness. Unmended, and hardly serving the purpose for which it had been meant, Rhino was treated with the deference of a discarded monument, children hiding their secrets in its belly. Some of the boys and girls used its belly as a poste restante, in whose care they left cryptic missives for one another. When he was young, Kalaman would sit astraddle on it, managing to draw lovely music out of the beast's wide flanks by beating them with sticks. Xusna, his pet monkey, imitated the human dancers as best as she could, her tongue out, eyes working overtime, in a bid to communicate one sexual innuendo or another. The point of all this is that I discovered a secret in Rhino's belly twice: once I found a thimble marked dark with monthly stains of old; on another occasion I came across a letter.

Now I looked away from Rhino. I let my orphaned gaze fall on Kalaman, features presently sporting a specter of worry. I have a certain fascination with anything that grows, and am partial to questions growing out of answers, like the branch of a tree shooting outwards as though it were an extra arm, or a fruit tree sprouting in the wild, roots entwining in the earth's entrails. What a bonanza: a letter waiting to be recovered in the stomach of a drum that had the shape of a rhino.

Out of the blue I asked, "Who has the papers for the apartment, you or I?" You never saw a more puzzled face than Kalaman's. I lit another cigarette.

"What has that to do with anything?" he asked.

"There is a bedrock truth in Somali tradition," I explained. "If a woman takes shelter in a man's house, and she refuses to leave of her own free will, the man may not force her out of the dwelling in which she has sought affection. If he does, then he prepares for a fine to be levied, to repair the honor of the woman thus slighted."

Kalaman confirmed hearing of the adage. But he argued that his and Sholoongo's situation was different. He questioned the thinking behind the attitude of Somali traditional society, and agreed with the sentiments of the wisdom, but not its spirit. It was one thing trying to find a way of discouraging the strong from treating the weak unfavorably and with impunity, it was another imposing a fine on a man in his victimized situation. He added, "Our case is dissimilar."

"But she is seeking affection?"

"A married woman," he interrupted me, "need not look for affection or for protection in another man's house. If anything, she should look for it in her fire-eating Moroccan husband's home and domain."

"Maybe we can save our family honor and hers too," I suggested, "if I offer a compromise. Suppose I step in, and become the nominal owner of your apartment. If you throw her out, you'll in part be absolved of blame, the place being not in your name but mine, and you a putative tenant." Mark you, I was conscious of how stupid I sounded even to myself.

"What of the pledge?"

"Pledges are binding on those who made them," I said. "The one 125 involving you and Sholoongo is not transferable. Even so, giving her a child was not in the original contract."

He got up. He looked unwell, as if a virus of worry had lodged itself in the nerves of his stomach, or bloodstream. He appeared bilious too. Half an hour later, he returned with his runaway stomach still intact.

Years and years ago . . .

Sholoongo took a walk in the woods, a duck trailing behind her. She and the duck vanished for a good while, and when next I set eyes on them Sholoongo was circling Rhino. She went on her knees as though in prayer, her neck moving rather clumsily like a pigeon's. She fumbled for something in her clothing. After examining the piece of paper she had in front of her with the attentiveness of a shortsighted person, Sholoongo deposited it in the belly of Rhino.

As I spoke, Kalaman grew short of breath. He might have been a little frightened too, like a child told to sleep in the dark. I could sense that he was afraid to ask what was in Rhino's belly.

Not apologizing for my behavior, I told him that, as soon as I ascertained that she was out of sight, I recovered two brief notes, both wrapped inside a seashell.

"What were the contents of the notes?"

I thought I sounded solemn like a mourner at his lover's funeral. I said, "I was more interested in one of them, which was not really a note, rather a cryptic drawing in pencil." In my memory I held the inanimate seashell close to my ears, to listen to the combined secrets of the wind and the sea.

"What kind of cryptic drawing?"

I described how it had been traced in pencil, of blown cheeks, lips colored red and a thumb-shaped projection pushing the cheeks from inside. I added, "The seashell is a memento from your youthful days, the one Fidow gave to you after killing a lion browsing in my orchard."

"You do not recall the content of the other note?"

"No."

He was sad. "Could the letter which you found in Rhino's belly have been the document my mother had accused Sholoongo of stealing from her, the one for which she was fingerprinted?"

I made a search-me gesture. My shoulders shrugged, as of their own accord, my eyebrows going up rather like a curtain the wind has slapped. We listened, in silence, to the evening's heat energy relaxing in the zinc roofing above our heads.

"If only to save you!" I said.

"Save me?" he wondered. "Save me from what? Or whom?"

"I wouldn't mind doing anything, wouldn't mind going insane, or murdering," I said. "If only to save you! I am saving my residual sanity by saving you. I would do anything to do that, murder if need be."

Kalaman dashed out of the room. In an instant the shower was running full blast. I didn't peek. I knew that he was going to be all right. Maybe his stomach might run. But the worst, I felt, seemed to be over.

But where, in my memory, had I mislaid the second note? If only . . . !

CHAPTER
SIX

Dawn preceded by a dream!

I could see clear signs of dawn. It was coming around a bend, as if being dug out of the tunneled darkness, and was emerging as a full-bodied daybreak out of the undecided hour. To it, there were intimations of mist, hollowed patches of foggy familiarity.

I sensed the ominous arrival of a couple of surprises too, the first in the shape of an ostrich, which issued a gentle *buu* call, then a harsher *tuu*. In all likelihood, the ostrich had just fed on a meager diet of seed heads of the season's tall grass, which I could also see from my window. Half asleep, in the high perch in the furthest corner, up in the treetop, undisturbed, there was another surprise delight, a large bird, most probably laden with birdy secrets buried in the sandy coloring of its pupils. But it was the ostrich on which my entire attention was now focused, as I recalled previous sightings of an ostrich speedily chasing its prey. Madoobe, Sholoongo's and Timir's father, had trained several as his bird-shepherds. He was of the informed view that ostriches could brace up to encounter the savage ferocity of a rhinoceros attacking. When fleeing, ostriches flung flying stones at their pursuers. Which brings me to the wisdom with the gist: Who dwells in a glass house mustn't invite the hostile sentiments of pebble throwers!

And I remembered that dawn had been preceded by a dream. In the dream, I am in a shop dealing in coagulated blood. There are two women, Damac's and Sholoongo's look-alikes, who are selling liters of the coagulated blood to Kalaman's look-alike. The women are talking amicably, but I can't follow the thread of the intricate narrative, whose bowline shares a complexity with another tale's clove hitch, the latter's granny knot reminding me of yet another story with its own reef knot. After insisting that I be served, I am shown a flower knot, dipped, according to Damac's look-alike, in noble blood. But apparently this is only for display, not for sale. Then I wake up.

I waited for my surprise visitor, wishing I could disown the dream, declare it "interfered-with," as if it were on a par with "contaminated blood." But why? No doubt self-protective, I was thinking how I wanted to safeguard my right to disregard the dream's insinuations, obviously not succumbing to the preposterous idea that *someone* had willed herself into my vision. But what was I to make of this, surely a premium of unpleasant associations so finely spun, the webbed mysteries to do with look-alikes of Kalaman, Sholoongo, and Damac? When next I napped, within half an hour of the earlier dream, and after seeing the ostrich and the large bird (I couldn't tell if these were part of the same dream), my daughter-in-law arrived to find the untilled territory of an exhausted mind, in the soil of whose unconscious she planted a spider's silk farm, my Damac!

On the other hand, in most of my dreams my daughter-in-law was pitiably drenched and in a depressive mood. Needing a generous supply of towels to dry, she often asked for a place to shelter from a pouring rain. She would drip like a faulty faucet, her cheeks prominently scarred, tribal scarifications resembling tears in a downward motion having been worked into her high cheeks. I am a pigeon, in my dreams with her in them, and she would plead that she had brought a message. "Trust the messenger," she would say, "not the message!"

I lay in bed a few inches away from Kalaman. His sleeping posture looked to me as if he were undergoing a pained spell of testicle-crushing torture. No sooner had I registered the thought, which left me helplessly debating with myself if there was anything I might do to alleviate Kalaman's pain, than I heard the makeshift rattle of a Toyota diesel pickup. I had a visitor, Damac.

I stood behind the drawn curtain, as if I were a naughty child waiting for his mother's return, knowing he would be punished. I made certain I could watch my daughter-in-law's movements without being seen, maybe hoping that I could assess the mood she was in, and prepare adequately for her. She stood nearly five-eight. At fifty-two, she was still good-looking. Now she was walking toward the wing of the bungalow where, awake, I waited, her every stride a terrible undertaking, a woman moving in the arrogant belief that she was being watched, was being vastly adored. Damac's bodily gestures, today as always, suggested that she slept and woke up in the full knowledge that she was the axis of her husband's world and that of her son as well.

She had the habit of arriving at ungodly hours. Like a child, she believed that the world woke up when she did. She expected you to receive her whenever she deigned to call on you, she expected to be pampered with your undivided welcome, ungodly hour or no. She never bothered to apologize for her eccentric behavior, pretending that what mattered was that she came. Used to being served on a regal platter by her husband, and treated with kid-glove care by Kalaman, Damac brought out a combination of her best silver and the most coveted gold when I was around. But she couldn't help turning up at an unearthly hour, and often behaving self-centeredly. Even with me.

I didn't share the view of my children, who considered her to be domineering, demanding, and difficult. I thought of her as a woman lacking in supreme self-appraisal. If anything, I would accuse her of overkill in matters of clothing and jewelry. Damac hid behind an array of dust-laden, desert-derived words, as illusive as mirages. She dressed to excess. "I am my husband Yaqut's publicity person, his walking advertisement, his talking billboard." In other words, she wore Yaqut's silver and gold handiwork. Casual acquaintances asked where she got the items of neckwear, especially foreign women. They saw, they were conquered, and they came to her shop to buy, each item unique. At home, she talked. Her husband listened. But she knew how best to pay the compliments due, and to whom. It was thanks to Yaqut, she boasted, that she stood heads above other women.

I could tell from the clothes she was wearing and from her bejeweled state that she was in ill humor. She was in a very elaborate getup consisting of a silk designer frock, an exquisite hand-beaded belt, and a gorgeous piece of silverwork, a collar necklace, items of splendor which were not meant so much to give full compliment to Yaqut, who

made them, as to bedeck their wearer, Damac, with the eyes of her beholder.

I compared her once to an ostrich capable of worrying and ultimately shepherding a most impossible herd into a state of total sub-
mission. She spoke as fast as an ostrich ran. Yaqut for his part would
watch her talk with the same dedication as an ostrich devotes to staring, in a mesmerized maternal state, at one of its chicks breaking free
of its shell. Yaqut, a father to her son! The woman was a genius in the
way she turned him around with her small finger. What a pity she
couldn't turn Sholoongo around with her middle one, given that the
small finger was busy attending to her husband.

I opened the door to wish her good morning, and waited. She remained still, her right foot ahead of her left, eyes blinking in feline
contemplation. "Where is he?" she asked.

I knew whom she meant. And it was not beyond her to walk past
me in the direction of the room referred to as Kalaman's. Which was
precisely what she did. But there was a slight stammer in her gait,
even though, to a casual observer not acquainted with her, she appeared to be as self-absorbed as a youth dancing in rhythm with his
own shadow.

"He's not in his usual room," I said.

She turned around squarely at the very corner where the two walls
met, one leading to his usual room, the other to mine, where Kalaman
was asleep. She stared at me. "Is he not well?"

For a moment I considered volunteering the information that
Kalaman's room had been used by *that* woman — Damac didn't speak
people's names when she loathed them — but I dismissed the idea as
distasteful. I said, "We shared my room."

This meant something was wrong. We seldom shared rooms
unless one of us was unwell. Nervous, and talking as fast as a football
commentator, she regulated the pitch of her voice to an inner tension.
"It's that stomach of his, is it? Running?"

"He's asleep," I responded.

Did I sound vexed? Maybe I was.

I said, "He was like a child having a nightmare. He continued mumbling something in his sleep, something to do with an impending national disaster of immeasurable consequences. Maybe Fidow's death has affected him."

She took that in with a good deal of self-restraint. Instead of heading in the direction of where he slept, she paced back and forth. Maybe she was considering her next move. For all I knew, she might have been asking herself whether I was hiding something from her. After all, she had the accursed habit of behaving unceremoniously. I was worried she might rub me the wrong way today, make me lose my temper with her, compel me to do something regrettable. We all knew her to be irrational when it came to her son or her husband, of whom she was protective.

"Would you like a cup of tea?" I asked.

I knew that my going into the kitchen to make tea or coffee for her would not meet with her approval. She was of the generation of women who associated these activities with a humbling of one's status. And as such, she could not bear the thought of me, her father-in-law, dirtying my hands, serving her. She had had a few tongues lashing her, and a lot more forefingers wagging at her, all because Yaqut attended to the house chores. It was he who took care of Kalaman right from when she weaned him. Did she feel as if others might accuse her of high-handedness if I too served her tea from my kitchen, because my housekeeper hadn't reported for work?

"Where is Zariba?" she said.

"I can cope with the making of tea or coffee," I said.

"These can wait," she suggested.

I had never known her to be overtly rude to me. She listened willingly to whatever I had to say, seldom interrupting me. I knew how difficult this must have been for her. She called on all her energies of self-persuasion for the two of us to get on. As part of her ploy to maintain her self-control, she wrapped herself with layers of static-charged tension. I felt the tremors of the tension, and advisedly kept a buffer distance between us.

In my anxiety to welcome her, I had forgotten to put on a more decent robe. Now I saw I had on only a flimsy nightshirt, the very one I had slept in. I stood my ground, though, thinking that I could not be expected to be woken up at an ungodly hour and to be demurely dressed, like a new bride forever prepared to be seen by her groom. In my cupped palm I strategically gathered a fistful of the material. This way I covered as much of my front as Adam's representational fig leaf might have done.

"You don't mind if we let Kalaman be?" I said.

I was in for a pleasanter surprise. "We'll let him be, for I would like the two of us to have a word or two before he awakes," she said. "There are a number of things that we need to sort out, you and I."

"See you shortly, then."

As well as clearing the mist in my brain, the hot shower assisted in opening the air passages of my sinuses. Morning showers, or, better still, morning dips in the river are as essential to me as ritual ones in the Ganges are to a sadhu. Mine was long and elaborate in every way. But I would rather I spared you some of the details of what I did in the shower, as they have no direct bearing on the tale unfolding.

I remembered how we first met, Damac and I. Yaqut had brought her along after the two of them had contracted a secret wedlock. It wasn't my place to question why they opted for a secret marriage, a form of matrimonial contract usually resorted to by couples likely to face opposition from one quarter or another. I suspected there was something not right with theirs being a secret wedding, but I didn't ask for an explanation. My son Yaqut silent, Damac held forth. She informed me they were married, but not *why*. Was she pregnant with the child of a man to whom she was betrothed?

A week later, she came to see me alone. She spoke and spoke. Because she was fretful, I didn't learn much. She inundated me with a flood of words. When I surfaced for breath, my hands went up in the gesture of a bad swimmer. I felt we wouldn't get down to the secrets agitating her mind in a single session. We had all the time in the world to know each other, I thought. And I welcomed her into the bosom of the family. I couldn't comprehend what troubled her. Was she fearful that some harm might come her fetus's way?

I suspected that Damac and Yaqut never presented themselves before a sheik. I suspected that the two of them never spoke the vow of the *nikaax* matrimony in the presence of a sheik, that they were never declared man and wife. The years have since vindicated my suspicions. I have often envied them their physical closeness, a man and a woman loving and trusting each other almost to the exclusion of all others. Don't ask how I could tell they were not husband and wife, only lovers. Drying myself with a towel, I wondered if she were a victim of blackmail. Sholoongo's?

Damac, my daughter-in-law, was in the bead business in those days. She dealt in amber, and its substitute, copal. She had a stall on a sidewalk in the center of Mogadiscio's Raqay district. To attract passersby, she shouted the praises of the articles she had on sale. When this failed, she made a public show of her copal, rubbing several beads together, generating electricity. A bit of smoke issuing forth attracted crowds. She sold seed necklaces on the side, ivory bracelets and similar knickknacks too. She had a large non-Somali clientele who bought her wares, commissioning her to obtain all manner of objets d'art for them.

On the afternoon of the day I asked her to come and see me alone, we sat on the porch, talking. During a pause in our conversation, we spotted a most handsome baby snake of the nonvenomous kind. This handsome affair lay in the grass of the untrimmed lawn as if taking the sun, a snake no thicker than a flexible cable. It was maybe a quarter of a meter in length. The snake was of the type Somali camel herdsmen feed on milk, and treat with pompous affection as one does a pet. I had barely thought of something humorous to allay her phobia (I, who truly fear snakes more than she) when she jumped over the banister, went round to where this gorgeous creature was performing a snake's idea of a somersault: and may the poor snake's soul be saved! Quick with her kick, she stepped on both ends of the unsuspecting length of rope. Result: knots of dead tissue.

My tongue was devoid of life for a while. Then I asked her, "But why?" I gave contradictory signals. I was raging inside with anger, but had got up in the manner of a football spectator applauding an extraordinary feat accomplished.

The signals confused her. Her lips parted, like friends who have had a nasty quarrel. She said, "I am pregnant," as if this explained everything. It didn't. For me.

I looked from the dead snake to Damac. What she did made no

sense. What manner of threat did the nonvenomous reptile present to the embryo in her? Death deforms. Death brings sadness to one's eyes. The snake's lifelessness affected me so. No longer alive, it was no longer good-looking, its corpse lying in the clumsy throes of a residual struggle. I thought that it would remain forever detained in a half-expressed motion, in a futile attempt to escape Damac's kick. Or was it meaning to do something in self-defense?

"How many months pregnant are you?"

"Three."

"Does Yaqut know?"

"Of course," she said.

I wondered if I had offended her honor by asking if Yaqut knew. During the brief pause, I recalled the speed with which she karate-kicked the snake to death. Pregnant women, I reminded myself as if wanting to exonerate her of blame, had schizophrenic eyes via whose topsy-turvydom they saw the world. Women in her state discerned the inadequacies of their own reasoning. There was no call for worry, no need to search for other explanations.

I congratulated her on her pregnancy.

Because her eyes were cast into a bronzy stillness which I found suspect, I remained unspeaking. The expression on her face darkened. Damac spoke in non sequiturs. She said, "Isn't there a proverb with the gist that the parent is the last person to know about the offspring's secret lives?"

I requested that she please explain herself.

"Because you may not know," she said, "although you are his father, that Yaqut, even if he deals in death by carving headstones, loves life." I waited. She went on, "I will love *my* child, *my* handsome baby boy."

My thoughts were busy with a possible interpretation. She was the one who wanted the child, who was, to her, "my child" and "my handsome baby boy." Did the two of them enter into the secret wedding contract before or after discovering that she was with child? Be it as it may, the news delighted me. Until then none of my other children had presented me with a grandchild. I said, "I don't want to be rude," and then trailed off.

"You'll have to be, sooner or later," she said, "considering that honeymoons with one's in-laws do not last forever. Let us clear the air. Let us get this or any other family-related business out of the way quickly. Ask. If I don't wish to reply to your rude question, I shall say so. Nobody makes me do what I do not voluntarily want to do."

I liked her. We were much of a muchness, she and I. Only she was gutsier, because younger, with a shorter past to fall back on. That she was a woman was a bonus. I love strong-headed women, they are more challenging. This decided me not to ask if she and Yaqut were man and wife. Nor did I put any irreverent queries to her, or inquire into her family background. I liked her. I found her *simpatica*. Nothing else mattered. I accepted who she became right in front of me. She was a woman constructed, as if to order, in a collage of squares, triangles, and zodiacal signs. These signs were, in turn, supported by lines crossing a ram's horns at the base, with a clover at the summit. A few words brought forth a Damac I welcomed, more of real flesh and bone and guts than many an in-law I've had to meet over the years.

"Have you been pregnant before?" I asked.

Her eyes detached themselves from the rest of her body. They roamed far and wide, returning after much grazing in the distant pasture of her fertile memory. She spoke in hyperbole, making a statement which turned out to be prophetic: "One pregnancy is enough."

Nearly thirty-four years later, and after my hot, hot shower, here she was in the living room by herself. She had woken up my housekeeper, who made her tea in the utilitarian kitchen. Young-looking as ever, for Damac one child was more than enough. But now she was worrying her lips sore. I bet she wasn't aware of that. I doubt if she remembered everything that passed between us on the day she stepped on the head of another *day*: to save the embryo of her future, Kalaman. If I were the boasting type I might have said that I could hear her thoughts, the humming quality of a honeybee going about its business while producing the sweet stuff. There was a lick of fondness in the way Damac and I conversed with each other.

But my housekeeper hovered in the kitchen door. I hate people standing in my blind spot. I get nervous. Conveniently I recalled that in Kalaman's and my paranoiac search for privacy the night before, I had locked Hanu up in one of the rooms. Now I instructed her to let him out, and suggested that she take him into the sparsely treed woods for a walk. When Damac and I were alone, I said, "Now, my dear!"

Damac once confided to someone we both know well that I could produce a squawk out of an obstinate bird just by staring at it so! Yet I was of the opinion that my demeanor to her was always faultlessly deferential. We've been through testing times, she and I. We have always deferred to each other's temperament. I knew Damac could be the acme of self-control, the envy of many.

I asked, "How many months after Kalaman's birth did that riffraff of a man, I forget his name now, accuse Yaqut of stealing a pair of shoes from the mosque?"

The silence was total. It was as if we were on the periphery of a hurricane. I worried when the hurricane might break upon us, blind as a bull to which a matador has shown a red cloth.

"Why do you ask?" she said.

"What was his name?"

"I don't wish to remember it," she stammered.

"If you are not telling his name," I said, wondering if I could render the hurricane inert, or change its course so as to make its mad eyes focus elsewhere, "then kindly remind me when the shameful accusation occurred!"

"I can't see what good will come out of this," she said. "Why, after an eternity, are you pulling him out of his lair, the beast?"

I said, "The date, please!"

The hurricane was active now. It had the name "Damac" written all over it. I knew it wasn't long before it would erupt with the abruptness of an earthquake, as devastating as Chernobyl's fallout. I waited.

But she changed the subject. "Are you trying to cause as much harm to me as you can?" she said furiously. "How dare you put up Sholoongo in Kalaman's room, here in your house, as your welcome guest?" She was most aggressive. Not flinching, I looked her straight in her storm-charged eyes. She went on, "And having humiliated me this way, how dare you ask me to remember one of the most shameful episodes in my life, of Yaqut unfairly accused of stealing a pair of shoes belonging to a riffraff, when he didn't?"

She was on a stallion of an aristocratic pedigree, all right. But she would have to dismount, the sooner the better, because I was decided no amount of addressing me as though I were a mule would distract me from uncovering the truth.

"You are right to challenge my fairness of judgment," I said. "You know I wouldn't compromise the loving sentiments for you and Yaqut as a family, or take them lightly. From my conversation two nights ago with Sholoongo, my impression was that she meant no harm, to you individually or as a family. If she harbored hateful sentiments, would she want to bear Kalaman's baby?"

"The bitch," she cursed, "the witch."

I wouldn't be deflected. "As for that riffraff of a man," I said, "I recall only the first half of his hyphenated nickname, an alias given on account of an escharous hand, with fingers seared into a singularly atrocious-looking stump having a pointed end. The man's hand resembled a scorpion's tail."

"Have mercy!" Damac appealed.

"It puzzles me so," I went on. "Why would bringing up this man's heinous name make you implode and then explode as if you were an Etna?"

"Some volcanoes erupt periodically, every so many years," she said. Her features were touched with tearful sadness. "I do it every thirty-odd years."

"You came close to losing your patience with me even in those days," I reminded her, "when I tried to get to the bottom of the ugly incident about the theft of a pair of shoes, a penny apiece. What's the true story? Because I never got to hear it."

She was in control again. "You'll have to ask Yaqut."

"Do I also have to talk to Yaqut about why you had Sholoongo's fingerprints taken?" I asked, now genuinely miffed. "What perfidies had the young girl committed for her fingerprints to be taken? What did she dispossess you of?"

Her whole body shaking, her teacup chattered on its saucer, for a good while teetering on the verge of falling off. She sat down, her hand trembling. She shivered, as though she were suffering from a chill or a fever.

She fought back. "What dishonors have I brought to the family, or to your person? Why must you dig up a dead matter? Why pay an untimely visit to a phase of my life of which I am ashamed?"

"I haven't accused you of anything. I want information."

"Yes. You are accusing me of something. Your tone does."

"What are you hiding?"

"What do you think?"

I changed tactics. "Would you rather Kalaman went insane?"

There were more brown deposits in her eyes than I had ever remarked, deposits the color of rust. Eyes of aged metal, her eyes, with an iron look. I didn't like what I caught sight of. I outstared her. Eventually her eyes blinked. I said, "Would you like to save Kalaman's life?"

I scented the odor of her unexpressed anger, starchily stiff, musty, the white stains mapping the boundaries of her ancient, now-dried sweat. Could it be that even though she was in an exquisite getup, my daughter-in-law had forgotten to shower before putting on her clothes? Were these indications of discord, signals of self-neglect?

I said, "We all love you. You've been a daughter-in-law to me. You and I have been closer to each other than I've been to some of my own children. But you and I disagree about Sholoongo, whom I do not believe to be a witch, or a bitch. What is it that she's done to earn your wrath? What are you hiding?"

"I don't like this conversation," she said and got up.

I wouldn't be bullied into silence. "It won't be long before we are done with this conversation. All the same, I want you to answer my question: what are you hiding?"

She looked at me with the put-upon aspect of a helpless woman in trouble up to her wide hips.

I said, "Have you distrusted Sholoongo ever since the day she took Kalaman into her feminine trust?"

She sat down, and held her head between her hands, sobbing.

"Is it true," I said, "that Arbaco, your good friend for many years, helped to find a midwife who got rid of an embarrassment, that is to say, a pregnancy?"

A strong smell penetrated my awareness. The odor coming in upon me pinched my lower lip, parching it. My tongue wet the lip which had fallen victim to this localized heat wave. She said, "Why are you talking about all this?"

"The truth, Damac," I said.

She lost herself in the train of a thought, and then finally emerged, looking sadder, a passenger of a wagon-lit who hadn't slept a wink the whole of the previous night. She said, "Did she tell it to you?"

For a moment I wasn't sure if she was referring to Sholoongo or to Arbaco. I said, "Does it matter how I've learnt of it? All pedestrian assumptions aside —"

She looked mean, vengeful. She said, "I am in possession of a couple of shocking facts too, I'll have you know. And if we are in the mood of letting the ugly secrets out, then let me remind you that I know about you and Sholoongo."

"Tell me," I said.

"The sun hasn't risen," she said. "The morning mist hangs over the river. An old man is enjoying his dip in the water when, quiet as an unrevealed secret, a young girl dives in and grabs the man in the groin. She takes him in her mouth. Right or wrong?"

I wouldn't ask her how she came by this bit of news, worried that she might suggest that I shouldn't descend so low as to draw pedestrian conclusions. This would not have done my spirits much good. Nor was there any point in putting very fine details on the tale, no point reminding her that I had kicked the young assailant in the mouth. And she bled profusely. Never mind that things kept hidden for years were coming out, secrets whose keeping had caused us anxiety, under whose pressure we abandoned the house of the sane in preference for the *lazaretto*, the house of the mad.

There was an extraordinarily long silence.

I had given Damac cold water and some vinegar to remove the tea stains from her dress. When she returned, I had her served with more heavily sugared tea, maybe to temper the bitterness in her mouth. I lit chains of cigarettes at which I pulled, the nicotine calming my nerves.

She said, "Sholoongo is not like you and me."

I was reminded of what white supremacists said about us Africans. I said, "Sholoongo can't be more than the total of her remembered thoughts." Obviously I was quoting someone, I can't say who. I added, "She is no more and no less than you or I. She is human, like you and me."

I made as if I would leave. She was offended.

"I'm referring to what happened years ago," she said.

Her voice was metal-like, sharp. It cut me short. I stood still. Hers was a voice commanding me to pay heed. I thought that maybe we hadn't much time left to clear up all the Sholoongo-related mess before I closed my eyes, before I departed, quiet as the wings of an eagle reaching for a slice of the heavens, dead.

"I've heard you out," she said. "Will you listen to me?"

"I hope you will moderate your views," I said.

"I won't accept any preconditions," she threatened.

"Only remember, when you speak of Sholoongo," I said, "that this inhumane society of ours, this our collective conscience that is the basis of our culture, has been most cruel to her as a child, as a human. She is a woman, for goodness' sake, another woman." I was ferocity itself, taking the world head-on.

"You're not listening to me," she said.

"Have you ever explained to anyone," I said, "how you could have had a teenager fingerprinted on some trumped-up charge that she had committed a theft? Did you have proof for that, evidence that would stand up in a court of law?"

Her face twitched, rather like the nose of a rabbit deciding if the odor it has picked up on the air is danger or food. "It wasn't a trumped-up charge," she said. "It wasn't."

"What did she steal?"

"You've obviously been misinformed," she said.

"Enlighten me, then," I said. "I am all ears."

I liked her, if I am to be fair, because she spoke her mind. But there was a difference to her today, no longer using the riders on which she usually relied to soften her blows. Her riders, of which she was fond, comprised of phrasal subterfuges like "You know I hate to disagree with you" or "You might be surprised to learn that —" This morning she was frankness itself. In my imagining, Damac was a turtle which, feeling impending danger, gave you its dorsal vertebrae so it wouldn't come to harm. Why hadn't she taken refuge in weeping, a ploy which might have disguised any noticeable blots, like a thick-nibbed fountain pen leaking globules of ink?

"There's a glut of will," I said by way of apology. "There are far too many strong minds working the same territory. Sholoongo is the territory we are all tilling, a most fertile soil, dark as the good earth is yielding. She is the territory, she is the cause, she is the source of much ill will. Each member of our immediate family is involved." I went on after a pause, "Add to this the fact that, in America, she has trained as a shape-shifter, able to tap into the energy of her shamanic powers. Shamans heal, they do not harm."

"The way *I* see it," Damac said, "being angry with society for treating her abysmally as a *duugan*, Sholoongo is a woman full of hate. There is nothing healing about her methods. She is vengeful, she means to harm. Death *is* she. Blackmail *is* she. You will see. Otherwise why feed Kalaman on her monthlies!"

"Why blame her? Why not blame Kalaman for doing what he did?"

"Blame a boy bewitched into an infatuation?" she shouted. "Are you going out of your mind? He was under her influence, in those days. He would've committed murder if she had told him to."

"Shamans heal!" I reminded her.

"Not *her!*"

"In a prognostic dream the night before her appearance in Kala-man's apartment, you claim that Sholoongo had willed her way into your unconscious. You say that you were invited to your son's wedding and, finding the bride to be absent, *you* stood in for her. You were wed-ded to your son. Now three pertinent queries. First: Why blame her for the tension in the country, as if she were responsible for people's com-mittal of collective suicide? Two: Did you see a face to which you could put her name? Three: How come you plucked Sholoongo's name out of a million others when you had not set eyes on her for twenty years? Is it possible that she had come to your shop and you didn't recognize her until after she had left? And then that night, your memory of her worked itself into your dream? Because she was here, in the country, when you had your nightmare. And four: Why blame her? Why not blame yourself?"

Calm, she reasoned, "I couldn't have seen her."

"What makes you so sure of yourself?"

"I would've recognized her body odor."

"You didn't know she was in Mogadiscio?"

"I was the last to know."

"And the first to raise the alarm?" I provoked her.

She was back to her unreasonable mood, shouting, "She is a witch and a bitch. Timir, her half brother, agrees with this view. Only he uses big words placed in scientific polythene for effect."

No point in pleading with her. My whole being alert and waiting, I was a cat that has chased a rat to its hiding hole. Cornered, Damac wrung the fingers of her hands as if wishing away a bad conscience. She sat in a half-leaning posture, like a mop stood in a bucket. She said, "What I can't fathom out is, why has she chosen my Kalaman to be the father of her baby?"

Her renewed fret disturbed my inner calm. I strove for the complacent air of a righteous man as I said, "It's all a matter of secrets, and of having the wherewithal to make something out of them. Wells are said by Somalis to contain secrets, of jinns residing in the mystery of their own reflections. Billowing smoke is believed to contain unknown quantities of secrets to be discovered in the blaze of a fire feeding on wet wood. The heady movement of a sunflower has secrets too. Only we don't concern ourselves with the secret behavior of a plant or a well or an animal until our lives are in danger. There are a million and one secrets embedded in everything we touch. Sadly, we're not aware of their existence. I too have asked Sholoongo why she chose Kalaman, and she refuses to explain."

"I would do anything to save Kalaman from her satanic clutch, anything," she said. "I would even kill, if that is the only alternative left to me." She sounded like any mother, firewood crackling in the pyre of her sacrificial love.

"My advice is talk, not kill."

"Talk to whom, *her?* Have you gone insane?"

"Talk to Kalaman," I counseled. "Tell him everything."

"Will any good come out of that?"

"Hold back no secrets from him."

The palms of her hands up, not convinced, she said, "Then?"

"Only by talking openly to Kalaman," I advised, "will you release him from the grip of fear, and the worry in his own heart and mind. Open up to him."

I sent my eyes on a furtive errand, concluding that the storm clouds had passed overhead, that no hurricane bearing Damac's name was likely to erupt. "As for Sholoongo's wish to have Kalaman's baby, we can find ways around it."

"No way," she swore.

The ubiquitous unpredictability of Damac's temper was there. I had obviously underestimated the extent of her anger. She was a forceful orator, with a colorful way of using her hands as if they were flags fluttering in the hurricane-stirred sandstorm. "Would *you* mate with her?"

"Would I *mate* with her?" I said. "But she is no animal!"

Her hands stopped gesticulating madly. "She is no different from animals, with whom a human mates!" Although brisk in their movements, her gestures were nevertheless courteous.

I decided not to rise to her provocation, conscious she was speaking in anger. Mate, indeed — as if she were describing the pairing of two animals for reproductive purposes, or the coupling of a human and an animal for lustful reasons. I said, "If mating with her, as you put it, would save Kalaman from ruin, I would do that too."

She dashed out of the living room.

Somewhere in the bungalow a radio began to play a blues song, which dripped with melancholy over the death of a lover. The singer's voice was soaked with regret, wishing he had not neglected his beloved. Damac was now back, having washed her face in cold water and applied a fresh coating of kohl to her eyelids.

"Secrecy is Sholoongo's condition," Damac said. "She is *it*, menstrual blood in a honey jar, a forefinger dipped in a thimble, here, taste *me*, she would say to young Kalaman."

"How do you know this?" I said.

"Let's not be pedestrian in our presumptions."

"You spied through a keyhole. I knew it!"

Neither denying nor challenging my speculation, she said, "If what that bitch of a witch did was not the crudest form of bewitching, I've no idea what is." Then Damac made a bizarre gesture as if she were protecting herself from being hit.

"Which came first," I asked, "the theft of the document, or Kalaman being fed on her preserved menstrual blood out of a honey jar — or was it out of a thimble?"

"Why are you tormenting me?"

"Am I? We're all entitled to our secrets," I said.

"Such secrets as Sholoongo's be damned!"

"Secrets define us, they mark us, they set us apart from all the others. The secrets which we preserve provide a key to who we are, deep down."

A smile pried open her mouth, gently fondling her lips. I knew instinctively and right away that I hadn't got her in the snare I had set. The smile lasted long enough for it to become something of a menace. We looked at each other across a gulf of silence which neither was prepared to break. I remembered Kalaman comparing secrets to growths on the body, boils never maturing to the pus-forming stage, at which they might burst. Then one day, one moment, something happens. The secret goes amok like an elephant gone mad. And the world is reduced to a headless Fidow, blood all over, bones and flesh ascatter, and none of us the wiser.

With a note of sarcasm in her voice, Damac said, "Good fortunes have an illogical way of vindicating one's memory of the evil times one has lived through." She faked a momentary hesitation, and for an instant I thought that she might faint. I rose to my feet, and stood by her toweringly. Our fingertips touched, my outstretched hand coming into contact with hers. Sensing a feebleness of will in her, I helped her into my rocking chair. Damac stayed still, not rocking.

I noticed that several morning birds had arrived, the birds communicating in chatty squawks. I felt a tickling sensation on my nape, but I dared not scratch it, lest I kill a butterfly. How did I know about the butterfly? I was sitting in front of a windowpane, and had seen it hesitate before alighting between the collar of my shirt and the upper rungs of my spine.

Then, with worrying eeriness, I sensed Kalaman's presence in the living room where his mother and I were. Hollow-eyed, like a bell's metal casing without a tongue to toll it, Damac resided wholly in the ill humor of her eyes.

I fled the scene.

I woke up, feeling half dead, in Nonno's room. But a very long, very hot shower resuscitated me. Only my eyes remained unfocused, as though I were looking through a pair of spectacles prescribed for someone much older.

Soon after coming out of the bedroom, fully dressed and feeling positively refreshed, I heard voices. Following the voices led me to the living room. There I met my mother and Nonno. It seemed they had exhausted themselves, and their topic too. They struck me like two boxers, both tired and neither winning, who wouldn't give up the fight. Where was my place in the fight? They were having their final round in a ring with no room for a third contestant. Nor did they need an adjudicator, not me anyway, considering that their contestation began long before I came into being. Nonno left the room, a man conceding that further talk wouldn't do either of them, or the topic, any good. We were ill at ease with each other for a second after his departure. But we soon worked a way out, availing ourselves of the morning's stir, by then well underway. Smiles. Hugs. Kisses. I can't remember who gave what to whom. Sobs, my mother's. A pat on the back, sympathetic mutterings, mine. We fell silent, to listen to wood being chopped outside. We listened to life being lived.

I sat down, not knowing what to do with my fragmented self. Highly uncoordinated images invaded my mind: a scatter of limbs, a loose wrist with no proximal or distal rows, the long bone of one of the limbs removing itself from all the tissues and flesh surrounding it. In short, *I* became a jigsaw puzzle of physical anomalies, one instant a man treading on broken glass, the next moment some altered form. I was chameleon-cautious. I took one step forward, half a step backward, conscious that I was undertaking a steep never-ending climb toward the summit of a self-definition. On account of a partial paralysis of the nerve muscle of my left eye, I was seeing everything twice.

Earlier, when I was showering, Nonno's housekeeper, Zariba, had urged me to "come quickly!" In her nervous rendering, she wanted me "to forestall any possible perversions, if this can be avoided," my mother being in a terrible humor and behaving "in a perverted manner, casting aspersions all around and throwing seeds of contempt at the earth on which Nonno stands." I had emerged, still dripping and with the soap not entirely washed off, as Zariba explained further that my mother was carrying a firearm. "She means to kill *someone*," the housekeeper couldn't tell who. I asked how she knew about the firearm. She hesitated at first and then admitted, after a little probing, to having taken a furtive peek from a vantage point. "For the good of all," she explained. She also confessed to having eavesdropped on Nonno and my mother.

A trifle giddy, burying my migraine in the embers of my calm, I looked away from my mother to Nonno fleeing. Then, after a decent interval, I tried my best to train my eyes on my mother's handbag. But seeing two bags, my right relaying what it saw, my left transmitting things in a diffused manner, I decided to disabuse her of her wrong assumptions: that no one knew that she was carrying a firearm or that she meant to kill Sholoongo.

As I said, I am not certain how things came to pass. I was confused. Did I, half bending, touch my lips to my mother's cheeks a second time? Did she half rise to receive it, and did we meet halfway? Not that it matters. At any rate, something to do with her scents, a perverse mix of traditional and imported ones — or could it be her overdressing, her overkill? — changed my attitude. I decided to make her angry, not placate her, assuming that an alteration in the temperature of our encounter was more likely to loosen up her tongue. If I were undeterred by questions of morality, she might talk freely. Knowing her — and this was clear to a baby of two — once she discerned my sense of discomfort my mother would assuage my sorrow. In fact she said, "I promise all will be all right shortly."

"Why are you carrying a firearm?" I asked.

She gave a start. She appeared as disabled as a falcon with broken wings. The home-thrust of my question had shocked us both, and my lips were atremble long after I had spoken the words, which felt very hot as they tumbled out.

But she recovered soon. "For my own protection."

"Such a small weapon won't frighten off the militias' and the regime's heavy guns, surely?" I challenged her. "Not a small firearm in a woman's handbag, a child's toy?"

"The shame of all unpardonables!" she lamented.

"Why do you say that?" I asked.

"Nonno has no business nosing into the contents of my bag," she said. Then she made a show of throwing a half-chewed toothpick into Nonno's ashtray, which floated with ash as well as stubbed cigarette butts. My mother's huff-snuff had its advantages, which she knew how to exploit to the maximum. She could derail a conversation by throwing her arms up in a rage, ranting and raving for hours on end until the other party abandoned pursuing the contours of an argument.

We knew each other, my mother and I. I said, "Why accuse Nonno of nosing into the contents of the bag, when he didn't? It would be helpful if you answered my question about the firearm. Why are you carrying it? Whom are you going to kill? That witch of a woman, the bitch?"

"It's no one's business if I carry a firearm."

"A firearm does not have any business in my mother's handbag," I said. "They say that you die by the gun if you carry one, or if you use a weapon to make any gains. In fact more people with firearms in their safes are killed, by others who are armed, than those not carrying any weapons at all. The militias and the thugs in the service of the dictator have bigger guns than you, and they are very brutal. So why are you carrying the child's toy?"

"Nonno nosing around?" she said. "Or Zariba eavesdropping?"

"My father might have hinted at the firearm," I said. "In fact he did. He spoke of a police officer cousin of yours who was acquiring a firearm for you. Was it not he who, years ago, abetted you by fingerprinting Sholoongo?"

Here she played her weaker-sex hand. She made a sound between a whimper and a sob. This was meant to throw our conversation off course. And she said, "What's the world coming to, respectable men putting their noses into the affairs of women?"

"If by women you're referring to Sholoongo and yourself," I said, "perhaps I should remind you that murder, when committed, will become our business, both women and men. We cannot blind ourselves to the commission of murder, since we won't be able to walk away from it."

"Where is she, anyway?"

My mother was hoping to draw me into a quagmire. I brought her back to a drier place, saying, "Sholoongo is not hiding anywhere on Nonno's estate."

"I wouldn't know how to believe him if he told me she was not."

"How do you mean?" I said.

"Because it is as if every single undertaking of Nonno's is a celebration of secrecy. The man has a penchant for secret-nurturing, secret-feeding, and secret-finding. He is not at all embarrassed to search for secrets among the Kleenexes in a woman's handbag. He must be proud of you. For in keeping with Nonno's tradition you never fail to discover a hiding place in any opening anywhere, teasing secrets out of trunks, a cupboard, from behind a tree, eavesdropping, overhearing people's talk."

"I do no such thing," I said weakly. "Nor does Nonno."

"He is your mentor, you his prize pupil and grandson."

I made no comment.

"His late wife knew of this," my mother went on, "and so does Zariba. Kathy, his American lover, spoke of it too. In a lot of ways, he shares a kinship with Sholoongo. Maybe this is why he sympathizes with her — because, like her, he too has gone to the precipice of death and come back. He too slept in death's thorny bed before he fled south. Now he lives in the horror of death catching up with him. They say he lives longer who harbors a secret wish to die. He will be eighty-four next year. From the look of it, he will survive us all, to bury us all, Sholoongo in collusion with him."

"Please!" I said.

Her face was crisscrossed with wrinkles. The stresses on her face were as prominent as the stretch marks on an old body. "After Sholoongo picked the lock of my jewelry box to lift a document of mine," my mother volunteered, "she came here. It was here that she hid for a day and a night."

Was my mother referring to the so-called letter Sholoongo left behind, secretly, in Rhino's belly? I was glad that Nonno remembered the incident so many years after it had happened. But would he be able to lay his hands on the document?

My mother said, "I've never spoken ill of Nonno. Nor do I wish to do so now. However, my skin is covered with goose pimples at the remembrance of a great many bizarre activities involving him. Some of these were so weird I could swear that he dabbles in magic, or that he is a man with life-and-death secrets to protect. Like Sholoongo."

The morning sun made good its promise. Ebullient in its youthful brightness, it was also hot as the temper of the young. The brightness formed the frontiers of the sun's reach, a half circle of shades stretching farther into the areas it had not touched, like the fingers of a hand, into the enclosure of yet another darker shape. The shapes put me in mind of a crescent, the wings of a hawk-eagle poised in its determination to descend in furious attack on its prey. No sooner had I revised my reading of the shadow's meaning than I heard my mother's voice, wet as cheeks soaked in tears.

"Love is cruel," she said.

"Irrational hate is more cruel," I said.

"Love wrings my heart dry of blood."

Love, I thought, is a mother armed. But I did not say it.

She said, "A sudden rush of blood renders me deaf at the memory of the humiliations which Sholoongo made you go through. I think of broad-daylight murder when I remember how she made you do what she made you do."

I got up. I went to take hold of my mother's handbag, which I opened. I pulled out the ancient firearm. But then I thought not of what the firearm might do, but of its beauty. I felt it with my fingers, unable to imagine that such a handsome thing could cause death. Would my mother use it to kill? I was not sure.

Nonetheless the firearm was creating much acrimony between us without her even pulling its trigger. Should I tell my mother that I knew a lot more about her than she credited me with, after having spoken to my father and Nonno? Earlier, I now suspected, Nonno had shaken her as if she were a fruit tree not yielding a fig of a manna. The poor thing was recovering from the shock of being shaken. I put the weapon back in her handbag, and set it down close to her.

She was in a folktale-telling mood. "There is a tale in which a fly catches sight of a beehive in an orchard. The fly offers half of his property for the right to dip his wings in the sweetness. They strike a deal which gives half of the fly's property to the queen bee, and which allows the fly to stay as long as he pleases in the honey. Eventually the fly tires of being in the honey, and wants out. A baby bee nearby asks what the fly will give, if helped. The fly lists many benefits. The baby bee is unimpressed. Finally the fly offers to escort her to a valley where honeyguides die by the million. 'Now you're talking,' the bee beams with delight. She helps him to get unstuck. The fly takes off, leaving behind him nothing but the ugly buzzing noise of an unfulfilled pledge in the baby bee's ears."

As if on cue, Zariba brought us tea and left.

I with a surprising suddenness thought how powerful my once-upon-a-time calf-love Sholoongo was, making us take each other on, making us tear into one another's viscera, impervious to the damage we were doing to ourselves. If she had power, I imagined this to be not animal power but the power of her personality. And if she were able to metamorphose into anything, she was in a position to do so only because we, my mother and I, were avowedly weaker than she. Not Nonno. Nor my father. Both were strong in the conviction of who they were, both agreeably more generous to her than either my mother or I. However, there was much sadness all around, my mother speaking with the slowness of an unseeing person negotiating blind bends, my mother who was known to cover a great deal of ground with her fast talk.

"Nothing makes sense anymore," I ventured.

"What doesn't make sense?" she asked.

"I cannot seem to follow the meaning of your folktales," I said, "nor do I see the relevance of my dreams, mysteries, secrets threaded into a weftage serving as a veil. Meanwhile you and Sholoongo trade insults, you and my father trade hush-hush confidences, you and Nonno exchange innuendoes. Now, is there any man, other than my father, who played in your life before I was born?"

This was a small matter for my mother. "None."

Then I remembered Nonno mentioning a man known by his alias Gacme-xume. And so I asked, "What's his real name?"

Even though she was clearly shaken, she wouldn't say anything. In fact she turned her back to me to make certain I didn't see her face.

"I shall make a point of asking my father."

Not a sound out of her.

"Let's try this. What document did Sholoongo steal?"

Her voice level, "It was my marriage certificate."

"Why?"

"You ask her yourself."

"Why bring it here? Why hide here for a day or two?"

"You'll have to put the question to her."

"Did she give it to Nonno, do you think, for safekeeping?"

"You ask her yourself."

My brain was a wire burning at one end. There was also an explosive mechanism attached to the other end. I didn't know when we might all blow up in the air. I asked, "Were you planning to divorce my father?"

"Of course not."

"Were you betrothed to another man, as his lawful wife?"

"What nonsense is this?"

"Why didn't you get a duplicate copy from the municipality, no sweat, if you were not planning to divorce my father and were not secretly betrothed to another man? What was the fuss?"

"You won't understand," she said.

"You wanted the original back?" I asked.

She didn't say anything.

"You wanted to punish her?"

"I doubt that you will ever understand."

"Why kill her now?"

She stayed motionless, not speaking.

"Why, Mother? Why?"

Shifty, the fingers of her hands laced together into a wringing pos ture. I took an absentminded sip of my tea, my gaze falling on the skim of weak milk floating on it. Undrunk, the stuff presently resembled a paranoiac's idea of a witch's distillation of prophylactic cures.

I said, "Do you know what it was like for me to come into a room where you and my father were, and to find you falling silent the moment I entered? Or changing the subject of your conversation? Do you know what it was like? The thought did cross my mind more than once that maybe you didn't want to have me. Or you were hiding something from me — maybe that I was an adopted child, and you wished me not to know that."

Her voice hard, "What a very cruel thing to say to me!"

"Starving a child of knowing the loving side of its parents is more cruel," I said. "You feed the child on self-mistrust. Paranoia eats into the heart of the unliked. In the end, such a child will imagine all kinds of untruths. Distrustful of humans, I sought the company of pets. When not with Nonno, who was more open with me than either of you, I ran errands for Fidow. Unloved, I fed on unhealthy diets of self-hate, when I came in and you fell silent."

My mother buried her head in her cupped hands, sobbing. I sat down beside her, but hadn't the courage to touch her. There was a spot of sunny brightness in a mandala of a solar circle and, surrounding it, a number of lighter shades with their own life-energies. She raised her head. We rearranged our bodies so as to embrace.

She must have held back a flood of tears, for her words, not her cheeks, were dripping with emotion. "We have done everything we have done out of love."

"Crying, loving, hating are all as natural as a mother loving her son to self-ruin." Now I kissed away her tears, tasting a touch of kohl. "Nonetheless I do not consider your attitude to have its origin in a healthy maternal sentiment. Not all the time. Open your mind and your heart to me, Mother. I am your one and only son."

She took my hands in hers, and kissed them. Then she stared at a dark smudge on the ball of my thumb, which I withdrew when I saw the worry on her face. I rubbed the kohl stains from her soaked cheeks, and eventually from my lips. I said, "The kettle-plain question, Mother, is why so much ugliness? Is it because true knowledge is gained through a kind of death? Or because true self-definition is attained through a total overhaul of one's identity? Name changing, a child outgrowing its parents, the maturing of something altogether new out of the old: where am I in all this?"

She might have said something if Nonno had not joined us. Then the three of us chatted amicably, making it a point to mention Fidow's name in our conversation. It was late morning when she left. But before doing so, she said, "We love you, your father and I."

My mind strayed soon after her departure. I took off skywards in the company of a crow which flew low. The crow kept the world in his sharp carrion-eater's vision, and the cosmos in the clutch of his claws.

It was high noon now. In the dining room, the residues of my mother's perfume mixed awkwardly and well with Nonno's smoke.

My imagination kept wanting to wander off. I would smell the whiff of gunpowder and would hear a shot. A day later, I would come upon the rotten stench of a corpse, Sholoongo's, lying in my room, unburied. I was sad to be conjuring up all manner of aberrations clad in tawdry anomalies, the produce of my fevered mind. The presence of firearms complicated matters. If there is beauty in death, there is beastliness in murdering the innocent. Many a person may see beauty in an elephant taking revenge on Fidow, whose unappeased ghost, now unchained, was bound to haunt our memories.

I was too strung up to sit still. I was so tense I could not bear the thought of standing either. I paced back and forth, regretting that I hadn't buried my head in the ostrich sand of parental confidence. What you don't know cannot harm you. Now, because I'd spoken, everyone's image seemed to suffer a dent. Was I being insensitive, merely distributing blame among my seniors? Had I laid censure at my parents' doors without knowing the full extent of what happened?

And there was the matter of Hanu, too. He sat not very far from where Nonno and I were, quiet as an eavesdropper, full of I-told-you-so posturing. It was as if he were sharing his simian secrets with us. Then we heard the soft whistle of a bird wading in the shallows of the river, and I saw Hanu's eyes sporting a sparkle of excitement in his startled stare. He sat up. Our curious eyes followed his

We had a mysterious visitor. A blackhead plover was now perched on the edge of the dining table. This enthralled Hanu, who made us ask ourselves questions as we listened to the bird's shrill whistle, as indistinct as the first utterance of a baby. Our newly arrived guest had strolled in, its crest reminding me of a hairstyle popular in the heyday of my infatuation with Sholoongo. The blackhead plover's red-eyed contemplative look had a sobering effect on the three of us, above all Hanu. He got up and left the room, tiptoeing out. He was as considerate as a parent going out of the room in which an ailing child has fallen asleep. Hanu meant to abandon center stage to the blackhead plover. I thought, how magnanimous.

We sat, the three of us, my grandfather, the *xidinxiito* plover, and I, in a suspicious silence, as if a new relationship were being forged between a species belonging to the unspeaking world and two inarticulate humans. I spoke my thought aloud: "But what on earth has made Hanu leave?"

"Maybe we should offer our guest a drink," Nonno said, half in earnest. The blackhead plover appeared as intimidated as a human finding himself in a place where the language was alien.

I said, "Shall we offer a lemonade, sugared?"

"Shall we?"

"Shall we pour it into a glass?"

But neither moved.

Nonno wondered, "Does the idea of a blackhead plover paying us a visit out of the mysterious nowhere disturb you in any way, Kalaman?"

"Why should it," I said, "when a stray cat walking in on me in my apartment does not?"

"Our visitor is no domesticated Hanu," Nonno reasoned, "a Hanu whom we pamper with a personal name and our affection. This *xidinxiito* plover is a freeborn, freethinking bird. Now what makes you think that he will receive our sugared indulgence in a jar, as served?"

My curiosity was aroused by a thread which had been tied to the bird's shank. Dangling from the shank was a tiny piece of paper, neatly folded up, very similar in shape to chits on which Koranic inscriptions, to form part of an amulet's charm, are written. Was the plover a message-carrying bird in our dining room? Contrary to Nonno's view, the bird was no free agent, roaming the winds at will and storming the desert's whirlwinds. Unless we freed him from the thread of his enslavement, he would remain in bondage.

Nonno's voice had in it a touch of humidity, which affected his delivery, making his words emerge curled up like the pages a fax machine spits out. "Somalis in their mythology," he said, "speak of the *xidinxiito* plover as having once been a member of the society of prey birds. One night, however, while the plovers slept, the other carnivorous birds devoured all the available provisions. Their king called a council meeting, at which the plovers debated whether to continue forming part of the society of prey birds or not. All those present pledged on oath never to fly with the other birds and never ever to eat flesh. To distinguish themselves from other prey birds, they elected not to abstain from eating during the hours of darkness. When they see anything in the dark, they repeat the oath. In chorus, they confirm that they are still bound by the not-meat-eating pledge. They keep a watchful night, lest they be cheated out of their share. A large number of them nowadays are purblind during daytime, but they rise from under a traveler's feet, crying loud the damnation *Gaalow!* We consider the *xidinxiito* to be an ill-omened bird."

I looked at the plover in curious awe, noting to myself that his shank folded away like a turtle's neck. It was as if it were disappearing in cautious self-preservation.

Somewhere in the kitchen the fridge shook. A grin of vaudeville richness crowned Nonno's features. Was a pleasant memory calling on him, in spite of the presence of the ill-omened bird?

Zariba came, carrying a tray. Bizarrely, she brought us three slices of avocado. For whom was the third cut of the fruit? Was it meant for the plover, or for Hanu? Before leaving the porch hurriedly, she shook her head in a desperate attempt to forget what she had witnessed.

"A visitor equally as mysterious as the blackhead plover arrived out of one of the sky's secret folds on the day you were born," he said. "A crow turned up as if in routine deference to your being born. Before the crow came a sparrow, tapping Morse code messages on dawn's windowpane." He repeated the story and what happened. I listened to it, fascinated, as I had listened many, many times before. I listened, my mouth filled with the buttery taste of the avocado, the pores of my whole body alert as ears. Aware that there were two of us paying him full attention, my grandfather's voice rose and fell in recognition of the significance of the tale he was telling.

In my grandfather's recall, the day I was born would be forever associated with a sparrow. The small, square-tailed bird pecked at his windowpane and uttered handsome trills in semitone Morse codes, trills ranging from three to five notes, insistent as the frightened bleating of a lost baby goat. This threw Nonno into a terrible fluster. My mother had been laboring at having me for more than forty-eight hours. There was little hope of bringing her dolorous pangs to a successful end before another day had lapsed. Anxious about the system of ditches he had dug, my grandfather had driven back to Afgoi after a two-day vigil, in expectation of averting untoward disasters to his irrigation plans. He had slept little in the night, but intended to get into his jalopy and be with my parents after sunup, to welcome the new baby. He awoke just before daybreak, to a bird pecking at his pane in dots and dashes and double-dashes. The message?

He remembered a dream he had had a couple of days earlier. In the dream, the baby had been born, with a face resembling a monkey's. This was his future grandson. And when he had tried to question the infant on why it had assumed this identity, the dream became too noisy, on account of the loud droning of bees, some lodging themselves in his ears. The following night he had a similar dream, but this time there was only a single bee, its elegant body poised, a ballerina about to curtsey, its head half bowing. The bee sported a waxy-looking spot of white on its outstretched aculeus. The bee pricked him with its poison, painful as though a tattooist had punctured a message in his skin. He read, "The key is buried in the half-living stump of a tamarind tree. You will make syrup out of its fruits, and you will make the baby take the pulp as a laxative." Then, like the switch of a bulb, his sight was turned off. Dreaming no more, he lay in bed, worried.

The following morning, as luck had it, Fidow stumbled on a mountain of elephant dung. Germinating in the dung there were tamarind seeds. Nonno sought the stars' counsel by gazing at them the entire night before planting a single seed. But why a monkey's face? Why the droning of bees? The journey between the bee in the dream and the bird pecking Morse dots and dashes of undecoded mysteries was shorter than the distance which separates illusion from reality.

Nonno did not speak of these to a living soul. He wouldn't say what these meant to him either. A drone of bees loud as humanity's collective cry? What of the nervous bird pecking at his window?

Woken up by the bird's Morse code messages, my future grandfather showered. He stood on the porch, his eyes lighting up at the decision that, in addition to tamarind seeds, he would take along a phial of honey from Fidow's harvest. He would also bring a manikin reputedly found in the second belly of a crocodile, and a cut of leather cured by Yaqut on which he had copied the Koranic sura The Opening.

He was on the road before sunrise. But scarcely had he crossed Afgoi's town boundary than he felt the engine of his car going dead. He stopped in front of a signboard saying MOGADISCIO 20 KM. My grandfather pushed the jalopy off the road and into the low shrubs, not anxious. The thought of walking back home, or of thumbing a lift to the city, did not occur to him as one might have expected. He took a couple of strides into the bushes in response to an urgent call of nature.

Upon returning to the jalopy vehicle, he had a passenger. Uninvited, a crow was seated in the other front seat, behaving like a house pet, appearing neither perturbed nor intimidated. The feathered creature, as a matter of fact, greeted him with a quizzical squawk, perhaps wondering why Nonno had not welcomed him. As though offended, the crow vacated the seat he had occupied till then, and balanced himself now on the metal framework of the van.

It took some time before my grandfather connected the bird who had pecked at his windowpane earlier to the crow now perched on the precarious framework of his jalopy, squawking with self-appraisal. Nonno got into his car, and in his absentmindedness turned on the ignition key. The engine caught at his first try, smooth as a miracle. He drove on, relegating all this to the status of a daydream complementing an earlier night vision, in which birds and bees had appeared. Empty of traffic, the tarmac road stretched ahead of them, silver with the mirage of a distant thirst.

There had been a fair amount of tension between Nonno and his son Yaqut ever since the young man quit school at fourteen to apprentice himself to an Italian engraver. Yaqut proved himself capable of dreaming up a series of vocations. Not yet twenty-two, a well-respected and skilled craftsman, still more devoted to his vocation as an engraver than to any other, Yaqut was a useful man around the house, and able to sink a well too. He wasn't the world's most articulate speaker, his active vocabulary in those days consisting of grunts, a plain yes, or a head-shaking no. He played the *kaman*, plucking the strings to the rhythm and scale of songs he himself composed.

The old man now stole a furtive glance at the crow. The bird was as contented-looking as a child, excited at the prospect of going on a festive outing. The question was, would the crow go with him into the compound where Damac was having her labor pangs? Or would he fly off into the unknown, leaving behind himself a mystery, some sort of an archaic link with pre-Islamic Somalia, a mythical creature elevated to the status of a deity?

"Here we are," my grandfather said as he maneuvered the jalopy vehicle, parking it. It was then that the feathered creature issued a most gentle squawk, which to my grandfather's ears sounded like "See you shortly." The squawk could equally have been "Thank you kindly," but my grandfather wasn't sure. But before he could think of the multiple significance of the word "crow" in Somali, the crow left, polite as a passenger showing gratitude for the offer of a lift.

As he repeated the story to me now for the nth time, I thought that Nonno had on an inexplicable expression, something which put me in mind of love going to seed. Was he regretting to himself how things had come to pass?

My grandfather found Yaqut making incisions on a slab of marble. My future father was working on a gravestone for "an Italian dead in *misericordia*," as my grandfather used to say. The young fellow's hands were clutching at his apron, tense. The place smelt lived-in; in fact there was another man asleep on the *alool* bed in the furthest corner, most likely a relation of Damac's from the countryside. The house was crawling with a great number of women, many of them making themselves useful. Yaqut met his father halfway, and offered a forearm, because his hands weren't clean enough to be shaken.

"I imagine you are anxious," ventured the father.

Yaqut nodded in the manner of a foreigner who, although he did not understand the language, wished to remain cordial. He was obviously nervous. Providing his father with a high stool to sit on, he appeared undecided whether or not to return to his work. How could a young man, soon to be a father, work on a gravestone for a dead Italian? Only some of the letters were engraved on the slab. Asked how things had been, Yaqut mumbled something to the effect that, to receive his payment, he had to deliver the headstone later that day. His father offered to make up for the loss, but Yaqut wouldn't hear of it, saying, "It would make Damac unhappy. We both prize our separateness. But thanks all the same."

After being served tea and biscuits by one of his daughters, my grandfather mentioned the good omen of the sparrow's predawn visit. Then he talked about the crow and how it had helped restart the engine of his jalopy. He might have spoken to a Chinese in a Mexican sign language, for he failed to draw any comment out of Yaqut on either of these renderings.

"Would you say," the old man asked, "that being a father matters more to you than your vocations, as a well-sinker, an engraver, or a man who commissions gravedigging?"

Not a single word out of Yaqut.

A few minutes later they were joined by two women, one of them Yaqut's oldest sister, the one to whom he was closest. She had brought a breakfast of fried liver for their father. The atmosphere jovial, they chatted frivolously. Arbaco, Damac's dearest friend, asked Yaqut if he was looking forward to becoming a father. Yaqut responded in a series of unlinked mnemonic words. Duufaan, Yaqut's eldest sister, being the only person aside from Damac able to untangle Yaqut's entwined noises, interpreted his wisdom in a string of words as disjointed as the rosary enumerating God's names of praise.

No sooner had the grandfather-to-be heaved forward as if to launch into an energetic talk than a griot's chanting voice stopped him in his tracks. The griot was making his traditional claim of a gift from a household blessed with a baby boy. How was it, though, that the griot knew, not only that it would be born soon, but that it would be a boy? For all intents and purposes the sounds emanating from the mother-in-labor room indicated that she hadn't even started to push, nor had her water broken.

Yaqut paid the griot handsomely.

My grandfather, in homage perhaps to the griot, listened, as if waiting for some kind of intimation of what was to be from Waaq, the ancient Somali sky god, imperfectly supplanted by Islam. As if on cue, the feathered creature was back and sitting on the highest branch of the fig tree in the center of the compound, issuing a squawk which to my grandfather's ears sounded like "Kalaman."

I was named Kalaman.

Yaqut was bubbly with delight.

His bubble began with a mere hint of a sound, something between a truncated grunt and a full-bodied syllable of a much longer word. Yaqut turned these into a tributary of sounds, an unintelligible river of noises breaking at the banks. What a joy to hear him, drowned as he was with the delight of being a father. He couldn't contain it. People deciphered the drift of his rejoicing as he kept saying "I am! I am!" But somehow he did not explain who or what he was.

He shouted, "No, no, no, no," hugging his own old man. It became clear later that he was bestowing the honorific title Nonno, Italian for Grandfather.

More griots arrived to chant blessings. An ample feast was promised, a sumptuous meal was offered, a goat was delivered to the door, and slaughtered, some of the meat going to the poor in its raw form, half of it cooked on improvised fires.

Duufaan called Nonno out. She appeared alarmed at the prospect of a crow attending at a birth. Nonno's searching gaze took in the ominous nearness of the crow, come to supervise the goings-on from close by.

Now the crow, with the smug confidence of an invited guest, joined the snarl of the activities. A number of people remarked on his incongruous presence among them. The women agreed to shoo him away. But Nonno intervened, the moment he noticed that vultures, hawks, and other everyday carnivores had arrived too. Only the crow made as if to distinguish himself from the other carrion eaters, come because of the possibility of receiving castaway meats. The crow joined the humans.

The news that I wouldn't make water, and wouldn't cry when spanked on the bottom, spread faster than the crow's ominous arrival. Yaqut's rollickings ceased. Again Nonno intervened. He spoke with bucolic simplicity to his daughter Duufaan, to make an unorthodox request: to go into the room where Damac had given birth. Traditionally men are not allowed to enter such a room for all of the forty days of the woman's confinement. But because of the special circumstances, Nonno was granted his request.

He might have been a reputable healer calling at a palace where the heir apparent had taken ill. He forged forward alone, and into Damac's room, his sleeves up and folded, his lips ashiver with the totemic powers of the crow, to whom we prayed long ago as our sky-god, the crow who was revered as a deity among the peoples of the Horn of Africa before the spread of Islam and Christianity.

Put it down to superstitious dread, but the crow would not follow Nonno into Damac's room, maybe because of the odd mixture of commiphora-*malmal*, incense, and other odors, smells crows consider to be repellent. The old man stepped in, head slightly bowed, eyes focusing, shoulders stooped. He took in that a couple of sticks had been driven into the uncemented floor, and that a screen had been draped to hide Damac from view.

I was in the midwife's lap. The midwife handed me over to Nonno. The hush in the room was total, all eyes fixed on him. Grandfather placed a tamarind seed on my lips, which stirred, opened, tongue out and then in, tasting, maybe naming the fruit and deciding it would have a little more of the pulp, if given. Nonno finger-fed me on a drop of wild honey, another of a tamarind drink. And I burst into a hearty cry. I made a flood of pee, abundant as the waters of the Shabelle River.

My grandfather might have been a magician who wanted not to divulge the secrets of his vocation, his livelihood. He handed me back to the midwife. An outburst of ululation greeted the handing over. But before leaving the room, he brought out of the folds of his clothing the sura of the Koran named *Faatixa*, The Opening, which Yaqut, his son, had copied in floriated Kufic style, together with the manikin recovered from the crocodile's belly. Nonno now offered these gifts to me, the newly born grandson whose curled-up long-nailed fingers accepted and held them in a possessive clutch. My grandfather might have been a nomad presenting his grandchild with a long hair plucked from a female camel, the *xuddun-xir*, a camel given to the newly born. This done, he left.

The smile returned to everyone else's lips. Yaqut from this day on would speak not in babbles but in words easily understood by everyone. The crow for his part descended from the height of his seclusion.

And there was rejoicing.

When at the end of the day the crow went back to the estate with my grandfather, his farmhands named the crow Madoobe. This is a descriptive name, concentrating more on the darkness of the bird's hue, but hardly alluding to divinity. The feathered creature responded to the villagers' welcome and teasing in squawks of amicability, demonstrably pleased. It was as though in an earlier existence he had known himself by that name, or he had known Nonno, or this particular village. But a number of the farmhands found the idea of a crow in their midst as distasteful as kissing an object of derision. Outside Nonno's hearing, some of them laughed their sides to splits at the sight of an old man standing over six foot tall, shoulders broad as a baobab's trunk, with a crow in tow.

Fidow said, "They are a grandfather and a grandchild."

Another farmhand reminded his audience of the eloquence of Somalis when they define a miracle as a donkey giving birth to a calf. This was a miracle, a crow not being stoned, but kept as a pet by one of our respected elders. Yet another farmhand asked my grandfather about the name given to his grandson. The name Kalaman produced a curious debate, some arguing it was Islamic, others that it was a pre-Islamic Somali name. One man, purporting to know more than the others, made what was taken as a facetious comment, "I think it has something to do with the ABC of the Arabic alphabet."

Walking away from the gathered crowd, the crow still in tow, my grandfather felt sad because no one linked Madoobe with an iconic significance, such as the ones which the presence of a chameleon evokes among other African communities. After all, crows are associated, in the ancient Somali mind, with a guarantee against death, as opposed to Islam and Christianity, faiths which offer the faithful a guarantee of afterlife!

Forty days later the crow vanished as mysteriously as he had arrived. He took off when my grandfather was returning from a visit to my parents' house to mark the end of the period of confinement. On this day an outing ritual is observed, and the newborn is brought out of the house for the first time. Wise men are chosen to perform this task. A secret wisdom is whispered in the ears of the newborn.

After becoming infatuated with Sholoongo and learning that her father was also called Madoobe, I asked my grandfather if the crow named Madoobe was my calf-love's altered nature.

"Only Allah knows!" he replied.

Then I asked, "What secrets did you whisper in my ears on the day you marked my readiness for the outside world with a ritual outing?"

"Just two words," said Nonno.

"What were they?"

"Birds soar!"

A small child asks his grandfather, "Can you think of any human being without known parents, with no grandfather and no grandmother either?"

"Only Adam fits the bill for Muslims and Christians."

"What of a person without a father?"

"Prophet Ciisa, known as Jesus among Christians."

"Any with a father but no mother?"

"I don't know of any, unless we think of Xaawa, otherwise known as Eve," says the child's grandfather. "But we'll have to assume a lot. We'll have to assume Adam to be her father, from whose rib the myths suppose she's been created."

And the child chants a hyperbole: *Mothers matter a lot! Fathers matter not!* He repeats this several times, breaking a toothpick every

time he sings it. Something activates the old man's mechanism of recall, and his eyes travel far, seeing things, remembering.

"What're you thinking?" the child asks the old man.

"I am thinking that myths are but a stew to spice up one's life,"
the old man responds.

CHAPTER EIGHT

I am Kalaman's mother. And for want of a more eloquent beginning I shall start with an incident which took place several months after Kalaman's third birthday, soon after weaning him.

He came in on me and Yaqut. He probably walked in on us in the stealthy attitude of a hunter surprising his intended victim, after marking the territory in which he operated with the frontiers of his quietness. Kalaman need not have bothered to shut the door quietly once he entered the room, because Yaqut and I, at any rate, were engrossed in each other, paying no attention to any noise other than the ones our sexually excited bodies were making. Goodness knows, because of our excitement, there was a throng of enthralled endearments which each addressed to the other, there were groans, there were moans too. We had the night-light burning, and maybe because we had forgotten to blow them out, a couple of candles were burning too. We had almost reached the summit of our lovemaking when I sensed the presence, among the candle's breeze-bent shadows, of someone or something casting a shadow without responding to the wind as candles do. There with us in the room I could see the exaggerated contours of a head. For a worrying moment, my frightened stare and the intruder's derring-do were locked in a knotted startle. I stared at the visitor's eyes, which might have belonged in an owl's facial disk, protuberances focused on us with more power than a human's eyes, diabolically beamed.

Anyway there he was, my Kalaman, more of a midget than a three-year-old. He was cross-eyed from concentrating his glare on

Yaqut, who had his back to him. Yaqut was in me, my nipple in his mouth. The young thing had his thumb pressing his cheek from the inside, and was emitting a small whistle from somewhere deep in his nasal cavity, a noise I put down to a feeling of sexual excitement, I don't know.

In my shock, everything took place as it does in an action replay, the gradualness of a delayed reaction assuming its own life. It was not long before I was overwhelmed by a sense of partial paralysis. I felt a nebulous numbness in every cell of my body, the message of what was occurring conveyed rather slowly to the so-far-unaffected parts of me, into which the feeling of helplessness now spread. This ended in my tongue, where the sense of necrosis was total. My temperature dropped to the freezing point. I pushed away Yaqut, who until then was unaware, pushed him away so I would embrace myself, cover my chest, my thighs, my sex, not with clothes, not definitely with Yaqut's otherness, but with a cosmic blindness. I didn't want to see, and didn't wish to be seen either. Not by Kalaman, nor by Yaqut. That was my feeling. A voyeur of a son at three!

Later that night Yaqut told me how he first remarked the chill in my feet before realizing what was happening, and how only after-wards he touched the goose pimples all over my thighs. My legs started to unclasp then, they let go of him little by little until he was no longer in me. To reclaim my body to myself, I freed my breast from his lips' fondness, in the way a mother removes from a sleeping baby's clasp a toy which might be dangerous. His manhood shrank to the life-less size of a supplementary sixth finger, empty of energy, devoid of memory, of sex.

Presently Kalaman stood apart from the candles' eerily moving shadows. And he was repeating a phrase, more of a command. He was repeating words which took me a long time to decipher, because of my current state of mind. He would chant, "Mummy, give me . . ." and, after a pause and a whimper, add the phrase " . . . a sibling!" Or he would whimper, and then chant the entire sequence without a pause. He would end the charade by burying his face in his small hands, and wait, as if catching his breath.

"What would you like Mummy to give you, Kalaman?" asked Yaqut, busy covering his indecency.

Before dashing out of the room, Kalaman would repeat, "Give me, give me, give me, gimme, gimme . . . a sibling!" For years, the walls of my memory reverberated with my son Kalaman making a gimme-gimme-Mummy-a-sibling plea.

Kalaman wanted us to give him siblings, if possible a younger brother and a younger sister, one of each, a normal enough request from a child growing up. It wasn't for lack of trying that we didn't. Only I was pregnant with Kalaman for a considerably long time, a day short of three hundred and ten. Perhaps this prolonged pregnancy ruined the lining of my womb. I am not at all regretting that I held him inside of me for the longest possible time. And there is no point in wishing away the fact that I breast-fed him for nearly three years, even though I was advised to wean him earlier. Why did I breast-feed him for such a long time? Because I did not want to let go of him, imagining that I was a tube being fondled by his fond lips, the ducts of my large nipples growing bigger at his touch. You see, I had two dwarf additional breasts way down on my abdomen. How it excited me to have them sucked, an indulgence my husband Yaqut was forever prepared to grant me. To suck, he would go down on his knees, and take my Tinies in his mouth, one at a time, in virtuous performance of a private ritual which we delighted in together. It was divine pleasure to have Kalaman at my breasts feeding, and at my feet my husband prostrated in worshipful adulation of my Dwarfines, head hidden in adoration between the little ones, fondling the milkless outlets. It was as if I had been blessed with a set of twins, one at each of my breasts, suckling. Any woman would have received a most delectable sensation to be handled with such veneration. "Down, further down please, kindly tease," I would say to Yaqut, "keep touching, keep teasing, more and more, tongue and all!" He would oblige, God bless him, until I rang like a bell. I would urge him to come. At my prompting, we would arrive together in monsoon moisture, his lips mustached with an opaque milkiness, my own wetness.

I was determined to keep the two of them all to myself. I was decided to make them wholly mine, Kalaman a fetus indisputably dependent on me for as long as I could hold on to him, and Yaqut totally mine, in secret trust of each other. He was home-bound, Yaqut was, because of his profession, Yaqut my warming pan. Bless the day I met the man, amen! I didn't let go of the fetus, because I didn't want anyone else to see my bodily secrets, my tiny, extra little breasts. The midwife would see, I used to fear, word would go around, and with gossip doing the rounds, either the Tinies would fall off of their own accord, or I would be labeled a witch.

After the baby's birth, and especially if it were a boy, I knew that the community of men would take over. But I didn't want to share my baby with anyone, not with the men in any case. For men had a way of indoctrinating boys, of whispering male secrets in their ears, as the mother lay on her back in an incapacitated state of bodily malfunction and numbness of mind, on account of having been infibulated. It takes us at least forty days, if not more, to heal, days in which women convalesce, days and nights which would afford the men time to conspire among themselves about the new arrival, days and nights when they might open and consult the Scriptures for divine guidance. My father-in-law Miftaax (later named Nnno-no-no by a then excited and stammering Yaqut) studied the stars, the respective position of the planets, the birds congregating around him, pecking, eating off his palm. He was a sight, with a crow in tow. Men did his bidding, the entire community likewise, because he was wealthy. He had a wicked tongue, which he lent to authoritative abuse when he chose to. He fed my son on all sorts of concoctions with a juju base, pure sorcery.

My son weaned, I couldn't tell what might become in the end of my two Supplementaries, now that Yaqut had the Mains at his beck and suck. I knew the day would come when the baby and I would be separated, he to follow the course of his own destiny and I mine. But in my imagination I remained the mother of twins, one of them old and my husband, the other my infant son. Even nowadays, when we make love, Yaqut suckles at my frontals one at a time. Lately, though, maybe because of Sholoongo, my cute Tininesses have proved dormant, ripe peaches drying on the tree which bore them. It is as if they are losing their plump abundance. Which is why it wouldn't surprise me any longer if I should wake up one morning to find them gone, a victim lying lifeless on the lap of Sholoongo-bewitched gravity. What would become of me then? I have had more nightmares of having my Lovelies exposed that I have worries of them vanishing without a proper exchange of good-byes. Everything is Sholoongo's doing. If she knew, she would do greater ill. Nobody like witches. Fires are built, pyres are fed on them. Witches burn to the quick. God forbid!

And even if no funeral pyre were lit, I would not want other people to know about me and them, my Tinies, whose existence complements mine. Before I am undressed by a physician to examine me, I am left with two choices: either the humiliation of being seen, or that of covering them with a bandage. Either way, doctors get to know of it. Until my teens my mother put on adhesive plasters, and I pretended I had dermoid cysts or some such puberty-related indisposition. But then I met Yaqut, who helped me to think of my original malediction as a fortuitous boon in disguise.

On balance, though, the Supplementaries have made a dent in my morale as a woman. It is more of a pity that I let go of the fetus, only for Nonno to name him Kalaman. As part of his goodwill gesture, Yaqut had awarded his father the distinguishing honor of naming the boy. But why call him Kalaman, a most absurd choice? The man is weird, choosing odd names for his offspring: Yaqut, Duufaan, and now Kalaman, all of them as attention-seeking as a woman baring her breasts at a camel bazaar.

I am described as a mean, calculating woman by people who, if they knew about my Additionals, might have described me as a many-breasted monster. I am surprised that not a large number of people know of my multiple mammae. Doctors tell on you, nurses exchange gossip at their cafeterias. Somalis being busybodies, many of the unemployed or underemployed manufacture talk, especially the men, who get up to all sorts of slanderous mischiefs. But there you are. I've known only one man lovingly and voluntarily. I couldn't say I knew the men who raped me, because I didn't. May the Lord's curse be upon them! I do not know if *the other* spoke about them. For he is a vengeful man, who admits to being a blackmailer. Curse his scorpionlike index finger. I would hate him more if he were to spread uglier gossip about my Lovelies!

As for a name, and Kalaman's in particular?

I compare my son's name to a sheet of water with arid scrawls in salt efflorescence. It is as though you are approaching the source of aqueous matter, and the mere thought gives you energy, making you invest all your will in pushing through the heat haze until you reach the coveted *bio*, the source of life, water. In mirage, though, despite the nearness of *bio* (the word means water in Somali), the vapor retreats the closer you get to it, moving farther and farther from you, making you suicidally thirstier.

If my son were called not Kalaman but any of the more commonplace Somali or Muslim designations, I doubt that my boy would have attracted as much attention to himself as he does now. Soon after meeting Sholoongo, the harbinger of evil, and after she pointed out to him the peculiar nature of his naming, I suggested to Nonno that we change the boy's name to something quite ordinary.

In those days, that evil woman (Sholoongo's own name is odder still, alluding to an ancient precapitalist form of banking among women; these contribute each to a collection, to share out once a week) was in everybody's conversation, her name caressing every male's lips. She induced nympholepsy in men, whatever their age or calling. With a mouth as watery as a succulent fruit, lips swollen as desire itself, she was no different from beasts with exposed natures. Her presence put the worry into women. This was the only time when I considered telling her that, in my Tinies, I had power over men too. I didn't like the bitch, least of all for running away with my son's name and playing with it as a playful she-dog might lock posteriors with a he-dog in cold, calculated deliberateness, just teasing.

Anyway: about Kalaman's name! That was my point, wasn't it?

I talked to Nonno on several occasions about changing the name too. One day, sounding clever and pleased with myself, I rehearsed what I was going to say to the old man. I perfected my strategy with the help of Yaqut, at whose prompting I improved on what I had. When face-to-face with Nonno, I compared the whole process to a mirage producing more thirst in the one espying it.

Nonno said, "Do you know where a camel stores up its water?"

I hadn't prepared myself for this kind of ambush, and in any case didn't know what my boy's being named Kalaman or Mohammed had to do with the topic at hand. At first I refused point-blank to fall for Nonno's strategy of subduing his interlocutors with the deflective powers of his style of intercourse. I am a city person and have had no reason to concern myself with camels or the men who herd them. "What if I said I hadn't the slightest idea?"

"That won't do," he said.

"Do they not store it in their humps?"

He shook his head no.

I felt as if he were training me for some sort of a sports contest. I was his young grandchild, a talented but lazy athlete, who required more encouragement, more intellectual vigor.

"What about its stomach?" I asked.

"Try again."

"I give up," I said.

"A camel," he said, "stores its water neither in its hump nor in its stomach but in its blood."

I confessed that his point eluded me.

"I knew it would," he said.

"Could you tell me what your point is?" I inquired.

"I'm hoping that you and Yaqut are intelligent enough to sort out the blood in the camel's vein from the water contained therein," he said. "I want you to imagine that the quantity of water has run low, because of the beast's consuming thirst."

"I still don't get your point," I insisted.

172 "I am constructing an allegory out of Kalaman, our boy's naming, and am employing the camel's blood-and-water mix as a metaphor, emblematic of a wider parabolic meaning."

"Maybe we should leave it at that," I said, "since I am not trained in cracking your mysterious talk in camel- and water-related imageries."

"You are the one who used the desert imagery," he accused me.

"Perhaps Yaqut will make sense of it."

Nonno said, his voice that of an impatient teacher whom ill luck has allotted a dumb pupil, "That's a good idea. Try the riddle on him."

I let the parable ride past me on a steed with human feet. A frog croaked. We were near a body of water, and I thought, I won't look at water, or think of camels or deserts, in the same way ever again after this. But I held my thoughts to myself. When I returned to my home-bound Yaqut and requested that he please decipher the blood-and-water message, he grinned a very mischievous grin. He shook his head in wonder. But no matter how hard I tried, no matter how much I pleaded, he wouldn't tell me what he made of the riddle. "Where was the secret in this?"

There is another area of contention between Nonno and myself.

This area is shiftier, more diffuse. Focus the spotlight on it, and it will illuminate a cupboard in which a few skeletons of dubious provenance are kept, Nonno's and my bone of contention. This has to do with the tamarind drink which, in place of a draught of goat's milk or my own divine-supplied mammary secretion, Kalaman was made to suck from a forefinger dipped in some juju juice which Nonno had brought along from Afgoi, juju country par excellence. There is also the matter of a crow and its cameo appearance. The incredibility of it all: the crow waited for Nonno outside the room where I had given birth to my Kalaman.

Ask Nonno pointed questions, and he fudges or talks in evasive waffle. He will ask, "Do you know why people nurse secrets, as if they were alcoholics prolonging the last sip of a drink? We're alienated, alienated from our bodies, from the sad sentiments in which our lives are swathed, as if our lives were prone to disappearances, like a child's writings on the sand." Do you make any sense of that? I don't. Let's hear him continue. "Because we are alienated from the epoch in which we live, the century waylaid by the Euro-saboteurs." Total, pure fudge, no sweetness in it anywhere. It is as if I were to answer the question "Who are you?" thus: "I am a woman born with two additional breasts, and I love to have them sucked." The waffle aside, Nonno, like Sholoongo, had been left for dead and survived. And if he is the kind of man he is and Yaqut is the kind of man he is to me, it is because they hang down heavily, an immensity neither knows how to handle.

But did Nonno put something in the tamarind drink on which he finger-fed Kalaman less than half an hour after his birth? We do not know, and he won't tell us. We ought to have asked where the drink came from. Who boiled the water, in the first place, with which the tamarind extract was mixed with teaspoonfuls of sugar? I wish I had known that Fidow had a hand in the making of the drink, Fidow who dabbled in Shiidliana wizardries, Fidow who, later, would feed Kalaman on prophylactics made out of weird combinations of doubtful origins. Nothing is as powerful as bewitching a baby at its inception. When my forty-day convalescence period ended and Nonno and I happened to be alone with Kalaman, I asked him to tell me more.

Nonno replied, "Fidow, my general factotum, found tamarind seeds germinating in a mountain of elephant dung, a bonanza weighing no less than two hundred kilograms and containing at least five thousand ready-to-plant tamarind seedlings. I suggested he bring five kilos of the stuff in a shovel, and planted these myself with my own hands. A priest blessed the planting, in an effort to appease the earth's spirits, and those of the trees."

I asked, "What aren't you telling me?"

For once Nonno appeared shocked. He said, "I am telling you that there are types of secrets which we choose not to disclose, secrets we prefer not to part with, secrets about dimly lit areas of one's lives, the lay of our bodies, the territories of our pain. These are curtained from public view or concern. Please do not press questions on me, do not insist that I answer them, lest I too be tempted to ask you what you think of as impertinent questions."

He sounded very threatening to me. (I had the same feeling when he hid in the convenience of the water-and-blood riddle when asked about Kalaman's name.) I knew I wasn't letting on what secrets I was holding back. I pondered in silence, waiting for him to continue.

"In fairness," he said, "I should say that when I gave an infusion of the tamarind drink to my first grandchild I believed I was offering it to him as a harbingered secret of survival."

"I am confused," I said.

"There is a subtext to all this," he said. "The subtext points at my own past, secrets I guard and of which I shall speak one day. But do not rush me, please. I am not ready."

More or less another water-in-the-camel's-blood? Or a small-mindedness passed off as wisdom? Physically there was so much of the man. But he could choose to be elusive, and you wouldn't know where he was, in the fudge. I couldn't unravel his riddles, or get to the bottom of his secrets. Nor, come to think of it, could I separate his water from Yaqut's blood, if you get my meaning!

I revisit these memories as I drive back to Mogadiscio. The checkpoints have multiplied since the morning. All kinds of uniforms stop you, ask you to get out of your vehicle and step aside, your hands where they can be seen. No one asks me to open my handbag, in which I have a small firearm.

As I drive straight to Kalaman's apartment, I think what an entangled existence our life has been: elephants seeking out the poachers who've murdered their kin; a young woman transforming her will into that of an enraged beast; a Kalaman fleeing his own apartment and taking refuge at Nonno's estate; a Yaqut refusing to get involved, arguing that, left to themselves, these matters will sort out themselves. The rest of the world is either looking on, indifferent, unbothered, or is concerned with the coming disaster, a war of the militias, if the dictator refuses to budge, a war to the finish, a country ruined.

I am thinking that even two persons sleeping in the same bed at the same time are on occasion held apart by the secret dreams they see on the screens of their unconscious. I am thinking that because all of us are holding our trump cards close to our chests, we can never know how best to serve this nation. I am thinking that whilst rivers burst their banks, while flying fishes assume the role of guides and frogs assume the role of the wise ancient men who admit to being misunderstood, while Kalaman is held hostage by a clutch of fingers of misgiving — I, Damac, shoot!

A woman the shape of a honey badger is dead and buried!

All his life Kalaman has lived in a state of perpetual anxiety. As a grown-up he has continued to suffer from the abject worry of not being on top of things. You wouldn't know from the way he behaves nowadays that he lacks the self-confidence to say what is irking him. He is adept at hiding this from most people, encircling himself with a large perimeter of untaken space and being reticent to the point of being rude. Observe him from close range, and especially when he isn't aware that your eyes are trained on him, and you will discern his awkwardnesses. Suspicious like an ostrich, he is watchful, unceasingly humming to himself an improvised tune. When he is on safer ground, he emits a clear sound, a signal like that of a crow warning of humans in the vicinity; among his familiars, he might signpost his worries, like a honeyguide alerting a hunter to the closeness of a bee's nest. Telling you nothing (does he tell me of the women he is with? does he tell me if that evil woman is putting up with him? does he tell if Qalin is aborting his baby?), he would insist on sharing your harvest of secrets. He is more intimate with Nonno than he is with me and Yaqut, maybe because we are in the position of his immediate responsibilities, whereas Nonno, as a grandparent, is at a remove, the tension between them not as palpable. Sure, he confides his worries to Nonno, no doubt about it. My relationship with Nonno has always been ambiguous, because I am bothered by the unchallengeable position he occupies in my son's scheme of priorities.

Oddly, Sholoongo stands to gain if she supplants Kalaman in Nonno's mind; or if the old man accedes to her advances. The woman is seeking to satiate an insatiable lust. Who knows, Yaqut and Kalaman may consent to wait on the sidelines while she is busy servicing Nonno. Sholoongo's designs on men are as dastardly as humankind's original perfidy. Do not misunderstand me: I love Nonno, in spite of his awfulnesses. I wish I could tell him and Kalaman too that my lifelong ill will toward Sholoongo has less to do with the document she stole, more with an earlier incident I had better not divulge at this instant.

If Nonno were here in my pickup truck and if he were to ask me to divulge this, my secret, I would offer him a folktale of an oriental quality for his troubles.

A hawk attacks a baby chick. The chick's mother hen defends with all her ferocious might. The hawk returns several more times. The old hen goes almost insane defending her chick, on one occasion encountering the assailant halfway, going for his eyes. Eventually, mother hen pokes the hawk in the eye, and he almost drops from the sky, the running blood half blinding him. But the hawk comes down in further ferocious swoops, more than ever determined to snatch away the baby chick — and maybe not spare the mother hen from harm either. A most savage confrontation takes place. The entire residents of the village come out to watch, the villagers taking sides, one section rooting for the fowl, the other applauding the hawk. Ultimately the mother hen wins. The hawk takes off and the heavens pour with the blood drops of vengeance.

I told him this tale just one week after I first met him. I remembered feeling intimidated, as he probed into my background during that encounter with double-pronged questions. To stonewall him, I stepped on the head of a baby snake. I was the hen, he the hawk in the tale, a mother defending her baby with all her maternal might.

He liked to have the last word, Nonno, as though he were able to have it even after death. To counter my tale, he told me one which takes place in a very distant land, where there is one of nature's marvels, in the shape of a cock with a comb the size of Kilimanjaro and a tail several meters long. (I've since learnt that this extraordinary cock does exist and in Japanese is called Shinotawaro.) The long-tailed cock arrives on the scene at the very instant when the fowl is about to surrender to the assailing hawk. The villagers make way for the newly arrived marvel, full of bewilderment and awe. Such are the powers associated with this huge and handsome cock, it takes him only an instant to trap the hawk with a mere twine of his many-stranded wondrous tail.

Does the Shinotawaro stand for Nonno? Most likely.

When I first met him, my father-in-law used to come into my dreams hardly invited. In the dreams, the poor arrived in hordes to be fed, the naked to be clothed, the sick to be healed, the limbless to have their missing organs restored. He was a miracle worker, in my visions. He had a hollow-ended voice, of the echoey kind. You thought that he was repeating every sound at least twice, for emphasis. Why did I not talk of those dreams to Yaqut? I hadn't the courage. I was afraid of my dreams being misconstrued, worried that they might be taken out of context and given a sexual meaning. If people knew I had Supplementaries, they might wonder if I wanted Nonno to join his son and grandson to take my Multiples in their lips. It could be the visitations were more mine than his, and that I worked him into my nocturnal visions. Aren't women, when raped, accused of cock-teasing?

Sure, he inspires a mix of adoration and awe in me, because of his size and his voice, both massive, with overflowing qualities like a silk robe. ("Thanks to the divine!" Kathy confided in me once, woman to woman. "I wouldn't dare ask you how much of Yaqut there is, quantitywise. But my goodness, Nonno is immense!")

Nonno was at one and the same time physically distant and near, placing himself out of your reach and then coming in upon you with the swiftness of a hawk in a furious descent. There was scarcely any part of my body that he hadn't touched or teased in one way or another. More recently I have spoken with Yaqut about Nonno and how his presence affects me: how I imagine the old man in my bed, and how my whole body breaks out in goose bumps suddenly sprouting as do tropical grasses after the heavy seasonal rains. Yaqut said he sensed it all along.

Apart from Sholoongo and the scorpion-fingered Gacme-xume, Nonno is the one person wielding unhealthy powers over me, powers likely to break my will in half. I compare his powers to the screws a blackmailer drills further and further into a victim's weak spot of flesh until the victim gives. I have a visceral distrust of their motives, a mistrust tucked away in the unreachable niches of the water in my blood. I am a mother hen defending her baby chick with all her ferocious might against the overpowering aggressiveness of a hawk, with blood for eyes. Mistakes abound, and the weaker you are, the more your mistakes, many imposed on you. Trust me, the mighty do not err in the same squeamish manner you and I do.

How much did I err dealing with Kalaman? For him the world was a keyhole, small, hard to get to and requiring him to go on his knees. Spying on us, Kalaman would risk being discovered. He hung about us, in wait of hearing things to tell Nonno. Later, he stayed up late into the night, eavesdropping on us or seeing us at *it*. "Give me," he would plead. "Gimme, gimme?" From the day he crept in on us making love and first mouthed the loathsome "gimme" plea until he was eight, I heard him relentlessly ask that we "give him" a sibling. Gimme a brother, gimme a sister! "We are content with you, we are satisfied and want no more," I would say. "We want no other baby, really, we do not wish to share our affection for you with another child or adult." But Kalaman would say he didn't mind sharing, that there was plenty of love to go around, with Nonno being near, within half an hour's bus ride.

"We will," one of us would say, promises made to a child who we hoped would forget it the following morning. A week would pass, at times months, and our son wouldn't speak of this undelivered pledge. Maybe he thought we were busy making the brother or sister out of the overflow of our respective hormones, or maybe he thought Yaqut would carve it out of his wood or marble pieces, or perhaps I might exchange a baby for one of my Supplementaries. Kalaman repeated his pleas when we celebrated his own birthday, or when a child was born in the area, to a neighbor, or if one of Nonno's farmhands was blessed with a baby.

"Where's the baby?" Kalaman would scream, touching my belly, pulling at my dwarf breasts. "Where have you hidden it? Tell it to come out."

We didn't know what to tell him, whether to admit that we had tried our best but failed. We promised to try again, even though we knew there was no chance of my having another baby. Kalaman loved making vows, he liked making pledges. With the tip of his forefinger to yours, a small incision of blood dotting it, he would make you touch blood to blood, as if sealing a pact of loyalty.

Now and then he abandoned himself to the irritable impression that we didn't love him enough. Otherwise, where was his younger sibling? Or, why were you less gregarious? Why didn't we come naked into the river with him, like Nonno and Fidow? What were we hiding from him? Why did we hardly tell him anything, how babies are made? Why did we never show our real selves to him, the way Nonno did?

Meanwhile we consulted gynecologists and medicine men, of the traditional and modern persuasion. The concoctions reduced my viscera to a rumble of noises loud as the heavens' violent throes of rainless thunder. These herbal mixtures upset my metabolism, my period becoming irregular. May the barren devil be confounded, for I was! I was pregnant. I was not. "Will you make up your mind?" Yaqut pleaded. It wasn't me. It was my body, as if it wanted to have a baby but also didn't want one.

We sought Nonno's opinion. He said, "Be honest with Kalaman."

"But we're not hiding anything from him. We've tried and tried and tried and haven't succeeded. We're not being dishonest."

"Tell him everything," he said. "Tell him what is what!"

I felt we were being unfairly accused of committing a crime. Not-telling and hiding were different aspects of the same thing, in a sense. But should we put down our not giving Kalaman a sibling to not telling? Were we hiding something from him, or were we simply unwilling to oblige the young boy's demands?

We took Kalaman into our confidence, and told him.

He said, "Then how did you make me?"

A parental prerogative mandated against telling him more. We resorted to an equally corrupt method: bribing him with chocolate and other indulgences. We bought his peace on a provisional basis. We paid a lot for a thorny pause among the padded silences of the haystacks. Bless the poor sod in the Somali folktale who, in a room he has darkened for that very purpose, raises his forefinger, only to learn once he emerges into the light of day that everybody has knowledge of what he's been up to, the fool! Curse the noon Sholoongo arrived at Arbaco's bidding, hugging an empty jar to her well-developed breasts (I couldn't believe she was only fourteen), asking, "Could you spare a spoonful of honey?" I did. I wish I hadn't.

Arbaco had earlier that morning, and unfairly, charged me with marrying into a family that sang psalms of praise to secrecy. Nonno and Yaqut, it is true, celebrated reticence with as much regard as a deity. It was as if they were raising monuments of worship to one's sense of discretion. Curse Arbaco who fell victim to one of Kalaman's daredevilries — but more about that another time.

Arbaco knew a lot about me, more than I cared to share with anyone else. She knew about Gacme-xume's blackmailing powers over me, why my blood relations kept their distance from me. But she knows nothing about two singularly significant secrets about me and Yaqut. Anyway we fell out, she and I, because she lacked the stamina to contain the ebb and flow of life's trust and secrets. Kalaman described her as a holed sieve, in at one end and out the other. He was wrong. I say this from the experience of knowing her almost all my life. For she never divulged the one confidence I had entrusted her with. Yet it was Arbaco who brought damnations into my life, who introduced me to Sholoongo, Timir, and their father.

Curse Sholoongo!

Whom Kalaman fed, and who in turn had been finger-fed on a concentrate of her monthlies, thimblefuls of the accursed stuff.

Curse her and the devil's day when she was conceived! Curse her and her diabolical intentions, curse her because she boasted that she could make him a younger brother if and when she put her mind to it, and nearly did: Sholoongo who filled his head with insane thoughts but emptied his pockets of everything he had, eating his potfuls of honey. It's no longer a guarded secret that she came very close to keeping her pledge to Kalaman by offering him a sibling. She became pregnant with Yaqut's child. Then she aborted it, with no help from me.

Curse her!

Curse her and her demonic vows! Curse the devil tempting the weak! Curse her too for making contact with Gacme-xume and for colluding with him, that evil blackmailer!

I didn't take notice of her physical presence at first, only of an undecided odor, a medley of smells, layers of scents which she wore to create an extraordinary effect. The wind in the apartment was straggly with a scatter of aromas, strong fragrances pointing to a most disharmonious state of mind, smells as distinct as mountain air, as aristocratic as sandalwood, or as specific in their intensity as Arabian skin oils. The different perfumes insinuated themselves into my brain, and interfered with my own thinking. My self-confidence may not have been as robust as I might have liked, but I felt strongly about Sholoongo.

I had a firearm in my handbag. My mood was that of a belligerent warrior, prepared to murder. The firearm was got for me by a distant cousin in the police force, who had been of use to me before, when I wanted Sholoongo's fingerprints taken. It was he who gave me a quick run-through of how a firearm functioned. With no bullets in, I pulled the trigger, bang-bang and all was fine, the ratel was as good as rotten dead! Carrying a firearm when you are not used to it weighs heavily on your conscience. And hiding it in my handbag amid the innocuous paraphernalia did not ease my worry. I brought it to Kalaman's

apartment on a just-in-case basis. Use it if threatened, or show it to
Sholoongo the way they did in gangster films. As a mother I needed to
defend my young, first with cunning, and only ultimately with my life.
The water was getting muddier. Because Gacme-xume was resurfacing
as if he too were driftwood. For how long were we guaranteed peace?

I hadn't rung the bell when the door was flung open. Had she been
expecting me? My heart missed a beat or two, and I recalled the police
officer cousin saying that firearms shoot quickly and kill those who are
of a cowardly nature! I stood there asking myself, was I brave or mad
enough to use a firearm? The door was soft on its hinges and creaked.
Was I trigger-unhappy?

Sholoongo stood aside to let me in, short as a witch is tall, a wizard
on stilts. She moved away with unease and I listened for sounds emanating from inside of me, inner whispers. I went in and pushed the
door shut, then followed her down the narrow corridor, wishing my
son would emerge out of one of the rooms, wrapped in a towel or a
robe; it would have delighted me more if Talaado had been there. But
I knew where my son was and that Talaado wouldn't be there either.
So where was the mother hen in me, chicken that I was!

"Where's Kalaman?" I asked.

"You know he isn't here, so why ask?" she said.

We were in the kitchen, the dining table separating us. Embarrassed, I looked away. I wanted to make sure I did not look nervous. I
was mother to the young man in danger. I recalled how I had thrown
out of Kalaman's life that arrogant fool of a Kenyan woman, who had
nothing good to say about Somalis, even though she claimed to be in
love with my son. I had told him he could not bring into our lives a
woman who had no respect for his people.

"Why must you always lie?" I went on the attack. It was my intention to fault her, blame her, somehow humiliate her before finally
shooting her. I tried my best not to flounder in the mire of my own
worries. There was no turning back. The weapon had been seen in my
handbag by more than one person, and it had better be used. Murder?
Suicide? Or were there other choices? If so, what were they? Many
more wicked thoughts than I care to put into words crossed my mind.
To weather the ordeals of the moment I convinced myself that self-
control never harmed anyone's viscera.

"I wish you'd grow up," she said. She sat down, full of dare.

I put my hand in my bag, as if touching base with the firearm. But I didn't pull it out, thinking that her death would be quicker if I surprised her, one moment alive, the second moment *finito*, dead! I had failed to act when it would've been more effective to shoot her at the entrance. Then I could've pretended that I had thought her a burglar. Still, there were many others we could blame her death on, the militias, for instance.

When I asked her the pedestrian question, "Why was the door locked?" I knew I was not going to pull the trigger for quite some time. I had hoped by provoking her to burrow open a tunnel in my head and go straight to the core of my memory's store — Sholoongo whom I associated in my mind with a posy-ring wrapped in a lick of her menstrual blood — and then shoot, but no! Here lay the origin, the source of my ominous fear, Sholoogo taking Kalaman into her feminine trust of blood. I couldn't bear the thought, couldn't speak of these matters straight to her face. How could I? So I charged her with minor crimes, with having stolen things precious to me. Instead of accusing her of dispossessing me of my son's affection, I accused her of thieving, of stealing my marriage certificate, which, as Kalaman had pointed out, I had no need of.

We circled around each other for some time. We ended up in the apartment's long corridor, within arm's reach of each other, my hand tucked in my bag in uninterrupted contact with the firearm. I thought, it is one thing killing a baby snake by smashing its head in, to stonewall a strong-willed Nonno, it is something else altogether pulling a trigger and murdering a human, in cold blood. Moreover she hadn't as yet incriminated herself or given me reason to humiliate her first before shooting her.

It was obvious I hadn't worked on my killer's instinct. Yaqut had become inured, maybe because he dealt in death, carving headstones, inscribing funeral messages of affection on marble. I was sure too that Nonno and Kalaman would be better at it, Kalaman who had experienced death in the company of Fidow, a professional killer. Could I hire one? Pay. Sit back and relax.

"Where were you the night before last?" I said.

She turned her back on me and walked away.

"I'm talking to you," I said, injecting a dose of menace into the artery of my voice. She paused, looked over her shoulder as if she were daring me to do something rash, and then continued walking. She turned left into the guest room, out of which she had emerged earlier, and then into the kitchen, where she sat down, her posture defiant. I stared at her, intuiting the relevant symbols and signs: we were two women conscious of our hostility for each other.

"Not in your son's bed."

"How could you tell such a lie?" I said. "You spent the night in my son's bed, the one he uses whenever he stays overnight at Nonno's place."

"He wasn't in it," she said.

"But why lie?"

"I spent a night in his room when he wasn't there," she said. "What's the big deal?"

"Where were you when Fidow was trampled by the elephant?"

"Don't be ridiculous," she said.

"Did you alter your nature into that of an elephant?"

"This is mindless madness!" she said.

"Where were you the night before then?"

Sholoongo's momentary rage separated itself from the tone of her voice, in which she had buried it. I wondered how she managed to make her anger stand apart from the rest of her. There was something self-sustaining about her disparate identities, her fragmented selves, breakaway miniselves in a federal togetherness. She was in control of her rages, I was not.

"And where's the document you stole?"

I began to wonder if she would kill me as I spoke, not I her. Lifeless, her eyes put me in mind of the seared knuckle of Gacme-xume's mutilated finger, hard as a tortoise's carapace. She didn't speak.

I said, "Years ago, I had your fingerprints taken. This time I will take your life."

She said, "You had me fingerprinted once and got away with it. Now you've come back with more heinous accusations. I am not going to take your nonsense anymore." Her voice went up and down in puffs, like the steam in a busy restaurant's kitchen, clouds of heat pursued into extinction by a parenthesis of vapor, and the active redness of gaseous flames whose tongues lick the rears of saucepans, casseroles, and kettles. "Imagine accusing me of bewitching Kalaman, or of making you grow two futilely dangling dwarf breasts!"

I shouted at the top of my lungs, "You are a ruthless, gutless bitch!" I was shaking all over, clutching my handbag closer to me, afraid perhaps that she might take the firearm from me, afraid that she might kill me.

"This is mindless madness!" she said again.

"And you are the cause of it," I said.

She reached for the door handle of the fridge, which she opened. Her feet held apart, she turned around. "Please let us be civil with each other," she said. "For once."

"You stay out of our lives," I said.

"Have you had lunch?" she asked.

I knew that Lambar hadn't been here for a couple of days, and was certain I wouldn't touch anything Sholoongo had cooked. I pointed at a yogurt cup in the still open fridge. We must have both been aware of the role that food-sharing played in people's relationships, as a measure of their mutual trust. She had a penchant for wild honey, my son for her blood, Nonno for tamarind juice, Yaqut for my Essentials, I for his. She would be having honey with tea in all probability, not tea with honey! "What are you having?"

The afternoon sun reflected in her malevolent smile. She said, "I'm tucking into a take-out Chinese meal, which you are most welcome to share. You don't have to fear, I won't serve you with foods I've *interfered* with."

It was an odd twist of fate, I remarked, that she was offering me food and drink in my son's place. The startled expression on her face hinted at her discomfort. She said, "Your son is his own man. Please remember that."

"I meant to say that you eat the food of those in whom you have trust," I said. I took a spoonful of the yogurt and asked, "Why are you here, in Kalaman's apartment?"

I was impressed that not a single twitch showed anywhere on her features.

She said, "I've asked Kalaman to give me a child."

"Why should he?"

She had an indeterminate expression between a grin and a

grimace, her diaphragm expanding with a portentous sigh of relief. She said, "Being his own man, I doubt that at his age he needs to seek his mother's approval."

"What will become of the baby if you bear one?" I asked.

Momentarily I was subject to fevers of demonic anger. I wished I could call back my murderous impulses from other times, surrender my mind to a temporary insanity, in order to kill.

"Maybe you and I have nothing to talk about," Sholoongo was saying. "It's Kalaman you should be speaking to if you must talk to someone about the baby, not me." After a pause, a smile broke on her cheeks, kettle-plain as the white of an egg.

Memories returned to me presently: of Nonno behaving as though he knew the contents of the document which young Sholoongo had stolen. He had made oblique references to it in our exchanges. I sat still and silent, wondering what to do to this evil woman or what to say to her. I felt that, for a while at least, no repartee would render my tongue active. I rose to my feet, a purblind woman sad to behold, my knees struggling to support the weight of my worries. A blank moment, followed by a fall. Who? Did I weaken at the knees? I woke to find Sholoongo towering over me, my upper arm in the grip of her right hand. She was helping me to sit, and had a glass of water pressed to my lips. It took me quite a while to regain my equilibrium and the use of my tongue. When I did, I said, "Why should he give you a baby?"

"Because," she responded, "years and years ago I made a promise that I would give him a sibling. I kept my end of the bargain, but it wasn't to be, because I miscarried. A pledge once made is as binding as an oath. I want to keep my word to Kalaman, cost what it might."

Again I lost touch with myself. Then an ugly memory raised its head like the proverbial forefinger in the folktale about the nature of secrets, a sad memory pointed at the core of my hurt. Sorrow overwhelmed me with a doomsday rancor. I remembered a quote from Bukhaari who said that on the Day of Resurrection lead would be poured into the ears of those who betrayed the secrets entrusted to them. My body, alas, was no longer in communication with my mind! Two hours later I woke up in Kalaman's bed alone, no Sholoongo in the apartment.

PART TWO

Kalaman felt oddly relieved, after throwing up all he had eaten.

It was as if he were vomiting not food but his nervous unease. He was under a most severe strain. He complained of a nerve-racking pain, half his head striking cymbals together, the other beating a precursory drumming with no rhythm or rationale. Asked what he thought was causing all this ache, he pointed to the moment when the feeling of nausea overcame him. He explained that he had fought the nausea even earlier, during his talk with his mother, managing to keep it at bay for at least an hour. It proved harder to fight it off once his mother had left. So he lay in bed, halfheartedly reminiscing.

The way Nonno saw it, Kalaman's undealt-with troubles began the instant he introduced a decisive element of blame-the-other into his guilt-ridden sorrow. "There are moments in a person's or a nation's life," the old man said, "when collapses can be avoided, even if at first they seem inevitable. The moments which matter come and, quite often, leave without one realizing. The climactic moments break on one rather in the manner of a hurricane with a mad eye, here now, gone the same instant, but with so much rubble and ruin left in its wake. And so very many memories: memories of hurt, of disappointment, of what-might-have-beens." Kalaman had a world of chances to put a stop to his mother's ruinous behavior; he had a universe of opportunities to speak to her before the hurricane struck, to deal a severing blow to the umbilicus and the placenta joining him to the things in his makeup which connected him to other persons. Something of a debilitated quality takes over the life of a Kalaman, who piques himself on his uniqueness, when he discovers that there is nothing special about his beginnings. As a result of this discovery, Kalaman did lose the ability to ride out his mother's stormy unreasonableness, or to make sense of Nonno's riddle-informed evasions.

Likewise, his mother could have intervened earlier and taken a crucial step in Kalaman's involvement with Sholoongo, or anyone else for that matter, in the years when the boy's life was in its early formation, being put together, as it were, out of the contributions his friends and family made to his general growth. Equally his father could have taken a keener interest yesterday in what went into the making up of today's Kalaman.

He was in a garrulous mood, Nonno was, he was expansive. He said, "Let's push aside Kalaman's doings and predicaments for a moment, and let's for a change talk about the entire country, and its impending collapse into blood-letting anarchy. And let's agree for what it is worth that our nation's predicament is our own predicament too, collectively and individually, each of us an accomplice in its ruin. Can anything be done to stop the country from fragmenting into family fiefdoms? I doubt that this is feasible at this stage. Because what is happening to the collective identity of the nation and in the individual lives of its people is not tiddlywinks, a game played with pieces of plastic made to jump into a container. What is happening is a life-and-death matter. The games are becoming more deadly on a daily basis. The bullets are out, the guns have been oiled, power at the center and power at the peripheries are both up for grabs, on battlefields which different claimants are prepared to fight on, and to win."

Was Nonno of the view that whoever wins power in his own family's fiefdom on the periphery is likely to take power at the center too?

"One doesn't preclude the other."

"And the dictator?"

"The dictator otherwise nicknamed 'the mayor of Mogadiscio' in reference to his political power base, which is confined to the metropolis?" he said. "He is no longer of relevance to the final outcome. The mad hurricane has gathered its momentum, and nothing short of a miracle can prevent the greatest damage from being unleashed. As for the tyrant himself? He will be swept aside by the ferocity of the hurricane, will bear on his person the brunt of the collective rage. You see,

I've never seen him as his own man, only as some cold-war automaton, guided by a remote control mechanism. Just before the Ogaden debacle, he changed masters, without adjusting himself to his new circumstances, a defeated man at the helm of a people desperate for a statesman. Siyad Barre might have prevented a worsening of the crisis if he had resigned then. He was a tragic figure, a victim of his own small-mindedness."

Kalaman could have brought an end to this rigmarole sooner too, if he had been true to his own instincts, honest to Talaado and his mother, or if he had been forthrightly frank with Sholoongo herself: the Somali collectivity could have reversed the coming decline. He had no right to blame his parents or Nonno or others for his own failures. Nor had he the right to blame Sholoongo, a classical *other*. You could apply the same yardstick against which you could assess the contributions others had made to the *construction* of the collapse, brick by destructive brick. Give people a chance to speak their pieces, and many will display their personal and collective hurts: Kalaman, his parents, Nonno, Fidow, the environment, the nonvocal animals, they all see themselves as ill used by the dictatorship. Press them further into the corner, ask them for their contribution to the struggle against one-man tyranny, and they fall silent, many unable to deny being accomplices in the ruin. Quick in self-defense, they blame the former colonialists, and they blame both the Soviet Union and the United States for bankrolling the cold warriors, gamers in weapons of mass destruction. Our challenge is to locate the metaphor for the collapse of the collective, following that of the individual.

Nonno was saying, "There is no further bottom to reach, when it comes to the self-esteem of many a peace-lover, a self-esteem that has gone as far down as a lintel posing as a mudsill. There is a martyr I mourn. If he had survived, Ismael Ali Giumaleh might have pulled us away from the precipice of self-savagery. We all participated in his funeral in our hundreds of thousands, many of us burying him in our hearts, out of love for what the man wanted to do. He worked so hard to prevent the clannish lot from moving their self-serving stones in order to uncover an exclusive life for their own, to the detriment of all others. The nation had invested all its hopes in Giumaleh, a man able not only to put together a viable opposition to the tyranny of the ruling autocracy, but to provide an alternative to the misguided politics of associating each militia grouping with a clan."

Kalaman remembered meeting him once, and liking him.

Nonno went on, "Displaying a hurt is tantamount to goalpost-shifting. Scorpions have their safe hiding places, so does a hurt. So do lies. Termites too have their way of hiding out in sandhills built with their own saliva, after they have destroyed one's timber construct. Mark my words, many of the self-serving men leading the armed militias are opportunists, former members of the tyrant's coterie, fellow conspirators of his or, worse still, corrupt yes-men, and potentially future tyrants. We can't all blame *the* one man, for we too are sharers in the censure."

There was nothing handsome about Kalaman today. The pain all over him and spreading made sure of that. His lips drooping, his mouth drooling, he didn't look intelligent either. Nor did he appear well heeled, or as charming as he used to be, a man, like Nonno, able to reach into areas of people's hearts, to affect them in a positive manner. He used to be of a malleable appearance, of the kind people fell in love with, assuming they could mold him into a friend to their liking. Qalin once said that he warmed her blood to the point where she felt cooled when he penetrated the center of her openings, deep, deep down.

Now Kalaman had the shivers. An instant later he was so hot the sheet covering him seemed to curl up at the edges, like a piece of paper close to a tongue of flame. His reflection in the mirror startled him. He had difficulty acknowledging his own face. So much change in such a short time, and such a loss of weight. Could a day's stubble be that preponderous? He felt alien to himself when he looked in the mirror, as though he were face-to-face with his nightmares, of which he had so far had several.

In one of them, Kalaman had come in on his mother chewing away at the soft ends of a human skull. Disturbed, he asked her whom the skull had belonged to, when alive. His mother explained that it once belonged in the head of a person from an "enemy clan." Would he like a bite of it? In another nightmare, he was a newt in the vast belly of a whale, at whose intestine it pulled in an effort to get out. The whale was branded with the identity of his mother's clan on one flank, on the other his father's. He was a prisoner in the whale's all-inclusiveness, a newt-man with no recognizable identity. His wish reclaim his deracinated, not-clan-based identity was denied. He was given the choice of dying at the hands of a nonmember of his mother's clan or his father's, or to roam in the belly of the whale as a newt. He chose to be a newt, preferring this to allying himself with the murderers.

It had been night. They had been at sea for a few days, fleeing from civil savagery. He saw his dearest friends, and they showed up decked in their clan identities. He was reminded of the fact that Nonno had once refused to have the name of his clan in his identity card, as was the custom in the Italian colony. He spent a while in detention, accused by the Italians of being an anarchist. Later he was released and issued a card with the word "British" marked in it, because he had come from the protectorate to the north, ruled at the time by Britain. Kalaman asked him, why did he prefer being "British" to having his clan identity? "Because 'British' is a political notion, alluding to the state, the Crown, et cetera," explained Nonno, "whereas being English, Welsh, Irish, or Scottish points to one's tribal provenance. One's 'Somaliness,' as opposed to being identified as belonging to a given clan, defines a political entity. The clan is nonpolitical, based as it is on one's primordial blood identity."

Intimate friends betraying one another on account of narcissistic differences, a man raping his sister-in-law and emptying her of her fetus just because the woman belonged to a different bloodline from his. Someone had earlier beaten a drum, a mob walking behind him, as they marched through the thoroughfares of the metropolis. They were chanting a nursery rhyme, invoking the sentiments of hatred against the clans from elsewhere.

He would rather he died a newt, and from suffocation, than be killed by a friend with an ancestral memory different from his own.

Kalaman woke up at last. And Nonno came to comfort him.

He went out for a jog.

He ran in what had been the woods of his childhood, sadly remarking the sandy dryness of the earth. The Shabelle River wore a jaw-fallen expression, like a boy deprived of the joy of play. He wished the madmen fighting over contending memories would realize how wars were linked to famines, how one came as a result of the other. Running back, he was a great deal sadder because, like a falling star bursting in utter brightness and then vanishing in a puff, he saw his mother holding a firearm to Sholoongo's head. The women were vicious to each other, his mother calling Sholoongo some terrible names just because she was born in the Ogaden. Sholoongo, in self-defense, threatened to blot Damac's name out of the screen of Kalaman's consciousness, "for I will kill you with my bare hands, and drink up your blood, out of spite." Finally he conjured up images of horror, a man whom he had never set eyes on, Gacme-xume.

He asked himself, had his mother killed Sholoongo?

Back from his bout of running, Kalaman came in on Nonno sitting by himself in the living room, hardly breathing and not at all moving. The old man might have been breaking wind, or ridding his body of a belch. Equally, he might have choked on a hiccup.

The ashtray within Nonno's reach was filled to bursting with cigarette-ends. However, Kalaman's attention dwelt longest on a figure sculptured in mysterious casualness out of cigarette ashes, a figure effigylike in its stature and yet so real, with hands folded across its chest, and seated majestically. Coming to, Nonno acknowledged Kalaman's presence by nodding his head. But he bent backwards, in the attitude of not wanting to breathe lest this upset the wholeness of the figure in ashes, the indulgent portrait of years of cigarette smoking.

Nonno said, "I've given up smoking."

"What are you planning to take up in place of smoking?"

Kalaman now studied the ash figure. It might have been a monument constructed as the old man's tribute to his years of nicotine intake, as part of his thank-you.

"Maybe I'll take up praying!"

Kalaman unlaced his running shoes. "Then you won't answer to Ma-tukade, your old nickname, as it will be invalidated by your giving up the habit?"

"Perhaps it's a way of acquiring a new identity," Nonno said with a mischievous grin giving a shine to his eyes.

"If you pray as obsessively as you smoked, yes!"

Nonno looked at the book which had lain open before him, as if waiting for something out of the ordinary to occur. Kalaman, for his part, massaged his toes, and wrinkled his nose at the odor associated with athletes' feet.

"How are you feeling?" Nonno asked, his furtive glance resting on the ashy image. He might have been speculating whether the wind would disfigure it, and how soon. Or he might have lost an item of talismanic worth till then buried in the ashes. The breeze made dents in the figure's top half, ruining it. The old man looked heartbroken, an artist watching his creation being demolished.

Kalaman accorded the loss a couple of seconds' silence, a man mourning the death of an idea. He said, "I would like to indulge myself in a protracted brainstorming soliloquy. Please interrupt me if I go off on a tangent, or if I am lacking in deference."

Nonno saluted this preamble with the complement of a nod.

Kalaman said, "I feel weighed down with an alloy of physical and mental incongruities, of a peculiar blend too cumbersome to define. One moment I am well, another moment I am mourning the death of someone dear to me, and the one following it I am in very high spirits, a bridegroom waiting for the imminent arrival of his bride. I am a citizen of a world stood on its head, where elephants behave in unexpected ways, but for the good of us all. With their drone, bees interfere with my visions. Honeyguides lead me to the source of the sweet stuff. Manikins emerge out of a crocodile's second belly. I am (in a dream) in a companionable camaraderie with flying fishes and a vast eighty-year-old man with a toad's face: we're having a tête-à-tête, the ancient man and I. A community feeds on a crackle of locusts, the very insects which, a season earlier, had ravaged its crops. Pigeons play their part in my life. Monkeys have their place too. Blackhead plovers are welcome as well. I am forewarned of death wherever I turn. Your life history is a pointer to death. So is Sholoongo's. So is the sighting of a heap of elephant bones. My question: In whom did I rise, riverlike?"

Kalaman laced his fingers and then unlaced them. Nonno, not smoking and not restless, listened. Kalaman went on:

"Enough has been said about Sholoongo. Enough about my mother's contemptuous suspicion of her. Enough about my cul-de-sac name. Enough about hyperboles purporting that mothers matter more to a child than a father. There is a Somali proverb that says that mothers are a certainty. To paraphrase: if there is a parent of whom we tend to be certain, it is the mother. But we are in an epoch in which mother-as-certainty no longer holds true: babies are abandoned in garbage bins. I read in a local paper the other day about a casualty of uncertainty, a mother committing suicide because her Somali-born daughter, now an American citizen, had borne a test-tube child. Why did the mother take her own life? Is it because she couldn't bear living any longer in a world where the mother-as-certainty was questioned, undermined as it was by the secret-derived science of today?"

He paused, to wonder why Nonno was sitting in provocative closeness to the ashtray filled to bursting with cigarettes, even after the ashy figure had been ruined.

"You remember the reaction of the Islamic world to the first American and Soviet claims that they had landed on the moon?" said Kalaman. "This was deemed by Islamists to be the mother of madness. Are we speaking of a community's certainty shaken to its rock foundation, the essence of its collective survival? What of ascertaining paternity, of DNA, blood-to-blood? Science-derived secrets have delved into this uncertainty, helping to push the frontiers of certainty."

Kalaman again laced his fingers in front of him and then unlaced them. The shadows his laced fingers cast put Nonno in mind of a cat's cradle, now opening, now closing. The old man nodded his head encouragingly.

"The question of paternity," Kalaman continued, "is of a different order in Somali society. You might have thought that because of the uncertainty associated with paternity (it is part of the Somali, and therefore Muslim, burial rite to mention the mother's name of the interred, given its certainty, but not the father's name), Somali society would moderate its ways. The male parent in matters governing a person's life is paramount. The father's name is added to that of the newborn, the father matters when it comes to inheritance of wealth. You remember how you and my mother took exception to my obsession with matters of paternity, not because Sholoongo had inspired me to such a daredevilry but because, by declaring that I would be adding my mother's name to mine, I was in essence questioning a universally accepted certainty, that I was Yaqut's son. In retrospect, I can appreciate why you both considered this to be an affront to my mother's integrity as a woman, a dastardly offense meant to undermine her personal honor."

Absentmindedly Nonno picked up a packet of cigarettes and pulled one out, which he placed between his lips. He was about to light it when he narrowed his eyes just in time. Now he put aside the packet and the lighter, grinning. In an instant, his lips were atremble. Was he praying?

Kalaman said, "Why did Sholoongo steal a document which my mother *claims* was her marriage certificate? Marriage to whom? What was Sholoongo's gain? Were my mother's friend Arbaco and Gacmexume, the perpetrator of evil deeds, both in the know? Were they party to the scheme? Were you, Nonno, privy to this secret, this conspiracy?"

Contrary to what Kalaman had expected, Nonno looked relieved. He stared at the young man, marveling at the anxious flow of his words as they emerged to gain a life of their own. He might have been thinking that clearing a backlog of uncertainties was the best way for Kalaman to rid himself of his fevered imagination. Especially since he appeared to be in total control of the narrative flux.

Kalaman again. "We've so far dug up many things. We may keep digging them up ad infinitum, till all the world's ratels are comfortably housed, each with its own lair, secure in its safe abode, unpestered and unafraid. But will we continue wallowing in our mud, as if we were pigs, not humans? Part of me wants no further probing to be done, the other part wants to get to the bottom of this, to place every grain of sand under a microscope of moral scrutiny. What if we dig further into the belly of the earth, what if we exhume corpses interred, Fidow's, Madoobe's et al? What will we learn? And to what end?"

Nonno's lips moved, the mouth of a fish in nervous feeding.

"We've all lived lives and done things of which we are bound to be ashamed," Kalaman went on. "We've all doctored the tales we tell about ourselves, tales which, by virtue of how we tell them, we domesticate to our logic. We seldom own up, if truth-telling is not to our advantage. It wasn't easy to grow up in a household in which your parents fall silent the moment they hear you coming. Were they withholding secrets for the good of their own only son, or for their own self-honor and sanity and survival?"

Toward the end of the speech, his voice underwent a considerable change, intimations of weariness suffusing his delivery, suppressed yawns, long vowels becoming needlessly shorter, consonants less well articulated. He now spoke in non sequitur. He said:

"Food is a principal component in the strategy of seduction, a youth feeding his calf-love on victuals of lust and chocolates of desire. It is the reverse of Eve's apple-giving, more likely a man's version of what occurred. Here the man coerces the woman, tempting her into sin. In this narrative, eating is associated with seduction and with death too — by death I mean a cessation of one state, the assumption of another. Death in the matter of name-changing, a man altering his name every so often and assuming the personality of an alias other."

Here Kalaman's vowels thickened, his consonants sounded much harsher. He talked so slowly Nonno was not certain if parts of Kalaman did not shut themselves off, like a tape recorder with battery problems. "I am . . ." he managed to say. He trailed off, his eyes closing as if from exhaustion. When they reopened, a migraine had gained entry into his distraught nerves via his sight. He collapsed. He was a child with whom sleep has caught up in the middle of talking.

Kalaman was astraddle the ambiguous divide between waking and sleep. Even so, Nonno's voice reached him, wavelets of sound from deep down an echoey hollowness.

The voice was saying, "You may treat this as an interim report on the part of your Nonno. Far be it from me to sit in judgment on an epoch, but I could be failing in my duty as an elder if I lied, conscious as I also am of the implications of my undertaking, which is formidable. There are souvenirs of uncertainty, memorative of the innocent times when one's logic-construct tended to fall apart at the recall of a boy doing all it took to express himself, a boy-child being led by a girl with whom he was infatuated further into questionable behavior. Now if the boy-child had emulated another of his gender, his mother might have accepted it, shrugging it off as part of a male child's growing up. She might have taken it all in with the starches of a *c'est la vie,* salted it, spiced it, sizzled it as brown as she prefers her onions and garlic done, and finally eaten a plateful of remorse, clean disregarding the consequences. She might have fallen back on the age-old wisdom that boy-children outgrow their years and their mentors. The boy-child's mother was upset not only because she didn't want her male child to do things at a female's bidding but because she didn't approve of a girl at puberty imposing her perverted feminine will on a boy four years her junior. The mother would argue that another male partner might have set impossible hurdles in the department of daredevilries, but he would most likely not have fed his playmate on a woman's monthlies. I doubt if the boy-child's mother realized that she was unfairly degrading her own sex by making such disparaging remarks about another of her gender, while exonerating her culpable son of blame. But that's altogether a different matter, with which we won't concern ourselves at present."

Kalaman, now in a time warp, thought about the civil war in Liberia. His memory revisited the videotaped scenes in which Samuel Doe, then president of that tragic country, was hacked to death in front of the cameras for the entire world to watch. The memories were as fresh as sores.

He gave a startle as if being awoken from sleep. He sat up, asking in a voice imbued with distrust, "Where am I?"

"An instant back you were in the land of memory," Nonno said. "An instant ago, you were supine, a man exorcising himself of guilt. But where are you now, or who are you? I am not certain where you are anymore, whether you are in the ebb tide or in the flow, whether you are a mere float or a flux of your fantasies, daydreaming."

He placed his hand gently first on Kalaman's head, then on the shoulder nearer him, the former to check if he had fever, the second touch to offer sympathy, assurances.

Kalaman went on, "Where's my mother, in all this?"

"Maybe she is just in another condition, as volatile as the tragic unfolding of the Somali people's collective descent into hell," said Nonno. "A land where reason does not reign, a condition of rage, an overwhelming condition of wrath."

"But it seems Sholoongo has vanished totally from my memory?"

"This proves my point, in fact."

"What's your point?"

"That Sholoongo is a condition too, a state of turbulence!"

"But why has she disappeared from my memory totally?"

"Maybe she has been supplanted by the tragic figures taking the national stage," Nonno said, "in which case she is relegated to a secondary position in the scheme of matters."

"Poor Somalia!"

"Absent in her presence, present in her absence," Nonno said, "Sholoongo assumes the different personae an actress assumes, while representing the full spectrum of human and animal possibilities. Not to worry. She is there, in *others!* As such she will live forever, because she will be remembered by others, for whatever motive."

A pinch of sadness touched Kalaman's face as he reviewed the past couple of hours in a flash. He drew comfort from lying snug in the spaciousness of Nonno's voice, a child warm in the solace-offering comfort of a thumb in its mouth.

"A flimsy fig leaf covers our person," Nonno was saying. "For a combination of climatic and cultural reasons we Africans lay ourselves open to accusations that we delight in the exposure of our bodies. I've heard it said that the Arabs, because they tend to be more jealous of their womenfolk, think that Somali females are underdressed, with their breasts and belly buttons showing, the contours of their womanness as prominent as a full moon. Our men swim naked in our rivers, the women at times go into the water fully dressed, in the very clothes in which they stand. Alone with each other, the women strip down, their breasts shiny like oil on the surface of water reflected in the moon's brightness."

The ebb and flow of Nonno's voice made Kalaman recall that he had been a newt, stuck inside a whale of cosmic dimensions. Nonno's voice again, but no burning cigarettes. "Sholoongo has a precipitate untameability about her. I also doubt that I've ever met a mouth as insatiable as hers, wanting to be filled with *something*."

Kalaman asked, "Her mouth? What about her mouth?"

Nonno surrendered himself to the rhythm of his own tale as he told it. "I recall the morning she broke through my defenses when, with a startling suddenness, she bounced out of the gray to take a good grip of *me*. I acted most decisively and, thank goodness, I brought the shameful charade to a stop."

Kalaman, as if in a state of delirium, was wondering what his blood relationship would have been to Sholoongo's children if she had had one each with Nonno and Yaqut, and one his own? Curse the blood that binds!

"I thought of Sholoongo as a calamitous condition, not as a person," continued Nonno, his voice gradually losing its tenebrous quality. "Think of her as a condition, then it will become clear how those exposed to the Sholoongo condition fall into two categories: a category of vulnerables, and a second category of those who are immune to the virus."

In his mind's eye, Kalaman was seeing a woman bent in a stoop, head in the water, mouth bulgy with the immensity of what was inside it, the man a mountain forever rising. Kalaman saw a substantial body of sperm, and baby fishes playfully gobbling it up, not a drop afloat.

Sandpaper rough, the voice said, "Would you like me to get you anything?"

Kalaman shook his head no.

"I take the view," Nonno said, "that women discharge their moral and civic responsibilities with a much healthier attitude than us men, and that women are more adept at keeping secrets than we men. A boy of Sholoongo's age might have spoken boastfully to all and sundry about his sexual exploits, if he had been party to as many adventures as she. At fourteen, because she was a woman, Sholoongo compared favorably with a man of forty when it came to preserving the integrity of her secrets."

A baby snake swish-swashing through wet grass: Damac?

"I should like to put forth one heretical notion," Nonno said.

"That what sets humans apart from other animals is not the generic ability to speak, or that we are capable of thinking in complicated mathematical equations, no. It is in the human's obedience to a set of tenets governing an overall behavior, taboo tenets that are observed, because they affect the community's life at large. I cannot imagine a world without taboos, a culture without its notion of right and wrong. Honors are maintained, pledges kept, gods worshipped. It is anathema to imagine a world in which there are no secrets. Secrets have a life energy, they keep us alive."

From an overnight stubble, Kalaman decided he was living!

"Perhaps you won't concur," Nonno's voice again, "but I believe that a balance is struck between what is permitted and what is not. This is how an ethos is established, how taboos are formulated. Thou shall not kill! This is my wife, therefore . . . ! This is my daughter-in-law, therefore . . . ! Your friend in preference to your blood! We reason, we construct a mechanism of self-restraints, of guides, we construct further constraints into our logic of being. Not to be misled by our primordial instincts, we formulate political platforms, we join parties, we vote. Compare these to the lattice in a wall, crossed laths overlooking an open space, the political merges with the personal, the good cancels out the bad. Since other animals haven't developed their sense of taboo insofar as we understand the notion, it follows that a bull may mate with his mother, a carrion bird feed on the flesh of its own offspring, and so on and so forth. It is only in exceptional cases that humans feed on other humans, to survive. Taboos cover a wide area. You are forbidden to eat certain foods. You are debarred from approaching places of worship without performing certain rites. When crowds, advancing the interests of a clan or fighting in the name of one, turn into a mob and, animal-like, kill and kill indiscriminately, then we are entering the area of taboo, of things not done under normal circumstances."

A one-eyed storm was gathered in Kalaman's head. He let go of Nonno's hand. Shifting in his bed, he guided his hand to a spot way up on his spine, and he touched pain.

"Fair is fair," Nonno was saying "Two highly apropos statements, two innocuous hyperboles, both attributed to you. The first is boiler-plate plain: *Blood is blood is blood!* The second hyperbole is a chorus of defiance: *Fathers matter not! Mothers matter a lot!* In my judgment, there is nothing untoward in either utterance, only why they were spoken, what prompted you to utter them in the first place. I shall take these one at a time."

Fidgeting, Kalaman's fingers felt more pain.

The voice reaching him drilled into him more nail-hard realities. "You cut your finger, you have a kind of blood. But that blood is different from the blood which defines a kinship. But a finger dipped in a woman's monthly elevates a waste to the status of a lust: that is taboo. To continue, but also to circumvent. Blood with a tissue of afterbirth covering it, is that blood divested of its inherent power? Fair is fair, blood is blood is blood, sperm is!"

Nonno's voice was like water seeping in. It found space in Kalaman's empty skull, in which it formed puddles. Now as Kalaman touched his forehead, he thought: My God, I'm leaking. And in the river flowing into Kalaman's head, a voice cast a gauntlet which was afloat with thoughts, thoughts as immense as the corpse of a hippo, buoying up other memories the years had buried under water.

More of Nonno's voice. "Suppose we delve into the matter of the document which Sholoongo stole? Suppose we find out her gain, why she stole it, where she put it? Suppose Arbaco and Gacme-xume are in secret conspiracy to blackmail your mother? As an animal with a high sense of taboo, will you be upset if you learn that you are somebody else's child, not Yaqut's? Will doubts shatter your certainties? What will become of your relationships with us, your kith and kin all your life? Will you kill me or your father if it turns out that your family is at war with ours, in the current struggle for political power?"

Kalaman heard a click in his head. He might have been listening to a tape recorder whose play button had switched itself off. His head filled with emptiness. He heard the wind whistling through his head, as if it were a skull empty of life.

Nonno decided Kalaman hadn't heard him right.

"I don't think I've got much longer to live," Nonno said, "especially now, after so much destruction. You might well ask, am I depriving myself of my daily nicotine intake because I am preparing for a type of death not very dissimilar to our country's? Will I explode in death? Will my death be peaceable or anarchic, full of unexpected twists like a turnstile's? You are my legatee, my grandson. It is fair that I die before you."

Kalaman dropped instantly into a deep well of reverie. He hid his head between his knees, and sat curled up. If I'm not Yaqut's biological child, whose son am I? If I am not Nonno's grandson, who is Nonno to me? What would become of his descriptive grandfatherly appellation, given to celebrate my birth?

He awoke hours later to the din of a dung beetle wanting to enter his right ear. He sat up in a startle. He now warmed to the one fragment of memory which had presented itself to him: a single link in the length of a chain joining the present to a past, the past to a future: blood to blood, blood to fairness, man to woman, and woman to man. Experiencing a sense of inner calm, he couldn't be bothered if the exchange between him and Nonno had taken place in the world of the living, a world of sperm-and-blood uncertainties. If the present was a predicament, the past a mystery, what of the future? No longer content with allegories, had Nonno told it how it was, and how things came to pass? What manner of tale was this? Slowly he found his way out of the fogginess of sleep and nightmares and uncertainties, and saw Nonno seated in his rocking chair. But who was the woman seated near him, the woman whose familiar scent was stirring his senses?

Talaado said, "Welcome back to the world of the living."

Kalaman and Talaado hugged awkwardly.

She sat on the edge of the bed, facing him. She bent, in his estimate, about a hundred and sixty degrees to effect a hug and a kiss. They were in this position for a considerably long time. As they fell apart, Nonno, who had been having a catnap, was woken up by the smacking sound of a kiss which had missed its intended target. Then Kalaman's hands groped for Talaado's. There was a slight tremor of static as they touched, his fevered fingers meeting her sweaty ones, for she had taken public transport and walked from the main road.

Kalaman got out of the utilitarian bed in the sitting room to walk, with Talaado supporting him, to a sofa on which they sat holding hands. Again they searched for each other in stealthy secretiveness, out of deference to Nonno.

The tremor in their touch, this time, was as hesitant as the uneven graphs of lightning on the distant horizon. Kalaman had no sadness in his eyes anymore, nor did he dwell in the mean territory of abject self-doubt.

Talaado asked how he was.

"I slept while the earth trembled," he said.

Talaado was puzzled. "How do you mean?"

"I slept while donkeys mated with calves," he said. "I slept and, with my eyes shut, my tongue in a cat's, watched while the union produced ostriches with sand in their eyes."

"Is this fever-talk?" she asked Nonno.

"That's poetry."

"A poem in riddle?"

"To show how pleased I am to see you," Kalaman said.

His mouth opened in a thin smile. He was happy. He kissed Talaado lightly on the tip of her nose. This made her squint a little, as he touched his lips to hers and caught her hot breath in his nostrils. The hairs in his nostrils trembled. He tasted groundnut in their kiss.

"How did you know I was here?" he asked.

"I went to your apartment," she said, "and found Sholoongo there, eating Chinese take-out alone, which she offered me. We ate and talked a little," Talaado said.

"Good for you!" Kalaman said.

She let him kiss her hand, a habit of his. He was sweetest after he had been sarcastic, or wicked. "But it felt weird, because I felt that she and I weren't alone in the apartment. Thinking it might have been you, I sneaked into your room and discovered your mother, asleep, her posture tortured like a baby who fell asleep crying."

"But she was all right, I mean my mother?"

"Apparently your mother had fainted from fatigue," Talaado said, "or something. I doubt that Sholoongo would have dared to serve her an interfered-with drink or food."

"What was it like talking to Sholoongo for you?"

"We had a surprisingly pleasant chat, she and I." Talaado was pleased with herself. "She filled me in on the essentials, that she had hoped to be given a baby in memory of the good days in your child-hood. She was sorry to have caused so much pain all around."

"She struck you positively?"

"We were delighted to make each other's acquaintance."

"So you liked her?"

"I couldn't help admiring the steadfastness of her mind."

"Why's that?"

"It takes guts to do what she's done," she said, "live the way she has, be the woman she is. And, my God, she has what it takes to live! Maybe she will see us all to our graves. The woman is energy, she contains so much pull, so much gravity. She will live until she is a hundred-plus!"

They both looked in Nonno's direction, Talaado half apologetic. Then she said: "It was she told me you were at Nonno's, and that you were a little under the weather. She suggested I come out to see you. She offered to lend me her rental car, but you know I don't drive."

"How did she know I was here?"

"I don't know. Maybe your mother told her. Or Qalin."

A smile spread itself on Talaado's cheeks as her eyes met Nonno's. He was stirring awake.

Kalaman to Nonno: "You see what happens when you don't take your siesta and talk and talk?"

206

"The pleasures of old age and of infancy," Nonno said, "consist in the joys of sleep, which seduces you with unequaled charm. When a baby, you sleep much longer; when old, you sleep as frequently as you please. You receive utter joy from your brief naps."

"I hope we didn't disturb you?"

"If you were my age," Nonno said, "you too would indulge in cat-naps. Why don't we sleep long? Because we don't like to think what might happen to the world if we abandoned ourselves into the lap of deep sleep, cuddled up in the comfort of our beds. I've been sleeping less and less lately, because I am afraid I might wake up and find Somalia totally obliterated from the map of my unconscious. If you young people indulge in a sound slumber, it is because your familiar-ity with the world is not imbued with as many contending memories as ours. Sleeping, the young postpone their future; waking, the old postpone their own or their country's deaths."

Talaado kept herself apart from Kalaman.

"Earlier," Nonno said, apropos a memory, "I lighted upon a dead rat with a syringe hanging from its flank, as though the poor animal had escaped from some science laboratory in the vicinity. There were signs of its struggle first with life and then with death. But what was a rat, with an unemptied third of a syringe of perfume, doing in our living room?"

Talaado listened, alert like a rank of taxis awaiting custom. She looked from the old man to Kalaman, to the door and back, as though expecting the arrival of someone who might solve the mystery of the dead rat.

Nonno said, his tone a soliloquist's, "I went to the kitchen meaning to remove the dreadful thing, perhaps to find a shovel to carry it, or to find Zariba and ask her to put it in the garbage bin. But when I returned carrying a broom and a dustpan, the dead rat had gone."

"I know the feeling!" Kalaman commented.

Talaado, though flabbergasted, was nonetheless amused by it all.

"Could this be the work of our *other* friend putting a loaded point across?" Kalaman said. "Or is this Hanu's idea, Hanu having fun? Because there is something of a shape-shifting quality to the story, a rat here and then not here. You wonder if you had imagined it all. But then you require time to develop your doubts."

"I saw a dead rat with a syringe in it, doubts be damned!"

"It is like imagining yourself to be a newt inside a whale never going ashore," Kalaman said. "Being as small as a whale is huge, you can't do much about it, surely not eat your way out of the whale. As a newt you are too small to matter, you are too little in the scheme of the whale's large bodily designs."

A twinkle of misdeed lit Nonno's eyes. His irises were very dark when you peered deep into them, but of a brown hue when you didn't. "We're not inventing our worries, Kalaman, are we?" he ventured.

"I see what you mean," Kalaman said.

Suddenly he felt itchy in the groin, but thought it impolite to scratch the area. Then he felt hot behind the ears, and again this embarrassed him, as if he were hiding an erection. Kalaman's voice was loose, so to speak, bouncy, like dice jumpily trotting down a tall stairway and avoiding your catch. He began relating an incident in which the streets of Mogadiscio were emptying, like a town being sacked by a defeated militia on the retreat, looting, pillaging. It had been raining. There had been lots of people standing in huddles, under large awnings. Kalaman knew many of the faces of the people fleeing, but hardly any of those who were not. He could hear an indistinct noise, between that of a baby crying and a crow answering a call. He chose to follow the crow, who took him to a clearing in the woods where a dead body lay. Hovering over the corpse was a fly the size of a human thumb. The crow pointed out to him that at the mouth of the wound which had caused the woman's death, there had been a single but prominent downward-pointing and three upward-pointing triangles, which met somewhere in the interlocked fashion of fingers entwined.

Talaado, Nonno, and Kalaman sat in ominous silence for a long time. Unable to follow what Nonno and Kalaman were talking about, Talaado said, "A dead rat. A dead woman, sporting a wound even flies fear to peck at. What's all this about?"

Eyes afire with fresh mischief, Nonno said, "Kalaman and I are planning to put on a vaudeville show, of vultures, crows, newts, elephants, and other beasts of totemic significance, animals whose presence portends death. To portray the tragedy that is Somalia!"

Talaado said nothing.

PART THREE

CHAPTER
NINE

As I showered and shaved, I thought ahead to my encounter with Arbaco, whom I hadn't seen for at least ten years. The truth was I had followed her progress in a ricochety way via Waliya, her daughter, lately one of Somalia's most up-and-coming fashion models. Waliya was a little over nine years my junior, many a man's idea of a pinup. The girl's name was quite often in one or another of the Italian tabloids. Both the rags and the *foto-romanzi* were keen on repeatedly feeding their lowbrow readers on a fantastic diet about a young Somali woman growing up in abject poverty in a mud hut "in darkest Africa, raised by a mother who was a Nureyev fan." The photograph of her idol the ballet dancer was said to have hung on her mud wall, suspended between a legendary act of leaping and a flamboyant pirouette finale. Nureyev was deemed to have brought joy to baby Waliya.

As a child I knew every crevice of Arbaco's wall, knew where a cockroach might have crept, knew where a gecko might have played hide-and-seek with a spider, the two competing to get the flying insects first. I do not recall a sighting of Nureyev. Nor did I hear the word "ballet" spoken in that house.

Make of the invented tale what you will. I, for one, can only assume that the Nureyev angle formed part of a young model's construction of an imagined identity. One must also assume that she was displeased with her pedestrian beginnings, to the extent where she had them expunged from her biography. Now, I do not wish to run down anyone, least of all a black woman born into a humble background who made good. Nor would I wish to belittle her efforts to look good, where it matters. The truth lay closer, where I could touch it. The truth lay with, or rather *in* Kathy, herself a Nureyev fan. The African-American Peace Corps volunteer, who put up with Nonno, told me how she had dreamt of making it to the big time as a ballet dancer, but didn't, because she suffered from a spinal condition known as scoliosis. The spinal problems began with rickets in early life, then developed into something serious later. Possibly I talked about all this to Arbaco, though I don't know why. Yet again, one or the other of them may have seen or heard of a photograph of the man, in Zariba's words, "with the bulge in the groin" who had pride of place on Kathy's wall. I trust that Arbaco would not have known what to make of a Nureyev, and would not have caught his importance in the world of ballet dancing. But then, who knows, knowledge travels in mysterious ways. In which case it makes sense to conclude that Arbaco gained access to Nureyev's secret essence, and passed it on to Waliya. No matter.

As backgrounds go, Arbaco belonged to a category of women a Somali sociologist of my acquaintance refers to as *floaters:* rural-born women, Joannie-come-to-town latter-day divorcees, with a primary school education or none at all, and most certainly no profession to speak of. As a group, these women are highly visible in the urban areas of Somalia. In fact they feature prominently in city entertainment, organizing *qaat*-chewing sessions in exchange for needed cash. They provide manifold services the urban elite with the wherewithal are prepared to pay handsomely for. The floaters are plied with gifts intended to forestall possible scandals. If you have a mind to sleep with a virgin plucked straight from the bucolic greenness, or are wanting to have sex with an unattached girl with skills to suit your city ways, then you hire a floater who will be only too pleased to use her moonshine capabilities to get you what you are after.

On the other hand, if you were fearful of rumors injurious to your reputation because of a one-night stand with an underage girl who was now with child, Arbaco was the floater you would go to. She'd find the obliging midwife and, in the event of unexpected complications, the physician to perform the abortion, or she would locate the discreet woman to look after the unfortunate girl-child until she was delivered of her misfortune. On payment of a small commission, she would arrange for the baby to be adopted.

Floaters serve as an integral part of Somali society's self-regulating mechanism. They are no saints, but cynical women, divorcees or widows, women on the margins of respectability, courtesans with loyalty only to their own self-interest. They operate in the full knowledge of what they are doing, mistrustful of men and women, and skeptical of the sanctity of matrimony. Secretive operatives, they hold no faith in the future, or in the prospect of the handsome prince who arrives in disguise with the frog's face!

Many of the floaters have a front. Arbaco's front was a legitimate trade. When I knew her, she was in the export-import business. She dealt in frankincense, myrrh, and spices. But she didn't have a shop. She didn't run a stall either. Dressed exquisitely in the most colorful getups, she went out, often in a taxi, to her appointments with high government officials. Otherwise she held court in her mud hut. Men came. Women went. The men, who came in droves, bought "something." As a child, I had no idea what was being sold, or bought. I know better now, know they were buying her silence, her intercession, in short, her favors, for which they paid extravagantly. They spoke to Arbaco in whispers when they were buying her services. In public, they talked to her normally. Sometimes a man would arrive in a car, alone. After a wait of a few minutes, a young woman would come, as if out of the dusty whirlwind, or a product of my imaginings. The woman would go giggly at the sight of the man behind the wheel, she would go soft at the center of her femininity. If they didn't go away together in the vehicle, I would see from my vantage spying-point that they went into Arbaco's house. She would make herself scarce, and come to call on my father and myself. Men demanded. She provided. Everybody was happy most of the time.

We had a special relationship, Arbaco and I. She loved giving me *baafs*. It delighted her to soap my body, rubbing it with oils afterwards. How I looked forward to these *baafs*, with me standing naked, facing her, as I held onto the V-cut of her frock, ogling her immensities, comparing them in my mind to other women's, Sholoongo's especially. She would shampoo my head, or rinse my hair in paraffin if she feared I might be infected with lice. She did this and more while my mother was busy pursuing her financial dreams, my father his artistic inclinations. I loved to be scrubbed clean by Arbaco. Above all, I took delight in her lack of the sense of taboo. I liked it when, naughty as a little girl, she squeezed my manhood in an effort to tease me into an erection. On one such occasion my father walked in on us. She was whispering an irreverence in my ears about the smallness of *me*, saying, "Where were you when Yaqut and Nonno got given their anchors, each of their things so heavy that, together, they could sink a dhow?" What a pity, my father had to put a stop to these *baafs*.

At the time I was interested in the beginnings of things. I used to ask Arbaco how babies began and where, what men and women did when they lowered the paraffin lamp's wick, what they were up to when you could only hear the odd moan, the odd word, before one of them or both wailed in painful rejoicing. I was also interested in motives. Why didn't Yaqut continue in me, the way Nonno had continued in him?

I cannot be sure, but maybe it was not she who whispered in a mischievous remark in my ear that maybe I was lucky not to suffer from a condition otherwise known as hydrocele, in which, deformed, the testicles become large and hang down weightily! She could be perceptive as only women could be. I asked Arbaco once how my mother explained why I was small down there. She pinched me on the you-know-where and said only, "You are lucky to be a boy!"

My body bathed and creamed, Arbaco used to take me to her place for a bit of fun, when my father was otherwise busy. I would lie side by side with her in her bed in the anteroom. My favorite hour for a cuddle was at siesta time. Not only were there few gentlemen callers, but she would magnanimously bring my erection to a near finish. I must have cut a boorish figure, falling asleep as I did a couple of times. Once when I stayed awake, and Arbaco's sleight of hand performed an untoward teasing, my manhood raised itself like a flag in formidable agitation, breathing like the glands of a gecko. I was in such an elated mood, I wondered where the rest of me was. Small against the immensity of Arbaco's breasts, I dropped into a well of a dream, and ended up wetting myself.

What would life have been like if I had never met her? What

would hers have been like if she had never met me? What we got up to was *pukka* outrageous. Weaned at the age of almost-three, I continued being suckled secretly by Arbaco until I was five-plus. She believed that breast-feeding a boy of the mature age of five would help remove the flaccidity in her uterovaginal tubing. I was the God-Have-Mercy boy, who drew a baby daughter out of her barrenness!

I made this claim after she became pregnant, and continued making it after she became a mother galore. I felt offended when I learnt of the arrangements they were making for a marriage of convenience with one of her midnight suitors. I felt slighted when they shrugged off my claims that I was the father of her baby.

"You'll take my daughter as your wife," one day Arbaco said, "when you are both grown up, and you'll bring me a wealthy dowry for her hand."

"Why would I pay anything for a hand?" I challenged.

"It is only a manner of speaking," explained my mother.

I found much of the adults' "manner of speaking" either confusing or misleading; at best it was a sophisticated way of keeping me in a child's place.

"If you became pregnant *because* you breast-fed me," I said, "would I still be able to receive Waliya's hand in marriage?"

"Why not?"

"Because she would be my daughter, wouldn't she?"

Arbaco and my mother were nonplused, my mother because she had never known of my being breast-fed secretly by her best friend, Arbaco because I was proving to be a nuisance. Even so, my mother ignored my indiscretions, deciding to postpone questioning her friend until I was out of the way, whereas Arbaco, speaking with a bold face, said, "For a woman to bear a man's child, and the Lord knows you are no man yet, the man and the woman have got to know each other physically."

I thought, here they go again, adults living in a world of pretend, a woman taking refuge in "a manner of speaking." I did know her body more than I knew my mother's, did know the curves on her back, knew about the birthmark on the inside of her right thigh. Was she saying this thing for a dare?

"Didn't we sleep together, naked, in the same bed?" I said.

"We didn't do anything to make you the father of my child, did we?" She sounded serious, offended, her voice raised like a stake. "Did we?"

I said, "I helped pull Waliya out of you through your nipples, didn't I? It took nine months and a week of hard work, from me. Every afternoon for nearly three hundred days." I was angry my "manner of speaking" was not as effective as an adult's.

My mother sided with Arbaco, one adult coming to the support of another. She said, the tone of her voice touched with sarcasm, "Kalaman, my dear, to bear your child, Arbaco will have had to make love with you."

As if she had never given me a lesson on the beginnings of things, Arbaco gave a hasty sketch of what happened between a man and a woman when they made love, what went into where. Livid, I sat listening and remembering not only how my parents did it but how Sholoongo and I went about it. Explaining, Arbaco almost touched me, but she confined herself to pointing in the general direction of my groin. Now I was seeing my mother's nipple in my father's lips; now I was a voyeur, spying on a man and a woman making love.

A week later, in a further attempt to safeguard my own fascination with myths, I reminded Arbaco and my mother that a man and a woman need not make love to produce a baby. To strengthen my argument I cited other myth-based precedents: a Jesus with no father, an Adam without either. I was being unbearably argumentative, becoming more of a nuisance with every passing second, making it impossible for Arbaco to breast-feed her baby in peace and for my mother to have it out with her friend for breast-feeding me secretly for two years. I hung around, as if I were hoping for a chance to feed.

I remember one occasion when Arbaco came close to hitting me, she was so annoyed with me. I walked in on her emptying her bowels. She was squatting on a pit latrine, in a most inconvenient posture for a woman heavy on top. When I entered without bothering to explain what I was there for, she asked rather angrily, "What on earth do you think you are doing?"

I unzipped my fly.

"Now what's that in aid of?" she said.

I didn't say anything.

In a voice meant to put the chill of fear into me, she said, "What do you want me to do with this ugly bit of male flesh?" Then she touched me, hurting me a little. "Looks to me like the extra sixth finger of a child just born, so small. My goodness, look." She squeezed it more, hurting me badly. "Are you really Yaqut's son?"

I paid no attention to what she said. I had rehearsed my lines, had numbered my cues in the order I would speak them, eager not to hesitate and not to be dissuaded from what I had set my mind on. "I want to father your baby," I shouted.

She pondered in silence for a long time. Then she said, "Zip up. I think I know just the right person who has the right kind of hole to accommodate your tininess."

Our conversation had a profound effect on my subsequent relations with human beings. It would take me a long time before I could approach any other woman.

Now I heard my name called.

I recognized Nonno's voice. Then I remembered where I was, in the bathroom, showering, reminiscing, calling back to mind a past shared with Arbaco. Nonno was saying that he was going out, because he had errands to run. He wouldn't be back until later in the afternoon. "Are you all right?"

"I too am planning to go out," I said.

"Giving Talaado a lift back to the city, are you?"

"Yes," I said. "After I've dropped her off, I will do a bit of lifting of stones, in the hope of uncovering a couple of scorpions hiding under the rocks."

"Mind you don't bring home a scorpion," he said.

"While looking under the stones, I might as well call on Arbaco too," I said, covering my nakedness with my cupped hands. "And if I have the time, I will call on my mother, at the shop."

"Take care," he said.

"I'll give your best wishes to Arbaco," I offered.

"Scorpion-bites have been known to be fatal," he warned me, "so take good care!" Then I heard his footsteps fade away.

Talaado and I managed to say a little to each other about what was bothering me, because we spent no less than five hours to cover a distance of thirty kilometers. We got stopped a number of times, and were instructed to get out of the vehicle and step aside. The trunk was searched for weapons, the hood for possible hand grenades and other small weapons. It was at one of the checkpoints, while waiting to get back to the vehicle, that we heard the names of Ali Mahdi and Aideed, the one a financier of the militia fighting to take Mogadiscio, the other a general in the army. "The tyrant's days are counted," said a man to his friends. "When he and his *faqash* are run out of the city, we will be a free people, ready to embrace the democratic will of our people!"

If Talaado and I didn't speak, it was because *her* people were not supposed to be *my* people. In the scheme of this sort of self-definition, my mother's people were different from my father's.

After dropping off Talaado, I went to call on Arbaco.

Who answered the outside gate herself. In all, it took her half a minute to work herself up into an enthralled state. We rubbed our chests against each other, in a fricative welcome of a reunion, as though we were cats. We walked into the villa together, my right hand in the clutch of her left and resting on her pelvic fat. She had on a *dirac* gown, a dress so transparent I could see the mounds of fat, rolls of flesh, goodness me, she had gotten out of shape, unbearably overweight. She slowed down to smile at me, almost twisting her ankle. So fat, she struck me as having a shorter neck than I remembered, and she was finding it difficult to move freely. At last we were in the living room, where there were two video players and a TV set, also a clutter of latter-day gadgets. A radio was on somewhere in one of the rooms.

"I wanted a six-bedroom *billa*," she was saying. "This was the only *billa* for sale in this neighborhood. But it has only four bedrooms, and no servants' quarters attached to it."

"How many of you are living here, in this four-bedroom villa?"

"Only me for now," she said.

"Does Waliya ever come?"

"She does," Arbaco said. "My daughter, otherwise known in this *billa* as Her Majesty, flies in, stays fussily for a day or at most two. She is in bed all day, up all night partying, showing off. The only good thing she does apart from meeting all my financial requirements is to contribute a hefty sum, in cash and in hard currency, to uplift the morale of our clan's armed militia. We have politicians of all manner knocking at our door, when she comes. She is a key contributor, as important to the clan as the hotelier who finances the running of the local wing of the USC, our militia grouping."

Now I understood why Waliya had to have a high political profile, why her mother needed six bedrooms for herself. Disturbed, I sipped at my soft drink, conscious of the extravagance as well as the wrong-headedness of those who come into wealth without working hard for it. We talked at length about Waliya, in passing about Nonno, then in general terms about my parents. I knew why she and my mother had fallen out: Arbaco had put me to her milkless breasts at the grown age of five, two years after my mother had herself weaned me controversially late at three. Eventually our tongues lighted on the multisyllabic mystery, Sholoongo.

"She came to see me," she said, "baggage and all."

"When?"

"I cannot remember." She shook her head. "A week ago?"

"Did you get to talk to her?"

"I arranged for my chauffeur to drive her to Nonno's, who I hoped would point her in your direction," she said. "The woman is besotted with you, she wants your baby, more than any woman has ever wanted to have your baby!"

"How did you find her?"

"You wouldn't have thought that she had come to bury her father," Arbaco said. "As soon as she walked in, she wanted to know everything about you. Were you married? Did you have any children? I told her that I lead a very busy life nowadays, that being Waliya's mother is a full-time job, and that many people, some of them white, come and see me and want to be friends with me. I offered her a room, but she didn't want it."

She had an impressive voice for a woman who had lost touch with her physical potential, being so obese. But at least she had something else going for her: eyes deep as a secret. At their coming into contact

219

with mine, I was convinced that they would unravel my thoughts in no time, throw aside all the waste and save the good bits for further analysis. I felt discomforted by the idea; I didn't know if I liked her.

"Did she tell you much about herself?" I asked. I wished she would switch off either the radio in the kitchen or the one in one of the bedrooms upstairs.

"You want to know what she told me?" she said. "She and I shared feminine secrets. Somehow your name kept popping up. So did your mother's, Nonno's, your father's. She told me lots of things I had no knowledge of."

"Like what?"

I stood weary at the entrance to her eyes. Would I make any inroads into her vaulted souvenir of secrets? As a floater, she had set her mind on her daughter making it good, when she could not. She was more than a floater, she was a genius facilitator, a clever manipulator of matters in her favor. She introduced her daughter to an Italian who hired her as a model. A floater and a facilitator. I would be interested in whether she introduced my parents to each other. Was either selling something? Was my mother being worried by a pregnancy? Or did my father go to Arbaco because of his "special circumstances," wanting a discreet woman arranged?

For a while she teased me, her censure rather amicable, saying why hadn't I visited her before presenting myself at her mercy and demanding that she share indiscretions with me. She said, "Only journalists and mendicants arrive unannounced, and suffer from the ill-bred behavior of demanding that you pay them all your attention."

I agreed she had a point there; and apologized.

"Sharing secrets is rather like making love." She was returning to a subject which was once of mutual interest to the two of us. "A gentleman doesn't unzip his fly and present his whatnot to a lady, if his intentions are healthy. There is an elaborate etiquette, rules of courtship, presents to be brought, flowers to be delivered, palms to be greased. There is foreplay too, a protracted kiss, and so on. Equally, the repository of a secret needs a bit of warning, he or she requires time to prepare to give up a secret. Like virginity, once you've parted with it, the loss of a secret is total."

Nonno used to say that secrets are like a farm, and must be tilled.

I would ask, how do you do that? If you are its repository, you will find out soon.

I apologized for not having alerted her in time. I said, "You know how things are. I am busy running a firm, you are busy looking after your daughter's concerns."

She said, "Would you like to marry my daughter, Waliya?"

The words caught in the cavity of my throat. It seemed a disaster was shaking hands in companionable camaraderie with a devil and making a pact. I scratched my head as though Sholoongo had contaminated us with her lice.

I could only ask, "Why me?"

"Men are only as useful as they are convenient."

She got up. I saw her very dark nipples, each as huge as a thumb and in their forward protrusion as attention-seeking as milk stains on a woman breast-feeding a baby.

"I am not pulling a fast one on you, or putting a firearm to your head to marry my daughter," she assured me. "You know she is worth a lot of money, and that I do not approve of her ways, nor of the company she keeps. I won't faint on you either. Now you may ask why my daughter, who lacks no opportunity to meet the best among men, why does she not find a man of her choice, and of whom I approve? (Not that she is bothered what I think of her choices, anyway.) The fact is, thousands of men propose to her daily. But I know men more than most, and I distrust them all. Not you. Also, you and she were pledged to each other, when you were both small. It is moreover remotely possible that if the two of you got together and married, your parents and I might become friends again. And I would like that, I liked being friends with your mother, whose friendship meant a lot to me. I miss her too, she was very dear to me."

I could somehow tell she wasn't done with her daughter.

"By the way, what would you like to drink? Whiskey?"

I remembered hearing that Waliya had more liquor in her body than blood. She would never wake up in a house that didn't cater for her dependency.

"This is fine," I said.

"I would've thought that computer programming and soft drinks didn't go well together," she said. "Modeling, you see, is the latest craze. If you make it into the big league, they pay you a lot, to make sure that you have a short life span. Waliya has her drinks heavily doctored. Her nightcaps lead to her dawn drinks, each of them in measures so heavy it would have killed you or me. Three fingers of whiskey and two of brandy mixed, and taken with a tumblerful of aqua vitae of the unrectified kind. Her nose is equally busy sniffing it all up, you never saw the variety of powdery stuff which comes here into this house, how much they go for. These give her bloodshot eyes."

"What's her interest in keeping in good standing among her immediate family?" I asked. "I wouldn't expect her to bother with this sort of lowly politics, bankrolling an armed militia movement."

"The idea is mine," she said, "the money Waliya's."

"But why?"

"It is part of my pension scheme," she said, "conceived to provide against the day when the dictator is run out of the city. Because I am interested in running for high office, maybe for mayor when the position is vacant. It will be great fun to fill the tyrant's boots. It is good for my CV."

A sad smile came from deep down in those eyes, a moist grin. Before I could change the subject back to what had brought me to her in the first place, Arbaco was showing me a pencil drawing in a glass frame. Could I guess who the artist might be? I stared at a face composed of a collage, I spotted a first set of fingers drawn end to end, and a second set with hands laced at the bend, the latter's fingers meeting at the joints. I saw vases filled with shades of light and dark brown, I saw a cat's cradle of such handsome symmetry I almost fell under its spell.

"Is this Waliya's?"

"She did it when under the influence," Arbaco said.

"Maybe she will take up drawing as a full-time profession, when she is done with modeling," I ventured. "She is highly talented. Like Sholoongo."

"What a dastardly thing to say."

"I mean no ill —" I started, and was interrupted.

Arbaco said, "Did you come driving?"

I nodded yes.

"Let's go for a drive in your car," she said. "Let's say things, let's talk about matters that I haven't spoken about for years. I prefer to do this kind of talking whilst in motion, lest I should foul up places, my daughter's, yours, Nonno's."

She requested that I sit out in the car and wait.

Dressed to the nines, her idea of bourgeois showwomanship, Arbaco was in an exalted state of mind, happy as a pampered only child born to elderly parents. In keeping with this new mood, she pressed her lips to my cheeks, purposefully indicating that we would always remain close, no matter the outcome of the impending crisis. Then she affected knowing a lot more than many others about what was happening, speaking as if she spent her nights cocooned in secretive conspiracy with the armed men and the politicians plotting the overthrow of the regime, and her days dispensing advice to the leadership of the militia and medicine to the wounded. She reminded me of when the Jabhadda was established in Rome at the insistence, among others, of her daughter and Ali Wardhiigley. She sounded as though she had more of a stake in the outcome of the ongoing struggle for power, like a woman who put all she had in the way of wealth into a sure-to-profit market shake-up.

Because she didn't tell me where we were headed as soon as I started the engine and drove, the vehicle, as if endowed with *nuuro* power, like a cow returning home after a day's grazing, took us back to Afgoi. Deep in thought, I misjudged the speed of the vehicle twice, unnecessarily changing gear from a low one to a high one.

"How do you explain Fidow's death?" she asked.

I said, "How does anyone explain a death like Fidow's?"

"How you fudge!" she commented. "If I didn't know the truth myself, I might have challenged anyone who argued that you were not Yaqut's son, or Nonno's grandchild."

I was in several minds all at once. I wanted to request that she repeat what she had said word for word, because I was finding it difficult to decide what she meant. I replayed it in my memory, and now couldn't tell if she had intended to confuse me. If she didn't know the truth herself, she might have — or was it, she might not have — challenged my being Yaqut's son, or Nonno's grandchild? I began to despair, rather disillusioned with her for making throwaway remarks such as these. I wished I could see into the truth. I wished I could see into her wells of eyes, eyes boasting a dark depth, eyes as unreachable as they proved to be misleading.

Slapping me amicably on my thigh, she said, "Take it easy!"

What did she mean, take it easy? How could I, when I was watching my world being pulled asunder by a throwaway remark? But it made no sense to ask her questions now, because we were at yet another checkpoint. She was recognized by one of the men in military uniform, and we were waved on with a smile. She commented, "One of our boys," as she acknowledged the smile with a wave.

She asked, "How's the old devil?"

I guessed who she meant. "Nonno looks a trifle exhausted," I replied.

"Is he too near the bucket to kick it?"

"We make sure there are no buckets, where he is about."

"Did you know that old Madoobe, Sholoongo's father," Arbaco said, "died from injuries to his whatnot, fatal wounds resulting from a kick received from a female donkey? I couldn't believe he would end up that way, cows, hens, and ostriches being one thing and female donkeys being deadly. He was found stark nude, on his back, his thing at half-mast, half an erection you might say. But dead all the same."

"Now what was a man of his age doing, standing stark naked behind a she-donkey at three in the morning?" I said, recalling how I had seen him mate with a heifer.

Her eyes again; then, "Not being a man, I wouldn't know."

"What wouldn't you know?"

"I have never experienced the urges of a man in heat," she said. "Many men get up to terribly perverse doings once aroused. Some never change their ways, the Fidows, the Madoobes, and the Nonnos of this world."

"Maybe animal power is in the ascendancy lately," I said, "what with elephants trekking across international boundaries to trample the man who massacred their herds, and she-donkeys avenging, killing, if only to reclaim their rights."

"What do you recall of your childhood years?" she asked.

She might have been a journalist interviewing a famous personality live, on a talk show. She made herself comfortable, her face widening with a put-on smile. She sat back, listening to the ramble in my talk as I roamed in the poorer palaces of my memory. I dwelt on how there was a logic to being a child like me, why I behaved the way I did when, why I became fascinated with the idea of rivers, of monkeys, why I imagined that bodies of water had a shape to them. Now I spoke with the contrived slowness of a fake medium, receiving inspiration from another source, outside of himself. I wasn't certain if I was making any sense to Arbaco, because with her limited education she might not have appreciated the growing-up dilemmas of a Kalaman, of a middle-class cast of mind, with a monkey for a pet, Nonno for a grandfather, a child who didn't worry where the next meal would come from, where he would sleep. I was on a tangent, thinking that the trouble with Somalia and much of Africa, in fact, the reason why there is so much civil strife erupting everywhere, is because there is no large middle-class constituency. The middle class are the first victims of an uprising. My tongue, tripping, stumbled on this generalization.

"Why are you silent?" she said. "What are you thinking?"

I paraphrased my thoughts about age-old traditions in which rivers are held sacred, seas are thought to have designs on a youth's ambition. I explained that it was in that spirit that I understood Nonno's fascination with farming and my father's recasting the shape of the universe of my infancy. The Shabelle River got the better of me, I went on, but then so did the idea of Madoobe's ostriches, although goodness knows I never saw them. I was fascinated watching Fidow as he dispossessed honeybees of their sweet stuff and crocodiles of the contents of their secret chambers. "It is the idea of worship which has kept me fascinated, the idea of shapes, how they are altered, and by what mechanisms."

"I knew once you started to talk like this, you'd lose me," she said.

"There is no reason why," I argued.

"I am not educated," she said. "I am a mere facilitator."

"I am sure your opinion on what's happening in the land is as valid as what any educated person says," I encouraged her, "despite your background."

Her eyes brightened. "I have opinions on the topic, yes. The trouble with us is a generational thing. On the one hand there are very many young people unemployed and unemployable, uneducated in the ways of our tradition, and unschooled in the modern ways either. On the other, you have a handful of very ambitious politicians. You put the two together, you have fire coming into direct contact with a combustible. You have a crisis on your hands, a problem exploding."

There was a silence.

I asked, "Where are we going?"

"You're doing just fine," she encouraged me.

She put her hand on mine. I saw her ill-formed dark nail, almost like mine. But hers had a crack at its center, just below its circular white half-moon. Had the metal end of a door, closing, given her that? I hurt mine spying.

"Where as we going?" I said. "Please tell me."

"We're treasure-trove hunting," she said.

I looked at her smooth wrinkles, rising in terraces toward a smoother forehead. The front of her head descended in more prominent waves, like a river's, toward her quadruple chin, which collapsed into several folds of loose skin ending in a roundness, no point to it at all.

We couldn't have been more than three kilometers away from Nonno's estate when I drove past two corpses lying by the roadside. You couldn't tell who the dead were, or who might have killed them and brought them here to one of the main roads. There were too many unaccounted-for dead bodies turning up in the environs of Mogadiscio of late. But why hadn't anybody bothered to bury them?

Arbaco instructed me to turn left, then right, then left, then two rights, then to park my car in the shade of a tree. I knew roughly where we were, in the eastern suburb of Afgoi, but I didn't know why. Alighting, she asked me to wait for her. Several children came out of the compound into which she had vanished. These stood crowding around the vehicle, some coming to my side of it and stretching their hands out. They rubbed their thumbs and forefingers together, the gesture of *bakhshiish*. I avoided making eye contact with any of them, my evasive gaze falling on a nest not very far away where two pigeons were busy pecking at each other's tails. I amused myself looking at the birds.

All of a sudden it occurred to me that an era of peace in Somalia was coming to an end. Attrition was taking its place, a deadly confrontation with tragic consequences to the civilian population: this had sadly, but truly, begun. We were being made to rethink our relationships, what Somalia meant to each of us, the smaller unit succeeding where the larger unit, that of nationhood, had failed. Peace has flown away, I thought, peace is in fright. Jaw-breaking wars are going on, mutinous communities taking on one another. What are the likes of me, the likes of Nonno, the likes of my parents, what are we to do? Arm ourselves, lower our stature and mental status to the common denominator's? Fight to the finish in order to keep what is ours, the income we've worked hard to earn, with the sweat of our brows, with the genius of our labor, the single-mindedness of our dedication, to make Somalia great? Are we all to seek refuge elsewhere, most likely abroad, to find a temporary haven? Yes, an epoch has resolved itself to a *finale!* Will Nonno, saddened by the tragic situation, let go? Will he die, thinking that no life is worth living anymore if one is no longer proud of one's Somaliness? But what have mansions of secrets to do with one's Somaliness? Didn't Nonno once remark that certain secrets are the product of their era and that one's attitude toward them changes with the passage of years?

I am clan-*faciis!* Fools, the lot!

When Arbaco reemerged she wasn't alone. A man with whom she had a kind of conspiratorial harmony was with her, the type of harmony informed by corruption. I could tell that they didn't trust each other either, like accomplices in a murder having no faith in one another. The man, who was sixty if a day, had about him the air of a blackmailer.

He chased away the children, one of whom referred to him as "father," but discouraged Arbaco from coming closer. And he stared at me for an eternity, the hardness in his eyes almost intimidating me. But he tired of staring and his look softened, and I began to notice that there was something quite familiar about him, as though I had known him. He had a bad hand! My eyes now shuttled in a startled journey between the man's face and his half-burnt hand. And memories were returning to me, of my father speaking of stones being lifted and of scorpions being dug up. I thought further ahead into a future in which a judge in a criminal court asked me why I had killed Gacme-xume.

My reply, "Because he smiled at me!" Or better still, "Because I cannot stand the thought of a man with a scorpion's tail for fingers."

Arbaco was back now, and spent a couple of minutes shooing away the children, many coming back soon after, like birds of prey hanging around in the vicinity of an abattoir. She told me that we should leave. Not only did I not want to go away, but I had the bizarre feeling that I wanted to murder. I was ready to kill! *How dare he?* I knew I was being rash, jumping to deadly conclusions. Would it not make better sense to probe into the identity of the man who had made my mother's life impossible? It was very clear from the urgency with which she invested her "Let's go!" that Arbaco didn't want me to delve further into the man's background, not while we were there and he was staring. But I wouldn't take my eyes away from the man's scorpioid finger, wishing I could settle scores with him there and then, this contemptible man who had accused my father of theft, my mother of deceit. But what was the true story? What was the man's version of the events?

Her hand on my right shoulder, she pleaded with me to drive off. True to her role as a facilitator, she didn't intend to complicate matters for either of her "clients." Then she said, "How much money do you have on you right this instant?"

I hadn't prepared myself for this. "Money, what money?"

"Times are hard and," Arbaco chin's pointed at the man waiting at the entrance, attentive as a soldier on sentry duty. "He is asking for some cash in advance."

"Who is he?" I asked.

"He has the original of a document," Arbaco said, "which is precious to your mother, and therefore precious to you too." She spoke slowly now, as if talking to an idiot. "The document makes her somebody else's wife. Your mother had a carbon copy of this document, for which she had Sholoongo fingerprinted when it went missing. This man is a blackmailer, that is who he is. I suggest we deal with him, cash in exchange for the piece of accursed paper."

My stomach turned, as if it were a grave in which a day-old corpse had stirred. I knew I shouldn't let my viscera get the better of me in a war of nerves, but I was in a weakened state of mind too. "How much money are we talking about?"

"Two million shillings," she said, looking furtively in the man's direction as though she were seeking his agreement. I could sense that she was sad. "I tried to make him surrender the document on trust, but he wants a deposit, at least a third of the sum before he would show it. Again and again he repeats that times are hard. Indeed times are not only hard but uncertain too. For everyone."

"How did he come by the document?" I asked.

From the sound of it, she was fed up with me, and unhappy too. "If we talk like this, we won't get anywhere. You and this man are both making it impossible for me to accomplish a facilitator's job. I shuffle and deal the cards, you play."

I decided there was no mileage in arguing with Arbaco. She was, after all, an intermediary, possibly with a commission waiting for her afterwards, but I doubted it. My quarrel was with Gacme-xume and I had better consult with Nonno before I did anything rash. Besides, my hate was turning into pity. I no longer wanted to kill him, only kick his teeth in.

I suggested Arbaco and I find a place out of his earshot so we could talk in peace. I drove away fast, the tires of my vehicle stirring so much dust you would have thought that a horde of hippopotami was having a wrestling bout with elephants.

I drove not in the direction whence we came. I drove toward Nonno's. Arbaco soon began to behave like an annoyed child. She stamped her feet on the car floor until the whole vehicle shook. She wanted me to stop at once. When I wouldn't, she screamed her head off, like a child in a tantrum. I drove on a bit more, her voice becoming hoarser the more obscenities she shouted. I braked all of a sudden and she fell forward. I was glad she wasn't hurt.

"There's no call for rudeness," she said after a while.

I had on my obligatory puzzled look. I said, "What hold has this man on my parents?"

Angry words, hot-tempered like bees, hovered too close to Arbaco's lips. I could see the bees were in an agitated state, prepared to sting. I cut the engine of the car.

"In my profession," she said, "I meet all sorts of people, men and women, seekers of fun. I also meet some who are in search of someone to solve their problems, men and women whom a misfortune has caught up with. I came to know your mother in circumstances not easy to explain. She came to me with a problem, a problem with a difference."

"What's a problem with a difference?"

"Hers was a difficult life to disentangle," said Arbaco, "a life in whose palatial web several flies had been caught. First to enter is a man proposing to marry her, whom she turns down. The man is not discouraged by her rebuffs. He returns time and again, pestering her. He makes a nuisance of himself, following her to the market, shadowing her to the cinema and back to where she was putting up, with her aunt, whose charge she was. One day Y.M.I. (let's call him by his initials, considering that he is recognized by them) meets her together with another man escorting her out of the movies. He doesn't ask about the man. Stung by the bees of jealousy, his fists fly at the man, quick as a nasty sting. Unfortunately, the other man is stronger, and Y.M.I. is beaten up badly. Nor will he accept any help from Damac. He quietly leaves.

"Damac doesn't hear from Y.M.I. for months. Then one day he turns up at her aunt's door, presenting himself as her husband. He is questioned by the aunt. Y.M.I. has the papers to prove that he and Damac were man and woman. He proffers a very regular-looking marriage certificate. No matter what Damac says, no one believes her, least of all her aunt. Before any action is taken, she is asked if she has known the man in the sexual sense. Damac responds in the negative. To call the man's bluff, your mother challenges him to produce two male witnesses. He does so, no trouble.

"Even if it is all a fabrication, why is it, Damac's aunt wonders, that Y.M.I. has picked her out of a million others? This is no lottery. What's the truth?

"In her self-exoneration, your mother makes no mention of the fight between Y.M.I. and her escort. One of the neighbors, who witnessed the fight, tells on her. Your mother is asked about the fight. Not knowing about the neighbor or what she told her aunt, Damac tries to keep the fistfight between the men secret. Her aunt tells her to leave the house. She is not even nineteen, the poor girl, and has nowhere to go.

"Down on her luck, she seeks out an old friend from her elementary school days. The friend is kind enough to provide her with a temporary accommodation in a house where she is room-sharing with another woman. When we see Damac next she is in the bead business, and is doing fine. At Y.M.I.'s instigation, the men in the marriage racket business put the screws on her. They want her to pay, and pay handsomely. She refuses. A different group of thugs arrives, apparently because Y.M.I. has by then lost the certificate in a card game, lost it to one Gacme-xume, who comes to collect the loot. Nothing doing. Several men, led by Gacme-xume and Y.M.I., gang-rape her. Word gets around. Finally I hear of it.

"I search her out," said Arbaco. "We talk, I promise to act as her facilitator. Confident of success, I follow a lead, the man's initials, Y.M.I. Now, I knew the initials in some other connection, maybe from some artwork, your father's. I do not recall why I suspected that Damac was pregnant. 'Just as it happens,' I say to her, 'I remember there is this man who is in your line of trade.' I hoped to Allah that the impostor's initials were leading me to him. Because if Yaqut was the culprit, I was decided to hand him over to the police. If Yaqut was not the blackmailer, then we were in luck. Then I organized for Yaqut to meet up with your mother at my place. Thank the Lord, he was not the impostor, and because Yaqut and she got on like a summer fly and honey, we were able to arrange for them to marry in a week. Even in my facilitation trade, I'll tell you a week is very fast. This was record facilitation time. Take it from me, it is!"

"And where does Gacme-xume come into this?"

"Gacme-xume belonged to the underworld in the fifties and sixties," said Arbaco, "a period when forging marriage certificates was a boom business. The impostor with the same initials as Yaqut's was a mate of his, a fellow thief in his den of secrets. True or not we do not know, but Gacme-xume claims that he had won the original "marriage certificate" as part settlement of a card game. The settlement included literally every stitch of clothing, every bit of anything worth pawning or selling or blackmailing with, everything the impostor owned. As I said, your mother wouldn't deal with any of them. But when Gacme-xume discovers that the woman is now married to Nonno's son, he reckons he can make a bounty out of a propertied man. What with one thing and another, there is that story about the theft of a pair of shoes from a mosque. I think this shoe business is a nail in the wrong coffin, if you follow my meaning."

Choking on the phlegm of my uncertain reaction, I started the vehicle, turning its nose in the direction of Mogadiscio. I drove, hardly paying attention to the checkpoints, at which I did not bother to stop. I dropped Arbaco off after thanking her and apologizing for my unwarranted behavior earlier. We would be in touch, I assured her. Then I drove straight back to Afgoi, to be sad in Nonno's company.

I sat in the west porch of Nonno's bungalow, waiting for him to return
with two million shillings. This money was to be paid in cash, on
receipt of a document, to a blackmailer who had it in his scorpioid
clutch. With his phenomenal sense of discretion, Nonno hadn't
pressed that I give more details than I was prepared to provide. Nonno
and I agreed after much to-ing and fro-ing that he would have the first
examination of the document. He insisted on this; I acquiesced. I
doubt that I withheld any information of pivotal significance. It was
unlike me to pour things out the way I had done, unlike me to tell him
everything that transpired between me and Arbaco. Then I told him
where to find Gacme-xume. Listening to me tell it all, I thought that
Nonno sat in the placidity of his self-confidence, a man in a clear mind
as to what he was meant to do and how he would go about it.

"A woman like Arbaco," he had said, "is not wholly of the underworld, even though she operates on the same principles as Gacme-
xume. Quite often she fishes in the same waters as he, for she is a
jetsam to his flotsam. I wish she had come to me earlier with these
indiscretions. Why didn't she? But never you mind!"

I asked him if he had known of the racket.

"One is always wiser after the event," he replied. "One may claim,
in retrospect, that one has had intimations of things, that one has
picked up whiffs of it in the air. I would go as far as admitting to having been suspicious, yes. But I had no nail-hard evidence. Otherwise, I
would have done something about it. I am not one to sit around doing
nothing. I would have dealt with it!"

"What intimations had you before today of all this?"

"I felt there was a secret which bound Yaqut and Damac, a secret which held them together," he said. "A pledge, perhaps, more solid than the words of a vow spoken to seal a matrimonial pact. I couldn't tell what it might be. But given that they were happy with each other, I let them be, thinking, what the hell!"

Following this, we spoke about Muslim marriage — about how, whereas the husband-to-be is present, the bride need not be there at all. She is required to be there in person only under special circumstances. Otherwise, she is represented by a male relation, who speaks on her behalf. We speculated how Damac's pesterer may have organized false witnesses, one of them claiming to be either her father or brother. The officiating priest may not have known of the deceit. When is a marriage described as *khudbo-sireed?*

"It is described as 'secret marriage,'" said Nonno, "when the two parties getting married travel a *masaafa* distance to avoid being detected. They defy the authority of the bride's family, who may have promised her hand to someone else, or override the family's objections, by marriage in secret outside the juridical boundaries of a *masaafa*. You need two male witnesses whom you present to the officiating judge, not a male relation. The nineteen-sixties saw many such secret matrimonies, as the ideas of family authority over the individual were being renegotiated, following society's fast transformation from a preponderantly nomadic and rural one to an urban one."

"Can we assume that the purported marriage between my mother and the pesterer took place between either him or an impostor and a false 'bride'?" I said. "She would have had to answer to Damac's name, the witnesses of dubious character swearing to the truth of her identity. My mother would not have known of the deceit until later, by which time the municipality would have issued a marriage certificate, which purported that she was Y.M.I.'s wife."

"I have known priests of dubious character too," Nonno said. "But that is not our main concern now." He appeared overwrought and exhausted. He might have been annoyed with himself, too, for not having caught out the deceit.

"The pesterer was in the marriage racket business, then?"

"Everything is possible in the underworld of thugs and Gacme-xumes and impostors."

I had an image of the items being priced in a room full of smoke where a card game was in progress. I said, "I have a vision of the marriage certificate being valued at an agreed price, and of Gacme-xume winning the hand cards up. He calls on my mother, Gacme-xume does, but she is uncooperative. He returns with some of his mates at a later date, and they gang-rape her. Pregnant, she is helpless. Arbaco enters the picture as a facilitator. Damac meets Yaqut. They are man and wife inside a week. Word gets to the riffraff. He comes back in expectation of a potential shakedown, because of who you are."

Nonno said, "So far so good." Encouragingly, "Go on!"

"Gacme-xume presents himself to Yaqut to collect," I continue speculating. "He receives a spit in the face. Stammering, Yaqut threatens him with murder. Because he operates in the shadier corners of human experience, Gacme-xume doesn't despair, not so easily, at any rate. He communicates his frustrations in a number of ways, directly to Damac and via duplicitous networks. He raises the dust of a storm. As part of their con game, a pair of shoes are stolen from a mosque. Yaqut is blamed for this. I presume this was done because of your nickname Ma-tukade, which places your son at a disadvantage among the attendants at the mosque. Then, maybe because Yaqut does not budge, nothing happens for a long time, and we hear not a word the riffraff, in fact we have no idea of his whereabouts until Sholoongo's return, her visit here. Did she look him up, with a helping hand from Arbaco? I cannot rule that out. We should pay whatever it takes to find out who was responsible for my mother's misery."

Silent, I was sad. I could do with therapeutic talking, but I was afraid I might make a fool of myself by promising to murder every single one of the men who had raped my mother. For there was I: Kalaman, the issue of a gang rape. What was there to say? I was conscious of my equivocal status, I was a changed man. Of that I was certain. Even so, I could not put my forefinger on the nature of these changes, which, it being too early, were still imprecise, vague.

I observed, with sadness, that tears had collected in the corners of Nonno's eyes, his gaze now adrift, off its own set course, like a boat about to go under. He began to shake. I couldn't tell why the tremor, but I put it down to a belated rage. Maybe this was taking hold of him in the way malarial bouts grip an overwrought body too tired to cope. His was the kind of anger with a stench. I could smell it from afar. The odor his rage emitted was so penetrative it took my memory back to Sholoongo's first afternoon in my apartment. It was unlike him to be so enraged, his every breath fraught with curses, his speech punctuated by inaudible damnation.

Barely a meter away from Nonno, I looked away from him, unseeing and, insofar as I was concerned, unseen. I might have been someone with eyes emptied of light and sight. It felt as if the blackness of my pupils was a shade paler than normal, my brain deprived of its strength, its characteristic human resolve. My head seemed peopled with monstrous beings, some half human, some belonging to the animal realm.

"As a citizen of the crossroads where several worlds meet," Nonno said, "you will find the weight of contradictory signs beginning to appear. You will come upon footpaths forking in all sorts of directions, signposts giving you confusing directions to where there is no return." I could see his lips moving, but I couldn't make out what he was saying. Ill at ease in my company, or so I thought, his eyes evasive, he looked withdrawn. He had known me as his grandson. Now I wasn't his grandchild anymore? There was I: the offspring of a gang rape. I had nothing of certainty linking me, as his own blood, to him. Maybe because he had no idea of what to do or say, Nonno left the porch with no explanation whatsoever.

While I waited for him to return from his money-gathering errand, the night arrived. I thought ahead with horror to the day when the world I had known until then and had taken for granted would be no more. Nonno not my grandfather. Yaqut not my father. I thought ahead to the moment when my mother would give me her version of what occurred. How would people react to the news that I was the issue of a gang rape? I didn't want sympathy or pity from anyone, I wanted to see palpable anger. Naturally, it would confound a lot of simpleminded, clan-obsessed persons who might feel cheated of their right to know the name of the rapist, my biological father, if only to

236

assign me to the one of the clans. If they pitied me, it would be because I was the poor sod who hadn't a blood family to be loyal to, to kill and die for, in this epoch of clan-kill-clan! I wondered how someone like Qalin, my deputy at the firm and once my lover, might react to this. How would my employees receive the news? I could only compare it in my experience to learning that X, a friend, had AIDS. We didn't know what to do, at least I didn't. So what do you say to someone afflicted with an identity crisis like mine, akin to AIDS in that it points to a kind of death?

Time and again my ideas were ambushed, I was thrown off course!

My thoughts were ambushed now by the sight of a shooting star in earthward motion. In Somali mythology, meteors are associated with jinns who, as tradition has it, were created two thousand years before Adam. Stories abound which ascribe to these pre-Adamite beings the genius of having been the architects of the pyramids during the reign of their king with the most enchantingly musical name Jinn ibn Januun. A wealthier harvest of tales spun out of jinn-related anecdotes tells of how the jinns' dwelling place was in the vicinity of a body of water. It is said that they frequent intersections of roads; that their favorite musical instrument is the flute. The *ghuul* is a special category of jinn, believed to appear in both human and animal forms. As well as being carnivorous, the *ghuuls* haunt the environs of tombs, hence their association with death. King Solomon is the most celebrated non-jinn king, whose dominion included possession of the keys to all the world's secret caves. According to the Koran, meteors are hurled at the jinns eavesdropping at the gates of heaven in an effort to discourage them from overhearing divine secrets.

My eye pressed to a keyhole, I could see Nonno in quarter profile, silhouetted against the half-light, his half-moons poised on his nose. He was writing from right to left, most likely in Arabic. In the look on his face, I could discern a seriousness of purpose. What was he up to?

Disregarding good manners, I walked into the room without bothering to knock. Nonno, I sensed, was in a perhaps-land, maybe that of his teens, a place from which he had been exiled for more than sixty years. What light there was in the room came through the door by which I had entered, from a corridor where a night-lamp, essential as an exit sign, was lit. On moving further, I upset the smoky compactness of the burning incense. Not even this distracted Nonno from his purposeful note-taking.

Like a juju man, he had all his wares around him, everything within reach. His books were open at specific pages. Within reach too, for consultation, there was a scatter of tiny pieces of paper, yellowed with the passage of years, scraps of scribbles piled on top of each other, memorabilia from half a century ago or more. The evening had gathered in his eyes. Though I could see him, he seemed unaware of my presence in the room.

From my vantage point directly behind him, I saw that he had written the letter K in Arabic. The K was joined to an L, then marked with the appropriate vowel-point for the sound he wished to achieve: accents of focus, of a skirmished relevance. His eyes were distant in the attitude of a man predicting final ruin. Here was I, the issue of a gang rape; here was Nonno, no longer my grandsire, working his way toward invoking a Koranic law to effect justice against men of dubious beginnings. We had lost everything precious to us. Maybe he was doing all he could to avert further disaster? To be sure, there was the odor of death in the air.

As I watched him, I pondered how different people reached into the pocketed depths of their souls. Some found firearms. Others sought the quietest recesses of their self-restraint, their reticence. And others traced the journeys of their souls in varied forms of study, now in figures and now in images, the secret keys to the mysteries of embryonic magic: the *kahanah*, the *darbul mandal*, the *faal*, the *darbul ramal*, finally the *dacwa*. These in their respective ways owed their origin to an inspired reading of the Holy Scriptures, the Prophet's Tradition, and the Saints.

Nonno tabulated the lists, as he wrote them out, into columns: letters of the Arabic alphabet, each with its value of *kahanah* as opposed to numbers, meanings of attributes or classes of attributes, the signs of the zodiac, the planets, and the "perfumed" letters. He copied out words like "cinnamon," a phrase like "red sandal." He encircled the names of the elements. He enumerated the titles of the jinns, taking ages to copy the *Qaypuush*, the *Twayush*, the *Danuush*, and the *Badyuush*. He was most patient when writing the value of the Number 20 against the letter K. Just below these, he wrote the Number 111. Opposite the letter L there was the Number 30, to the right of it God's attribute *Latiif* and the correlated Number 129. Now the letter M, valued at 40, abreast God's attribute *Maalik*. But I lost interest in what he was doing when I noticed that he looked immensely sad, as though something was eluding him, like a blur in the distance receding the closer one got to it.

As a child I used to think of the unraveling of magic and all the related mysteries as being comparable to an extremely large manikin holding in its abdomen several more, the smallest in the second smallest, that one in the third smallest, and so on and so forth. Timir, on the day he called at my office, had argued, I now remembered, that if magic essentially had to do with one's occult control, then taboo *is* magic's correlate, magic having a secret influence, and taboo affording privileged status to the thing interdicted. Interpreted thus I asked myself if Nonno was accessing the occult world through a magic rite involving the copying of letters and numbers and their correlates.

To check, I looked at what he was doing. I saw that he had written down *Kahf* (sura xviii), *Kaahin* (sura lxix, 42), *Laxd*. Below these he wrote and then underlined the phrase *Kanzul Makhfi* (said to be the secret treasure, *Kanzul Makhfi* being a term used by the Sufis for the essence and personality of God). Presently Nonno copied down a combination of mysterious numbers and letters, then organized these into tables, under columns, in fours, fives, sixes, and nines. He also drew a strange set of diagrams. Maybe these were charms, which those in the know think of highly; others doubt their significance, calling them balderdash. I didn't know what to think. I quit the room.

Even so I could hear Nonno's voice from where I was, in the corridor. But I wasn't certain if he was invoking the name of Sulaiman (Solomon) or beseeching aid for Kalaman. King Solomon has a revered standing among the practitioners of the science of magic, Solomon the king whom Allah helped "subject the wind blowing strongly" in order for "the devils to dive for him in the sea and to bring forth from it jewels," Solomon upon whom Allah "bestowed knowledge in judging men" and whom Allah taught to speak "in the language of birds and other matters."

When I looked in on him later, Nonno was turning the house upside down. He was going into areas of the house which he hadn't set foot in for ages. He was opening and closing cupboards, he was emptying drawers and leaving things where they fell, a man in flight who wanted nothing to do either with the room or the mess. Now and then he emerged, dragging out metal cases. He broke the locks, because he had no keys to open the locks anymore. But what was he looking for? Why was he searching with so much haste, as though it were a matter of life and death to locate it?

The hammer was out, the hammer going mad, bang-bang-bang, chests falling to the floor and being picked up, the metal end of the chest echoing with the violent onslaught of the hammer. Hitting the hardest he could, Nonno missed his target: *Ouch!* He cursed, paused, sucked the hurt forefinger. He stared at his thumbnail, gashed, yes, but not bleeding. He forced one of the ancient padlocks open. He rummaged in the interior. Nothing. Another dramatic pause, as brief as the ephemeral nature of parental rage. Then my senses were invaded afresh by further disparate noises: cabinets being ransacked, cupboards being demolished, kicked at. Because they failed to deliver the promises memory had invested in them? Further curses, more pronounced lamentations. Had Nonno lost his mental equilibrium? Was he looking for it among the items in his chest of drawers, in his metal cases? Somalis say that, out of despair, a man may look for his camel in a milk container, hoping to find it there. "Curse the day!"

It was for my own peace of mind that I asked if I could be of any assistance. Because, knowing him, he would do his utmost not to involve me, especially if getting me involved meant possible peril.

As we stood unspeaking in the midst of the ruin he had wrought upon everything within view, I wondered if we were not witnessing, within the confines of the house, a replica of the civil disorder occurring without. Nor would he say anything to me. He might have been a man deposited by his misfortune on the outskirts of madness, thinking of the change coming around the bend in the blind spot, where his past had been. I remembered that as a young man, Nonno had replaced the letters *s* and *b* in his name Misbaax with the letters *f* and *t*, a journey long and short at the same time, Misbaax, "light" in Arabic, becoming Miftaax, "a key"!

"What are you looking for with such fury?" I asked.

His voice shaking, he replied, "I am searching for the first identity card the Italian colonial authorities issued to me in my true names, mine and my father's and my grandfather's, in that order. Curse the day!"

"Will you please tell me why you are looking for it?"

He disregarded my question, saying, "Tragedies have a humor to them too. In fact, such was the Italian clerk's ignorance that I am described in that first Identity Card as *Inglese*, apparently because I hailed from what was then the British Somaliland Protectorate. His superior officer, when signing the ID card, crosses out the word *Inglese* and in its place writes in his clumsy hand the word *Brittanico*. Other Somalis of my acquaintance had their clan names where I had *Brittanico*. Fancy that!"

"Why are you looking for it now?"

"I thought I might as well put my life in some order," he said. "A man of my age, after all, might as well be prepared for all eventualities." He looked absentmindedly at a paper he held away from himself, at trombone distance. He searched for and found a pair of reading spectacles, which he placed on the bridge of his nose. Then he picked up a second and a third paper, with Italian writing on them. From where I stood I could see what these were, title deeds to the estate, bought the Lord knows when. He was a man comparing the details of the past with the minutiae of the present ensconced in the manifold possibilities of the future.

"Take a good look at these," he said.

My heart missed a beat, then ran off with my worries, upwards, until it came past my Adam's apple into my mouth. There I managed to detain it, thanks to having had the foresight to bite my tongue, which now hurt.

What was I holding in my trembling hands and looking at? I had before me a single sheet the years had been unkind to, a carbon copy of a document, which Nonno's mad search had unearthed. If I couldn't read it, it was because I felt the approaching storm which had begun to brew in my head the moment the sheet was proffered. I was staring at a form of death. Death was arriving from a blind bend, and there was nothing I could do to prevent its coming. I did what I could to postpone its arrival, which was why I read as slowly as an *analfabeta* does, speaking the individual letters. My mother's name was given as the wife in the marriage certificate, and in the space for "husband" the name *Yussuf Mohamoud Isaaq* was given. The document was in pedantic Italian, with renderings in flowery Arabic. It was dated sixteen months before my birth.

"How did you come by it?" I asked.

"Sholoongo left it in Rhino's belly, years ago," he said. "I remember retrieving it. Not wanting to read it then, for reasons I cannot fathom now, I put it away, intending to return to it. Is it possible I never bothered to scrutinize this document because I believed her to be innocent of blame? You see, I mistrusted your mother. That, in my opinion, made Sholoongo a victim of your mother's slander."

"What are we going to do with Sholoongo now?" I said.

"Leave her to me," he suggested. "I'll deal with her."

All of a sudden I collapsed into a chair between one bilious moment and another. When my eyes encountered Nonno's, I saw death being forecast, death being anticipated, I saw death stalking the entire country, pursuing it with the determination of an elephant gone amok.

"There are many myths," Nonno said, "myths bestowing unparalleled importance on the idea of motherhood, the certainty of mothers." He paused. "The best illustration I can think of is the Somali parable about the Milky Way. Do you know it?"

"The Milky Way myth?"

"An ingrate son beats his mother to near death," said Nonno, narrating the parable, "and then, as though meaning to finish her off, pulls her along a rocky surface in the scorching heat of noon. The woman is badly hurt, her skin breaks, bleeds, her bones ache, she faints. Heartlessly cruel, the young fellow drags her until she is a dead weight, a lifeless being bearing no resemblance to herself alive. The woman's sister, his maternal aunt, asks that he allow her to give the woman a decent burial. Pleading, the aunt looks up at the heavens and invokes God's sense of justice. The son won't hear of it, saying she is food fit for vultures.

"Again his aunt pleads, and again she looks up at the heavens as she speaks. The sky darkens with clouds, there is unseasonal thunder, there is lightning. The son is struck with epilepsy. He dies an agonizing death, in horrific misery and loneliness, and his corpse is dragged across the heavens. We say that the act is etched on the body of the sky in purgatorial remembrance of all the mothers who suffer unkindnesses meted out to them by their offspring."

Silent, his gaze filled to bursting with tears.

I spoke the words with the deliberateness of a sadhu speaking his mantra. "Fathers matter not. Mothers matter a lot. Fathers matter not. Mothers matter a lot."

Nonno closed and opened his eyes to the rhythm of the spoken mantra. His eyes were awash not so much with lachrymose sadness as with sightlessness. Now he held his breath in terrifying suspense, perhaps waiting for the well of his eyes to be drained of the fluid that was blinding him. Eager to engage my attention, he stood still, making sure I heard every single word. He wiped away the moisture from his cheeks.

"Motherhood," he said, "is the off-and-on light in the darkness of night, a firefly in joyous dizziness and rejoicing, now here, now there, and everywhere. Our problem as a society is that we pay mothers only lip service, nothing else. In fact, the crisis that is coming to a head in the shape of civil strife would not be breaking on us if we'd offered women-as-mothers their due worth, respect and affection, a brightness celebrating motherhood, a monument erected in worship of women."

Suddenly like a tropical night his eyes dimmed. Then with equal abruptness, as if the veil of darkness had been lifted, his face opened up, vistas of historico-theological awareness. As though inspired with atavistic irrationality, he rose to his feet and went around and around, repeating again and again, "Fathers matter not. Mothers matter a lot!" He looked every bit his age now. He had grown afternoon shad-

243

ows under his morning-gray eyes. It seemed to me as if he were planning death, the removal of riffraff dirt. He blinked with the nervous tension of an exhausted cat.

Tea. More tea. Hot stuff too.

In the meanwhile we roamed in our respective imaginations. We wandered in a mythical territory peopled by an Adam without parents, an Eve without a mother, a Jesus without a father. We talked of miracle babies born to beings from the animal realm. We invoked the authority of the moon, which Egyptian priests of old referred to as the Mother of the Universe. We recalled how, in India, a girl-child having her first monthly is described as bearing a flower.

My wanderlust led me further afield. I came upon Yaqut, named for a highly respected Islamic theologian, who entertained a most vivacious interest in inanimate things. My wanderings led me to Damac, a woman with the sting of a bee, the foresight and the determination of a honeyguide. Happy, her natural kindness is overwhelming, as is that of a contented woman. We tried to avoid Sholoongo, but she wouldn't be avoided, insisting that she too was a woman, even if unfulfilled. I didn't know what to think of her, having none of the healing powers of a shaman!

Then there was a long silence. But, restless, I couldn't bear the quietness, especially after spotting Nonno's sorrow in the unfocused quality of his look. Maybe I was quoting someone, for I said, "Like life, every story has logic. I wonder, does death have a rationale? The life of a young brute, dragging his mother dead across rocky footpaths, is emblematically turned into a parable. The brow of the heavens is marked with his shame."

He said, "The dead, we are told, hear nothing."

"Do the living hear anything?" I asked. "Did the young fool?"

"The living listen to stories, which they tell to others in the hope of weaving strands of their personalities into the mysteries of the tale."

I asked myself if I should interpret his statement as an indication of his preparedness to let go, after putting his life in some order. I took a gentle grip of his large hand in my small one and tightened my clasp around his fingers. I said, "What about the dying?"

"If they are lucky," he said, "the dying are so attuned to what is happening that they can hear the sound of a cricket, or a mosquito buzzing in their ear. Like your grandmother. We had lain side by side all day, she and I, alone in our bedroom. Not only was she conscious that she would be dying that day, but she could have specified when she would expire."

I was very glad I was still his grandson, and was moved when he talked of *my* grandmother, meaning his late wife, the mother of Yaqut. Nonno was a certainty.

I said, "Do you know when you are to let go in advance, and will you?"

"The day that I have organized my ragtag of ideas into some order, I will let go," he said. "I've lived for an eternity of years. Because of this I have so many loose threads to tie together into a neater shape. I can't tell how much time I require."

He then looked about himself, maybe wondering why he was where he was. One moment he had the expression of a man too tired to invest energy in this day-to-day living; the next moment he was a visitor saying his good-byes but who wasn't gone. Everything he did hinted at the contradiction: his posture, the way he held his body a little off his chair, as if he might get up at any instant, leave, and let go. Besides, it was taking me a long time to get used to the idea of a non-smoking Nonno, an entity as outré as a naked man in a mosque. Bizarrely I thought of pleading with him to go back to the habit of smoking, light one and puff on it, let the smoke curl up, a chimney of cigarettes held filter tip to filter tip. What the hell!

Two men, both strong and wide-shouldered, were preceded into the room by their own shadows. Their shadows were preceded in equal measure by their whispers. Nonno welcomed the two men in.

One of them, Yarow, the son of the late Fidow, had given his hair a crew-cut look, as if in haste. The other man, who would remain nameless to me, had on a pair of hand-me-down shorts and a dirty

T-shirt with a huge tear in the back. He was all muscle, veins rolling snakelike when he moved. I didn't know who he was. Even so, he bore a certain physical resemblance to my idea of a thug. He had a roughness to his manners, an uncouthness to his tongue. He looked ruthless, sadistic, sporting a set of artificial front teeth of the cheapest metal. He had the habit of grinning. When he did so, it seemed as if his entire face stood back from the rest of him. Then you spotted the wryness of his grimace. You knew he was there for an extrajudicial purpose.

No one said anything about murder. And yet I felt the word "death" hanging in the air. Had Yarow Fidow's companion been assigned to murder Gacme-xume, plain and simple? All his fee paid in advance, in cash, no questions entertained?

Yarow Fidow's features were etched with a look of worried expectancy. He listened to Nonno as the old man pontificated on a point of detail. Then he turned to his companion and gave a shortened version of what he had heard. Then he looked again at Nonno, who spoke some more, this time offering directions. Because much of their conversation was in soft whispers, I suspected that he was giving them instructions to lead them to where the supposed victim lived. You might have thought, from the way he gesticulated, that he was taking them from a projected scene of death to a part of the woods where the corpse might be safely hidden. I caught the name of the victim — an alias, to be precise: *Hangaroole?* Translated, the alias meant Arachnida. I was now sure they were talking about Gacme-xume.

It had been agreed that I would stay out of Nonno's and Yarow Fidow's arrangements, that I would withdraw into the privileged privacy of my room while they held their conference within a few feet of me. For the sake of pretense I even pushed the door to my room shut against the possibility of anyone suspecting that I was overhearing their talk.

A tremor had informed my voice as I said to Yarow, "My condolence, Yarow!" We shook hands. He was at least fifteen years my senior, as private a man as his father had been gregarious. I liked him. We got on well, maybe because we seldom met. After my words of commiseration, I hardly knew what to say to him, on account of the deadpan expression on his face.

He mumbled his thanks, adding, "We'll all die sooner or later." Then Nonno, Yarow, and the unnamed man exchanged a quiet look. I am sure we all thought about Gacme-xume in our different ways.

Nonno said to Yarow, "You know what you're expected to do?"

Both men nodded.

To give them more privacy, I went outside for a few minutes, confident that Nonno and the two men would discuss the salient details while I was out of their hearing. Just in case. We were preparing ourselves for the possibility of a murder charge. The old man pointed out, in a whisper, that they oughtn't to let me hear either of them mention the name of the victim. All hush. And then boom, bang, and dead. Whereas I, his legatee and grandson, would pretend not be privy to any of this. In a sense the whole thing derived its origin from Nonno's wish to "organize his ragtag of ideas into some order" before letting go. If something went terribly awry, the old man would take the full blame. He was prepared to hang. "Compare your long years ahead of you to mine, which are as short as a midday shadow, compact, curled up at one's feet," he explained.

To make his communion with Yarow and his companion less awkward, Nonno switched off almost all the lights in the area of their hush-hush operation. They stood in the dimness of the outer porch, with two or three small yellow and red bulbs. The dim yellow light was meant to discourage mosquitoes from coming into the area at all.

While listening for them to go away I imagined all sorts of scenarios. In one, Nonno was betrayed by Fidow's son. In another, the foreign-looking thug struck a deal with his supposed victim, who came to us to take his vengeance. All that night I would have in my vision two bones crossed, signs indicating danger, death.

Suddenly nervous, Yarow and his companion were eager to leave. Neither said anything to me as they walked past my door, although they knew that I was there. When I last set eyes on my mother, she too was planning somebody's murder. Did I begin in death, in the thought of a man fleeing it, coming south and changing his name? Then deciding not only that his dying-time had arrived but that others must come with him too? Did I start in death, in my mother planning to kill every single one of the thugs who gang-raped her?

Yarow said good-night to Nonno. The other man did not say anything at all. Then I heard their footsteps. These receded and then totally faded as they walked away. The ignition of Yarow's car failed to catch, the engine refusing to turn over.

I thought it odd that Yarow's companion didn't look Somali. Was he a foreigner who had come to this country following Fidow's death, on instructions from his Kenyan masters, to look into Yarow's father's encounter with an elephant of misfortune and miscalculation?

After many attempts the car started.

The door was let go. It shut on Nonno's silence.

A dust storm: whirly, powerful, life-endangering.

Something is falling, a coin dropping into a tin can. For an instant the world is reduced to a tingly, gentle twinkle of two pieces of metal touching. I see fingerprints of complicity, I see ample evidence of a crime perpetrated, I spy traces of proof. In my paranoia, I imagine court cases. I think of runaway scandals, my name in the newspapers, Nonno's too, my mother being mentioned. I stare at the grooves, the turns, the curves in the prints, as if hoping to read therein the identity of the person to whose hand the prints belong. Prints are a mystery to those who know not how to decipher them.

Taking care not to make any noise, I knocked on Nonno's door. No answer. When I pushed the door open a little I could see that he was lying in bed, sheets covering him. I pulled the door to. I switched off the lights in the room, although I didn't know to what purpose. After all, the old man may have decided to let go, now that he had saved the honor of his household. Restless and unable to sleep, I moved in the bungalow, quiet as a cat in search of a place where no other of its kind would insist on sharing the food with it.

I fell asleep at about four to the hooting of an owl.

CHAPTER
ELEVEN

Half awake, I rubbed the veins of my wrist. I hurt.

The room was a little too dark. I imagined seeing dark figures, one of them with a discal face like an owl's. I saw a long line of termites crawling out of the powdered hideout of their penchant for destruction. I watched these "white ants" as they carried on their foreheads the evidence of what was to them a considerable booty, each ant quick-paced as a warrior returning home with the medal of his gain. I listened for the susurration of white death, thinking what it must be like to a termite, forever busy tearing apart, eating into the foundations which others had built. For a couple of minutes I busied my mind with other matters. I was under a mental stress. I felt a sudden gnawing at my bowels.

Now I lay on my back in utter discomfort. I was unable to massage the stiffness out of my right shoulder. The ache would not be soothed, neither would the knots of my muscular discomfort be smoothed. In all likelihood my muscles had twisted themselves out of shape while I tossed and turned in the turmoil of my brief sleep. All the veins leading to my neck pained. To locate the source of my physical agony, I explored my body, touching here and there. There were bumps on my skin, maybe insect bites. Had the ants joined me in my bed, and got under the sheets? I itched! I touched the areas of my body which had sustained so many bites the night before. And my eyes opened. Fully.

I put the lights on. Nonno was not in bed any longer. I contemplated a parade of white ants forming a never-ending line. They were busily eating their way into the timber legs of the bed I had lain on, performing their duty with dedicated industriousness. It was not long, I feared, before they got to me. I itched all over, a couple of the ants traveling to and fro across my person and over it. They bit me in the most impossible of spots, corners, nooks and crannies of my person I couldn't get to even with the help of a back-scratcher. The white ants left me with a physical and mental unease: mental because they made me think of the mindless havoc currently being visited on the nation. (I reminded myself that if I were an ant, I would do other than what they were doing. But then, I would behave in the same way, wouldn't I, and commit unheard-of atrocities and unpardonable roguery if I were one the vigilantes, or besotted with the idea of power like the ambitious cowboy politicians? I would rather I destroyed what I wasn't allowed to take, like the vigilantes!) The ants marked my body with polygonal and polyhedral messages I couldn't decipher. Exploring further, I touched what felt like fresh eruptions of eczema, at which my fingers pulled. I held the folds of eczema-induced loose skin, as if in the palm of my memory. The night itched. The night miaowed. The night hooted a doomsday call, dark as an owl's face is round. I must have gone back to sleep for a couple of hours, because when I woke up, the morning had dawned. Itchy and very irritable, I scratched my scrotum with renewed vigor, my vengeance.

I suffered a severe bout of flatulence. As if it might help, I altered my position, my body half raising itself. Now it sent forth an issue of warm wind, its odor of a rotten ugliness. This put me in mind of a corpse decomposing in a swamp. I was overwhelmed by a feeling of beleaguerment. I thought, do I contain an iota of humanness worth saving?

There I was, helpless, dumbfounded, tyrannized — the summation, the symbol of many a Somali in a worse condition than I was. I wasn't what I had always believed myself to be, a man able to locate his truth in half truth, and able to live with the contradictions. But I was ahead of myself: showering before I showered, shaving before I shaved, shuffling into my clothes to drive in a westerly direction and park the car in front of the compound in which Gacme-xume lived.

My eyes were moist: drops of vapor distilled from the morning's phosphorescence. Miragelike in reflection, the memories of the previous day's sorrow gathered in a state of utter disorder, like the hem of a funeral robe coming undone!

After showering I searched for Nonno. Failing to find him, I looked for Zariba, his housekeeper. At my insistence, she told me that he had gone in his jalopy long before dawn broke, with two men. But she wouldn't say who the men might be, or where the three of them went. She volunteered that there was some urgency to their departure.

I got into my car, driving as fast as I could, and parked near enough to Gacme-xume's compound, at a vantage spot where I could spy on the movements of the people entering and leaving the compound. "Spy" is the wrong word, considering that mine was the only vehicle in sight, like a hippo taking a dip in a shallow pond. I was trying to make sense of the patterning of the tasks those entering the compound or exiting performed, confident that I would know if death, cast in the shape of a Yarow, had visited overnight! But there was nothing unusual, nothing suggestive of death, as I watched women tending a fire just built, men brushing their teeth and clearing their systems of the previous night's residues: of saliva still gluey with sleep, of phlegm blocking their respiratory passages.

I hadn't been there long when it dawned on me that there was a funereal slowness to the occupants' bodily gestures, a lethargy to their gait, their postures. Now a fresh group of people arrived: the women with their faces partly hidden from view, the men walking in rows of three, eyes downcast, their silence suggesting sadness, the sudden loss of someone dear. I saw that a couple of men moved briskly. This helped me deduce that they were professional grave-diggers, bringing in a litter on which a corpse might be placed. In fact, one of them was carrying into the compound the standard *subeeci-xariir* cloth with which the dead body's bier is covered.

Several of the passersby took an interest in me sitting in a vehicle and watching the people's movements. One of them had a gun. Because I am averse to gun-wielders, whom I suspect are capable of causing a lot of havoc, I thought paranoiacally that he had looked at me in a threatening way. He exchanged a few words with his unarmed

251

companion before deciding to let me be. I told myself that I had better find a good enough pretext in case anyone walked up to me and asked what I was doing there. But soon enough I abandoned the idea of asking anyone if someone had died, and how. Mark you, I was now worried some of the kids might remember seeing me yesterday or, worse still, one of the neighbors might recognize the vehicle, or my face.

Had Gacme-xume been murdered? Why I was set upon by an onslaught of guilt, if I had been prepared to kill the man myself? How did he meet his death? Was he stabbed with a knife? Did he die a slow, dolorous death? Had a pistol done the job? Or was he taken away for a drive in a car and drowned in the river, his corpse brought out and left in open view of this very street? His family wasn't likely to insist on a postmortem examination of his body. They would bury him within the same day, before the tropical heat took its toll. No one would question the cause of death unless there was evidence of tampering, of knifewounds or ugly marks on the corpse. Would Gacme-xume's death be traced to our family, by one route or another, maybe an incident linking him to the theft of a pair of shoes as far back as thirty years? I doubted it.

The early signs of a migraine pounded on the entrance to my forehead. To keep the headache at bay I closed my eyes. When the threat of pain abated, I opened my eyes. I saw a man running after a small boy of about seven. The boy had in his hand a medium-size duffel bag, which I recognized from the night before, being the one Yarow had taken away the cash in. How odd, I thought. The boy being chased, possibly one of the urchins whom I had seen the previous day (he may have been one of Gacme-xume's children for all I knew), was pleading as he fled the stick the older man running after him was brandishing. The young boy referred to the man as "Uncle." A closer look at the man revealed an uncanny resemblance to Gacme-xume. Promising he would give up the bag, the boy was pleading not to be beaten. But his thin legs got caught in a thorny mess in the dirt road. As he ran around and around, the thorny mess hampered his speed, for he dragged it along as he escaped. Now he bent down to disengage his leg from the thorny bush. As he took a moment to study the crisscrosses of bleeding spots on his shin, the man was on top of him. He darted out his left hand, grabbed the boy by the wrist, and then *whack!*

I reacted as though *I* was being hit. I flinched. In fact my right hand rose, as if blocking the cane. But I did not cry. Neither did the little boy. For he held on bravely for a moment to the bag's strap before finally letting go. Then he stood firm as his body received more blows. The boy then watched the man unzip the bag, look inside, and take out wads of money held together with rubber bands. "Uncle" ran out of stamina, but not of ambition, as he paused to give the boy an ungenerous wad of cash. He said to the boy, "That's all you and your mother will get from me!" They might have been muggers sharing a poor haul!

Then Uncle, who had a heat-dried unhealthy look about him, saw me. He turned away, his grimace a bit guilt-ridden, his cheeks rimmed with a bristle of stiffness. My eye contact with him inspired in me an ugly sadness. I thought what a small-minded, mean people we were, Somalis, selling one another for wads of valueless currencies. The bag slung across his left side, Uncle moved away, his walk as clumsy as the waddle of a duck. The boy saw me. It struck me that he recognized me from yesterday. He hurried away, after Uncle. I couldn't tell if he would report me, to Uncle or someone else, or if he was afraid I might be after his booty. He fled, his every step invested with negative energy.

I was having to alter my notions of death. Not only was I capable of stepping out of my own body, but I sensed the intimations of a storm brewing inside of me. I was about to start my engine and drive off, when I saw at least seven goats clustered together in companionable gregariousness. These came out of the compound and, guided by their own sense of *nuuro*, ambled straight toward a trash bin to the left of where I was parked. One of them rammed into the bin to knock it down, the noise drawing the attention of other passersby. I watched the goats feed on the debris. This consisted of bones with no meat on them and of old shirts with no buttons. There were also ancient shoes, curled up stiffly and sporting huge tears where the buckles had been, shoes as hard as bunions and as deformed in their death as the calluses on the toes of the people who wore them. Apart from the shoes, another item held my attention, a small shoulder bag with ALITALIA printed on its ribs. This had once belonged to me. To get their teeth into it, the goats were goring each other with their horns, the better to

253

have a chance to eat the labels, my name in clear handwriting and in permanent brown ink. Was Gacme-xume murdered by his own brother for the money in these bags? Did the Uncle who had dispossessed the boy of the bag have a hand in the riffraff's death? Cynical, Somalis say that the shoes of a dead man are more useful than he. Maybe this was the case of a man less useful alive, the riffraff, than an old, worn pair of shoes!

I wanted to get away. I turned the key in the ignition. Again, a sudden storm was upon me. I was momentarily engulfed in an onrush of rising dust, the whole world going up around me in a thunderous scatter of debris, a whirlwind of so very many irreconcilables, a noisy mix of sand and bones and paper.

I sat in the car. I was a storm-beaten, lonely man. I was sad. I was mournful. I grieved, not because Gacme-xume had been murdered, or that his family had traded his worthless life for a handful of cash, something many Somalis would do in an age of material greed and soullessness.

I grieved for my country!

From my vantage point, I decided that my father's head had something of the shape of a tamarind seed, compact, wholly intact. The idea of him, my love of him, grew tall in the tree of my imagination, healthy, and shady. Half of his face was in the sun, the other half out of it.

I also thought that his features had a durability about them, the blessed marvel of a mortal surviving an earthquake, the earth's frequent tremors, its fits and starts, meteors aimed at eavesdroppers. In place of sperm, I thought it was the river of his humanity which flowed into my blood, a more precious thing, everlasting in my memory. Though his penis was not bestowed on me as Nonno's had been on him, his kindness was, my delightful remembrance of what he meant to me as a child, a shaper of life and an artist, coaxing things into being. I wouldn't have wanted to exchange him for any other man, as my father, thank you! Because his mouth stayed open, his lips forever moving, my father put me in mind of a saltwater fish feeding in springwater. How I loved him, the certainty that was Yaqut! With him, I observed, even the pigeons were alive with excitement, like children at a *ciid* festivity. Busily pecking at bonbonlike grains, they were enthralled, celebrating my presence at my parents' house.

Presently he turned around. On seeing me, he came forward, his hand outstretched. He was red-eyed, perhaps from lack of sleep. Shaking hands with him, I sensed the intaglio of an open sore on the palm of my right hand. Not that it was a big gash, only a very small superficial cut, its shape matching that of a key. I had no idea how I had come by the sore. However, I had a vague memory of ants gnawing at me. I also remembered feeling a burning sensation when showering earlier.

After a cursory embrace, our shoulders ended up touching. My father said, "I haven't had as many visitors in a day as I've had this morning." He sounded like a bad actor, mouthing the words of a terribly pedestrian script.

"Has Nonno been to see you too?" I asked.

My father said, "Nonno came quite early in the morning, to bring both good and bad news. He was joined here by Yarow and his sidekick, whose name I couldn't catch. He had a foreign name and didn't say a thing."

There was something lighthearted about his manner, a man no longer bearing a burden. But he restrained himself from fully letting go, his voice sounding like the echo of a foghorn from afar. "How low have we sunk lately," he said, "to receive the news of a man's death, and to mark his expiration with celebrations."

In memory, I was back in the dream of the locusts, the community mindlessly feeding on the insects which had devastated their crops. "How tragically sad!"

I didn't bother to ask who had died, certain that I knew a lot more than he about how the murder had been organized. At best, my father had received secondhand news from Nonno or Yarow. He did not look happy, only relieved for having been spared, for not having had to bump off the riffraff himself. The phrase "my father" was now weighty, with moral as well as political responsibility bearing on it, notions I might not have linked to the relationship between a biological son and father. What else could I call him? I had known no other father, and been closer to Yaqut than my thumb is to my forefinger.

I followed him to the courtyard where his worktable stood. It had a few tools on it. Looking closely, I detected a hand-on-heart jamboree of a joy: in the tools, so to speak. They appeared rested, in repose, content. *Sadness was he*, the sun in his eyes at half-mast, a derrick of darkness moving to and fro between the spars of solar reflection. I concluded that Gacme-xume's death had given him a well-deserved relief. Else why was he in his Friday best, in clothes which smelt of mothballs? His posture suggested that of a villager going to the big city, shoes pinching him because of the recently reinforced heelplates. The hard metal came into crushing contact with the pigeons' nibblings, leveling them into the cemented floor. I hurt!

There was the faint sound of bells ringing.

I asked my father to explained what happened.

I could hear the wingbeat of his thoughts, a hawk spreading its furtive gaze upon the land below as it climbed the better to survey the scene. He said, "A stone has been lifted . . . !" Then he trailed off, the glitter of his eyes' mischief fixed on the confetti the pigeons were pecking on. He waited, as if he had spoken the first line of a riddle, the idea being that I should run with it and provide him with the unspoken half.

". . . and the scorpion killed?"

"With the sting gone . . ."

". . . the corpse interred!"

"With all evidence removed . . . !"

After a pause, I added, "It's a wise offspring . . ."

". . . who has faith in his father . . ."

". . . whose secrets are, to him, a treasure trove!"

Now the idea of him was no more as evergreen as a tamarind tree, no more was he standing high and tall, or supplying one with the sweetest of shades. He had the appearance of a cactus, with more thorns to its flanks than it had flowers. He changed yet again to assume the shape of a baobab tree, wearing the sad habit of a man whose hair had gone gray overnight, a man resigned to his unhappy fate.

"Perhaps you ought not to know about the riffraff," he said. Absentmindedly he picked up a wedge-shaped instrument, with which he filed his nails, one at a time.

"Do you know at whose hands he died?" I asked.

"Not Yarow's," he said.

"Did Yarow's companion do him in?"

"No."

"Who, then?"

"Nonno assures me," he said, "that he didn't meet his death at the hands of anyone remotely linked to us. Greed killed him, the greed of those sharing the den of infamy with him — his own brother with the help of his cousins."

I told him where I had just come from.

"Did anything transpire?"

I told him that I had seen a group of companionable goats eagerly feeding on a shoulder bag with ALITALIA on its side. But I withheld the bit about the label with my name in ink, which was voraciously consumed by the goat.

"The man deserved to die," was all my father would say. He fell silent, his head bent in concentration, as he stared at the palatial dwelling-place of the pigeons and today's provision of royal bonbons. "It's my understanding," he went on, affording himself a moment in which he looked up at me, "that Gacme-xume died at the hands of a couple of armed bandits who got away with only a quarter of the extortion money given to him just after midnight."

Silent, he picked up a silver box no bigger than a beauty kit. A tiny Yale padlock hung on it. The silver box was clearly the pride of his workmanship, wrought so exquisitely you couldn't help being impressed with the achievement. Now he made a ceremony out of handing it over to me, as though he were entrusting to me a confidence upon whose keeping our lives depended. I received first the box, then the key as though they were trust deeds a father bequeaths to his beloved son. Now I looked from the key to my palm, comparing the cuts impressed upon it with the grooves of the key. The grooves matched with miraculous precision. It was as though I had fallen asleep with this very key in the clutch of my hand the previous night.

Don't ask me why, but I dared not turn the key in the lock, dared not pull open the silver box, fearful that I would be dealing with a world larger than the one I had known so far. But what secrets did the silver box contain? I said, "What about my mother?"

As I waited for his answer, I studied the cut on my palm where the blood had dried and the bruised skin had gone slightly darker. My father had the uncertain look of a fish caught between two high wavecrests. He seemed hollow-eyed, the sun shooting youthful rays through to the brown of his irises. As I looked into his eyes, the image came to me of a pestle of light standing crookedly in the mortar of my father's noon.

"Where to begin!" he said.

He was as subtle as an ant altering course, now a little to the left, now a little to the right, until the dark, menacing shapes recede, and the ant is out of danger.

"I am adult enough now," I said.

He fell silent, thinking.

"I can take anything," I assured him.

"Aren't I aware of that!" he said.

"Maybe I know a lot more than you think," I said.

"There's a lot more that I don't know myself," he said.

Something else was happening here too. Our exchanges, whatever else one might say about them, were like the exchanges of two persons in near collision, face-to-face in a narrow corridor, each attempting to move out of the other's way. One of them smiles, the other responds likewise.

"Certain secrets benefit from being told when you have prepared their recipients for them," he said. "I understand that you have received a couple of shocking revelations. My question is, how much more can you take?"

"As much as you're ready to part with," I said. "Nonno has already told me a number of the things you are going to tell me today. I know, for instance, that I am not your biological son. I know that my mother was the victim of a gang rape. That for years she was blackmailed, because a rogue forged a certificate which purported to make her the wife of someone other than yourself. I know that I am the issue of the gang rape."

His hand reached out to me, in sympathy. We touched.

"So you are aware of the fact that, as our luck had it, Arbaco arranged for us to meet," he said, "because one of the rapist's initials were the same as mine. A fortuitous chance presented her with as good a starting point as any. Your mother told what had come to pass. I didn't hesitate. I said, let's be husband and wife, and we were man and wife." He fell silent, watching a spider's acrobatics as it balanced its elegant body on a singularly thin silvery thread. We waited, wondering if the spider would lose its equilibrium, and if so, how far down it would go before it picked itself up and climbed to safety.

"You were man and wife inside a week," I said.

Now we focused on a gecko, which was readying itself for attack, its belly tightly hugging the wall, eyes trained on the moving spider. The gecko pounced and missed, the spider jumped out of the way, safe. The gecko fell earthward, in the end touching down near our feet. Then it ran up the same wall in fright, no longer in pursuit of the spider, but wanting to survive.

"Who said we married inside a week?" he said.

"Did you not?"

I sat watching, my stare a hiatus in the ebb of a mirage receding.

"We've never married," he confessed. "Your mother and I have never married."

"Never?" I said.

His thirsty tongue licking his parched lips. "No."

I saw in my mind's eye the image of a lie daubed over with layers of a secret. I imagined it might take a lifetime to clean the stains of layers of falsehoods, superimposed on others of reticence. "But you've always been enviably happy?" I asked.

"I don't know about that," he said.

I remembered Nonno telling me years ago how he suspected that my parents were hiding something. I couldn't recall who told me that they had got married inside a week. Was it Nonno? Was it Arbaco? What great courage on their part, I thought!

"It doesn't matter," I said.

"What?"

"It doesn't matter whether you married or not," I said.

"Well!" He shrugged his shoulders.

"You are my father, and I love you," I said. We touched.

His diaphragm expanding, he said: "I love you most dearly too, and have loved your mother all these years more than I might have loved her if she had been my wife." Presently his eyes were wells

259

drowned in the tears of abundant emotion. Not wiping the tears away, he let the moisture run down his cheeks, like a child unbothered by the mucus staining his face. I too had difficulty holding back my tears. I sniffed and, for a moment, felt as though my heart dislodged itself from my body. I had a hand with only thumbs, no fingers, a hand not taking proper care of the things with which its fate entrusted it. Then something of a blur rose before my eyes, a blur as huge as a wall, with openings in it, my father saying, "We had no faith in anyone, your mother and I. We're truly sorry if we locked you out, but then we had no choice but to exclude everybody from knowing our secrets. Can you imagine a man and a woman living in sin, as they say, in a tradition-ally Muslim society such as ours? We would have been stoned to death, and the perpetrators of the crime of gang rape would have been allowed to go scot-free."

At the center of my desolation lay a fever!

"It was fun bathing you, though," he said.

I nearly said, it was fun being bathed by you, but didn't.

He continued, "And I drew pleasure from being in constant phys-ical contact with you. Understandably your mother had a certain am-bivalence toward you, forever remembering the humiliation of the rape, which brought along with it an overwhelming neurosis. It was tragic to study a revulsion etching itself on her face whenever your gestures put her in mind of how you were conceived. We talked it through. Goodness knows it took a very long time before she accepted you. At first she could not even bear the thought of holding you to her breast. Only after seeing more and more of me in you, and less and less of any of the rapists, could she relax in your presence."

I said before a hush could settle, "I wish I could get my hands on them to kill them all. They don't deserve to live, they deserve to die."

"It wouldn't serve any purpose punishing beasts like them," he said, "for they are no different from millions of others, criminals in cahoots. I was more interested in Damac healing, and in the three of us staying close, a well-knit unit of love and affection, trusting and loving, not avenging. Your mother used to be on the perilously jagged precipice of a nervous breakdown. I am glad that we have survived the suicide attempts. We've been through a great deal together, your mother and I, sharing insomnia as long as a year of sleepless nights, her tempers as short as the noon shadows, our souls submerged, mere voices drowned by others much louder, more tenebrous."

My father talked on and on, and I, silent, listened in an attempt to catch at the byzantine traps of his tale: images conjured up out of sounds and words meant to represent his humanity, his healing powers.

"What's in the box?" I asked.

He said, "Why don't you open it and find out?"

I turned the key in the lock the proper way. The padlock gave. I took out a piece of paper folded up and streaked with flour and old-age stains, evidence of the years when it was first folded up and put there. I had to be very careful lest I tear it, because the paper had gone as stiff as a corpse in rigor mortis in parts. My father focused his stare on me. I don't know why I hadn't as yet told him about the carbon copy of the certificate, which purported to prove that my mother was the spouse of some Yussuf Mohamoud Isaaq, a certificate which Nonno's frantic search for his true identity card had unearthed from the bowels of his secretful past.

I read the letter I had in my hand several times, noting that it was dated six months after the false marriage certificate. The writer, who penned it in the royal "we," had as much self-pride as an eagle had of flight. I wondered to myself if this would be considered evidence in a court of law, and if I could have these men prosecuted for their crime. But how could one prove a crime committed so long ago? Anyway, here is the text.

Dear Damac:

Whether we like it or not, a woman's body has its timetable, and before many more crescents have grown to full-fledged moons, we will have come to make our claim, our fair dividend from having been your husband as stated in the document in my possession. We are delighted that you are doing well in your bead business. We're not asking for much, only a third of your monthly take, that's all. We'll send someone round, he'll make himself known to you. He has a slightly damaged hand and

*goes by his nickname Gacme-xume. As a matter of fact he'll be
the one to bring this note to you in person.*

*What if you don't pay up after we've initiated the contact? It
will be unwise of you to reject this kind intercession, for then
we'll show our wild streak. We know where you live, we know
where you run your bead business. We'll intercept you on your
way home or away from it and we will humiliate you bodily. We
suggest you pay up. And soon. If not, your life will be one long
nightmare. Remember you are a woman! Remember that you
are responsible for what happens, should it occur to you to refuse
to cooperate with us.*

Y.M.I.

I came out of the well of shock to find my father's lower lip hanging down in silent concentration. There was a long line of saliva dangling down from his lip, clear like the albumen of an egg in the top
half shell.

I drove. I heard a soft patter, a sound akin to canned applause, cued
slightly off key. I tapped gently on the horn of my vehicle, drawing
out of it a tuneless rhythm. To supplement the sounds, I spoke these
words to the beating of my klaxon: *Mothers matter a lot! Yaqut matters
too!*

I was on my way to the center of the city. I was intending to call at
my mother's shop, to assure her that I loved her most dearly, a son forever loyal to the love which bound us together as a family. I was sad
too, sad that the phrases "my father" or "grandfather" sounded re-
monstrative whenever I said them. It was like learning a new language in which the words "father" and "grandfather" had a charged
quality about them, in which "mother" was imbued with other significances.

Again I heard a soft clapping, and someone was speaking Yaqut's
name, another rooting loudly in appreciation for a deed well done.
More and more people joined in, everybody in the hall was turning
around to look at him, *my* father, Yaqut! I thought that it is a wise fa-

ther who knows when to tell what to his son. It is a wise parent who digs up the skeletons of a secret at the proper time, or knows when to allude to a scorpion by its name.

Surrounded by the uncertainties of life, my parents were wise to encircle themselves with a thread visible only to themselves, and which bound them together, a man and a woman who made a secret pact, their vows forever sealed in silence. "I owe my sanity to the fact that I deal with death on a daily basis," my father had once said, "carving mourning words on marble, copying funereal phrases on a board. These moderate my fears of death, they help dull my nerves to them, they keep my sorrowful life in check."

I parked. I got out. I found my mother. She was alone in the shop, doing her sums. I pushed the door shut and put up the sign SHOP CLOSED, then switched on the lights inside. I gave her the longest hug, the warmest kiss. Ever.

She wept. I wept. We hugged for a long while. No one ever felt a love so pure in its pristine primitivity as we did. A son filled to bursting with latent filial affection. A mother trembling leaflike with the urge of her maternal love.

We talked at length and freely, my mother and I.

We touched on taboo areas, subjects which many a Somali son would never discuss with his mother openly. We stirred the pot of memory. We fed the pyre with our combustible past, uttering our valedictory words. We rid ourselves of the ill will which we might have held in our bosoms. We sought each other's pardon. We applauded Yaqut's exemplary generosity to both of us. Lest we be misunderstood, we managed to remember our appreciation of Nonno's understanding kindness too.

At some point my mother said, "Yaqut was a godsend to a woman in my state of feverish need. I might have conjured him up if he hadn't existed. But he was there, a healer of wounds, a mender of my shattered self-reflections, a bringer together of all my fragmented selves. He used to tape my fragmented parts together nightly, daily, never failing in his determination to make me whole again. I was a candle beam, he the light within its penumbra. I was the twilight, he a virtuoso of vintage godliness. I doubt that either of us would have survived if it hadn't been for his selflessness. Only once, in all the thirty-odd years that Yaqut and I have been together, did he lose his temper with me, only the once, the one and only time."

"When was that?" I said. "Or rather why?"

"Sholoongo had arrived. This coincided with a period when we were at a crisis point," my mother said. "Because I had been miserable to live in daily and nightly agony when the men who had gang-raped me remained unpunished. I had acquired a firearm to this end, decided to take my revenge. But Yaqut wouldn't hear of it, arguing that hate reigns unwisely. He said that he would rather I healed than have these men brought to book. What was the point of doing so in a place where the word 'justice' meant nothing to the judge, the lawyer, the jury, and the criminal? We had savage rows. After one such fight, I didn't come home for a couple of days for fear of having another quarrel. After all, it hurt to see pain on his face."

Silence. I had such a momentous epiphany, thinking ahead!

"I have no idea how that witch of a woman knew I wasn't home that afternoon," she said. "Nor would your father know how she willed her way into her bed, with him in it. *There* between his tossings, she was: that was how he put it. Of course I didn't believe him. Do you take me for a fool? I argued. Could he not tell the difference between my body odor and hers? But she was *there* between my fits and starts, quieter than a vowel. How poetic!"

"Did that period overlap with the times in which she took me in her feminine trust?" I asked, remembering it had been she, my mother, who had first used the phrase "feminine trust" when referring to what was going on between Sholoongo and myself.

"Don't let's remember the ugly aspects of our past!" she pleaded. "For if the truth be spoken, it was so wonderful to go home and find Yaqut loving you as his own son, and taking handsome care of you, that I didn't wish to continue the fight. Yaqut has remained the beacon of my affection, the houselight in my tumultuous nights, caring for me and you as though we were both his children."

On the other hand, if my father and I were two babies at my mother's multiple outlets, me at her big nipples and my father at the midget ones, then it followed, didn't it, that we were her children? But why did they not have their own baby?

"You remember how often you pestered us with your gimme-a-sibling plea," she said. "Well, it wasn't for lack of trying, it wasn't."

Now we hugged. Now we kissed. "I have a triad of unshaken loyalties," she said, "you and Yaqut and Nonno, and I imagine my faith in these three allegiances would be all the more solidified if we sealed it with a sacred trust — the fact that Yaqut and I have never married, and aren't planning to. The sacred trust of a family secret."

In the silence that came after this, a disjointed body of ideas entered my mind. I felt cold to the bone, then was warm as the blood circulating in the veins of my self-doubt. I surprised even myself as I said: "I suppose it is high time I married Talaado and gave you a grandchild, and made Yaqut *another* Nonno!"

My mother cried with a hoopla joy. She danced around the shop, hopping about. We wept and wept out of happiness. Then we hugged for a much, much longer period this time.

And Sholoongo?

Between lovers: a secret tension.

This is all the more so if dealing with a fluke of a day in my life and Nonno's. For I, Sholoongo, on this my fluke day, with all my faculties functioning at their optimum, do hereby declare that I slipped into one ancient man's bed, namely Nonno, even if the bed was actually Kalaman's, it being the one the young man used when putting up at Grandfather Nonno's estate. If I mention Kalaman as the putative user of the bed, it is because beds have a place of juridical importance in Islam when it comes to determining paternity. Without going off on a tangent, I should like to quote from Prophet Mohammed's tradition here. In order to disentangle the knots in the blood of a baby under dispute between two claimant fathers, the Prophet passed a landmark judgment in which he said, "The baby is the bed's." I take this to mean that whichever of the two men owned the bed was the child's father. I am no jurist, and far be it from me to suggest that the Prophet or learned Islamists would give a moment's heed to my sinful use of the sacred tradition. But my point, for what it is worth, is that since Nonno and I were in a bed associated for sleeping purposes with his grandson, the baby, if I should bear one, would be the child of Kalaman, not its putative biological parent, namely Nonno.

Something else entered into my calculations when I slipped into Nonno's bed as the ancient man was busy negotiating a difficult bend in a catnap. I was aware that Nonno would think a hundred times before throwing me out of his house, or before rudely turning down my advances. I reckoned he might plead with me, but he would never bring himself to demand point-blank that I "scram out of his sight" as Kalaman might if I dared slip into *his* bed. Nonno was of the old world, his operating principle being that a gentleman, out of deference to tradition, does not lightly earn for himself the wrath of *nabsi.* I was confident as I went about the business of getting into bed with Nonno that I would have my way with him one way or the other. I knew that Kathy had had hers with him, fully conscious of his old-world sensibilities. With *nabsi*-wrath paramount in his assessments, he wouldn't send me off without a fair hearing.

How he rose at my teasing touch! My goodness: what an erection of singular handsomeness, Nonno's. I wish the world could see what I saw, a sex of stupendous smoothness as if oiled, veined, a well-rooted body of muscles, collagen, and elastic fiber, these expanding up into a mushroom-shaped dome. At my touch, it rose to meet me, hardening with the pressures of excitement, and due also to the blood level rising. What a shame, too, that in this hour of terrible happenings, of men with scorpioid associations being bumped off, and of the entire Nonno lineage in resultant turmoil, I pursue a stain no bigger than a fly, a live active stain, jellylike in its consistency, clear as sunshine at siesta time. I ask for your Spanish pardon as I take the stand and reveal that I am privy to a death. No, I am not an accessory to the committal of the murder. Moreover if you kindly hold your ostriches, nobody has died, not yet. This much I can confirm. But someone will die soon. Anyway!

I was in Nonno's bed, naked. I sat up, the sheet covering the old man's body, save his sex, which I kept teasing, whose opening I touched again and again in an up and down motion. Why he was in Kalaman's bed I couldn't tell. Maybe he had wet his bed, as some men in their second or third childhoods do, on account of their prostate condition. Myself, I enjoyed the sense of privacy Nonno's estate afforded me: a room for him, many others for guests. I was thinking how people like Nonno have a set of arrangements of the musical-chair sort, Kalaman sleeping in a bed of his, Nonno's, and the old man taking his siesta in his grandson's. This was luxury galore, something a handful of Somalis had at their disposal.

Nonno now awoke with the slowness of a tortoise bringing its head out into view. It struck me that he had no idea where he might be, who I was, or what was happening to him. He might have been dreaming all this up, conjuring into existence a Sholoongo doing the *daba-gur*. Stories abound in Somalia of men performing the *daba-gur* on women, men who, with the woman asleep, insinuate themselves into her bed. The term suggests a gathering of the sleeping woman's robe, and of gradually making an entry from behind, without her consent. Fearful that were she to scream foul she might be condemned for leading the man on, many a woman will submit to this rape of the simulated sort. Damned if they shout for help, and damned and raped if they remain quiet. In such a bind, few of the women on whom the *daba-gur* is practiced succeed in shooing the rapist away.

Of course, mine wasn't a *daba-gur*, for I wasn't approaching Nonno from behind but from the front. It would be *hor-gur*, only I have to coin the term myself, given that no such concept exists in Somali, even though we know it happens. Talk of being unfair to women! I can assure you that even if there was no word to describe what I, a woman, was doing to Nonno, a man, the fact is that the perpetrator of the act and the victim are both supposed to dwell in a world of pretend, both supposed to participate in a simulation. The woman, to bring it to an end, fusses, threatening to cry for help. The man, to bring it to fruition, employs all kinds of tactics, including promising to marry. But we did no such thing, Nonno and I.

When he came to and realized what was afoot, he complained of the fog in his vision, at a stroke affecting a feeling of helplessness. Falling for his deflective strategy, I requested that he tell me what was ailing his eyes. He explained that, because of a hurt in his eyes, he felt as though his vision had been halved. Now, I had never known anyone suffering from a sudden partial eclipse of vision. I inquired what, in his view, might have caused it. Not enlightening me, he was as elusive as ever, speaking in riddles. He said, "An eternity is anathema by another name."

My hand was by my side. He was flaccid.

"How do you mean?" I said.

"I am a candle burning at both ends," he said, "and which is extinguished by the blowing breeze working directly upon it, under direct orders from other natural phenomena operating within its vicinity. My vision is a candle put out by a forefinger coming into contact with a thumb!"

He was in command. I was spellbound, listening to him. He talked about death, his own and my father's. He alluded to a she-donkey kicking the life out of a man who had stooped to do the *daba-gur* on her. He referred to Fidow's two-way traffic, one carriageway leading him to men, the other to women. Now flaccid, there was something unattractive about him. Even if unaroused, he was big, capable of filling my cupped hands with it. No matter what I did, he refused to rise to my coaxing fingers.

I was set ablaze with vertiginous lust. I was wet down below, eager to be penetrated. Now I was no longer certain of my physical status, my body saying one thing, the mind disapproving. I suppose I saw more of a variety of men and women in my thirty-odd years of life than most, saw a number of them in various degrees of undress. However, I have yet to meet manhoods as exquisite-looking as Nonno's, or for that matter Yaqut's; or a body with as many outlets as Damac's; nor have I run into a man endowed with a belly button as deep as Kalaman's. I know what I'm saying. For I've been the alumna of the three men, even if not Damac's, whom I never got to know in that way.

Lovemaking, at its premium, places demands on the bodily mechanisms of the participants. Nonno was an inactive nonparticipant, half rising at my coaxing but going flaccid as soon as I relaxed. Something was saddening me, though: that I might have been eavesdropping on Nonno's death throes, that I was the last person to see him alive, the last person to give joy to his partially impaired vision. At one point I sensed his physicalness disintegrating right before my very eyes, like milk going bad, the white particles parting with the watery bits, the milk look-alikes undecidedly going hither and thither. No matter.

Now I recalled surprising him one morning before sunrise. This would have been a little over two decades ago. I grabbed him by his sex. My jaws hurt at the memory, at the ferocity of his kick, more hard-hitting than a donkey in heat. As I said, no matter! Because that was years ago. Today I would see to it that I got what I was after. Only

I had to pursue him with the same predatory tendencies which, in the end, helped me persuade Kalaman to take thimblefuls of my feminine trust. Not speaking, the rhythm of his breathing had undergone a substantial change. I touched him. He rose abundantly, his eyes still shut. He was as immense as a mountain rising out the mist from the beyond, his sex sculpted to please this beholder's eyes.

His mouth opened and shut in the manner of a bull chewing the dusky dream of the day's cud. The man might have been having a wet dream. As I lifted my hind up, prepared to put him inside of me, he shifted his position slightly to the left, clearly in an effort to help. I thought that the *hor-gur* was working. He was letting me have my way. Compatriots of the land of pretend, we were also citizens of the world of stocktaking.

He came. So did I. Tired, breathing heavily, his features collapsed as though they had been constructed out of logs of wood which a great fire had eaten into. The suddenness of it all. I imagined if he had opened his eyes, I might have seen the steel in his gentlemanly resolve, obvious that his mind was in control of his body, able to make it do what he pleased. No trouble at all.

I lay prostrate where I was. In a little while I was poised right above him, a vulture ready to perch or fly off in self-preservation. Mine was a predator's greed, success crowning it the first time. Would he give me a second chance? What would I become, a second-time *hor-gur* rapist? What the hell! His sex flaccid, no amount of coaxing or cajoling getting him up, I told myself that he had gone limp on me out of spite. What a bore!

With his back to me in a way that afforded him partial vision of me (a quarter vision, considering the circumstances) I put him whole in my mouth. Soon enough, Nonno was in his distended state. What the heck, I was a bad loser. To turn the tables, I did something to prick his gentleman's conscience. I took him out of my mouth, then started to masturbate right there and then, my forefinger actively going to and fro in rhythmic concause with my moans and groans, the self-fingering crescendo of my defiance increasing in volume louder and louder until he couldn't stand the sad sight and the unbearableness of a young woman drawing sexual pleasure from nothing better than her own forefinger. I told you he was a gentleman. Why, soon after, we were making love.

But he would not eject in me.

What manner of a gentleman was he? He would come close to bursting forth with a torrent of spermal eruption, then hold it back. Why this meanness? Why the spitefulness? The likelihood of my bearing a baby on the basis of one single effort was minimal. I was more interested in what he might release in me than either his genes or the genesis of his strained state of mind. I wanted to bear a child, anybody's baby. Nonno knew it, knew that Kalaman wouldn't give me a moment of his sex-time. Why did he reach deep inside me, approach a climax, and then hold back? This was criminal.

"You may come in me," I reminded him.

I felt his body hesitating. I felt a terrible sense of awe in the way he held himself askew and away from me, half of him barely touching me, as though he were about to break wind.

"I would rather I didn't come in you," he said, sounding ever so mysterious. There was a glimmer of mischief burning in his eyes. "I contain waste," he explained, "as if my spermal sense has gone awry, infected with germicide. In point of fact you wouldn't want to have anything to do with me, if you knew!"

"How do you mean?" I said, wondering to myself if he were making a veiled reference to one form or the other of the many contagious sexual diseases one keeps hearing about. Might he be suffering from one unheard-of, one that was uniquely of his own making?

"I will release it into you if you want me to," he said.

If he is HIV-positive, so is my Maghreb fire-eating husband! Besides it's been my ill luck to keep courting men on the verge of extinction, myself a returnee from the precipice of death, surviving it thanks to the kindness of a wolf, the maternal instinct of a lioness, the protective motherliness of an ostrich.

"Please, come in me!" I pleaded with him.

"You may regret it," he warned, no doubt a little bothered.

"Why do you say I might regret it?" I said.

271

"I know you will regret it in due course," he assured me.

For a moment he stared up at a spot on the ceiling the way blind people fix their eyes on an item. Was he accessing a secret? Was he conjuring up a magic potential? Now he touched me where I tickled, at the very center of my womanness. How his finger teased me with such elegant gentleness! He fondled the tip of an area which might have been my clitoris if I hadn't been infibulated, wherein I might have been easily aroused. His expertise in matters of the body had no equal, once he put his mind to arousing me. He rubbed my spine up and down, in an ever so divine way. It was as though he was reinventing a past with another woman, once more living through exciting times of lovemaking. With one of his hands tickling me and the other minimizing the exhaustion in my vertebral column, I was overcome with an inexplicable urge to be taken. I felt as if I were dispossessed of the power to act. I submitted myself to his handling of my body, he who knew its magical working more than any other person including myself. Despite the soaring joy, my now alert faculties picked out a most peculiar sound, soft, hypnotic. I was under the spell of termites, moving in their susurratory dedication to demolish structures. I came in tremors of divine absolution.

I itched.

We took a very long pause after we came, I first, then he. We lay side by side, neither speaking. I listened to the rhythm of his breathing. I was bothered by its unevenness. I thought that maybe, because of his age, a few moments of rest would do him wonders. Scarcely had I spoken a word to suggest that he rest than I remarked that he was not breathing anymore. I placed my open palm close to his eyes, then nearer his nose in expectation of catching evidence of his breathing. Nothing.

Had he willed himself to death?

I was in a panic. I thought, bless the misguided. O Almighty!

But I decided that this could not be. Because Nonno's life, if it was as strong as his will, could not have ended in a faint whimper, just like that. Unless! Unless he was playing a pretend-game of the wickedest sort, if the Lord would pardon my indiscretion. Had I not held him in the dark recesses of my body only a few minutes ago? Hadn't his sex generated such sufficient nervous energy within its muscular might, its cartilaginous vigor? Had I not taken him in whole, muscle, tissue, erection, and all?

Imagine the irony. Even though he could not will his mind to let go, yet he was prepared to leave this world for good while still in his distended state. How ludicrous! I wouldn't permit him to walk out on me that way, without bidding me farewell as he ought to, I his bed companion, I the sharer of his secrets. I would not let him, thank you! Meanwhile his diaphragmal quietness measured the extent of a century of my waiting.

I had heard it said that before enacting one of their cavalier misdeeds, many an elderly person boasted of having had intimations of their pending demise. Nonno, however, did not strike me as a man whom death would woo away to an afterlife in which he had hardly invested as laid down by Islamic doctrine. For he prayed not. He fasted not. He bothered not to call at the Black Stone in Mecca, although he had the financial means to do so, and more. Nonno dead? That sounded like a bad joke; it wouldn't raise a laugh. I would not think it far-fetched if someone told me that he had played a prank on the Archangel of Death. It was not beyond him to do so. He was such a teaser. Why, he told me once that he could hear the future in the drone of a bee caught in a glass turned upside down. But to explode in a mighty eruption, in the climax of his orgasm, and then quit? This was tickle-teasing fun. I would be in the local paper, as having brought death on. I would be described as a witch come from America, a *duugan*, originally from the Ogaden, empowered to use the white man's juju to supplement my powers.

He lay on his back, ungathered like a fishnet drying in a windswept land. I took hold of his callused fingers, massaging them one at a time, as if I were hoping this would bring back life into the rest of him. A motionless mass of flesh and heavy bones, there was a lot of him to take at one go. I didn't panic, though. I wasn't in the least worried that I might be implicated in his death.

No sound out of him yet. Nor, try as I might, could I work out how his body managed, like the weather in some countries, to go from being hot and sunny one moment to being plunged into the depths of winter. Was there the slimmest hope in a trillion that all wasn't as I

273

had imagined? Because there was a part of him which was rising, going up, stiffening, its head nodding in acknowledgment of a life force within. His sex was in its distended state. Hallelujah! He was upright, tower-of-Pisa erect! Was it possible for death to disable all the other organs and limbs of a man except his penis? I scoured in the undusted corners of my memory for an instance in fiction or real life in which a dead man's erection outlived him. In the Japanese film *The Empire of the Senses*, a man collapses in the midst of lovemaking. But does he lose his stiffness? I held Nonno's erection with one hand, and with my free one I rubbed at its mushroom-structured head, transferring the smudge of his slime to my own. I drew a dwarfed solace from envisaging a future in which I was a mother to Nonno's detrition.

I thought ahead, and saw a baby, mine. I could hear myself in my imagination as I told my friends the number of hours *she* had slept the previous night, how well *she* had fed. It gave me pleasure to talk about her, my one and only daughter, the one and only girl of her kind in the universe; it gave me joy to have a hallucinatory mirth. Now I watched myself walk down an airline ladder twenty-odd years hence, to bring my daughter back for her first visit ever to the land of my birth. A baby, who was the produce of Nonno's concentrate, which rose inside of me like yeast into a living miracle. Would I introduce her to her blood, to Nonno? No. I couldn't care an owl's hoot if he had died, or what became of Yaqut, Damac, the lot. From Nonno I got what I was after, the correct amount of sperm having the appropriate count in strength. How relieved I was to walk in this make-believe world, lost as I was in the labyrinths of my capital joy, my motherhood.

Then came thoughts dark as a fertile night, which closed in on me, managing to create in my mind something of a partial eclipse. One instant the sun was feeding on itself, like a mother bird eating its own fledgling, and in the next it was the moon whose face displayed neither a tree nor a bird glowing on its mythic wisdom.

Then I gave a start: because Nonno spoke.

"Touch me some more!" he said.

When I wouldn't, he took my hand and guided it toward the very organ upon which he had been unable to exercise his will, the decision to die. Obliging I knew not why, my fingers curled around his erection like a flag choking a mast. I held the nodding head of his obstinacy in the cuddle of my hesitant grip. I let the heart of his sex rise and fall. I let the raw energy of his insatiableness breathe in me, like a lizard's throat. Sure enough, he was living. *E come,* as an Italian might exclaim. *E come!*

How very perverse of me to have felt closer to Nonno now than to anyone else at any other time. Yet I hated the man, hated him viscerally, and wouldn't have hesitated to plunge a knife in him for all his sins the moment we finished this lovemaking charade. Mark you, there was a part of me that was in awe of his powers of articulation. He said, "All that death does is to deny you the opportunity to reinvent your life as you live it. Because dying, you cease to dream." I couldn't be sure if I was misquoting him or if I was quoting somebody else, Timir. "You must be content with others' dreams, visions which are not continued in you." Would his death bring about a discontinuity?

Yawning with the soporific desires of a man having his siesta's share of daydreams, Nonno put forth a question. "Is living truth or is death?"

Not that I was overwhelmed with a terrible unhappiness. But I was not certain which would please me more, a dead Nonno or a living one.

His erection expanded, reaching out into all the perimeters of my open palm. I felt encroached upon, my whole body felt invaded. I choked, as though I had him in my mouth. There was something like a rattling sound in my throat, a cluster of sounds, worries wanting to be born.

If there was continuity in the sense I now understood it, then truth was to be discovered in Nonno's erection. I thought of monuments and of statues in windswept squares, statues brown with bird droppings, gory with gouged-out eye sockets. I thought of all the betrayals of history, all the treacheries. Thought that in memory of women very few mementos of stone were erected, no minarets. That most statues resembled phalluses, a child's drawing exercises of male representations. How absurd: to continue in the truth of Nonno's erection!

"I hurt badly!" he said.

I let go of his erection. "Where do you hurt?"

"I hurt in the eyes," he said. "Summer one moment, and on its heels a sudden winter, with frostbite more bitter than any the world has known." He was limp, that was what he was. After such a labored erection, such lifelessness. I wondered if there was anything I could do for him.

"Touch me!" he said.

"Where?" I asked.

"Wake me!"

I obliged. His eyes opened with the gentlest of smiles. But why was it that his eyes didn't appear to me as if they were the principal source of his pains? I had other worldly preoccupations, wishing that I could stand on my feet, put on my clothes in haste, and leave. But I just couldn't. I felt I was to witness an event of extraordinary significance.

True to the drill of my female body, I required time to unwind, reminding myself of the telltale aloneness of a womb in wait. A womb is a curse! A woman is a womb, a woman is a curse, the sensing of an ominous crisis coming to a head. I was faced with the usual dilemma, my heart wanting one thing, my mind another. I felt as if the woman in me didn't know what *she* wanted, and as if the person in me didn't wish to have anything to do with Nonno.

"How come you hurt in the eyes?" I asked.

"We go back a long way, my eyes and I," he said.

"You do? How so?"

"We go back to my teens," he said, "when I was growing up in the city of Berbera in the north and learning to be a Koranic scholar. We go back, my eyes and I, to a specific day during the dusky moments in which my destiny placed a curse on itself."

"A curse?"

"A malediction as devastating as the impulse of my youth," he said. "I had to flee a communal rage, flee southwards. I ended up here on the Shabelle's riverbank. There were deaths. I had to take certain vows, which if I broke, would mean further curses, maybe partial blindness!"

Attracted though I was to the tale and its teller, I wasn't able to follow it. In view of the seriousness of the matter, I deemed it part of my honor-bound obligation to cover my nakedness. I was not sure if the angels said to eavesdrop on the last words of the dying would mind seeing me the way I was, a woman with a body so much out of shape. Never mind the sins that Nonno and I had just committed in flagrant disobedience of the Islamic creed.

He opened his eyes a tiny fraction as he said, "I felt terribly humbled by the curse, I felt terribly humbled by the fact that I had the choice to shun it, provided I kept true to the vow. That I would never again dabble in magic."

I realized how little I knew of Nonno's past. I realized that the little I knew was not of much help. I had heard it said, among the villagers in the midst of whom he lived, that he had influence over birds, whom he could gather at will. I had heard it circulated that he spoke to the birds in their respective tongues, like King Solomon before him.

He sat up, his eyes still half closed. I do not know what got into me, but I wanted a wet cuddle, I wanted a wet foreplay. I put my nipple rather unceremoniously into his mouth. He might have been a man in his eighties remembering his first suckle, his tongue active in its pulsing motions, my nipple in, his diaphragm out, and so on and so on. He wouldn't let go until I began to leak the moisture of my lust. Whereupon *he* rose.

I lay across him. We formed a cross, his forefinger in me, my cupped hand clutching him. Throwing his head back as if in amusement, he asked, "Could you put your ears close to my chest and tell me what you hear?"

"I can hear streams of water dropping down from a great height," I said. "Such is the water's power I foam at the mouth in acknowledgment of its force."

Miffed, he accused me of speaking falsehoods.

"What did you expect me to hear?" I asked.

His features were bright like loose gravel after a shower in the summer. He said, "I had hoped you would hear a wisdom to the effect that death is in the shift of emphasis!"

"In the what?"

"The shift of emphasis!"

I did not get his meaning. I told him so.

He continued, "I had hoped you would confirm that death is in a whirlpool of an ungathered wreck as well as in the rush of a waterfall. That it is in the vapor of a distilled mirage."

I wondered if he was repeating to himself speeches from scenes of his involvement with magic. Was he rehearsing his role according to a set pattern of exchanges, as part of a rite of self-redemption?

"One of my teachers used to say," he said, "that death is not a fire going out, or a glow losing its shine. Rather it is like a lemon peel, now dry and curling at the edges. Another of my revered instructors used to say that death is an egg rotting acridly."

He hoisted himself on his elbows, pulling my head a little too heavy-handedly towards his erection. He said, "Death is the spartan squeeze of a ripe fruit!"

"Could death be a lock giving?" I asked.

The fact that I joined him in the playfulness, that I was prepared to participate in his definitions, delighted him so! He took my head in his hands and held it. He kissed me on the forehead. We made a most ravenous love. He came in immense bursts, emitting ugly sounds not too dissimilar to the gargles a diesel engine makes first thing in the morning. He wanted an encore, more and more and encore. At some point he got up to go the toilet. It occurred to me then that he was moving with the unhealthy slowness of a man suffering from excessive fatness in his blood.

"What does all this talk about death mean?" I asked.

"A storm has been gusting up within me since your arrival," he said. "My head has been whirling, my lungs have been overworking themselves in fury. For days now I've watched a whirlwind of dust rising up, Kalaman the mad dervish dancing to alien piping from secret flutes. Yours is the forefinger on the hole, you the stirrer of this ill wind, you the author of all this turbulence."

He seemed riven by an inner pain, driven by the force of what he had to say. His voice worrying in its importunity, he repeated, "A woman forewarned is a woman saved!" Then I heard the buzzing nervousness of a fly too frightened to perch anywhere. Or was it a bee, detained in a glass turned upside down?

278

I said, "In this fly-buzzing atmosphere of fright and tension, am I the stirrer of the excrement? Or a dispensable victim of a condition? Why are you speaking such threats?"

"I wish you wouldn't take things personally," he said.

He lay on his back, his hands serving as a pillow. Had he already fallen asleep? Now was my chance. As I sneaked out of the room, my mind juxtaposed my memory of the Arab shepherd's tale with another equally fascinating Spanish folk wisdom: One corpse, three living secrets! Retrieving my underpants from the sheets' tangles, I picked up my brassiere from under the bed. I bent down to recover my hairbrush, repeating the adage to myself: One corpse, three living secrets.

I left as quietly as I had come, afraid that the truth of Nonno's erection, not to mention his death, might catch up with me sooner than I was prepared to acknowledge.

I itched!

I itched where it was inconvenient to itch, between my legs!

I itched at a spot in my crotch. The spot was very hard to get to. Moreover it was impossible to disregard the irritation as I drove my rental car on a narrow so-called highway where you required your full concentration and a lot more if you did not wish to end up in a ditch by the roadside or in the bushes to either side of the carriageway. How I wished I could purge the itching worries out of my thoughts, or give my crotch a good nail-powered scrubbing, to my pointed fingers' content.

I couldn't be certain when I began to itch, although I guess it must have been sometime soon after I decided to leave. I think it was then that I registered a quaint sensation, in the attitude of someone getting into scrapes with his own body. It started with suspect moisture, originating somewhere in my sex. It all started in the unlikely form of two irregular blotches of running wetness going down the hairier parts of my crotch, eventually separating into two distinct forks, one following the contours of my right thigh, the other the muscular angles of my left. I had just taken the resolve to leave. There was no point getting caught up in guilt. Besides, I wasn't acquitting myself well, not putting up a viable resistance to Nonno's challenges. He was making a fool of me. Was it then that I heard a most peculiar sound, of termites marching and eating their way through the earth's fundament? Or could it have been a bee behaving in the nervous jitteriness of one caught in a cup turned upside down? It might equally have been the call of a bird, a chirpy, chatty parrotlike bird chanting phrases intended to denigrate me, a parrot repeating phrases like "self-serving bitch," a Nonno-trained parrot.

"Would you stay awhile if I asked you to?" he said.

I knew I should have, but I said I wouldn't. After all, I had what I wanted, thanks to my *hor-gur*, to my stimulated rape, woman to man!

Nonno suggested I lie down beside him "for my own good."

"The cheek of it all!" I said.

"Please," he said, "for the sake of the baby."

"You are an ineffectual bastard," I said. "I am off. I am going. After all, I've got what I came here for, I had you by your sods, and I won't be persuaded to listen to you any more."

"For the baby's sake," he said. "Stay."

"Do you never listen?" I challenged him. "You know the proverb, don't you, that the skin of a frog, no matter how long it remains submerged in the water, will never become soft? You won't change. You and your obsessions, your predilections for secrets, your penchant for keeping them, pretending as if this is for the general good of society. You know what's wrong with our people? Where there is no individual justice, there can be no communal justice, certainly no possibility of democracy. You are a murderer, run south. I am from the Ogaden, come south. I am a sinned upon, fed to wolves. Grow up, Ancient Man. Take this my rambling as your first lesson."

You couldn't persuade him to let go when he set his mind on something. He said, "It would be inauspicious if you went. I advise you to remain in a horizontal position."

"Why?"

"Lest you waste *it* all."

"You're losing your senses in your old age," I said.

"I know what I'm talking about."

He put me in mind of a Somali tale in which a foolish husband accuses his wife of miscarrying several of their babies because of the downward direction her vagina faces.

"See you some time, Doddo!" I said.

"Have trust in me, young woman," he warned. "I know what I am talking about." When I would not pay heed to his counsel, he repeated it in a slightly different way. "Give me the benefit of our combined misgiving."

His extended hand reached for mine, but I shunned contact with him, moving away. I had no idea what devil had got into me, why I wouldn't listen to him. I just wanted to be away.

"Bye-bye, old fart," I jeered.

Then I dripped!

I dripped like a faucet with a slow leak. Then itched much more ferociously than before, a hairy scratch at the inside of my groin, as though an insect had found its way into my clothes. I didn't know how to put one foot ahead of the other. In my attempt to contain the flow, I held my thighs tighter together. I waddled out of the room, the insides of my thighs rubbing against each other. My thighs, touching, made a sound similar to a duck chewing a rubber ball. I wish I had paid heed to his counsel.

I got to my car and for a good while drove it. I felt as uncomfortable as a person sleeping on a bed another has peed on. I smelt a most venomous odor coming from between my thighs, and wondered if I would drain like a tap, if my womanly sap would flow away into a dead river choked with scrogs.

No sooner had I entered Kalaman's flat than I rushed straight into the bathroom. Fortunately it was free. I stood under the shower, fully clothed, the water boiling, jets of it descending upon me every which direction. I scrubbed the itchy segments of my privates with a loofah belonging most probably to Kalaman. I turned off the shower to oil every crevice and cranny of my body, applying Vaseline to the less hairy holes. Deriving not much relief out of these attempts, I considered spraying my body with an insecticide. I decided against the idea, washed and washed, repeating the same process half a dozen times. I dried myself, washing away more and more of the residual stains of Nonno's emissions.

I oozed. I held my legs closer together and tighter in the uncomfortable posture of a young girl sore from a recent infibulation. None of this was doing my ego any good. The thought that I might still be with child was now bedeviled with serious doubts, the idea slipping away from me like a stolen item returned to its lawful owner. I entertained the barnacle of a paranoiac notion: that such was Nonno's contempt of me that he emptied into me sperm crawling with insects. What prosaic justice!

Silence in the apartment. I continued to ooze the slime of my accursed discharge, dripping on and on. I went almost insane with self-hate. I was a couple of meters short of the door to my room when the telephone rang, only I couldn't summon myself out of my sense of awe.

I gained my room at last. There everything smelt of my phlegmy discharge. And to complicate matters, there was a peppery sting to the itching. Wholly naked, I rolled and rolled like a cow having its turn in the hot sand after quenching its thirst. Not that the rolling in the heat of the sand did me any good. Now I was full of self-loathing. I picked up objects with sharp edges, pencils, pens, any items with the shape of a phallus. I scratched and scratched.

Fearful of the approach of an attack of vertigo, I half crouched. I tore madly at my insides, dragging my claws at the walls of my person, my sex. Then I smelt a bizarre odor. This reminded me of menstrual blood. At last I heard a faint, ugly, moist sound, like gum boots getting stuck to the bottom of a swamp.

Had Nonno filled me with self-loathing? Was my body refusing to hold it? The thought that my body was resisting against Nonno's poison provided me with a short-lived sense of comfort, an instant of respite. Soon enough I saw the shape of my discharge: a spider's web, etched on the inside of my thighs. I had a number of unsavory thoughts knocking on the door to my brain. No matter, I won't speak of these!

I busied myself with my packing as soon as I stopped oozing the slime of my mysterious discharge. My back ached, my thighs were glued together with glutinous stuff, my head throbbed with the pain of thinking, I had difficulties moving about, I was finding the whole experience very unpleasant. I thought, What a fool I was not to have paid heed to Nonno!

Then I heard the key turn in the outside door. There were footsteps, first determined, then hesitant, Kalaman wondering if I was in. I allowed a decent interval between the time they entered and the time I let them know that I was in the guest room. A little later, I joined him and Talaado in the kitchen.

They were wrapped in each other's legs and arms, each fingering the other's whatevers. I made some appropriate noises before entering the kitchen. They wouldn't disengage until I was on top of them.

"Is anything amiss?" Kalaman said.

"I itch," I said.

He wasn't certain he heard me right. "You what?"

"I itch!" I repeated.

He appeared confused. He looked about himself in distress. He seemed concerned for a moment or two, then shook his head as though he were clearing up the clogs of miscomprehension, obstructions blocking the passages to the center of his brain. He was Nonno's grandson by upbringing. He said, "Am I permitted to ask an indiscreet question?"

"You may *not* ask where I itch," I said.

This did not please him at all. Talaado, for her part, appeared disinterested. She took a seat and looked out of the kitchen door, uninvolved. I hate women who are possessive in that coquettish way. Out of spite, I was being vindictive and was not going to let them enjoy themselves, necking and fingering each other's elegances when I was feeling miserable. "And I smell!" I said.

"Is it too impolite of me to ask where the lice are?"

"You're a pompous ass," I said, "and you know it."

"But where are the lice?" he asked. "Could they be the cause of your itch?" He looked terribly pleased with himself.

I changed the subject. "Won't you offer us a drink?"

The kitchen became too small for him as he moved about, opening the fridge, emptying the cupboards of half their contents, and putting all manner of labeled and unlabeled bottles on the table right in front of me. "What would you like?"

"I am in the mood to celebrate," I said.

"That's wonderful," he said. His hand reached for a bottle of Italian wine, which must have cost him a great deal if he bought it in Mogadiscio, where alcohol is inordinately expensive. He took Talaado's hand in his free one and he kissed it.

"Why don't you ask what I am celebrating?"

I watched him look for a corkscrew.

Things were building to a thunderhead which I felt would explode sooner or later. I could sense that. However, I was decided not to let him determine when the storm might break and over whose head.

"Only in spirit am I pleased to join you in celebrating whatever it is that you are celebrating," he said, "and I won't begrudge you a bottle of Italian wine, which I should've offered to you on the day you first insinuated yourself into my apartment and my affairs."

I looked in Talaado's direction, unsure if she would join us, wondering if she drank wine or did not touch liquor at all. But I must say I was surprised to hear him say, "I'm afraid I am not having any wine, though."

"You are a bore!" I said.

"I'm planning to have an early night," he explained, "and red wine tends to afflict me with a hangover and a grogginess the following morning."

"Why, what's happening early tomorrow?"

"Maybe you've forgotten," he said, "that Timir is getting married tomorrow morning?" Kalaman is such a sweet guy, he wouldn't rub more salt in the wound he had helped to open.

"I had no idea he had found a woman," I said.

"The things you forget!" said Talaado sarcastically.

"I haven't forgotten, for instance," I said, "that this young man's parents have never married, and that he is not Yaqut's biological son." No dice, no eyes rolling either!

He was in terrible humor. "What're you celebrating?"

I was getting a bad deal out of my exchanges with him.

I said, "I've just come back from Nonno's."

"How was he?"

"We've enjoyed ourselves," I said.

He beamed a smile of complacency. "The trouble with Nonno," he said, "is that everyone enjoys themselves when they are with him, rain or sunshine. I am glad he entertained you."

Here I reminded myself to play this particular trump card by the secret code as established of old and in the tradition of Nonno's family. In other words, I wouldn't divulge the secret to be cherished or suffered in private, even if we talked of other things that may or may not be pertinent to the topic at hand.

"We had a great time, Nonno and I," I said.

He looked surprised. "You did?"

"We did so until some impediment or other began to impose a blind man's burden on his vision," I said. "I would describe the impediments as untoward inconveniences. It's terrible to be ancient and blind too."

Then I dripped most savagely.

A worrying thought, meanwhile, stalked Kalaman's partly shadowed features. I suspect he understood what I was talking about, for he was up on his feet and ready to go to Afgoi right away.

"He was handsome too, and heavy below." I spoke these taunts with a view to further torturing him and to making him realize that I had had my way with Nonno, that I had made love to him when he, Kalaman, wouldn't acquiesce to my request to give me a baby.

Clearly overwhelmed with worries, Kalaman sat down in the very chair his mother had sat in when her knees had gone suddenly weak. He put me in mind of his mother, his body inclined to one side, like a lean-to with which a recent storm has tampered. He was charmingly frightened. Then he got up so abruptly that he upset the table at which we sat, the bottle of wine tilting forward. But I caught it in time.

"Kalaman?" Talaado said, getting involved.

"Yes?"

"You've forgotten to mention the rumor about Timir," she said, looking from him to me, mischievous, like a little girl refusing to part with a girlish secret.

"What about him?" I asked anxiously.

"A man whose description matches Timir's," Kalaman said, "has been blown up sky-high as he drove his rental car. The rumor is that he is dead."

I sat silently for a short while, and then spoke bitterly about my half brother. "Why does he have to die today? Why couldn't he wait until I am gone?"

"I wish you never came," Kalaman stammered at last and lurched clumsily forward as though he might strike me in the face. He was out of the kitchen, perhaps hoping that he was out of my life forever. Talaado followed him as a foolish woman in love follows the man she loves.

"I may not be here when you get back," I told them. "I am leaving first thing tomorrow morning, remember. Thanks for having me, and thank Nonno for me too."

Kalaman was back in the kitchen doorway. He spaced his words in an effort not to stutter. "Perhaps you could tell me something."

"What?" I said, eager to let them know I had it off with the old fart.

I was shocked to hear Kalaman say, "How did you get into my apartment the first day, without a key, and with no one letting you in?"

"You are a bore!" I said.

He and Talaado left without saying good-bye.

I itched. I was alone.

Dressed in a loose silk robe, Nonno is facing Mecca.

He is praying, the first time I've ever seen him perform this most important of Islamic rituals. The room is awash with blazing light, as though Nonno means to prove himself worthy of the devotions passing through his lips, in suspirious communication with the Supreme. As he prays, his gesticulations are expansive, his execution of the praying ritual putting me in mind of a blind man reacquainting himself with his surroundings, given his new condition. Standing just outside the door, and seeing without being seen, I am a fly on the wall. I watch him with earthy fascination.

As I take in the significance of what is happening, I recall Nonno saying not long ago that it is in the nature of knots to come undone, and in the nature of buried things to be dug up by Time. Are we to deduce from these dicta that it is in the nature of humans to countenance humility in worshipful self-expression in moments of personal and national crisis, when we are on the verge of death, our nation is on the precipice of collapse, the country in turmoil, and the entire continent being taken to a land of virtual ruin, a land without memories? Do we prostrate ourselves before our Creator in a tardy expectation of being pardoned, saved, our lives put right, when for years we have spoken in the periphrastics of self-delusion, speaking of family allegiances while advancing our personal interests?

The awesomeness of lighting on Nonno in his valedictory cast of mind so overwhelms me that I feel terribly unbalanced. I am tempted to join him. But I hesitate, replaying Sholoongo's demonic voice in my memory. I ask myself if the thought of seeing him in worshipful gesture upset her impish character. I may never find out what did happen between the two of them, given Nonno's penchant for privacy and Sholoongo's predilection for trafficking in falsehoods and scandals.

Waiting for him to absolve himself of all the sins of all his years, I step outside into the night. I listen to the night as it speaks to itself in the multiplicity of nature's tongues: trees dancing in the lush splendor of their greenness; mammals howling in the language in which mammals mate; the river doing what it is best at, going where the tide is taking it; the moon watching its reflection in the placidity of the water. I decide on the basis of what I see, what I hear, and what I sense that all is well with Nonno, and there is no cause for worry.

I pick my name off the nocturnal wind, clear as a camel bell. Nonno is calling out my name. I gargle my response. I wonder if something is after all the matter with him. The timbre of his voice worries me. It is dry. It cracks like wood in the jaws of fire. His voice, I remark to myself, has lost its woodpecker quality. Reentering, I find him waiting for me. He is standing erect, not praying. In fact his prayer mat is leaning against the wall.

He moves toward me with the quietness of an electric float. Only there is something not right with the way he carries himself, a little to the side, like a float that can't sit upright. We hug. As we do so, I look more closely: his eyes are bothering him. He strikes me as having at best a peripheral vision. I deduce this from the way he inclines his whole body in the posture of someone suffering from a stiff neck. I am convinced of this, but I continue to pay attention to him. Yes, it is the angle at which he holds his head. It is as though he wishes not to keep shifting if he wants me to be in his view.

Letting go of him, I walk away. We sit down.

The room, now that it has been prayed in, feels different. It takes me a bit of time to work out why. The furniture has been shifted so as to accommodate Nonno's worshipful disposition. I also remark how he now stands apart from the furniture around him, as the unsighted tend to do, giving room in order for them to be rewarded with larger space. He is alone in his isolation, prominent in his physicalness. I have always known Nonno to be physically outgoing when in his withdrawn state of mind. Today he is no extrovert.

"Come," I say. I lead him to the farthest corner, where his bed is. He pushes away my hand the moment his knee comes into contact with the frame of the bed. I discern in his movements a secret mindfulness of the partially sighted, his mouth making munching sounds of nervous chewing, like a baby's. His clumsiness dispossesses him of his rosary. I retrieve it for him. I tell him that I've had pleasant talks with my parents. I tell him not to worry. All is well.

He asks, "Have you seen Sholoongo?

"Yes," I say.

Nonno nods his head, then he says "Bless the day!" I think that is a new one. He is not in his "Curse the day" mood. After all, he prays nowadays, and means not to offend the sensibilities of the Scribes, two angels, one on either side of a person, who are assigned the job of noting down the activities of every individual. Bless the day, indeed!

"Has anything happened?" I ask.

"My eyes have *happened!*" he says.

I pull up a chair, placing myself within reach of his bed. He talks. I listen. His voice, however, hasn't a bounce in it, more like a plank of wood that has been in the rain all day. There is no resonance to it, only thuds flat. His stare is as soft as sawdust. It is as if Berbera, the Somali coastal city of his birth, has somehow insinuated itself into him, causing the natural flair of the southern lilt, which he has picked up, to vanish in a vaporous denial. His speech pattern has slowed down very significantly. The press of my inner anxiety prevents me from asking questions or demanding explanations. His face is swollen, his breathing is arrhythmic. The veins on the back of his hand stand out, wiggly. They are as prominent as the sweat beads of a runner in a marathon competition.

He says, "I hurt badly in the eyes."

I take his large right hand in mine. I touch pain in his farmer's calluses, which dominate the fleshy boundaries of his once soft palm. Examining them closely, I conclude that there are no squiggly mysteries of what you might call life-, heart-, and head-lines. Nor are there divine digitals totaling ninety-nine, Allah's honorific designations.

"You'll be all right," I assure him.

"Bless the day," he says, "for I am no child."

"Of course not."

He whispers secrets to the Almighty, showering blessings on the day, his thumb busy going up and down, pausing as it counts the rosary on the joints of the forefinger. He looks, shades spread across his cheeks horizontally, stepladders leading him, nowadays a praying man, upwards, toward the heavens of a recent self-appraisal. "I conduct well," he says, "in case you have forgotten."

In my memory of how he conducts well, I remember my father telling me about Nonno's late wife, who nagged him that he had better not keep altering his name. How, at any rate, he had better not answer to his nickname Ma-tukade, a descriptive provocation meaning the one who does not say his prayers. She wondered, what if the angels, Munkar and Nakir, who sit in wait for the recently departed in the darkness of the tomb with a list of questions, what if they asked him what his name was, and what if he replied, Ma-tukade? Or worse still, what if they inquired as to why he was nicknamed Ma-tukade? What would his response be? Tongue in cheek, Nonno retorted that he would tell the good angels that he had been *grounded* against his will.

"How come you conduct well?" I ask.

"My deeds are wrapped in thunder and lightning," he says, sounding like his usual self, not the cowed, cautious, do-not-sin-at-any-cost born-again Muslim fundamentalists. "All my life," he goes on, "I have made sure that my deeds are charged with the extraordinary static of secrecy, in celebratory deference to higher powers."

I call on another memory, one in which Nonno speaks of feeling almost *ungrounded!* This was in reference to when he spent half a year in a National Security detention center where he was tortured. He wouldn't break, despite the heavy-handed treatment administered to him in the presence of high officials. (A rumor attributed to Arbaco had it that Nonno was hauled in because he had won a manhood competition between himself and a highly placed official in the National Security Service. Nonno had won it "penis flaccid," as Arbaco put it.)

Released, the old man was asked to explain why the electric shock treatment did not break his will whereas it broke the will of all the others. Nonno retorted that he had withstood the Security's methods because he was grounded.

"Sooner or later I won't be all right," he says.

It is curious how off-course our exchanges are starting to sound to me. I think: if his eyes are the center of his hurt, why, that can be dealt with! But what precisely is he suffering from, an identity crisis, considering that he has mislaid the only ID card issued to him in his name?

He gathers his robe of silk around himself. He gets to his feet, slowly and painstakingly. Looming large, he leans a little to the side, tower of Pisan proclivity. He looks away from me in a very abrupt manner. I think, have I offended him? Or is he responding to an edict with a source which he cannot locate, a source within himself, or without, a edict which boasts a diabolical association with Sholoongo, or one blessed with a divine backing? Walking away, he sways like a washing-line blowing in the breeze. He takes a step forward, then another, every step more of an effort than the one preceding it. I ask if I can help. He says no. I get up and reach for him in spite of what he has said, and in spite of myself. This time he doesn't tell me to let go of him. I hold him in my grasp in much the same manner you hold a child full of play, to restrain him.

"I hate the idea of pain," he says.

I remain silent with a demure air of empathy.

"I hate the hurt in the eyes," he says. "Bless the day!"

He moves away with the exhausted slowness of a man wading through a swamp. He lifts his feet off the ground one at a time, then puts them down as though he might not be able to pick them up again. I go with him to the lavatory. As he prepares his body effortfully to sit, he pushes my hand away, demanding that I let go of him. I oblige. He pushes me away. I wonder if I should stick around. He insists that I leave him alone in the toilet. I do so, leaving the door ajar, just in case. I go back to the sitting room, waiting for a sign or a sound from him.

He is back with me in ten minutes. He prays for long. He says his devotions. He takes a break from his praying, and we talk some more.

"My eyes *happened!* May Allah bless the day," he says.

"Your eyes happened? How?"

"Because of a piece of ruled white paper, yellow with old age, a paper which had, fringing it, humidity stains curling its corners. I had preserved it for sixty-odd years, not knowing what value it might have one day. I had it with me when I fled southwards, to come here. At first it felt bone dry. I opened it with tremendous care, not wishing to break it into triangular pieces. And there I was remembering the sequences of the letters I had copied down so very many, many years ago. There I was breaking a vow. There I was hearing my Koranic instructor's edict in my memory, hearing his curse, 'May the memory of your felony lodge in your partial blindness!'"

"What had you done to earn the curse?"

"My instructor believed that I had tampered with magical scrawls when I worked with them," he said, "but I don't recall much of what he had accused me of!" He fell silent, obviously dejected.

"Did you tamper with a magical text?" I asked.

He disregarded my question. "I can't recall much. Except there was suddenly an explosion inside my head, fragments of blazing brightness after a detonation. Then in a moment or so, total darkness. More like a bulb that bursts, with wires sticking out any which way. Or like the darkness coming after a searchlight has been turned off. And then . . . !"

We touch. I commiserate with him.

"I was sure," he says, "I saw a hand in the corner of the good side of my vision, as it moved away after it had switched off a light inside my head. Then came a susurration of termites in their march toward destruction. This was replaced by a din of noises, a drone of bees. On the heel of the drone came a piercing pain emanating from somewhere in my brain. It was as though a vein in my brain had snapped, there had been a hemorrhage, a pain that, within a matter of seconds, penetrated to all the nerves leading to and from my eye sockets. A tunnel of darkness drilled through my head. This affected my sight in a

decisive way before another, final earth-shattering explosion of brightness occurred. All was light, the cosmos analogous with light. Then total
darkness. I woke up finally to several realities at once. I had more or
less lost my sight, in the precise manner in which my Koranic instructor had predicted it would happen. My eyes! What a malediction!"

"I wish I had been here!" I say.

"A chill tore through my flesh," he continues.

"Was this before or after Sholoongo?"

Obligingly he answers, "After her visit."

I wait for him to continue. He goes on, returning to his earlier
narration, saying, "There was drumming in my chest, my head dust-
stirring like a dervish doing a whirl of ecstatic dancing. My heart
pumped not blood but water, tributaries of worry, arteries of icy water,
a flood of curses coursing through my whole body. My knees knocked
against each other from the cold within, my feet were swollen with
the liquid residing in them. I collapsed, a tent losing support, a sprawl
of robes, my legs stiff like the poles of a Bedouin's dismantled home.
Then I fell asleep."

His face now has a hallowed look. His eye sockets put me in mind
of sun-dried prunes, so deep are their depressions. The wrinkles are
wide and as irregular as a footpath in a valley. "How do you feel?" I ask.

"Bless the day, for the spring in my gait is returning," he says. "I
would like to get up and walk about a little while I can." But he doesn't
rise. When I try to help him, he pushes me away. It appears to me that
he is behaving like a baby asking for something and then forgetting
what he has asked for soon after. I notice a change in his breathing,
too, again like a child falling asleep in the middle of play, with no fore-
warning.

He wakes up with a sudden jerk of the knee. I start. We smile at each
other grudgingly. Our hands touch in the way some African communities touch noses when greeting one another. I ask, "Sholoongo?
What of her?"

His tongue trembles with the anticipatory horror, I am sure, of remembering what had transpired between Sholoongo and himself. I
think of her as a woman who has made each of us inquire into the

meaning of truth, and how to distinguish our find from other categories of truth. I think of her as the shaman who has come not to heal but to dispossess us of our secret ill wills. I compare her, wrongheadedly, to one's idea of the clan: a notion difficult to locate, slippery, contradictory, temperamental, testing one's capacity to remain patient during one's trying times.

"Some mysteries are best left alone," he says.

I give Nonno a no-nonsense look. However, I doubt that he can see it. He has an odd expression, suggesting that one side of his face has been affected by paralysis, the other in full working order. Touching the cheek that has suffered this most sudden paralysis, I try to remember who likened Nonno to a woman. Because he is hard at the center, soft on the peripheries.

I probe further. "What about Sholoongo?"

At his bidding, I help him to gather his robe around the lower part of his body so he may sit up without feeling too exposed. But his hands fuss about in the area of his body, which has often caused him to be wary.

"She slipped into my bed," he says, "and I let her. I thought to myself that in a world turned upside down, in which brothers are gathering deadly weapons to kill brothers, a world with no sense of morality, a society with no sense of taboos, no knowing where we are ending up and what has become of us — I asked myself, is it worth my while to remain true to my moral sense, when no one is?"

There is a sizzling sound in the background, a fizzy noise, like the distilled water in a car battery coming to a boil.

He goes on, "We had a covenant binding us, Sholoongo and I, from long before she left for the States. The date of the covenant goes back to the period when she was small, really."

He takes a calming hold of himself, showing more of the brown than the white of his eyes, his pupils tucked in, hidden from my stare. He says, "She arrived shortly after the fog had lodged itself in my sight. I decided to be magnanimous, I decided to be indifferent to her baby-centered obsessions. I did what I had to do. We met and made love in the world of pretend, the world of simulated rape in reverse. The woman taking the man, in a bed not usually associated with him.

Why didn't I turn her out? Because I wished to absolve our family of any *nabsi*-related ill luck."

With hardly any light emanating from his eyes, his voice sounds slightly off key, like a tape recorder with weak batteries. It pains me to listen to its jarring lower ranges.

"Sholoongo's insanity knows no bounds," I say.

"Where is she now?" he asks.

"She is at my place, packing."

"What did she look like when you last set eyes on her?"

"She looked awful," I say.

"I wish she had heeded my counsel," he says.

I say I don't understand.

"Maybe it is better that we leave things alone," he says.

"Nonno, what're you talking about?"

"Anyhow, one must be kind to those who are less fortunate than oneself," he says, "if one wishes to enjoy fully the fruits of one's fortuity." Do I sense a shine to his smile, an impish grin?

"I've wondered if her bodily odors have their origin not in her human ancestry but in an animal one," I say, remembering the acridity. "She smelt like a wolf when I saw her, awful!"

Hereon his eyes become livid spots, as shapeless as death itself. A part of me begins to wonder if Nonno knows when he might die, and if so would he tell me? But what purpose will my knowing serve? I am in despair, but I do not speak of it. I am silent. I wait anxiously.

He hiccups. I think about omens that are not portentous. Worries invade my tranquillity. Nonno hiccups again and again. I stir agitatedly, not knowing what to do with myself. I rise to my feet, I sit down, I pace about the room.

"Would you like a glass of tamarind drink, chilled?"

He nods his head.

I fetch him a glass of tamarind juice, chilled. Clumsy like a village woman wearing her first high heels, I walk unevenly, my ankles twisting every which way, and aching too. I stretch my hand with the drink out to him. Nonno motions me to let him be. I oblige. He sits upright, taking in more air than his expanded chest expels. He remains in that distended posture without exhaling, then all of a sudden stirs with vigor, only to stay motionless again for an extended period of time.

Am I bearing witness to a bird's wing thrashing the wind to its *finalissimo?*

He speaks!

"About your parents," he says.

"What about them?"

Silent, he takes a sip of the chilled tamarind juice. He tilts his head a little at an angle so he can hold me in his peripheral gaze as he drinks. The position of his head affords me a view of the desert sand of Berbera in his eyes.

"I've made it clear to them," he says, "that despite what has transpired, I love them very, very much, and love you a great deal too. I've told them you that are my grandson and legatee, the one to inherit my estate intact."

He falls quiet to make himself comfortable, his hands raised as though in mock flight, a bird in two minds whether to ride the wind or to humble its excessive demands by having its feet firmly on the ground.

I mean to say, How very grandfatherly of you! But I can't.

He speaks painfully slowly, all the time tilting his head back slightly, and shaking it in the jumpy gesture of a swimmer emptying residual water out of his ears. "With my vision impaired," he says, "my hopes of Somalia surviving the disasters are nil. Like me — and I am on my deathbed — she is as good as gone. It is a tragedy that the country which many generations have strived to shape is being destroyed piecemeal right in front of our unseeing eyes. Cursed, I have become blind, because I've failed to read the warning signals. Our people have not heeded the signs portending the coming catastrophes. I am as good as gone. Our country is as good as gone. My advice to you is make of your life what you may."

"We love you too," I say. I feel the words failing me.

"Here," he says, giving me a key.

"What does the key open?"

"Wills, testaments, documents, all my wealth," he says.

The key fits the grooves etched on my palm, identical.

A most weird silence hangs down from the ceiling, at which Nonno's peripheral sight stares for what it is worth. I say after a long time: "We'll all miss you terribly." I speak these words because the silence in which we sit frightens me. Nor can I think of what to say, or whether to remain quiet.

He nods his head vigorously. He then spreads his hands, palms up: a lizard with a belly exposed to the sun. I hear the sleepy rustle of the trees outside. This decides me to accept his death with the magnanimous attitude of a devotee dying, confident that he will live on in me, in my parents, in the memory of those who have loved him, in the trees, in his woods, in his patch of the river, in Hanu, in all those who have been fortunate enough to know him.

He has his naughty boy's grin in his eyes.

"I *read* something?" He speaks in a non sequitur, then silence.

"And then *it* happened?"

He isn't making it easy for me. Nor can I follow his meaning. Will I ever get to hear of *what* happened, when, why, and to whom? He will be buried with many of his secrets, his intimations, his judgments. Of what clan, he would be asked, and he would shrug his shoulders and take refuge in a waffle of words. "I can't bear the thought of generalizing. I am a person, a clan is a mob. Talk to me, sell things to me, I am reasonable. Clans are not." I wish many of the fighters visiting havoc on people's lives had been born with the luck to hear him. "If we had many like him, there would be no civil strife," Talaado said earlier that day. "A hardworking, honest, lovable Nonno. A century will die with him, one's idea of tolerance, of magnanimity, these will die with him too."

I abandon my rambling thoughts, and ask, "Tell me *what* happened, Nonno?"

He tells me the same story. However, the words he employs are not the same. He says, "I heard a tiny explosion in my eyes, no different from a bulb bursting, once it has rendered its thousand hours' worth of service."

"And then?"

"And then Sholoongo came to see me," he says. He adds in a judicious tone of voice, "You came in on me, and I was on my knees, in full praying gear, full of worship. After so much sin, so much vacillation, after wanting to have a taste of everything that life affords the living: I go on my knees, in prostration, humbled to the powers above me."

"What I am to make of all this?" I say.

He gives thought to my question. He replies, "I reckon that everything has to do with the authority, the wherewithal to manipulate other people's destinies. In my teens, not humbled then, I was molded of the same clay as a madcap scientist, the sort that is familiar from films or fiction. You know the type? A madcap of a scientist, with too much knowledge for his own good and too little sense, who has the urge to remake the universe in the cast of his rigid formula. Power-hungry, I guessed that by replacing a set of magical codes with some of my own making, I might rule the wind and the birds which ride upon it."

His body tenses. Has something caught in his throat? Is he choking on an abrupt intake of air? He is having difficulty breathing, and there is a surge of tension in the upper part of his body, like floodwater in a river's throat. I get up to bend over him. I take his wrist. I measure his pulse as best I can. Everything seems to be in working order.

"Shall I call for a doctor?" I inquire.

"No need."

"Shall I call a priest?" I ask. "Fetch my parents?"

"No need."

"How do you feel?" I whisper.

I see a tiny light, no bigger than a pilot, going on in his eyes and then off. His pulse in my grip, his heart races faster, as though it belongs to an athlete chesting the ribbon of triumph.

"I feel weird," he says, "as if, inside of me, the sharper end of a feather is being scratchily dragged against my heart. I have no pain, though, thank God. I also itch. But then, so did Sholoongo. How bizarre!"

"Would you like me to do anything?" I ask.

"Bless the day," he says. "No, thank you!"

His head moves, as though in an effort to shake it in disbelief. It jerks. It makes an awkward angle. But before completing the circle, something in Nonno collapses. He dies, his eyes still open, his heart racing in its competitiveness to outrun another heart, that of life.

One corpse. Three secrets.